James T. Hughes

JASPER SPRING

Cover photograph, courtesy of Katie Vanbalen.
Illustrated by John Gritts.

© 2016 James T. Hughes
All Rights Reserved.

No part of this publication may be reproduced, stored in a retrieval system, or transmitted, in any form or by any means, electronic, mechanical, photocopying, recording, or otherwise, without the written permission of the author.

First published by Dog Ear Publishing
4011 Vincennes Rd
Indianapolis, IN 46268
www.dogearpublishing.net

ISBN: 978-1-4575-5001-0

This book is printed on acid-free paper.

This book is a work of fiction. Places, events, and situations in this book are purely fictional and any resemblance to actual persons, living or dead, is coincidental.

Printed in the United States of America

For Pam and Tyler

Beautiful Jasper Park is an ironic setting for arson and the ideal stage for moments of truth, the coming together of three scarred people. Ever present in this family's journey is the abundant Jasper Spring, flowing steadily through seasons' vibrant and growing, dark and oppressive—nature above the ashes—whispering:
"This mountain will green again."

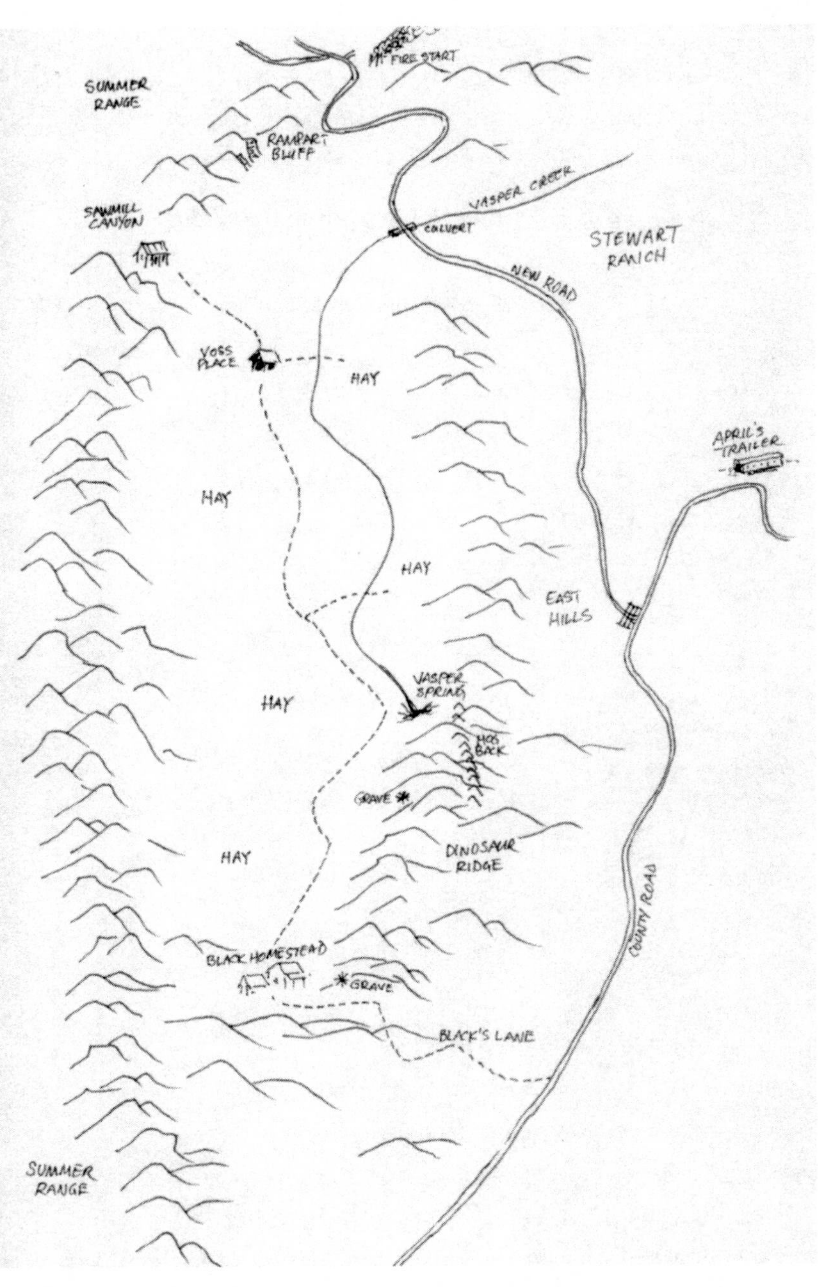
FIRE START
SUMMER RANGE
RAMPART BLUFF
VASPER CREEK
SAWMILL CANYON
CULVERT
STEWART RANCH
NEW ROAD
VOSS PLACE
HAY
APRIL'S TRAILER
HAY
HAY
EAST HILLS
VASPER SPRING
HAY
HOG BACK
GRAVE
DINOSAUR RIDGE
HAY
COUNTY ROAD
BLACK HOMESTEAD
GRAVE
BLACK'S LANE
SUMMER RANGE

"Poets for the earth...scream in the night."

—Dougie MacLean, *Celtic musician*

Untold Contentment

The ad read: "Pups, Border Collie. Out of working parents. Imported grandfather." The address was unclear but across the Palmer divide; sprawling, arid, short grass—Tucker remembered.

That night he dialed the number.

"Yep."

"Do the parents work cattle?" It had never before mattered.

"The mother can…"

Tucker heard the close clatter of plates and chewing. Suppertime. "You want me to call back?"

"Why?"

"You are eating."

"Jack. The dad, has never seen a cow. Woolies think he has the plague."

He never before cared. "How many are there, and what kind of coat?"

"Damn fashionable." The man's mouth cleared but he took another bite and was hard to follow, "*Harum washalous*—same outfit on every day—*los chaloose, shinazz*—"

The phone dimmed, as though something had stretched the distant lines, then crackled and came sharply back.

"Hell of a fashion statement. There are eight. Them damn burrs fall out pretty good."

Never before an issue.

"How far from Marshal are you?"

"People here know good dogs. These are damn good dogs. Two is picked. Jack has some tan, some might get some tan. Otherwise black and white."

"Where are you?"

"Seventy-two miles east a town, then a few other turns."

"Far out—"

"Too far out for it to rain, not far enough the wind don't blow." He had a smaller mouthful but the wires began to sag and sing. "You need a crackerjack dog—you better get here soon. Just put the ad out. The lady has a fancy history; her dad is from Scotland. A bunch of ranchers out of Stapleton kicked in big money and had him shipped here. Biggest border I ever seen."

Tucker sat blinking.

The man stopped his eating.

"How many boy and girl?"

A vacillating hum and whistle came from the receiver, a chop chop and squeal from the earpiece, refined interruption.

"All male and just two little jugs. One's been picked."

"How much?"

"*Chiowizzits*ifty—They'd be more but I have another litter coming."

Tucker strained to hear. He leaned back and his chair made a sound like a foretelling chuckle. "Too fancy for me. I'm just a farmer, with a few cows—"

"*Hell,*" the man challenged. "You got stock, one a these will do the work of three hired men, three riders. And they don't complain. They want to work and know a lot better… How far do you think you'd get with a hired human?"

Tucker bent forward to the desk, the chair repeated its creak, and Alice came to listen; the blood from Scotland had a bit of a hook in it. He thought of cool green and cloudy weather: small flocks of sheep: people and animals with their feet in the grass. Alice nodded.

"I will swing by tomorrow."

"It'd have to be early *too wet to farm* but I got things to do."

After many repeats for the drawn and careening connection, Tucker drew a doubtful map leading further to the north and east than he had ever been. With a nervous finger Alice traced the instruction.

"You have me lost."

"We will have to leave in the pitch dark of the morning."

Now that they had decided, they each felt a mild undoing, a scant urgency tugging at the last of their evening.

Alice lay looking at the ceiling, haunted by patches in the plaster—faint queasiness, restlessness, not leaving her alone. She remembered their previous dog, Billie, and his recent departure. Billie had grown to be their family and ally, brought to them after only two years of marriage. And now, as if to coincide with his old age and death, her first pregnancy, the coming true of her and Tucker's long-awaited hopes. The dog had a rough coat that easily gathered dust and burrs. Sable from his nose to the tip of his tail, he was a mixed breed of English-German shepherd and Aussie. Alice lay quietly, not believing he was gone.

The early adoption of Billie had been abrupt and not well planned. The puppy dove headlong into their welcome. As sinful a model who ever ruined rugs, he ate the fringe off the front of the sofa. Even the porch was not safe. Through the open window, Alice heard gnawing, frenetic scuffling. Billie had extended his jaw beyond its limit and was hanging by his teeth, as if by little fish-hooks, about the base of a porch post.

"No, no, *bad.*"

She recalled her swelling affection for his apologizing eyes.

First he chased moths, then the fluttering sparrows... One late afternoon, to the sound of great dissension and panic in the chickens, Tucker had come rushing around the shop's corner. He threw a glove. She remembered her husband's open smile at the puppy's tucked and wooly retreat.

"Bad dog."

More than a year passed. As sudden as the adoption, Billy took on self-appointed tasks, like a surplus of energy at last with a purpose: functions bordering on make-believe. He announced the obvious approach of any car or truck. Each evening and without supervision he gathered the birds he had once accosted and held them in their house until someone shut the door. They both watched in quiet amazement as a stern authority began to lead. But if he did anything with slow confidence and deliberation—he did it privately. For eleven years he would have given his life on their behalf, but guarded no children, no heirs. The emptiness Alice had felt was twofold, both for man and dog.

She began turning over in bed; the shadows outside the window caused her to stop midway. The light of moon and stars cast a silhouette of the upstairs dormers on the gray leaves of the hedge. Alice pictured them, directly above her and Tucker's shared sleeping, two vacant windows reflecting the night. She rested a hand on her stomach and felt herself breathing; she grew conscious of the rhythm, and her want to keep it even and calm.

Would the new puppy be anything like Billie? Would she think of it differently, now that she was expecting—their long-awaited goal...prayer—to come true? Alice slipped one leg out from under the bedcovers, then the other. She stood softly, not wanting to wake Tucker, and stepped barefoot to the window.

Work in the corral had become Billie's calling. With Tucker or her at his side, especially her, he was fearless. He rarely stared into a cow's eyes, but would snarl and grip the cow's heel so firmly she would shake the entire leg and momentarily limp. As his intensity compounded, he bit too high and his timing faltered, resulting in severe kicks to his chest or mouth. He would cry out, never stopping his duty.

In the open field his power diminished. He barked even more frequently and would lose his heading. Large numbers of cattle or belligerent mother cows intimidated him. He needed someone horseback near to hold things together, to secure his direction and resolve.

Only seven years old and his clear, expressive eyes grew cloudy. They sensed a whisper in his joints and cotton in his hearing. At nine, a hoof broke two of his front teeth. Alice minced aspirin to sprinkle in his food. His look became troubled and brooding. A highlight of gray grew on his cheeks. Still, like an old boxer, if either of them went for the corral, he would pass and lead with a lowly swishing tail.

The day arrived. After a dusty midday gather, Tucker moved the truck from the fierce sun and tucked it under a nearby ash. He called the crippled dog and helped him onto the seat. Alice was horseback on Daisy. Once loaded the dog sat up and tried to see the corral through the smudged rear glass. Never before had he not been allowed to help. His ears went up, but his failing eyes surely could not see. Alice had expected howls or pleading barks. After the sorting of heifers into secondary pens, she had looked over and the silhouette of the dog was gone.

Without work their old friend lost all vigor. His eyes no longer grew bright when either of them called. He began to walk with an imperceptible hunch, as though something pained him on the inside. Eventually, when he rose he would stagger. There was sadness in his tail. One cool spring morning he scooted himself under the porch as if to hide, escape all imperfection, and fell asleep. In the dimness well behind the step and beside the body, her husband had found a china sugar bowl, chipped and without a lid, half buried in the forgotten dirt.

Tucker dug a hole in the red clay hill overlooking the barn, then made a marker for the grave out of slate and chiseled in the name *Bill, Billie.*

Alice didn't suffer wholly Billie's death. It was spring. They were still young. A new dog would surely come. Most important, the dream of having their first child had just awakened and would easily flourish.

Standing at the window, she could see the dim outline of the chicken house through the tree branches, pictured the hens fluffed and nestled for the night in the straw. Pulling on the window shade's bottom rail, she eased it down and in the darkness found her way back to lie beside her husband.

Tucker awoke at three. A clock glowed on the dresser by the bed. All the room was black but for the clock and the leak from the shade over the window. The shade was new. Alice kept it pulled now so she could go back to sleep on most mornings.

Her breathing changed. "I think I'm going to get sick," she slurred.

"I do not like this sickness."

"Maybe I shouldn't go. It's no good...getting sick on the road."

"The drive might settle your, settle your thoughts."

"I *am* happy."

He heard a sigh and could feel a release of tension.

"Don't get one with white around their eyes. We have too much snow."

He began to dress in the dark, listening.

"Check for a dark mouth, make sure they look back at you with good attention. Wait for them to finish playing and see who will hold their eyes still."

He could not see her at all, just a voice from the bed, restless, with notions stirring.

"Don't be in a hurry. Look them all over. Even the little female."

He found her and kissed her, then left for the kitchen.

While waiting for the coffee he could hear her in the bathroom—getting sick. He sliced bread for sandwiches and filled a thermos. He had no desire to eat, but sat for a moment to sip lightly from the steaming bottle, careful not to burn his mouth.

To the fragrance of coffee she appeared in the bright doorway, completely dressed. "A dog will be with us a long time. You don't want one that runs and hides." She stood with a smooth, frail face over coarse shirt and worn jeans. The pregnancy did not show. "On the other hand, you don't want something too rough, one that fights, is too hard on all the others."

The grayness began to lift, Tucker realized, a pink returning to her lips, more traces of shine in her hair.

"Find out how the parents are with children. They need to be good with children."

"You better come," he said.

"All right."

Toward dawn they left the pavement. The road began to curve and the lights of the truck swept the open hills on either side. At junctions the dust eddied and overtook them in two distinct beams. More dips and bigger gravel made the cab chatter. Items fell from the dash. No matter what the speed, Tucker felt a discord throbbing up through the tires. The light increased and he saw into the box that sat between them; Alice had folded together a ragged and discarded coat to make a bed. One of his. A dog would know his scent early.

She did not show but she had told him. He tried hard not to think about it: inspired by a feeling about luck and destiny, the rugged path. He thought of horses and cattle or dogs and sheep, tall hay, straight trees. When he watched her walk, it drove holes in his thinking. She did not show—but she *did*. Only twice in his life would he live here; off balance by an untold contentment. They did not talk, such a jagged trail.

One hundred miles to the north, beyond the divide, Tucker knew there were great sheep ranches. His father first took him there when he was very small. The thought of how he had choked at the startling, pungent smell of sheep lay close and disturbing. His breakfast had come up and spoiled his shirt while his father watched. The mean looks from the sheep men urged him to swallow the bitterness. He had seen the dogs gathering and their hot smiles and how they ran on the backs of huge lots of packed-together sheep. He felt the wool in their claws and the taste in their mouths—searching for fresher air. The whistles, gestures, the imperceptible growls and sparing words propelled by the men charged him with fright and interest. They spoke in a foreign tongue. The swirling of the sheep and their herders, the vague, strange sounds from the people, had brought dizziness, a pull on his stomach no longer from any smell, a blotch in his future, mysterious and older than explanation.

The drive home had been quiet and uneasy, filled with phantom beasts: a slight boy groping for a missing key. His gloves lay beside him, child size, very small and well used with fingertips bent over and puckered.

The sheepherder's hands had been waxy and darker.

"Isn't any gloves—Don't wear gloves... How come?"

"So they can better get a grasp, hang on to the wool," his father had said.

Tucker flicked the truck lights off, the curves and humps slowly diminishing. The rocks sunk or grew smaller, her face white yet brilliant with an inside promise, an expansion of their world. He watched her look into the box and adjust the ragged coat, as if making a twofold nest.

Tucker grew certain, by afternoon the nest would hold a new puppy.

Skies of Possibility

Alice, her sickness easing as they headed northeast, glanced down at Tucker's already wrinkled map, and her thoughts lost touch with its vaguely sketched lines. She imagined Tucker as a father, and already knew how different things would be. He would be the very opposite of what her own father had been.

Mr. Harrington remained as chief janitor at the creamery. After a long history in traveling sales, two attempts with his own store of durable goods, and one short period as a textile clerk—he had finally settled into endless scrubbing of the painted concrete floor, repeated steamy rinsing of the stainless vats where they made the cottage cheese. Vats so large a man could drown in one. In the winter he suffered from a fungus on his hands from all the soap and water. He often had sores in his mouth. Alice's mother said it was a chronic yeast infection.

Alice's young home had never been steady, many strange beds and ceilings, a window to an ever-changing countryside, usually the outskirts of a small town where her father had renewed his glamorous ramblings as a salesman. She always had her own room, while her brothers shared. He sold pots and pans, vacuum cleaners, encyclopedias, knives; twice he set up an appliance store. Sales and repair. He had no mechanical ability, and the repair side was a fumbling pretense; it drew customers to his door. Her childhood memory was ingrained with big talk around many different kitchen tables, support that soured and turned to opposition. With each new place, hopeful sight, the support rebounded…until she entered junior high. She was growing a frail beauty. Her hair began to glisten, her legs as if she wore tights, her walk: a movement so unlike her brothers—even her mother—she began to capture glances. The recurring scale for her father's encouragement began to teeter; the family's belief in any future success fell flat. Her mother's opposition suddenly bore down with finality, bouncing heavily on the table and thudding to a halt. The flamboyant salesman could no longer sell anything in his own home. After their last move, Alice entered high school and Mr. Harrington took work at the creamery.

Out the pickup window, the day grew bright and the scenery level, the box between them like a long, drawn-out pause, holding the space. As if driving over a barren table, mile after mile across the Palmer Divide, Alice found no livestock, no buildings, only an expanse of short and ungrazed grass, a different future unfolding…

By the time they were seniors, Tucker thought Alice was the most attractive girl in the entire school, her soft brown hair split and curved above her forehead like a heart, her face tender, open. "It was that delicate manner of yours," he told her once, "for the simplest of actions: tying your shoe or straightening your collar, opening a book." This pulled on his composure, making him feel off center. When he saw her among their peers he thought of a precarious glass, too close to the edge, too breakable. "I knew you knew that I was watching," he said, "but I saw no reason you would want me."

Tucker Black was exactly what drew her interest, the Black name contiguous with an angular nook in the Front Range, a high basin that caught more rain, a hidden valley and hills with a wealth of resource. His people in the local cemetery dated back to the late 1800s: timber men, dairymen, farmers, ranchers: resolute, resourceful, and *not* rich. People who built sawmills, barns, houses—things to hold—a firm porch to stand and see from, so different from the floating parade of promises and failures which fluttered about her father. And she liked him, his glide. He was tall and square-shouldered, he spoke softly, and a slow accord followed him when he walked or moved his arms. He had manners. He always removed his hat when in a building, a strict gentleman when it came to opening doors for others or making a conscious effort to listen. He smiled broadly with his white teeth and direct eyes, his handshake unaggressive. When he smiled at Alice she could feel something surface, not so subtle or polite. Her legs tingled and a heat would gather at the top of her forehead.

Not once, Tucker confided, did he remotely consider asking her out. Not until her mother's incisive push. Mrs. Harrington was a stranger to him before they met on Main Street, her mother a slender, graying woman. She had approached him, he said, *with purpose in her step.* "I've heard about your father."

"Good morning." Alice pictured Tucker leaning lightly forward, nodding his hat, her mother's quick, hard look, dry lips and stringent mouth—too many disappointments, too many years without a plan.

"You *are* Tucker Black?"

"Yes, ma'am."

With crisp movements, the sharp point of her fingers touching the tip of her nose. She always had a spotless handkerchief tucked in her sleeve. "What happened to him? You're so young."

"He had a heart condition. We have known for a long time."

"That doesn't make it any easier." Not a single thread escaping the tie in her hair.

"We have our place," he said, thinking of the coming summer. He had no idea, then, who the woman was.

"You and my youngest are in the same class. My girl *Alice* has told me how tall you were."

The ground sloped. Tucker took a step.

"Give my condolences to your mother. I don't know how you'll do it, how you'll take care of—*all that place*. You are such a young man."

His feet planted. No need to explain. He looked to the west: his inborn home and the root to his future, alive in his heart like a child or a parent.

"Thank you, I will."

She was not finished.

"You'll be out of school soon. You and my only girl will be going your separate ways."

After that, Alice noticed Tucker's walk taking a new turn. They spoke several times. Toward the last days of school Tucker brought her to the valley. On a Saturday morning they crested the final hill to look down on the buildings. Arms from the mountain curved down, as though with hands to shelter the backsides of a settlement. Long established, nestled in trees, the hay land spread below them like a rich spill. She could feel the transformation; his smile lost reserve, his eyes with intent. Life with direction. Much higher than the town, higher stratus of air unfurled in her lungs, pressed on her vision—a lifelong picture over a fabric of green. Like an opening curtain to a greater clarity…skies of possibility…

The Choosing

Closure of the Quonset door resounded. In the heights of the building, milk-colored panels filtered the light as if through paper or linen. The floor's expanse was littered with straw; dusty machinery sat parked in the corners. At one end stood a wobbly stack of bright green bales. Immediately they heard the sounds. As though stuck in a barrel, puppy barks and squeals echoed off the ceiling near the hay. Bales had been pulled out to form a circle, a forgotten wall of confinement. Some of the twine had been gnawed. Hay spilled freshly on the layered and faded straw. Puppies were wrestling and jumping in the green spill, the new toy in a mammoth house of entertainment: two of the most adventurous chased among the wheels of a dismantled tractor, charging each other with wild tumbles. The people marched forward and one of the players heard the crunch of their steps, bringing a disease of distraction. All broke free to greet and gallop in unison. Several tripped and rolled while they scurried forward. Until now unnoticed, an adult female dog hopped down from high on the stack. Five of the litter at once altered their course and rudely attached themselves to her underside. She stood wagging her tail, showing a clear but surmountable irritation at the sharp teeth and multiple sucking sounds coming from underneath.

Tucker and Alice sat on opposite intact bales and studied the dogs for a long time, futilely brushing stems from their short, fuzzy backs and white-tipped tails, curled up and whirling.

He was slow to abandon his deeper concern, *their very first child*, reminded of Alice's walk, the bumping of the long gravel road. Tucker found himself watching...*her*, far more than the choices.

As if to dissemble the true purpose of the morning, they identified each small bundle by some subtle mark or trait. Alice gave them names. Fluff, Tall, Timid, Tilly, Brute. Looking down into the maze, the cistern of wriggles—mock prudence, pretend ferocity—Tucker felt empty of energy. There were too many.

. . . awaited hopes now so close...

Abruptly interrupted, their forgotten host knelt forward, searching, then plucked out the two already spoken for and tied a short length of twine around each neck. His thick fingers handled them callously, but with an underlying kindness. Returning them to the floor, they fussed and rolled, growling, yapping for the sudden collar. The unexpectedly young man gruffly rose: from the back side his neck stood out short and strong with shoulders hunched and muscled, but when he turned, his face contradicted—deep brown and lean with an outstanding smoothness. The long wires of the night before had given him a mask. Now an almost brooding silent, his presence faded.

One by one, Alice held the others in her lap and gently maneuvered them onto their backs. Tucker stepped over to sit by her side, catching the glitter in every eye. As they settled, each looked back at her *intently*. She lightly stroked their naked bellies and the paws grew limp, the hind legs splayed out like bird wings, a gape of trust.

Tucker sensed his own hat tipping down, as if for a nod of instant sleep.

She hunched over them and strings of her hair came loose. The intricacy of choosing wore on her mouth. Each puppy broke its calm, paddling and biting at the special hair.

A manner of sudden impatience overtook their company, a disturbing mixture of pride and even shy apprehension. Tucker glanced at the layer of T-shirts below his collar, lightly wondering who washed his clothes. He watched him brush his sleeves and begin looking toward the door.

"How old is the father, the one you call *Jack*?" Tucker asked.

"Four."

Tucker also stood, then considered the only parent they had seen. She had returned to the safety of the haystack, lying on a high bench with her head resting above crossed front legs, a serene observer.

"How old is she?"

"Seven…the one with the prize blood… It's a *fact*, the granddad's from Scotland—I told you about everyone pitching in. This might be her last litter." He oddly jerked his head. He swept alfalfa leaves from his shirttail. "You want to see her work?"

Tucker looked up at her wide blaze, the delicate matching feet.

"That's okay."

He turned to Alice, then back to the pressure of the man. "You mind if we stay here alone? We want to take our time."

"No trouble. *Yep*. I'm damn busy. Stay all day. I have to leave here at ten—" He headed down the long path for the door, a bowed-armed shamble. Another view of his back, *hunched…* Tucker imagined he wasn't quite ready to lose one of the litter. At the very last moment the mother dog leapt down from the hay and disappeared into the sunlight behind him.

Finally, after much playing and handling, the puppies began to pile up in exhaustion, pushing against the tidy edge of a bale, squirming themselves into sleep. Except two: one female and a male with a darker head, no string attached. They lay on their sides separate of the others, panting, heads nodding with their eyes closed.

With a spray of hair on each side, Alice turned suddenly white and more than tired.

"Pick one of these..."

She stood with a stagger, an obvious faint, familiar pale.

"I've got to take care of myself."

Tucker rose too and held out his hands. *Only one need.*

She denied them.

"I'll be all right."

Alice brushed her hair back and shook her head, as though to rid herself of a thought, still weaving.

"I'll be in the truck. You stay..."

Tucker sat again, placing his elbows on his knees and his chin in his hands *Dreams revived. After waiting thirteen years. As if something now were very achievable—almost immediately achievable.* He heard the door close. Slowly, very slowly, he reconsidered the choices.

After the loss of Billie, she would do the naming.

He settled on the two lying out by themselves. The male dog had a narrow blaze and a small ring of white around his muzzle. Compared to his blue-eyed siblings the face looked black. The white had been saved for his chest and collar and the tip of his tail; he revealed no hint of brown or tan. Tucker touched both noses with a long stem of hay. Their eyes reopened. The little girl rolled hers toward him, without shifting her head, heaving her ribs. Shortly she rose and went to lie with her brothers and sisters. The other sat upright and focused—mouth closed. Tucker knelt in the broken hay and pulled his hat off. The black face looked back at him, and the puppy's spine straightened like the pulling of a string: not the soft look of adoration or subservience: a strong face, glistening gaze.

A primordial dark eye.

He cradled the young thing in his hands and hurriedly left the shelter of the building.

Convalescence

Such a fragile pregnancy...

She didn't carry the baby very long. A nurse came. Some of the far neighbors didn't even know that she had been pregnant. They brought cakes and cookies, cards and notes, plates of homemade salami and sausage: food for the heart.

"She is such a slight girl—" many of them said to Tucker.

It would have been a daughter.

Alice kept the bedroom shade drawn, night and day. The early morning visits of condoling people dwindled, at last leaving them alone. Before wrapping the very small stillborn, they locked the new puppy in the chicken house, then buried the baby girl on the hill high above Billie, just below the rocks where the ridge began like the immense back to a dinosaur. Alice sat in the thin grass with her back curved. She held her knees together with folded arms, facing west, out across the valley. Red eyes, red soil at her feet. Tucker searched below the rocks of the ridge, balancing, slipping on flakes of shale like huge broken dishes. The clatter made by his footsteps was the single sound as he returned to Alice. He gripped a large plate in each hand. He built a small pyramid, like the pinnacle of an overlook to green fields: a place to rest...and feel safe.

At the base of the formation Jasper Spring flowed, gushed from under the ledge as if being pumped, the interior cavern huffing like a muffled seaside, a vague ventricle to the earth. Immediately the creek emerged, willows, wild plum, chokecherry. Lower there were vine-covered cottonwoods and a few pines, their dark-needled tops proud above the sprawl of leaves. The water traversed the broadest part of the hay bottoms. When farmed the near soil had a harsh red clay tone graduating in arcs and waves to a deep brown, then black. The black continued to the far tree line and became sandy but no lighter: a thick, damp wealth, deeper than any plow.

The shaken Alice took in the valley as if welcome rays from the sun, convalescing.

Rising steeply from this richness, the north slope had widely scattered old-growth pines—tall, straight, thin bark—towering above the young saplings and underbrush, sound, without limb for thirty feet. Once the stream crossed the farmland it remained at the foot of the slope, a softer seam in the floor. Spruce and aspen now clustered beside the channel of the creek. The aspen spread. Colonies climbed the first bench to crest and dwindle. A high field lay in a tilt, a distinctive table planted in oats. Above the grain, much taller than the crowding trees, stood the imperial sisters, noticeably humanlike: guardians: two granite spires reminding of an ancient force, remnant slough from the mountain above.

"You shouldn't have told my mother." Her mouth quivered. "I didn't want them to come. I didn't want to see anyone."

The warmth of the morning began to push air up the ridge, a wake of event.

"I am sorry."

He squatted beside the laced-together shards and his mind changed. "They had to know. They *would* know." He looked at her unblinking, but she did not turn to him.

At last she responded, "They have eyes, but they do not see…who we are. They don't see where we are."

The legacy—

Alice's face lost its openness, her mouth any want for words. But her eyes continued combing the valley, the living stream with its growth—like a distant note of suffering and understanding only she could hear.

Tucker looked out, his vision narrowed, burning with the brightness. He knew what she meant. How she felt? The hay had been cut, all was put by but the oats; it had been another good year, the grass on the eastside taller than a horse's knee. He *thought* he knew…with pangs of doubt. Torn, Tucker didn't have his parents; maybe that was easier.

Alice, suffering—the day in front of her too hard to bear—escaped into the past, an earlier time when the valley was fresh and unmarred, when Tucker's mother had still been alive.

The young man and the valley were attached; this she knew with a certainty—the first moment and morning when he chose to take her there—and the valley quickly enveloped her. They drove past the buildings and skirted the edge of rife fields. Alice remembered her admiration. She remembered how the rock formations shielded the sun, and the overwhelming mountain and table that bounded the early day. They approached a row of trees lining a creek and Tucker parked. Bluebirds twittered and cooed just outside the shadows. He had carried a blanket and she a limp basket with handles. He mentioned a spring, then led her up the bank to stay above its beginning. Her shoes were slippery and she went down. With disarming directness he tugged on her hand; she slipped again but he kept her from falling. More carefully he chose a pathway over the ledge and back into the darkness of the trees, where she could hear the surge, the intoxicating whisper, and see the first fantails of water. She had forgotten the name…then in his voice it came to her… *Jasper Spring.* A musky odor came from inside. He let her listen, then led her back into the half sun, where he spread the blanket and they sat and ate a light lunch. Birds, trees, water—absorbed by the sounds they spoke very little. Before them wound the bush and pines, crossing the lowland, following a flow from deep within the ridge. Spirit of solitude.

Alice had felt two powers folding around her, a power in herself. She stood and her eyes left the line of the stream and slowly began climbing the mountain. The high table had been freshly farmed and the seed was late to come, dark soil with a delicate fuzz of green. She began to grow a vision. An inviolable life, meaningful, clean, thankful, family gathered together taking food. A place to grow and fill in the blanks. A place to nest.

Tucker rose too and interrupted her view. He took her hands and kissed her and all fell away—her mother and father and brothers—all the houses and towns. More than heat in her forehead it passed up her front, now high enough to press against his chest and waist. Her breath stopped, then returned in slight, shallow pulses. Her eyes drifted over his shoulder.

She felt Tucker's hold tighten around her fingers.

"We will be here soon, very soon," he said.

Tucker kissed her again, quickly leading her through the shade to the hidden ruins of an old building, with a caution not to let her trip. Under the canopy of a large willow, partly buried in leaves and tuft, she watched him trace the foundation.

Her eyes cleared. Precisely laid rock held back the bank, a square enclosure with an opening down near the water, cool and mossy.

"What a chilly place."

"There had been a pipe from the spring running continuously over and between the cans of milk. A cool room. A springhouse." He held his hands out, forming the roof and walls. "When the house was full they took a wagonload to town."

"How long ago?"

The sound of water increased in her ears. She tasted milk and cold tin.

"When my father was just a child...they sold the milkers and went to raising grain for the mine horses...and the military. This whole bottom was in oats and barley. The milk wagons turned into grain wagons; they built granaries instead of milking sheds. Then they stopped using horses. We went to raising food for people again."

She could see him thinking of more to tell but without inclination.

Alice glanced up toward the blanket...then back to the motion in front of her; several levels turned to confusion. She imagined wagons filled with grain and Tucker searching for something in the stream bed. Much more dwelt in this place than what she first saw: busy people harvesting and hauling things to market. Was he looking for fish among the polished rocks?

"They are all black? The cattle?"

He smiled and seemed a little surprised. "Not always.... We cannot cross here—" he looked at her shoes "—the boulders are too slick." He spoke loudly for the close trickle and bubbling, as though under a fountain.

They had climbed above the ledge and stopped for a moment, looking down upon where they had picnicked, to catch the last luscious note from the spring. She remembered feeling quiet but not awkward.

"My mother is not well. I do not think you should meet her today."

He had opened her door and she again sat in his car as he drove slowly to the buildings.

"We lived…we lived in a different town almost every year," she told him. "I like staying in one place. I like it here." She believed his attention. "I am the last at home; my brothers have all moved away."

"I know Joseph."

"Charlie has learned how to weld."

"And the oldest, has he gone on to school?"

"Not yet, he drives a truck for the creamery. Not one of us wants to sell…" She turned to the side with a mood of disinterest.

They had approached his home, the gathering of improvements, and Alice bent forward. Her hand touched the dash.

"Your sister—is she in school?" Alice asked.

"Valerie married. Her husband did not want to be out here. They live along the Yakima—Washington State—in a town called Grandview."

Rather than pass below the barn and corrals, he took the drive that circled the house. The small yard in front had been freshly mowed. Plump robins were hopping and picking in the light rows of tattered green. Tall tulips were spent, losing their petals beside the step. She touched the dash again; the house was not big, wood-sided, a well-kept two-story with dormer windows and shallow eaves, white curtains.

Imagining a spirit, a person in the upstairs, she noticed a brick chimney and stained shakes, a litter of leaves, a small octagonal window high in the gable end.

Artifacts of the human hearth.

Therein stood the porch—covered, safe—surveyor of all the valley and the endless sky.

She remembered how the following weekend he took her all the way to Marshal, out to supper and they danced. The next morning he introduced her to his mother. In a matter of a week the hay had grown six inches. There were different flowers blooming in the yard. They sat in the kitchen and made small talk for a long while. The older woman had long, loosely bound hair, not a heavy gunmetal gray, but a lifting—*radiant*—white. Sun came in the window, catching waves of this hair and the corner of the table. She wore a cheerful paisley dress, calf length and full. Much of the time Alice could feel her watching. Her overused hands were carefully laced together with an aura of content.

At last she rose and rattled the lids to the wood range. The tool to lift them appeared in her hand as though by magic, or ever-present in the deep folds of her dress.

"I haven't made bread for a month. I don't care for that new thing," she referred across the room. There sat a bland appliance with the spiral of electric elements.

"Bread from a wood-fired oven—" She inhaled weakly and staggered, bending at the waist and seeming to float, as though puzzling over some distant trouble.

Alice felt a stamina gathering under the snowy hair, spreading downward. She glanced at the woman's undersized feet. His mother drew herself *nearly* straight.

"It smells much better."

Tucker tipped forward in agreement.

Alice began to smile with concern.

She sat down heavily and faced her son. "Fetch me some wood— p-l-e-a-s-e."

He left and the two waited in silence for a moment, looking away from one another. Alice pondered the whiff of a laundry soap and some type of lavender fragrance, then the sparse tidiness of the surrounding room. She passed along the dark woodwork, the sheer curtains—the glass-covered print of a bay horse.

His mother sharply intervened, age and feebleness shed, pulling on Alice with all her force. "This country is changing...changing more than you can realize." She took a breath, not to gather her thoughts but to empower their expression. "Tucker doesn't see it. It is coming—"

Alice felt nervous.

The small mouth and creased lip continued speaking with a cadence and tone she would not forget. "He is going to need help to hold it together. Are you going to be his help?"

Tucker filled the doorway. He came into the room with a balanced armload, certain not to spill any crumbs, very sturdy and upright. Alice waited for him to turn away and place the split pieces in the box beside the stove, then nodded firmly.

"I better get pitch. I better get kindling."

They were alone again, with the fresh smell of pine. Now weary, the voice came from a deep place, a draining strength, and hurried:

"I won't be making much more bread." She looked through Alice and with gaunt shoulders pressed down on her own lap. "I haven't got much time." She pulled away, then focused on Alice's smooth young face. "Girl. You can have this house, but for yourself—and him...you better fill it."

Thrown together, the newlywed Alice and Tucker chose to share. Their involution hungered and met. As if by fate their purpose united, superimposed. They painted the house and built a new garden fence. They planted fruit trees of a special hardiness. They gathered wood with a confidence. Alice fit. All grew together. She embraced the sense of place, the landscape, the need, and the gentle man. In small touches and increments Tucker eased, conformed to her lead. They swelled and wound together. She became his girl—a deep link—no other—his mate. His star in the heaven. He became her artist, depicting the valley and its inhabitants, her connection. Each a teacher of the other's fulfillment. Her engagement convoluted—his softness—masculine whole—his caretaking, giving. Female and male: attracted opposites walking in the same footprint. Their solitudes mingled. They awoke believing the same things.

Young Prince

The new dog, unnamed, was still not allowed into the house; he had not yet unfolded and become a member in their lives. And now, Alice did not want him.

Tucker partitioned off one end of the chicken house. He put a peach crate on its side and draped a blanket over the top. The original coat lay as padding on the inside. This was the young dog's space: his safe haven from the threatening howl of coyotes, the passing shadow of hawks and owls, even eagles: his protection from the wind and rain, the coming snow and cold. In the evenings, this is where he received his food.

Each morning, Tucker would open the door and greet him on the high threshold, then welcome him out. The dog followed him everywhere, but avoided the house, and for the first days left at the sound of any engine. He was fearless of horses. Tucker put a line on as throttle and kept him from around their legs. Pulling on the restraint, the dog's small eyes brightened; he backed up with a quivering yawn of discipline and pulled again, over and over. Horse, Tucker's mount, snorted and stomped his feet. Alice's mare Daisy affirmed her rule with a display of cruel stained teeth and snapping tail. Tucker had to load him on the back of the wagon six times before he would stay and they could rattle down the valley to the stack yards. Once the wagon was packed with hay, the dog rode on top of the bales, a clear preference to the empty bouncing. They slowly returned to the buildings. Tucker left the pickup idling in direct line with the porch, then either moved to the passenger side, or walked back to climb on the hay and join the dog. Already dressed for the weather, Alice descended the steps and replaced him as the driver.

The collie's first encounter with cattle, and the young dog lost all self-control. He dove from the trailer directly into their pushing presence and vaporous heads. A deadly shuffle of hooves, humped backs—a drowned murmur and Tucker thought the dog was lost. Calling out, he followed, searching low. *Whissht.* The hoof of a friendly cow knocked Tucker's hat off. *Kump*, a vile strike to his rib. Alice stopped the engine while Tucker searched for the flexing pup. Tucker could hear snarls and intent movement from underneath. The small dog crouched, whipping from tire to tire, baring his miniature range of ivory at the horde of legs. Wincing, Tucker scooped him up. Back at the barn, Tucker staggered a moment in the privacy of a calving bay, then abruptly gagged, leaving a puddle of his morning meal in a layer of pale straw. He spit-hacked up a clot of blood, still trying to find a balance.

In nice weather he and the dog rode together to the feed grounds, swaying as if attached. Weeks passed before the oblong lump in Tucker's side finally shrank and disappeared.

* * *

Before bed each night Alice kissed Tucker: a conflicting embrace. For three months after the loss of the baby, she did not welcome his touch. He waited, hoping she would at least give the dog a name.

Tucker buried himself in teaching, getting to know his new companion. He kept eight newly weaned calves in the corral.

When leaving the house he carried a guarded numbness, then opened the chicken house door to an eager face, a minimal substitution. He patted the welcome head with a gloved hand, but felt a curling heaviness in his own breath. Before feeding he would weave through the young cattle with the dog on a short leash. They were curious while the dog was tense, glaring back. For five cool mornings they briefly walked among them; Tucker frequently needed to tug to keep the collie in motion. On the sixth morning the calves felt frisky and brave. Two skittered about with their tails in the air, then bawled and made a callow charge at the dog. The pup jerked the line from Tucker's hand and ran to the far end of the corral; in an instant the two calves began leaping and bucking in random pursuit. Snugging his haunches, the puppy escaped under the rail, then turned and crouched, a disquieting quiver to his lip. They all stopped. Tucker felt a pressure—like an overhead weight—too much for the calves and they quickly forgot the dog's presence. As if to regain their status, they butted each other with hard boney heads. Their hooves kicked up bits of frosty ground. Dragging elbows the small collie crept back in...riveted, keen eyes. The two stopped playing, but would not move for his entrenched effort, his glazed stare. Tucker stepped closer. Nothing moved.

"Walk up," he said.

The dog seemed frozen.

"Walk up." This time steam rose around the words. Nothing moved.

"Sh-sh-h.

"Chu-chu-chu."

The dog exploded, leapt into their faces, biting foreheads and hooking an ear. The two calves cut and bellowed in retreat, broke into the others. The entire eight panicked and ran headlong into the corral gate, which splintered and swung open, allowing them to gallop and scatter from the now empty pen into the sudden rustle of tall winter grass, the juvenile dog beginning to stop and jump, jump so he could see above the reed-like stems, might see where he had lost them all.

Tucker blinked with surprise and swung his chin to a tingle of nerves. He inhaled deeply on the sharply filtered morning air.

Snow fell and after feeding he left for town to run errands. Tucker allowed the dog to be by himself. Without leash or collar he was free in the yard, his door of the chicken house wired open. Paw prints soon went to the door where the hens were, still not wanting to get their feet wet. The disturbed snow at their entrance, clear evidence that the dog had sat and looked in at the queer birds. Tracks headed for the barn and corral, then angled away. He had been told to *stay out* when Tucker was not with him. He made adult tracks though his body was half grown; his trail went to the near end of the loafing shed and disappeared under the protection of its roof to reappear at the far end. The lone prints looped from building to building: granary, icehouse, root cellar, machine shed, and Tucker's shop: each loop approached the house but never passed a certain radius.

Alice came from inside and swept away the thin drifts in the shade of the porch. She swept the sunny steps. All was clear but the packed snow from Tucker's boots. She swept again—eroded islands too stubborn for the broom—she returned with a small shovel intended for ashes and noticed the sign in the yard. For a moment she thought there was a child, a young thing drawing grand patterns in the clean snow, as if the porch were the center of an inverted daisy. She straightened and looked for the dog. At length he trotted from the gaping darkness of the wood shed. As soon as he entered the light, their eyes met. His tail went down and he halted his search and discovery. All the white between them made him squint, look deceivingly understanding and wise.

"Hey."

A warm breath on a chilly morning.

His tail rose, as if in answer, and the white plume slowly waved.

"Hey," she said again.

He was yet to bloom, but not his tail. He waved, spoke to her gracefully.

"Hey—you."

The approach began stiffly, graduating to a tentative skip, his first entrance to the circle—the circle of view about the steps. He did not climb them. She watched his voice relax, again dragging in the snow.

"I don't dislike you."

She regarded him closely. His trailing fluff made him look like a fox, though his feet were too big and his ears too small. She remembered his age and finally smiled.

"Come on." She bent her slender fingers inward, to draw him.

He abruptly arched over the steps and commenced wagging his whole body to press against her legs. To contain him, she sat down and stroked his head, his coat a vigorous cool from being in the snow, a fresh purity. Unbroken flakes fell on her arm. He stilled and looked away, as though suddenly absent, now distantly dreaming.

She followed his profile and stopped petting. She pulled his chin around to hold, his dark face closed and strong, as though somehow impaired—or superior, as if he didn't need to breathe. The blue eyes of puppyhood had turned amber.

"Perhaps I should name you *Prince*," she said.

That night her kiss had clear intention, reaching. She wrapped her small body around Tucker and drew him in.

Tucker awoke in the predawn, listening, hearing the sound of sleep. He carried his clothes to the kitchen and dressed silently. He took his hat, vest, and coat from the hooks beside the door and entered the frozen night. Blind fingers snapped the buttons to his vest and zipped the coat, finding gloves in its pocket. As he left the porch, the night began to open. There were stars and a minuscule moon, a glow in the east. The south slopes had thawed and the crusty snow made his strides sure and quick; the chill and bitterness of winter did not yet feel defeating. High up the ridge he bent forward, puffing, increasing his step. By the grave it had grown light enough he could see his breath.

His own sound receded. The eastern horizon grew in definition; stars disappeared. The sky between buttes slowly gathered color. Standing with the shale plates at his feet, he could feel the planet move, an incomprehensible giant thing… This special section of the earth rolling toward the sun—then rolling away.

He returned to the yard well before sunrise, and quietly released the new dog from his space in the chicken house. Alice had named him Tommie.

A Quiet, Well-Ordered Place

Unable to find a complete book, Tucker was hungry for any knowledge on the instinct of herding—practicing alone, pulled forward. He searched out information: reading pamphlets, small booklets from the veterinarian, flyers pinned among the bulletins at the livestock auction. His understanding began to center around balance…and *eye*.

Once Tommie had the respect of the calves, they would crowd against the corral fence and group for him. One day Tucker gently wedged himself between the rough planks and this tight bunching of calves. Everything backed away. At first the cattle tried to divide but the young dog's four light feet skipped out in a mindless response. They were trapped, without space or gap for breaking away. Tucker watched: this new motion quick and unbound yet connected, like the reciprocating movement of a nimble crank and piston, ready to wheel around and keep things contained. The collie's need to have them together began to root, become smooth, a suddenly organized urge. Tucker held his arms out and walked backward in a slow curve through the main corral; he felt the calves being held at a steady distance, as if by an elastic, invisible band. If one tried to split, the dog caught them with an immediate swing. Twice he flashed his teeth, no bark, no voice from the man. At the end of the pen Tucker turned and headed back, this time leaving a trail in the dirt like a snake. The dog's eyes remarkably *affixed* to the tiny herd. Like opposite poles to a compass, the human moved and his assistant balanced.

By the third morning of working the cattle the corral had turned into a ballroom floor. Tucker like an airplane, arms extended and backing in curves and figure eights, Tommie a reflection, reading every detail. An unknown waltz, a mesmerizing dance. Tucker was the lead with his tall form and broad hat. The animals held at his feet completely captive—secondary to dog and man, and their ripening alliance.

* * *

The yard froze quickly with the dusk of shorter days. In the dimness, Tucker closely followed Tom toward the chicken house entrance, for the dog's feeding and place to sleep. He was not quite eight months old. The white of the collie's collar captured light and led his way. Tucker carried a tin bowl of food and a pitcher filled with fresh water. He opened the black of the outbuilding doorway and turned to sit on the unpainted sill. The collie eagerly ate with the bowl near his boots, content with his lonely place to spend the night. When Tommie finished, Tucker stood, but the dog didn't leap into the dark room, an unexpected change from his daily habit. He remained by the empty container waving his tail, as if still hungry. Tucker reached in and felt for the water dish. He found nothing and could not place the old coat or blanket. He could barely discern the empty peach crate set against the far wall.

"No good night here," he said. Though nearly dark, he could see the dog's eyes. The sound of his simple phrase faded slowly: *no good night here.* His lips remained parted and he pushed his hat up…

Alice stood across the well-lit kitchen with her back to him, a large wooden cutting board in her hands, still dripping. She placed it beside the sink. "The bedding was filthy. I washed it. And still had to comb and brush—get the fur out. Also the dust from the chickens."

"Yes."

It seemed immediate—she held a knife and two yellow onions. "He has already tested, how he will fit."

Tucker could feel his eyes smiling.

Alice began slicing and dicing the onions. "Aren't you going to ask where I made his bed?"

"May I let him come in?"

"Of course." Without using her hands she swung a rope of hair over her shoulder.

Tucker smiled openly, "I'm sure you chose a good place."

"It's in the washroom, hidden by the linen cupboard. Confining, but I think it's what he wants." Alice turned, bits of onion on her hands, her eyes beginning to pool. "We've never kept a dog—never kept a dog we didn't have sleep in this home…"

For the next several months Alice took over his feeding. Though her touch was infrequent, when indoors Tommie was often beside her, lying by her chair or sitting nearby when she stood at the counter. He seemed never underfoot or in the way, but a follower, a shadow. The prime environment, the place to fill.

When her fine fingers combed the dog's fur he stopped all motion and turned away, a distinct composure very different from the tie he had with Tucker, a full swing from masculine strength to the tenderness of untold touch and acceptance.

Despite Alice's private manner and Tucker's reserve, their young working companion became a neighborhood marker. Crisp black and white—no blended tones or fading transition—the collie's sharp contrast in color drew focus. He stood in their threshold, not filling a space, but reminder of what was lacking. And he had style, a working ability and flare that attracted attention. His history as a predator-turned-guardian brought an unsettling pleasure to those who watched.

On his first fall gathering of cattle, the land brimmed with health and plenty. Late rains had fallen and the brown hills were supple that day, without dust, the regrowth of the low-lying hay bright and washy.

A car stopped on the county road and its door opened. A man balanced on the doorsill sighting an old-fashioned movie camera over the roof. He moved to the rear bumper in clear avoidance of the glossy paint and the angle of the high-altitude sun. He pressed his legs against the trunk, giving himself two free hands. He paused for a lesser distance as the herd began its traverse below the tree line. Where he had parked revealed care and purpose. His lens caught the carved definition between loose grassed hills and dense alfalfa. Only a fragment of the stone spires peered above the beginning ridge. Over the mountain hung a tolling mixture of cloud and blue. To his left, cottonwoods fluttered their leaves in the road ditch.

Horseback, Tucker brought the yearling steers first. The cattle were all black. He rode a black horse with a broad white blaze and held the front flanks—as if he had planned the colors. Tommie kept the stragglers up in light little sweeps and pushes. At length the throng approached and smelled the alfalfa. The dog ceased. The cattle spilled around the horse and rider and off the ripe slopes in thick, fluid shapes like mercury on sand. Briefly they spread, a few ran and bucked, then all stopped to bury their heads in the tremendous green.

Tucker made a wide swing through the tender plants and caught a glimpse of the dog's white socks. They were already stained and his belly hair had begun to cake and cling together. The cattle left a trail of crushed growth too lavish and soft to stand again. Steam rose around their heads. The horse snorted and nodded.

"Horse," he muttered, "I can taste it too…"

Tucker's eyes were drawn from the field—diagonally—to catch the sheen of a clean and polished car on the bordering road. The car was not moving. Though far beyond the range of speech, he recognized the bare-headed figure in the open air, Glen Simmons, the creamery foreman, strangely leaning and semi-hunched. With a jerk-like nod of his broad hat, Tucker returned to the herd and the challenge at hand.

Now the work began. The rich, moist clover and legume could easily turn to calamity, a toxin in disguise. Tucker felt the *strong absence* of his wife's help. He had a picture of Daisy, Alice's ardent mare, pressing with remarkable force: using rolling eyes and nipping teeth, shaping lips and ears into gestures of scorn.

Something wrong with the day —rustled the green. It had been strange for her to make excuses. He vaguely wondered if Alice were fighting a sickness…after such a long time—he starkly remembered: some mornings she would be sick twice, as if host to a constrained clock, ticking with an overload of worry and doubt.

Another chance for a child.

Without warning, Tucker practiced a hiss and hoot, slapping his thigh with a broken length of cinch. His horse butted the cattle's sides with its chest. Tucker extended his arm and slapped at their rumps: a crowd of gluttonous magnets on an iron field. He felt an off-balance, *uneasy anger*.

Without his young helper it would have been hopeless. The dog crept in, gripping heels; his chin tinted green like his socks. One or more steers kicked the air and others turned to face him. The collie paused with a glimmering eye. At a chosen instant the dog sprang up to sting brows or pinch an ear, without wrath. No one fought. Tucker watched, his anger receding, as a sluggish backing then quick retreat began to expand. The cattle clearly remembered this hornet-like capacity, the past bewilderment of bitten noses and clashing teeth. A pattern developed. The collie triggered motion and Horse kept it trotting. Tucker tugged on the reins while significant numbers gained speed and momentum. Within minutes the stalking, the hesitations shortened to a flow and the yearlings began to scuttle in waves larger and larger. For one hundred yards they trailed across the flat without direction, no more heeling; the simple, quick following presence of dog-horse-man kept them moving.

"Tom!" Tucker called. Once he had the dog's readiness he spoke as if they were in a small room. "Come out—out." His chin and hat swung left and the left collar of his vest tipped down.

Tom made a wide arc, loping through the resistant hay. Before he reached the opposite side of the cattle, Tucker whistled him in. Once the leaders began to turn, he whistled him to stop. Six times, after going left or right, the collie had to return to help Tucker on the horse. He panted now, tongue growing long, eager eyes with a pressure as though stuffed with heat.

From the horse's height, Tucker could see his partner striving through the difficult growth, no sweaty face, no sign of restraint, no low breeze. He felt a sharp rift in the plan; two levels of grimness pulled on his cheeks. Tucker thrust Horse into the yearlings, flailing the cinch and slapping it so loudly it burned through his pants.

Should have Alice... No, no.

Two more cars stopped along the gravel.

At last the wide flat began to slope down and lose sight of the road, ending at a long, rusty fence with an open gate. Further lay a dish-shaped pasture of pale wild grass. Horse and his extraordinary teammate guided everyone through the gate like water through the narrows in a stream. Afterward, they spread as if a delta.

The people on the road followed with turning heads; the rider with his dog passed close enough to see faces, then descended the incline behind the cattle and disappeared. Just before sinking from view, Tucker glanced over and caught Glen relaxing his camera. The eyes of any outlander remained ignorant of the fence and valley beyond. Witness now, a quiet, well-ordered place.

Cobwebs

Jasper Spring in the approach of winter: a steamy flow, moss-covered rocks, icicles hanging from the near branches—another child was growing well before Tucker's awareness. Though she believed he now knew—*guessed?*—she chose the fresh air and close to the spring as the place to tell him. They did not pack for a cold picnic, but planned a brief visit, to again see the stream in such a changed season. They came alone, as a couple, quietly returning to the place so important. Sitting side by side on the ledge above, nearest the water, Alice opened her down coat and drew Tucker's hand to press inside, the warm inside.

He stood—"Are you sure?"—then pulled her up by both wrists.

"I know what is happening inside my own body… It is definite—*you* already knew." She could see their words steaming, like the bubbling of the creek. Her fur-lined hood drooped around her neck, as though a tray for the moist air. Frost began to form in the hair beside her cheeks. Tucker lifted his hat and placed it on the close rock shelf. They held each other tightly, very tightly…signal of an expression hard for her to trace. Then they kissed. Alice imagined a tremor in his lips.

"It will happen… *This time*, it will happen."

Unlike before, on the heel of three months, Alice insisted they get the crib down from the attic. She watched her husband struggle to fit it through the opening, as if the hatch door had been built for a smaller people. He passed all the sections down, then descended the ladder with a box of hardware under one arm. His hair and ears were tangled with spider web, and shirt and pants with large smudges of dust. After a cleaning with a damp cloth, most of the components appeared brand-new, the painted wood still a bright creamy white. Valerie had been the last infant to use it as a bed.

In Tucker's absence, Alice rewashed every detailed part with soapy water and a soft brush. All the lathe work she dried and polished with a strip of old towel, as though polishing the glossy toe of a shoe. On closer inspection she found chips in the paint on the headboard and the side rail that lowered. She made tentative plans to sand and repaint, then visualized a very small girl, standing and hammering with a metal cup, or some early toy. Her hand passed over the roughness: they could have been made by a boy. Her memory had skipped—Valerie was the oldest. The last person to lie in this crib had been her husband.

"I think I will leave the marks," she said aloud.

She bought, and double-washed in a special softener, enough cloth diapers to fill a whole strand of the clothesline. She watched them sun themselves and flutter in the March breeze. Alice gathered them in a basket and imagined a young person trailing her. She turned abruptly and the child vanished. *"Oh-oh—"* feeling her breath catch, like an echo to the secret surprise. Tommie lay watching from beside the garden gate. She felt tears in her eyes at the thought of a small brother and sister playing on the still brown but sunlit grass. The collie trotted to be by her side as if knowing her dreams. They returned to the house, each in turn following the other.

In the fifth month, the hope fell: from so high: *too* high. Alice followed the brittle vessel, shattering with it. And *after*: awake in the small hours of the morning, she felt her body pressing down, the core of her body like broken pieces compacted together, lying still, trying to resist, brace against another clench. The prayer she clung to, now a vapor. *Where was*—she didn't want to hear his breathing. She lay quietly, waiting for him to rise like clockwork and go to the kitchen and make coffee, then turn the light out to drink in the darkness. Maybe then she could feel alone, rest, even fall asleep. She lay on the bed, empty of force. Gray and dismal daylight began to define the walls.

Hesitant, the black-and-white dog ventured forward in the still sunless room and placed his chin on the rumpled quilt. With his nose, he tried to lift Alice's ivory hand. She pulled it away, moaning. Then she shook her head with her eyes closed. Withered sobs exhaled, began refreshed. Silently backing away, Tommie returned to his pacing, beginning to cry himself, whimper, studying the dark boards of the burnished floor as though needing to bury something, the worn, tight joints too hard and barren.

Tucker awoke from his aimlessness. He entered the slightly open door and from the bedroom window found the barn roof, the corral fence, the sawdust pile...all in sepia tone, distorted by the ripple of glass and a wave of sorrow, the outdoor light electric and numb. Standing unshaven and gray like a stone, he felt a current, a draw, the permanent stifling closure of a door—barrier to dreams fulfilled.

This time he *knew*: the hurt would run much deeper and longer, absolute, beyond his reach. Tucker could deal with the loss of children, eventually, but he couldn't deal with—couldn't see or find the passage.

He pushed Tommie out of the room and down the hall and across the rolling kitchen linoleum. He swung open the flimsy screen. "Go on," he said softly, without moving his lips. In a breath of thin, clear air Tucker watched him stand on the steps, then with a visible tension in his movement lay on the top plank, without sigh, wrapping his thick tail around as if he were cold. Tucker couldn't help but notice the eyes, as though fiercely bound to something hidden in the rank grass of the east yard: listening. In a long moment they closed and the dog relaxed.

Following his early chores and returning to the house, she had risen. "Good morning," he offered. Without an answer, he tried to kiss her, renew their touch...as though she had no heart or lung, only icy lips. The thought of more words entered Tucker's head, but formed into blank phrases. He couldn't deny her withdrawing to other rooms, her discomfort whenever he was near. The dog tried again to nuzzle her hand, and received—*nothing*.

In the dim tack room of the barn, Daisy's saddle grew dust and the brow band of her bridle filled with cobwebs. Tucker counted the years by loss. Thirteen years of marriage and the loss of Billie. Followed by a few hopeful months like a cruel tease—burial on the high ridge—barrenness, rising, for nearly two years of uneasy recovery and continued trying…as though pulled forward by an unstoppable flow—*damn the second tease, damn, DAMN*—then the pinnacle of expectation impossible to stop—turning to cobwebs. Fifteen years, turning to cobwebs.

Discovered

Working and learning with the collie Alice had named Tommie became Tucker's compensation, his avoidance. Spring; then summer. The usefulness and structure of this fascination began to take hold and expand, well separate of his greatest concern: the need to attract and embrace—simply understand. Grief indelible... The dog was there for so many things. A mere collie who mingled in the hushed memory, the landmark happenings of Alice and Tucker's middle life.

By the time the collie was four years old, Glen Simmons had shown his movies of Tommie working cattle to nearly all the creamery employees, and several of the township ranchers. In consequence, Tucker was asked by the Hendersons to help gather the Crooked Oaks. The Conlon brothers invited him for the Highland Allotment. And notorious Spruce Draw, the Nelsons.

Alice never rode.

Tucker knew well it was not Horse and man the neighbors were after.

His fellow stockmen and women most valued the border collie in brush, deadfall, thick timber. In the sweep to bring in the big herds over a rolling and immense land, a camouflage of snags, dark possibilities for deep concealment, lay in wait. Secret places of heavy forest growth: ravines like tunnels under a weave of boughs and bridging vine, shadowy cliffs obscured by thorns and slides of rock, and the wind-thrown spruce—tree after tree—broken-uprooted in a confusion of litter and draping moss. Most of these catches, horses and riders had unwillingly learned. In Tucker's memory they were like holes in a net, an invitation for the clever and lurking: sometimes fearful or lame: to duck away…find refuge.

The day they helped the Nelsons gather at Spruce Draw, it began with Tucker watching the collie slip through silently where a most capable horse would stumble and thrash, possibly come to a halt in a tangle of gear and flailing jockey. The Nelsons' herd was rainbow in color. Whatever the breed, without apparent effort the dog dislodged *all* cattle, no matter how shrewd or silent. Some quickly sensed his slyness and hid behind screens of jack pine, or crusted in mud, blended with the black bark of ancient trunks, steaming, more still than a tree. Tucker could barely follow as they might try to hide again, but the dog's ease—his darting over harsh rock and below fallen logs, daring and quick—always succeeded. Many of the animals panicked over this ghostlike pursuit, surrendering in a mad dash, as though suddenly frantic and falsely expecting a less predatory horse and rider.

On this gather, little went smoothly. The Nelsons' cattle were the most contentious, and the terrain of their allotment well known for its severity. And the Nelsons—their replacement yearlings were especially persistent in an effort to fly apart, scatter like birds or pellets shot from a gun. Tucker smiled with surprise at the early dust cloud of hooves, the precarious races, teams of horses and *family members only*, in a desperate skirmish—four adults and six grown children riding like their cattle. Now is when he held back. With such wild handling, it became essential that the collie's craft remain in the brush. Even the most headstrong cow or yearling could not cut to the side and disappear. Tucker and Horse accompanied, but how the dog managed was rarely seen, with a stealth and quiet: trembling fugitives beginning to mill, deep in their cover, then with a sudden rush, burst forward to attempt a new hiding. Relentless push after push. They eventually surrendered into the open, in permanent avoidance of the blinding spruce and tangle of undergrowth. At last the family met them, still riding with a mood of fierceness, but the fury exhausted: a sweaty posse of horses and glistening faces—pressing the continuation of a very broken and disorderly trail.

On the last leg, at the end and with the cattle now calm, Tucker felt his hat was the broadest, the nodding imperceptible. The two elder Nelsons riding beside him followed the collie, their eyes in notice of wherever he might be: a respect and admiration...with a slight smile...without a word.

Home, putting away Horse's pungent and polished tack, Tucker's glance caught the dull coating of Alice's nearby saddle, then stalled on the figure of Tommie standing in the entrance. With a new level of partnership, he considered the inhuman feet and legs, an undaunted athletic source: a remarkable power—such power and finesse—to push, coax—he wished—*anyone* from hiding.

* * *

A road was being built on the far side of the high mountain, unknown to the foothills or eastern plain. When the air was right, Tucker could stand in the yard and hear the sputter and rev of distant machines.

Alice stood separate, on the level of the porch. "The sound carries," she said, with Tommie hugging her side and hoping to be noticed. "The scrape and clang of steel against rock—*I hate it.*" The dog sank, beyond anyone's reach.

Though faint, the sound was cutting, a drain on Tucker's temper. He kept looking toward the mountain, expecting to see a billow of smoke or drifting dust. He felt the life in the forest withdraw.

Coming deep from the interior, as though entering through a back door, the construction dissected the heart of the timber reserve, little-known country. It crossed the western ranges and wound east, through trackless land of virgin parks, imperious trees, stopping just before the crest of the front rampart, just beyond view from the Blacks' homestead. Distant, but close, a remaining and hidden erosion.

Not even Tucker's grandfather had cut wood so high, most of the mountain face too steep and over the top too far for his horses.

"The country above is for the quiet of feet, hooves," Tucker muttered, his eyes on the dog. "Not machines." The collie made an imprint in his mind, rising from the porch floor with his ears nervously perked, as though disturbed by the words, as though knowing Tucker and Alice's distressed agreement—still without warmth.

After the road they sold timber. For two seasons Tucker felt the subtle invasion of the valley's aura, a dim intermittent echo of fluctuant saws and engines. Silence came when the snow grew deep, and the valley could once again breathe.

The following summer, bands of elk came and went. The second summer, they came and stayed for a much longer time.

* * *

Tommie was there the shimmering summer Ray came to them. High pockets of hay land were ripening, the alfalfa heavy with blossom; resplendent grass heads waved as tall as a man's chest. The dog sat upright on the seat beside Tucker—an August afternoon he would always remember. Though with room by the window, Tommie perched in the middle, looking straight ahead. They drove a trail that skirted the upper edge of the fields. The dry hills began to close in. As if following the bank to a large river, the rippling hay turned and disappeared. The fence between path and field was drowned, engulfed; no visible strands but a short curious string of uneven post tops. They curved to see more of the hidden flow and the collie grew more attentive. At once they came to a stark row of pitch and cedar, drooping wires, the growth smashed and trampled on both sides. The thick and thin and lumpy posts stood like oddly-shaped people abruptly undressed. Not thirty yards further lay snapped wood and strung barbs, as flat as the grass. A bright August day and far into the field were large patches with nothing remaining to waver.

Tucker pressed on the clutch and engaged the brake; the truck ceased its motion with a soft groaning. He tipped forward, studying the far reaches of the hay. He felt behind the seat and shook his head. He clicked off the engine, then immediately stepped out and looked into the bed. From under fence tools and short rolls of wire, he untangled an axe, but did not lift it out. At first notice it looked as though a troop had meandered through making multiple passes with a scythe, leaving a clear line, revealing just how wealthy the crop. Tucker lowered himself into the truck, and leaned back. He rapped the steering wheel with the heel of his hand. A luxurious forest clipped to its edge. Slender blue-green stems had a climbing understory of dark leaves, crowding, reaching for more height. Some seed heads *were* missing—and flowers had been snipped, yet most lay bruised and shriveled, churned and trampled, as though those responsible had not considered it food, merely a place to bed and play and wallow, and leave their waste.

The dog and driver could smell the cause. The truck continued up the track until the last of the field was visible. There were no more signs of elk, and the hay stood clean and untouched.

At the base of the opposite hill Tucker caught a glint of something metallic, a stirring in the tall grass.

As though struck by an arrow, Tommie slid from his wolf-eyed attention to a driving interest and vivid excitement. He rose and began pumping the dusty seat with all four feet. The hair on his shoulder ruffled. Tucker felt something too: a hazard, a sharpness, concealed at the edge of the cover.

He took the axe and carefully followed the dog, who led blindly through the clutching growth. The plants parted and came together as they each passed. In the depths the pull increased with the weight of blossoms and healthy vines around his feet and legs. Tucker enjoyed this pulling, holding the axe up as if needing to keep it above water. A sudden change occurred in the collie; he began to leap so he could see. His worried tail went up and he leapt as though emerging from a viscous fluid—the tail beginning to wave in rapid circles and figure eights. The jumps grew higher and a little desperate. Suddenly all confusion vanished. The dog had found a definite scent and pounced forward, with Tucker high-stepping and lurching in his trail.

"N-o... N-o!" a muffled shriek.

For less than a second Tommie stood above this voice with his tail erect and madly spinning like a wild feather, then began poking with his nose. Tucker still could not see but heard the sound of struggle and gasping—exasperation. The dog had the voice pinned, his nose darted everywhere, and his tongue began to loll then lick. Tucker came near and relaxed his axe, swinging it to the ground. A child rolled but the dog persisted, never touching with his paws, skipping around and over, swarming about the face and neck, leaving a dampness, as though clearing away all effort to speak and breathe. The boy's look of fear and need to escape changed to surprise. The collie's frantic hovering allowed no chance for the young boy to gain his balance and rise.

"Enough—Tom."

The boy sat up in the wrestled hay, wiping his cheeks, pushing his wetted hair back, eyelashes matted from all the cool burrowing. Blond and blue.

Tommie was beside himself, prancing, a continuous white-tipped flurry; only a short hesitation, then the boy went down again.

This time laughter and faint squeals, a complex welcome.

Tucker smiled.

"*Tommie*—enough!"

Tucker called him away and had him sit. The dog only panted after work and when hot. He panted now. His eyes shone, glittering and determined, while his tail flapped and struggled in the snarl of grass.

"*Where,* where did you come from?"

Tucker looked seriously down at the boy, re-drying his neck and ears.

He stood, as if the fun were ending, not bothering to brush off.

"I live…I live in that trailer on the other side of the road."

The field occurred in motion, sloshing in all directions.

His eyelashes came together in star points, as if he had come from a salty ocean. His breathing was unsteady. "Where the sharp corner is."

Tucker knew the place: a solitary and dilapidated trailer house, crowding the county right-of-way. People there came and went, it was several miles to the northeast, a considerable distance for a boy on foot.

"*How* did you get here?"

"My bike."

Without expression the boy shrugged and pointed.

Tucker could find nothing but the pleasure of clover fading to brome; they stood near the edge of the structured planting.

"What bike?"

The boy held his wind. His eyes watered a fresh blue, as though they belonged in a young girl's face. He pointed again. His shirt clung and pulled about his chest and neck in pronounced opposition to the loose fit of his pants. He drew straighter. "It don't have a stand." He began to follow the line of his own arm, a mild but ungroomed cleanliness to his size and shape.

Tucker released the collie—spilling with impatience. The dog immediately buzzed in circles around the strange clothes, nuzzling hands, unrelenting, making the intruder weave then trip. Soon he reared and went for the perfect face and Tucker said *no,* so he stayed with the hands.

In the thinning grass lay a fat-tired bike with rust-pitted chrome handlebars and a chrome chain guard and tattered seat, the paint weathered and chipped. Tucker considered the surrounding hills and shook his head.

"I come through that gate along the road into your top pastures. I—"

The dog, like a brimming distraction, began to tickle. The boy pulled his arms up.

"I didn't—I didn't go through no bottom…I…didn't come by no buildings."

Still without expression he tried to pet Tommie. The collie's own affections constantly interfered. Between all the dog's frenzy, Tucker absorbed more face and guessed the boy to be about ten years old. He needed a haircut. Tucker studied the bike again, then along the horizon.

Too many wriggles.

"Tommie—SIT!"

The dog's legs folded and he leaned against his catch, looking up, his restraint on a tether.

The boy waited for Tucker's eye, then repeated his point. "I come down that ridge and into that trail you been on."

"What is your name?"

"R-Ray..." The boy turned and reviewed the hay. Something pure and individual.

Tucker turned too, as if it were the first time he had seen it: a sea of timothy: numberless seed heads drifting and swaying in the summer afternoon.

"What are you doing?"

"I—I come to see what this colored grass was about."

Ray strained to raise his bike while the dog sat and watched, now settled, yet panting and intent.

"It makes you dizzy."

The bike was for someone older.

"I-I...never seen that color." He balanced on the cracked and sun-bleached seat, and in the same motion pressed down on a pedal, moving forward. With an incomplete smile, "I better be gone—"

Tucker watched him bounce around the upper boundary until he hit a dead furrow and crashed to the ground. Up again, he continued until he found the path that smoothed out and he quickly gathered speed. He wove around the truck, then stood and pedaled faster. The shimmering flow of hay in the foreground hid all but the handlebars. A blond boy bobbing up and down in the silvery green. Tucker could see his hair parting.

"We will see him again," he said to the dog's back. "*This boy* knows at least two ways into the valley."

Tucker watched him pass where the elk had been and received a glimpse of his clumsy steed, kicking up a haze as it made the bend. The dog stopped panting and closed his mouth.

Tears in the Tea

Tommie sat at a distance, a black-and-white collie by a chicken house stoop, well across the yard, well apart from the house.

Alice ventured out for the second time, joining the ordinary items and gloves she had gathered below the garden, near the smallest of the apple trees. Three buckets of water sat to one side of the trunk. They seemed an interruption to the view, while her other things were lost in the grass. She wore no hat—feeling herself an outstanding pale, even her clothes, a harsh reflection of the sun. In her mind Alice had welcomed the coming shade. She felt anxious to reach the comfort and cover of the private little orchard.

Quickly kneeling under the shortest and stiffest-looking tree, she stayed bent to the side to keep from tangling her hair in the crooked lower limbs. She pulled the rough leather of a matching glove over her left fingers. This gave her a padded grip on a light steel bar. The bar was two feet in length. Even through the leather she could feel the weight of something cool and unforgiving. Before taking hold of the opposite tool, she paused, studying the frailty of her bare hand. Her slim fingers had a bluish tint. They made a determined wrap around the dark wooden handle of one of Tucker's hammers: a ball and peen:

aged and corroded but polished from use and frequent cleanings by a rag. The grip on the bar felt muffled while the grip on the hammer felt close and secure. At the start of her task, she had the remote vision that her arms were disconnected: one hand bare and one hand clothed, going different directions.

The basin for the tree had long grown in with grass. Closely clipped, it now resembled a large bowl of sod and interwoven root. Following the drip line traced by the shadow of the overhead branches, Alice began pounding the steel rod into the thickly carpeted dirt...over and over. She lay the hammer down. In her repeated effort to extrude this bar, she began by stirring it in a circle. The shaft rolled and bit at her unprotected palm.

Steel against steel. *Tap, tap, tap*. Then quiet. She looked back at the honeycomb of holes beginning to circle the tree. She felt Tucker's presence. Out of the corner of her eye, she could see his full length stand in the bright doorway to the shop.

He had said something about a boy...on a bicycle.

She bent further down and caught the scent of dry dirt and newly torn roots. Her progress turned suddenly halting, but led her on, as though with a jagged and single mind of its own. The buckets she had set out earlier were placed in an arch. As Alice continued, this galvanized curve began to pinch her in the basin. At last the bar struck the closest pail with a dull clang and threw a splash of water. One knee to her pant leg developed a pattern of large dots.

Tucker's form took action, like a pedaling across the yard.

She tried to tip and twist the buckets further away without standing. The fingers to the one glove became dark and cool, while her hair caught in a spur from the lowest branch.

She felt a baffling discomfort over his approach. *Boys pedaling*.

Each bucket had a feed sack draped over its edge from the inside, like a wick to draw moisture and share it with air. This merely added to her difficulty in pushing them away, an added drag, awkwardness turning to irritation she could not describe.

Tucker lifted two of the buckets in a single sweep.

Weakness spread through the small of her back, then her right shoulder. A creeping disturbance flickered through her hands. This standing above her, so tall and straight. What could it be? As if *she* were a drying fruit, one lacking success: Alice scrunched down from the limb, then shifted to the side and sat back on her heels.

Intrusions, boys on bicycles.

She tucked at the lump in her snagged hair.

"What is this?" he asked.

"The water won't go in."

"I heard you pounding, but what is this?" He lifted the sack from the remaining bucket, revealing a bulge, an outline of soggy contents like a suspicious dead weight.

Carefully gathered humus and soil, an erosion from below the corral. He lifted it higher, with dribbling brown fluid exactly as intended.

"Manure tea."

"What? … Oh." He tried to smile "An unfound brew?" He lowered the sack again and it bubbled slightly, then sank for a continuing steep.

She didn't want to know about boys.

Alice looked nervously about, as if in search of an outside source to draw his attention, pull him away from this *help*.

He had other things, callings from all sides, mountains of—projects, plans.

"The leaves are smaller than the others. And it is not growing up." Her voice felt a new inflection, new levels of nerves.

Will we ever be all right?

Tucker lifted the last bucket further out. It slopped on his boots. He stood with an obvious silence.

Alice picked up the rod and hammer and returned to her tapping. "The water can't get in. It just sits and evaporates." Strength now came into her hands and clarity with the sound.

"It is tight. These roots won't let anything through," he said.

She felt the quiver of an added misalignment.

More strings of brown hair fell free from her barrette.

"I should get a spade and plow up the grass," he offered.

"It's just one tree, the others are fine."

"I could break it up—the sod—and shake out the dirt…put on a mulch…"

"Other basins have sand. This has clay."

"Would a covering be good, something to snuff—something to keep the grass from coming back?"

"This has clay."

His arms and hands had a look like he needed a shovel, an item to poke, pry at the ground. While she hammered.

"I think you have a good idea."

"This little thing needs a boost. My mix will get through." She kept pounding as she spoke, giving an offset emphasis to the spacing of her words. "I, know-this, will-work."

"The trailer is already hitched. A load of bark and chips—" he paused, as though she might rest and discuss "—could help the struggle with so much root and hold in the wet."

"Too much turpentine," as if tapping out a message, "this is working."

Tucker turned, she could feel a stiffness, and now against all reason her mouth would not function. He was leaving; she watched his arms counter the swing of his legs and her message stopped. With a stirring motion Alice twisted the rod, attempting to pull it out, and tore a layer of thin skin in the creases of her right palm. Her hand quickly drew into a fist. As it burned she watched his walk: narrow hips and wide shoulders, a classic design. Too upright? She hurriedly snugged the unused glove over her lightly bloodied fingers. Tall and stable. A silhouette.

Tucker's boots crossed the porch and entered the house.

The black-and-white collie sat by the chicken house stoop.

Now she jerked at the rod: dwindling force, dwindling purpose. Why was she all alone? The dog looked suddenly foreign, its colors like an alien flag, uninvolved, motionless and observant as though knowing to stay away.

As if she had had her eyes closed, Tucker appeared over her head welding a pruning shear. He snipped at small limbs, deftly catching and gathering them in his other hand, a spray of leaves and reddish stems. Alice backed out from under him as though worried over the sharpness of the scissors-like tool. She watched for a moment: his ability to reach almost the highest of the limbs. Frowning for no cause, she brought forward a container of her tea and began to pour. The loose bag pulled the tension of the water to the side and it spilled in a thin fan, dark but transparent, about the series of holes closest to Tucker's feet. Rich nutrients with a sediment of quartz. She caught the bright wiggle of four smaller apples in his bounty of clipped branches.

"What are you doing?"

"There are too many limbs rubbing on each other—"

"But the apples?"

He looked at them, hanging, now separate of the tree.

"Like your mix, the sun needs to get through."

She shook her head, dropping the bucket with a clank from the handle.

"The wind makes them bump, one against the other." He gestured to the tree's center now hidden by his arm. "Where they cross, the bark is getting bruised and scuffed."

"You shouldn't chop off the apples."

"They did—I don't—"

"I can't fertilize and have you chop off the apples."

"Competition." His voice came to a standstill. It had not been interrupted. He did not shrug. His hat tipped forward.

"No matter," her lips quick and carrying them all the wrong places. "It's not the season to prune. This time of year the wounds do not harden and winter and fungus can get in and it can kill it. And you ought to know."

"Seems like too much product without enough sun."

"I won't have you cutting…not now." She could see the limbs and leaves squeezing together in his grasp, the dangle of a few—very few small round ornaments. The shears came down beside his leg, open and limp. Alice watched them close, with an evenness.

"This is the only dwarf," he said.

She finally glanced into his eyes.

"I do not know about the leaves, but it is bred so it will not grow very tall. Haralson: a dwarf," he repeated.

"What do you know about apple trees?"

His eyes—they blinked and he looked away. A sleeve came up and touched his nose.

"Nothing… I am glad you are out here."

"They aren't *bred*, they are grafted."

He repeated his turning, this time very smoothly, but heavily, as though something intangible and withdrawn were now pressing down through his hips. His hips. Not hers. The secret of her wounded hand kept burning through the glove. Alice shuddered. She went from strong to weak—then blank. Where was her memory? With a bitter pulse in her chest she wanted to call-shout something beautiful and passionate. She still needed him. She still wanted him…?

Tucker

Stop

He laid the small bundle of trimmings by the rusty barrel for burning trash on the back edge of the lawn. He didn't return the pruning shears to the utility drawer beside the kitchen sink, rattle them with the well-known clutter of thumbtacks, tangled shoelaces, sewing awl, chrome scissors too dull to cut paper, but headed directly for the shop. This skip, deviation from her prediction brought a falling apart and folding in, panic over the unfaithful. Like a force of the landscape she felt a ridge of loneliness and complexity rising between her and whatever he did. The door closed behind him. She remembered the soft click and frictionless turning of worn hardware, her hands on the verge of flying away.

The black-and-white collie sat. Then curled its tail and lay down, the only one of its kind, a surreal picture of pristine calm and anchored patience.

Alice began to cry: *tears in the tea.*

Welcome Guest

From the low fields, Tommie was first to notice a movement high on the lane. As if triggered by a voice, Tucker looked up and at once discovered a little stick thing with wheels against the skyline, and the small boy. The dog stayed near the tractor until the bridge, then began to weave forward and swing away from their course, as if for a better view. Though distant, Tucker knew who and what it was as it sped down the final slope, then suddenly slowed and labored in the loose dirt and sand behind the shop. Generations of rain and wear had created a softness, now a comedy of effort, as if driving into a pot of honey. Spokes pulled up sand and the boy stood to gain power and keep pushing forward.

Tucker pondered: *Should he allow the collie to run ahead?*

The bike would get knocked down or a tail pinched under its tires.

As if he were concerned over a coming traffic, Tucker pulled to the side of his hay field road and invited his companion to hop on the wagon. "Load up," he directed without looking. Seconds later he turned to study the dog—standing on four spread feet, swaying and absorbing the ruts with his total attention one-quarter mile away. The tractor patiently putted. The wheels slowly turned. The collie's self-control was impeccable, as long as his paws were off the ground.

They drove between mowed fields, picked clean and already beginning to re-green. Tucker watched the clouds in the east building, white, yet heavy in their form, still a bright blue behind. He saw the able rider pull from the mire, then quickly turn to be swallowed by the structures of the farmyard. The boy disappeared. Not sure what this motion meant, the dog's ears went up, his mouth opened and closed. Tucker lightly nudged the front of his hat. Bouncing-leaning into an apparition of happiness.

Put-put-put.

Ray could hear nothing but his own panting and the distant tractor. The only motion: chickens fluffing in the powder under a bush with drooping limbs. Where was the dog? Disappointed, he let the bike drop. The chain slapped and clanged against its guard.

Alice heard the break in the quiet and glanced out the window. Standing in full sun, with a bike around his legs, was a shining blond boy. The rear wheel coasted slowly, a calm glitter of spokes. The boy looked from building to building, then centered on the house. Something about this entry, this slice in the silence, Alice felt he could see directly through the window to where she stood. She drew in her breath. Without thinking she quickly hid behind the curtain and the frame, peeking out to see him untangle his legs and shake his hair back—take a few steps forward, only to stop again and reconsider. His face was tan and too hidden by the light hair. Breathing more easily, Alice felt the need to tuck it back so she could know— She folded and stroked the curtain, like pulling away her own soft brown hair, and watched his indecision. She heard the muffled tractor coming and saw him listening, searching through the barrier of trees to find the source.

They approached the end of the hay land, and Tucker again pulled to the edge of the road. He turned to the dog, who was mesmerized and still swaying as if his feet were buckled to the floor of the wagon. His tail swept the dust.

"You can go."

With a great leap from the platform, he hit the ground in a powerful lope and his sleek nose pointed and his neck stretched out like a racehorse, raising the dry until he left the road to make a straight line over ditches and under fences.

Alice watched the young face grimace then collapse. She saw his recognition and immediate cheer. The sudden flurry of a wild friendship was pressing, knocking the boy one way, then the other. He clearly wanted to reach down and pat, even hug the exuberant dog, but the long black-and-white body would not hold still: rearing and diving. For a moment the boy appeared to be lightly choking, wishing to talk. The nose bounced off his hands and touched his mouth.

"I remember—I remember your name—"

Ray felt the surprise of a fresh wetness on his lips and grinned, wiping them with the back of his hand. He tried for the dog's collar. "It's Tom," he said loudly.

All hullabaloo slowed.

"Or *Tommie,*" he said most clearly, as if meant for someone else to hear.

The dog was set back, stopped for an instant, and Ray could have caught him. All he wanted was to look into the handsome face, remember the magnetic eyes.

Alice watched as the dog began again, only more controlled and with the hint of an intention. He made charges at the house, to return over and over, firmly brushing against Ray's legs, taking his balance and causing a step.

She relaxed.

All Ray could see or think of was the collie. He soon forgot almost everything else. He knew he was outside and had re-found the love of a stranger. The vibrant sight and touch of this dog, his mission—complete.

Without knowing, the boy was being coaxed closer and closer to the steps leading up to Alice.

Like a ghost she found a different window.

At last he grew tired of being bumped and wanted to touch. *"Tommie. Sit,"* he said with an uncertain thrust, and a broad smile.

At once the dog sat and waved its tail, some distance away, directly between Ray and the climb to the entrance.

Ray came forward and knelt, finally able to stroke the dark head, still not thinking of the porch.

Alice slipped further behind the curtain. She was able to see the blue of his eyes.

The prince turned squeamish, wanting a release. He pulled his ears tight to his head and gave one solitary bark, spinning, to bound into the shade and nearer—

The peculiarity of such an immediate woof made her wince. She could hear the click of his paws on the hardened wood. He barked again. She twisted to hide entirely, lean her back against the wall. *"Oh, Tommie,"* she whispered. In the near instant she could hear shoes, light and very different from the boots of Tucker.

After the crawl of the tractor, Tucker made big strides across the yard, stopping before the path in the lawn. He and the dog regarded each other. Tommie stayed beside the boy and the door, looking proud of his prize and where they stood.

"What are you carrying on about?" Tucker said lowly. He met the boy. His tone lifted. "This dog never talks. And will not when you want him to."

With the sound of Tucker's voice, Alice vanished deep inside the house. In hurried passing she jarred the glass shade to the desk lamp. It wobbled precariously with a threat to fall and burst.

Tucker understood the dog's wish, his urge to introduce Alice, yet in the shadow of the porch he felt a bleakness. He wanted the boy back in the sun. He cared for a better picture before such a remarkable presence disappeared, pedaled away, for the second time.

Ray made a face that Tucker clearly remembered, a defeated expression, as though the fun were ending.

"He is a good dog."

Tucker watched: a thread to the boy's interest seemed to tighten and pull to the surface. Ray stooped to pat Tommie's side, never turning away from Tucker or dropping his eyes to see what he was touching.

"He's a good dog—Tommie is."

Tucker tipped his head back and rubbed his throat. The broad hat kept his mouth under cover.

"You know his name?"

"You talked—you talked at him when we was up in the pasture, when I—I was here the first time...I know your names. You're Mister Black and this is Tom—Tommie."

The boy's eyes flashed diagonally up, then slid to the floor. He knelt, showing a clear but halting desire to put his arm around the dog's neck.

"I sure think he's—sure like him."

"He has a *thing* for you."

Ray's bare arm slid around and he fingered the clean white to the collie's chest.

Even without sun, Tucker studied his face, two blue pools under a golden tree. He stepped onto the porch and extended his hand. "Ray?"

The boy rose and their fingers touched. There was no grip. He went back to the floor and held Tommie, who nuzzled his free hand until both were on him. Tucker felt a sudden awkwardness. He moved to the side and left the steps uncluttered.

"People know *him*, not me."

The man's company was hard and the dog's was easy. Though Ray now knelt, Tucker could feel a growing conflict. Ray did not want to release what he had come to see and touch.

"I never seen a dog like this." With a shrug he stood, sadness in the droop of his arms. His eyes covered the yard, in obvious search for more than his bike.

The collie's soft fur and tail wormed in front of him. A cloud shadow displaced the sun and passed over the buildings; the roof creaked, quickly cooling the porch.

Tucker peered in the window. "Alice? Alice *has* to be home. Did you knock?"

"No sir."

Tucker knocked, as though it were not his home.

"Have you had your dinner?"

No answer.

The dog turned sideways and braced to stop an exit.

At the very least she had to see him.

He knocked again and opened the door a fraction. The same weight as in Ray's arms snubbed his voice. Tucker did not call out.

No faltering in the collie; he wedged his nose in the gap in the door and went straight away for her figure, waiting and expectant in the dimly lit hallway. She heard a sudden brush and thumping on the wainscot.

"You, *you*," Alice said softly.

After the dog's lead, Tucker swung the door wide. "You better come in. I know she is here."

Amazed that Ray went first, or even entered, Tucker felt the disappearance of Tommie's tail, as though it were a suction. He followed and closed the door. He hung his hat on one of an empty row of wire hooks and lay his gloves on the dark wood floor, taking care to keep them separate from a small oval rug. At the same time Alice walked in with the dog at her side—serious and stretching up like he wanted to be as tall as the people and give her courage. She would not meet Tucker's face and fiddled with her hair. She looked at Ray; the blond now parted with a mild lift in each direction, a clean image. In the presence of Alice the boy looked bigger and older.

Her hands trembled, unprepared.

"This is *the* Ray.

"Not too much surprise? I think he came to see Tommie. He came on his bike. It is very quiet." Tucker made a gesture toward the table. "He has not had his dinner."

"Pleased to meet you," swallowed Alice, her voice thin and withheld.

She did not quite smile. Her regard had an experimental friendliness, a passing welcome, a definite shyness.

"This is Alice."

Ray looked down to his friend—then to her and back again. The dog's eyes reflected a manner encouraging. Tommie left her side and nuzzled Ray's hand, then returned to Alice.

"I sometimes don't eat—lunch."

Tucker set the table. Ray sat with his back to the window, his arm almost touching the wide ruffles of a drape. Tommie waited on the edge of a large braided rug with his back to the door. The wainscot came down the hall, varnished and marked by age, passing behind the desk and under high rows of very familiar books, to break and signify how the room had once been divided. Tucker considered the warm floor, the kitchen range—though the oak chairs were unmatching—all blended to provide a useful space to group and renew. He watched Alice slice cold beef and bring a slightly heated bowl of rice. She stopped and studied her own wrists and hands, then the boy at the table.

Gathered together taking food.

"This won't do."

She took away what she had brought and went back to a bustling in the kitchen. This time the pots and dishes clashed and she allowed the cupboard doors to clap shut.

Tucker rose to help yet saw no place to enter this terse activity, the boy like an expression of clarity and across the room one of confusion. Ray's bright presence magnified...renewed Tucker's vision of Alice. With a fresh perspective he was beginning to understand her eroded confidence, the distortion of the girl still living out of reach. Ray: the pure unbroken human heart, and what it could offer, unsoiled or divided or confused: unlost. Tucker massaged his own bare forehead, then met the dog's face and slowly nodded.

"What grade are you in?"

"I would—I woulda be starting seventh—" he put his hands in his lap and leaned his chest against the table "—they held me back. I'll do it again, I'll do sixth again. We been moving—moving all over."

Alice glanced over her shoulder and dropped a spoon.

"Your folks know where you are? Do they know you are here?" asked Tucker.

"M-Mom's between jobs. She's looking for work—right now."

He watched the boy's very brown arms come into view, to brush the hair away. They were faintly covered with dust.

"You need to wash?"

"No sir."

Tucker had washed at the creek. Next time he would be a better example and they would clean their hands together.

Alice came with a steaming pan of macaroni and melted cheese. In one pass she carried bread and butter and a bowl of beans, balanced on her arm like a practiced waitress; the other hand held a bottle of milk with individual napkins scissored between her fingers. She delivered a hot plate of sliced meat and sat looking from one end of the table to the other, only to rise again and return with a jar of jam and extra silverware. She allowed Tucker to serve himself, then gathered the prepared dishes in a semicircle around the boy's plate. She served him a generous portion of macaroni and scooted the remaining dishes closer, bottles and jars bumped together. He looked up in bewilderment and the blue eyes made her stop.

"Make out your meal," said Tucker.

He did not know the meaning.

Ray slowly began to see more than the dog. She still didn't smile but her lips parted and he could see she was a very pretty lady, so light and quick, with slim hands, a character and experience around her eyes that made him feel important. He began to eat.

Alice watched him chew and closed her eyes.

Tommie lay down and placed his chin on his paws, breathing deeply.

The big man rose to collect his hat and gloves and say he was grateful.

Ray also stood and pushed his chair back in place, then turned to the window. "It's—it's getting cloudy." The drifting patches of shadow had turned into small patches of sun.

"They are coming from the east," Tucker said. "I am going. It could rain this afternoon."

Ray felt the light pass away. The cloud stayed longer than before and the indoor space faded to an unexpected dimness. He felt a new power in the sky and Tucker's forecast, but as if the man had no interest, nothing to do with the weather. He listened to his deep voice thanking Alice again. Tommie went directly to stand beside the tall man's boots.

She rested her chin in her hand and accepted this politeness, a tired kind of softness.

"Lunch *was* good," Ray heard coming from his own lips.

He had never thanked anyone for food before. He just took it.

"You are very welcome."

A tapering angle of sun swept over the window, as though a whole day were passing in a single sweep. Abruptly he wanted out from behind the table; his feet caught in the legs of the chairs. The stumbling brought his hair down and he shook it back.

"What do you got to do, Mister Black?"

Tucker's fingers pressed the fold in his hat. "I still have horse hay to put in the lower shed."

"Can—" He took his place beside the man, like a twin to the dog.

Alice seemed to agree, take *his* side.

Tucker looked down and stroked the brim, then up, with eyes that bore straight and without any blink. "You can go." He put his hat on and opened the door, his followers in step. "What does your father do?"

"I—I don't got a dad."

The door closed behind them.

Alice lay her head on the table.

Orphan in the Rain

Upon leaving the house—as though not his own choice—Ray found himself riding on a wagon, the dog at his side. His legs hung over the edge and were dangling. Within moments, contentment with the present and the near future overcame him; he was unable to think. He watched the valley go by as if plunged into a dream, gently bumping with the pleasure of the collie's coat leaning against him. One side he looked up the mountain, the big pines were spaced—with very large trunks, like the mothers and fathers of what grew beneath. Then he turned his head slowly, traversing the heart of Jasper Park, as if to savor the hay land, smooth and trim. Jasper Spring came from the foot of the ridge. It curved like a deep green thread, growing taller with trees and scratching a line in his mind: he would not forget. The sky above the sharp ridge was now covered in cloud, a shifting darkness. The high rocks looked like a fortress. He put his bare arm around the dog, abruptly hungry for warmth.

Now a distraction, an interruption to his half-dream, he caught the man studying the sky. It remained blue above the mountain but the sun had disappeared. Tucker's head went from left to right; then with a reflex dip of his hat, he bent forward, to pull a little further on the throttle. Ray watched him stroke each sleeve of his shirt, then briskly brush his completely hidden arms.

They passed by a bridge and the spruce and aspen began, adding to the cool. The leaves fluttered weakly as they bumped along. The tractor sounded muted. They joined the sound of water. After some distance they came to an opening with a gray barn roofed in long, rough boards. Ray had never seen a roof like this; the boards were speckled and fringed with a faded moss. Opposite the barn stood a tall, open shed, no corrals, only a loose cage-like netting of wire enclosing a small yard in front. Ray could see machinery tucked inside and an overhead mow stuffed with bright green hay. The overripe grass lay flattened out front. Elsewhere it stood higher than the tractor hood. Sitting on the wagon, Ray could see but half of the barn, unclear doors and openings to a once busy place. He smelled the sweet baled hay and the grass underneath the wheels. The tires rolled up below him with a twist of green in their tread.

Tucker opened a tall, floppy gate and drove alongside the hay storage. He parked very close. He stood on the seat, then stepped to the tractor tire and hoisted himself into the loft. Ray remained sitting and Tucker left his sight for a moment. He reappeared shaking his head and carrying several burlap bags.

"I forgot jackets. If it rains…all we have with us are feed sacks."

Ray and the dog and man heard the first rumble, distant, and the leaves above the creek quivered. The blue had gone. The light drew flat, a gleaning of definition. They left the yard and continued on a two-track, then down a long slope to ford the stream, the same deep thread coming from the spring.

At last, Ray discovered the abandoned house: overgrown, wading under a group of trees very different and broader than all the others. It stood square and erect with boarded windows weathered a somber brown, like dark eyes without a purpose. The floor and half the railing of a huge porch were swallowed by the summer's growth, as though suffering in flood or melting evenly from the ground up.

Ray felt the dog stiffen. Water fanned and rippled over worn rocks, still deep enough his arm left the warmth of fur and both hands gripped the edge of the wagon. Just before the roughness of the water, the collie spread his feet and yawned, then pressed a shoulder into Ray's ribs. Ray felt the strong urge to jump and let them cross without him.

"Hold on," Tucker turned and called.

As if with the same breath, Ray heard a closer rumble from the sky, prolonged and groaning. They started bouncing in jolts, and splashing overpowered the skyward sound. He raised his legs and held tightly, watching the water turn white and churn around the turning wheels. The motion of the trees brought his eyes up. More than leaves, whole limbs and the pointed spruce were swaying and shaking. A sudden draft crossed his face, and the dog's coat parted and swirled. Tucker ducked his hat and the brim went down like a flap of cardboard. Leaving the stream, the tractor climbed the bank and a calm returned. They entered the open to a total quiet, as though the just present gusting and excitement had been imagined. No longer a track or road, the field bore smooth as a table and Tucker changed gears. Ray could hear the rapid crunch of the stubble as they approached a cluster of bales, crisp square dots below an outline of clean hills. The valley had narrowed and this field felt sheltered. The gray air flashed, a neon glimmer without location, and in the same moment the tractor ceased, as if a wire had been cut. He could see the man's lips and read several numbers. They stopped at nine. The thunder clashed and moaned with a deep vibration. The dog drove its pointed nose under Ray's arm and bore weight against his chest. He watched the collie's ears move up and down as though listening but not wanting to hear.

They began moving again, then soon parked among a thick group of bales. Tucker drew the strings together and swung them onto the trailer. Ray dragged them to the side while the dog went back and forth across the polished wagon, never in the way. After three stops the man stepped onto the bed and made a stack along the front edge. Ray watched as he laced them together with a certain pattern. He was not big enough to lift much, so slid them closer.

Tucker faintly smiled. "Next time I will have gloves for you."

Ray looked into the changing weather, as though the voice he had heard was not in his language, then returned to his struggle with another bale.

They both watched the clouds lowering and becoming very moody. A large bank began to stir and eddy against the mountains.

KABOOM! —sizzling light directly above. Ray felt Tucker's hands thrusting him down beside the stack, then immediately leaving him—the man leapt from the wagon, returning with an armload of gunnysacks. He threw them into Ray's lap: "You stay down."

Tommie huddled with him, sniffing at the air as if smelling the static, sniffing the future. They began to move, not with panic but the turnaround was sharp and they wove between the bales with a sense of hurry. Ray could not see what was pulling him. The sound seemed padded. The smooth and level of the receding field felt artificial. He saw the wind in the trees above the crossing, then watched it follow the creek and reach out and touch; a current in the stubble and one of the sacks blew from the wagon. Ray suddenly clung to the mixture of a soft dog and coarse burlap. Like an opening roof the rain began, not a timid sprinkle or leading patter but a rush and hard pelting and he pulled the sacks over his arms and head. The rolling stopped and Tucker appeared through the blur of water and spray, snatching a sack away and placing his hat on Ray's head. Blinking, Ray could see the instantaneous change in the man's dry hair—a vivifying glaze streaming down his face.

Again in tow, almost at once he felt them tip from the field and descend the bank to the other water, Tommie's fur like a coated mop and the burlap a dirty sieve, the corner of the hat a downspout onto his leg. This new incline made the water run under him and dam against the hay. The partial stack quavered and bounced in unison but one top cube lost its balance and splashed into the stream, rolling with a dragging float until it caught against a boulder.

They approached the buildings, and the rain lost its force, still steady but the view had gained space.

Tommie attached himself more closely than ever to the boy.

Still driving, Tucker stood and looked behind, seeing them as one, wet to the core. Tucker parked and trotted back to the wagon. Beyond his own clinging pants and squishy boots, this snuggled pair appeared much worse. He jumped up to Ray's height, then swung him into the loft as though he had strings. The loose hat wobbled but never fell. He picked up Tommie, who submitted with great discomfort, his soaked ears clutching his own head, and helped him reach and scuffle onto the dry boards at Ray's feet. Tucker caught another series of flashes, deflections of light, with a long count to the fibrous rumble. He backed the wagon into an open bay, then came to stand under the protection of the eaves, directly below the feet of the boy and dog. Behind and above, he felt a shake and could hear ears flap, barely audible through the drumming on the roof.

The bales in the field, now heavy with water, would need several days of sun—and a breeze.

Without Tucker's knowing, Ray looked down at his bare head and broad shoulders, clearly drawn through the wet shirt. In that moment all chill vanished. The boy's eyes looked as if they were burning; big hot tears rolled down his cheeks as though drops of rain bleeding from the strange hat and his matted hair. The dog pressed against him, with a heavy shine...a smoldering expression not easy to interpret.

Tucker craned, his neck stiffened and turned up toward the boy. Sacks hung about his small frame like wet rags. The hat continued to drip. It ran down his arms and dripped from individual fingers. Now more than ever his eyes had a marine look, like he had *lived* in water.

Ray touched his arms and the soggy burlap, shouting with a weak effort at cheer, "They don't itch no more!" The green sticky dust on his pants and shoes turned gradually dark and combined with the wet.

The dog shook again.

The rain came in waves.

Tucker stepped up on the tongue to the rake and searched for gaps in the boards to the platform so he could pull himself up. The collie kissed his vulnerable face. Tucker made a low growl so he would back away and give room. The boy had also come closer. They both moved away. He pulled his chest over the sharp edge, then flung his leg up and without hesitation gained his feet. He couldn't straighten completely under the rafters. The dry and sticky crushed leaves and stems covered much of his front; like bentonite it greased his saturated gloves. In the darkness of the mow he collected more sacks and slapped them against the wall before returning to Ray. He smiled to feel the warmth under the roof, trapped, still lingering from the volume of dry hay. He wadded up a cleaner bag and lifted away Ray's hat, only to stop in midair. He could sense a recovering heat under the flattened yellow hair. The hat returned to its place. The clinging sacks were removed and he began with a gentle circular motion, then changed to back and forth, the burlap rolling on the boy's skin but drawing moisture from his clothes.

"I know this scratches but you have got to get dry." Though close, he had to speak loudly for the beating and streaming on the roof.

Ray submitted to his touch as if he were another dog. Tucker felt a roughness and power in his own hands but heard no complaint.

After much rubbing he had the boy sit between bales and draped dry sacks over his shoulders and legs, like packing a grotesque figurine, allowing ample space for the large hat. He watched Ray shuffle his position, trying to avoid pokes from the brittle hay, then settle. He looked warm but only a little dry. The dog sat on his feet. Tucker dried his own hair, then rested beside the boy, pulling the brown rags up and about his neck and back like an insufficient shawl. Together they looked out into the rain, a union of meager comfort and solid security.

"Behind the barn, across the way, there is a house." Tucker noticed a faint but unmistakable nod through the extension of the hat. "This is the old Voss place." He paused, sensing a passing of the storm. The roof began to quiet; the ceiling of cloud occurred thinner and brighter.

"It was a good place. Very protected but the winter days are short...so close to the mountain the sun is blocked." He caught a dreamy quality to the boy's blue eyes.

Tommie rose, then returned and sat with a heavier pressing on Ray's ankles.

Ray blinked, a sudden and unusual clearness in his head. He listened to the roof. He had never so enjoyed the sound of weather, removed and now so welcome: what rain was and would always be.

He did not want it to stop.

Again distracted, he felt the man leaning forward to place his elbows on his knees, and the close flicker then lift of the dog's ragged ears. Ray heard the engine of a truck. It splashed over the flooded grass and parked, facing them with a serious Alice peering through flapping wipers. Streaks of light came down around the soaked barn and shed, and the rain grew to less than a tickle, no more than a smattering of shining pinpoints between tarnished buildings. Ray felt suddenly drawn and pale, as though from a returning numbness and shiver. Alice left the wipers going. The boy could see her shoes getting wet as she brought coats and towels to within their reach. He gave the hat back and dried his face and thoroughly scoured his head with one of the towels. He could smell the hat in the towel, that of lightly oiled hair: not just the smell of sweat but of a tall, straight walk, a solitary purpose.

Somehow moved, he touched his own eyes...then touched again. When they were down from the mow, the black barn roof was beginning to steam. Tucker slogged through the wet, carrying him on his hip. Ray memorized the paint-less farm, a steamy wealth of tone and color. He pretended to be settled against the trunk of a tree rather than a walking person. Just before entering the warm and dry of the pickup cab, he looked up—beyond the cover of the man's hat and damp brow—and felt a crystal emptiness in the coming blue.

Tucker paused; then returned from closing the tall gate he had opened before the storm. He would cling to this partial image of two figures waiting for their driver, behind sunlit and water-spotted glass...long brown waves of hair, feminine shoulders...near the center and base of the picture, a gnarled, unknown tangle—

Tucker twisted back to see the old house and recall its life. He turned again; then several steps further lowered himself to sit beside the boy. "My mother and father lived here when they were young," he whispered.

* * *

The death of Tucker's parents had hurried his marriage. Valerie briefly returned and they buried their mother, then had the wedding in the same visit. The ceremony was small and weighted with the loss of both his parents. He was but twenty, Alice nineteen. Valerie stood beside him as his only family. Alice's brothers were of different sizes and shapes but their necks and faces nearly identical. None had the black hair of their father. They wavered in a solemn row with matching suits differently tailored. Alice glowed.

Tucker remembered wandering at the hub of the buildings and watching his sister's car climb the hill. *His single sibling—as tottering children running on the grand veranda—they had fallen and cried together, shaded by the yet-to-be abandoned Voss roof and its arching trees… and now standing in a different yard…*the car left so slowly it disturbed no dust. At the crest she had stopped and waved from the open window. He raised his arm and hand high but kept it still.

Too long of lane.

It proceeded again and the dust began to roll.

What will have happened before he sees her again?

The car sped along the skyline with a cloud hovering.

He had a vision then: the fading structure of mother and father and brother and sister: changes in her face.

One last turn, small and obscured by its own exhaust, dipping from view for his wave, he brought his arm down.

New beginnings and new resolve, a sustained level of drive and energy. His goal then had been to have Jasper Park complete and perfect so they could grow. Perfect fields, tight, straight fences, fresh, square buildings, everything with a niche. Defense against outside chaos.

Alice had tried to slow him, soothe his torment, seeming to know life would fall into place, the hurry would pass. More family would come.

Home

Tucker often thought of the *old* Jasper Park when his grandfather reigned: calm winter snows, blue-green summer, cleansing rains...*gathering thunder*—a soundness—children at the feet of couples. The raveling began when his grandparents took a road trip, one bountiful fall, and never returned. While driving their Ford sedan and viewing the Columbia River, a one-ton truck met them head-on. The other driver had been drinking.

With this sudden void, his uncle and aunt chose to move, gather their young family in search of an unfound wealth. And like a subtle change in the climate, the discovery of his father's disability wound to the surface.

Alastair's twenty-eighth year marked their leaving of the Voss house, and the start of a seriously failing health. He again lived in the building where he had been born.

When Tucker's father was a baby, he nearly died from a dreadful fever. No one knew the full extent of the damage until Alastair himself was the head of a family. As though set by an interior timer, his physical capabilities fell into sharp decline. Tucker's young world was led by a man who was very slow at crossing the yard, with a rigid back and eyes off the ground, a walk of excruciating patience. He often stopped to lean on the corral fence and put his foot on the bottom rail. If near a woodpile or an implement, they provided a seat and he would tell a story. He did not use a cane. Tucker had the overwhelming urge to run circles around him and not to listen. As though with an innate hand on his shoulder, he held back; a natural impulse told him there was an end to this time and he believed his father had much to tell. He spoke of horses and their varying character: trees, the ones to leave to grow tall and stronger: farming, opening the deep earth to take in moisture and seed and return with sustenance: myriad grass, the stimulating graze from cleft feet.

In strange riddles he spoke of his curse-like failing.

"I hope I haven't sinned so that you will have to pay," a marble look to his depleted cheeks, "so that you will be deprived..."

Alistair's indirect guidance—concerning rules for living—confused Tucker's young mind. Over time the boy grew to understand and his father's wisdom settled into place. A collection of milestones and monuments to a loving map.

Not yet able, Tucker watched the buildings fall into disrepair, the fences grow loose and begin to list. At nine, *almost as old as Ray was now,* Tucker learned to keep a saw sharp and he and his mother cut and piled the wood for their winter heat. His father taught him how to splice wire and his mother how to tamp a post. He taught himself two ways for bracing a corner. At eleven they hired a man from town to help with the haying. Tucker drove a tractor and did all that he was allowed.

The time came when his father rarely left the house. More and more he spoke of his short fall—his being sickly—as though it had thrown the Park off center, out of round. Before each meal he swallowed pills unhurried and willful. When he sat for long periods his back lost its stiffness, bending forward as though his spine had become elastic. Sometimes he would lean sharply to the side, getting lower and lower until a sudden spasm of correction pulled him upright. Tucker denied his expressions of guilt. He reliably gripped his father's weakening hand when coming to or leaving the table. He became his father's arms, his father's speed.

His sister helped. She was older. He forgave her for wanting to escape. Friends, school, other places drew her away. Valerie married very young.

Tucker and his mother did much together; they fed, they fenced, they maintained and repaired machinery; but it all began to show, things began to fall: wires and planks broken, cattle in the wrong pasture, shingles missing. Implements not parked in their proper place with flat tires and robbed parts, rusty tools left out on the bench. The paint on the south face of the house curled and flaked. Winters, he had to do chores before and after school and still do book work. Calving forced them to hire another man, but he was part time and they suffered losses like never before—death lay in the grainy snow behind the barn, or paled and softened in the icy waters of the creek. His mother's hands grew bent and cracked and touched her own face like a stranger's, evoking premature age. The dilapidation reflected in her eye, a frustrated, beaten soul. She perpetually wore a scarf and tied it snugly under her chin.

Opposite his sister he was driven to remain. His sense of place and obligation grew warm. As he stood taller and more able, he felt the rise to a draft, like the fanning of an ember. He had entered a race to get big enough…competent and organized so he could rebuild the base, bring back vigor and tidiness to their lives—allow his mother rest, make his father again smile. He wished for her to undish her shoulders, comb her hair free, and cream her hands. This same race lashed him headlong into a communion with the valley, all the land, as if to a point of reeling demarcation—the leap over a chasm to another side.

He had legs like a deer: a limber age: *and now remembered the summer storms of youth*—pouring rains...

Himself as a boy...*and another boy*?

Caught, drenched together, under a vibrant thunder—the voice of a parent easing all confusion.

Reading Lessons

Ray started school and could only come on the weekends. He might miss several, then come for two in a row, both days. The weather had to be dry so he could travel on the bike. There was no plan, no discussion; he would just arrive at midmorning and he and the dog Tommie would find each other with an elaborate greeting—regardless if it had been three weeks or one night.

With each visit Alice came more quickly. She met him on the porch. They would talk while Ray waited for Tucker, who rarely remained in the yard. Alice began taking care to know just where and how long in absence her husband might be. Ray sat with the dog on the toe of the steps. Her feelings of stress began to relax: like a never known leisure creeping in from the side. She found herself also waiting, without hurry. She began to lean on the porch post and carefully absorb his presence, listening to an outer voice and movement, knowing his want for an eager companion—a welcoming space and the free air. His hair had been trimmed. He buried his face in the white of the dog's collar, and she admired the shape of his head, the tone to his skin. His clothes came in odd combinations, un-ironed, often of improper fit and badly worn out. The growing form underneath made them pleasant, no matter the mismatch or raggedness. She felt a vague stirring, and flashed to the thought of a young apple tree with its sod-bound roots.

They talked quietly below the shroud of the collie's approval.

"I almost forgot. Tucker...Tucker has bought...these gloves for you—"

Canvas-backed, still stapled together with their tag from the hardware, Ray took them gingerly, turning them over and over, without a word.

"Take them apart and see if they fit."

The boy pulled the staple cautiously and tucked it and the cardboard in his front pocket. He slipped the gloves on and worked his fingers.

"They fit nice." He smelled them.

As though from an allergy, redness marred the quality of his eyes. He hopped up and traced his steps back to the bike. Alice watched him fold the fresh leather and meticulously pinch them between the fender and the front fork. He never brought them back.

Each morning grew earlier and earlier.

"How is school?"

"Not so good."

He gave his attendant an added hug.

"I'm gettin'—getting behind in my reading." He rolled his regard past her face and looked across the clean yard.

Everything in its place. Everything in repair. As though something she had never noticed.

She lowered her brow, a motion to lift—root out the hidden with her own nose.

"I got trouble, sittin' behind a desk."

Her chin rose. "I'm sure, in fall weather like—" She felt the sun on her low back and hip and lost her assertiveness: like the letting go of a guarded item...in a fierce grip. "It's hard...reading...but it is a very good thing."

"Sure."

"Did your mother read to you when you were small?"

The blue eyes now roving and evasive, "Maybe...no..."

"Has she found work?"

"I-I—think so."

He began to squirm and the dog licked his ear. "You bugger." He cast an oblique look to Alice and his face turned a little ruddy.

"I'd like to meet her."

He was silent and now Alice began to shift and feel unsteady. She reached down to touch Tommie. The dog's softness forgave her.

She diverted the subject. "I have books, stories, that might pull you along, help you learn." She stepped back and folded her arms.

He looked at her directly.

She felt a returning clench: a recurring knot of anxiety...then a loosening. "If you come tomorrow, I'll have something. I'll have a couple." Alice again bent down to pet the dog. He kept the boy close.

They each had a hand on him.

"It'd have to be simple...easy... I'm *bad,*" he said.

The next morning she came through the door with four volumes held against her breast. Their cloth jackets were of dark earth shades and different sizes, thick and thin. She immediately saw his concern over the collie's absence. He would not stand still and stayed well clear of the porch.

"He and Tucker are together. They are bringing cattle down."

She went to the shaded edge and pointed with her face to the sway in the rampart. One arm balanced books and the other hand pulled at her hair, her mind still a little absent from what she had been reading. "They'll be back, soon after noon."

He continued an agitated shuffle, to and fro, out of reach.

She awoke and realized he might leave. "It used to take at least two riders. Now Tucker and Horse barely need go." She hoped to get some kind of loop, tie an anchor.

He backed away, a flourished disturbance in his eyes. "You *shoulda* told me. I *shouldna* come." He said words like these to someone else.

With a tinge of panic, she wished for the dog to come skipping around the house and stabilize the moment. She herself blushed.

He wouldn't be this way with Tucker.

"I didn't know. It's the weather. He moved it up one day."

Her mind had played the morning several times, not thinking she would lose him, just because, without the— She made a supreme effort to avow a body language, her guileless intention, all choice was his.

"Can't you feel it?" She held her free hand out, touching the unseen, the invisible. "The weather is on the change. Soon we'll have our first snow."

He took two paces forward.

She wrinkled her forehead. "The sky was tawny this morning. The light is a little chalky." She rubbed her thumb and fingers together.

He looked at her closely, as if impressed with a pretty knowing—in and around the corners of her eyes. He reached out, like he should touch the air also, feel its texture. "How do you know?"

"Smell it. Can you smell it? The snow—" She inhaled…to the slow awakening of her own attraction…then smiled. She was not quivering.

He sniffed, "I don't smell anything," then came onto the porch.

"Well, Tucker thinks it is going to rain and turn into snow. It would be good to get things brought home. I like having them back where I can see them." She passed him, and went down to stand on the ground and away from the roof, exactly where he had stood, so she could see more pasture. "I feel it in my joints." Still cradling books and with grass under her feet, she faced him, massaging her shoulder. "You don't feel it?"

He shook his head. She caught him looking for his bike, as though worrying over its worn-out tires and the effects of snow. Then he searched the sky behind her. He returned to the top step but didn't come down, curling his upper lip. Deep snow and the bike would not do well.

With ease she reentered the porch. Returning to his level she passed him again and stood in the center of the floor, thumbing through the books. "I bet the wind will come up before nightfall."

She had him turning.

"Anyway, they'll be back soon." Pulling a particular book to the top, "I have some stories. It's still too cool to be out here. We can go in and you tell me what you like." The door opened and she went inside and he followed as if there had never been a question. They sat at the spotless table where they ate. Ray could easily look out the window. There was no conversation, no choosing. Alice allowed no lull. She began reading from a collection of short stories with a calm, smooth voice. Early she led him to a dialogue between two men and a boy. Showing amazement, he watched her face as it changed with each character and her mode even more, sundry masculine words given flavor and distinction as though she had practiced or the pages were blank and it all came from her head. Alice twisted her brow and crinkled her nose; she puffed out her cheeks; she folded her tongue to one side and spoke with exaggerated dryness. She sounded old, then young. Though her eyes rarely left the pages, she felt Ray watching and not blinking, swallowed by her creation, as though he *believed* she was the author.

The concern he would have to read to her surely wandered away. His hands slowly pursued the edge of the table, listening. The chair whispered and he faced the window. He was not seeing beyond the glass.

He had been turned this way for some time when she began leaving the book in glances, underlining her place with a sideways palm, surprised at his relaxation, his captivity. Since the haircut his wave had become more pronounced. She saw a matching arc, an outward curve in the manner of his boyish nose. Alice could not help but wonder how it would be as a man's.

* * *

Tucker tucked his pants in his boots whenever he rode. Mounted on Horse, he dropped from the dark forest trail and into the canyon a half mile above the Voss place. Two Angus pair immediately followed in single file, then three more. Their hooves turned up thin black earth mixed with needles and leaves of the north slope, no dust stirred. He had Horse lope to the edge of the clearing as the cattle passed—not paying any notice. They now had a mind-set. This was their day to head home. Cows led a tapering jumble of calves steadily past and down the route toward a well-known security. Horse stood for a moment, then shifted his weight to a single hip, leaving Tucker off square.

"Horse," with a light pull on the rein, "stand up." He spoke very clearly. The horse backed onto a pad of coarse sedge and rested evenly. This platform of green had been used before. Tucker straightened his knees to stand in the stirrups, then sat again, placing both hands on the horn with each rein between the fingers of one glove. More cattle came. His lips were moving but he made no sound.

After a long, tedious string of beasts, Horse's head began to doze, a break in the count and Tucker could see the inattention in his ears. Once again several calves came abreast, attempting to get ahead: all the rest were linked head to tail, head to tail, like a monotonous train with no vision to the side. As the numbers in the herd continued, the severe drop from the trees became more difficult. Cows rocked back on their hocks and slid, hooves grated against slabs of stone, and the year-old tuft collected at the bottom of great steps. At last they began to dwindle, four or five pair, one pair, big spaces in between. For a long time he waited in silence. Horse's head fell in notches.

Higher, the aspen had a hint of color, in this place only a paleness. Tucker remembered the timbering. His grandfather skidded to this very same clearing. Here, with the help of the bank and log ramps, they loaded massive wagons. They chained whole trees to the rear axles as a cumbersome drag and brake. He looked up the trail and beyond, then cocked his head. Big white-barked trees stood on either side. The distinguishing bark of aspen, pale quivering leaves, stretched up the hill like a lace, an accent to the darker pine. His ancestors had opened up this dim slope, making room for a new and changed growth. The definite fade of deciduous leaves sketched the steep trail of labor and the pattern of their harvest. He could hear the crosscut, the ax, the jingle of the horses, sense the same smell as under his saddle and the sap and pitch of pine, all a vision to be passed on. He felt the heat of his own muscle, the sweat of his father's father still present in the air. His jaw flexed, as shun to the void that would follow him…and his Alice.

"This is too easy," Tucker said aloud.

The long, sheer head before him remained adrift, one furry ear pivoted like a periscope to tender the message.

"We shall get fat."

Up the mountain he heard a great thrashing. Horse lifted his head. A calf bawled and a cow bellowed. In jolts the commotion came nearer, first on one side, then the other, never in the trail. Abruptly the calf wheeled forward, then darted across the path only to stall in a leafless teepee of fallen trees.

Tucker caught glimpses of the dog, a silent performance through brush and litter much too thick for a horse, a swiftly moving shadow. The calf lowered its head and stood still, as though buried from sight. Tommie approached, then stared into its face; he turned to climb logs and weave through deadfall, disappearing. With an even greater thrashing another bellow echoed. Large limbs snapped and popped. Briefly a cow shot into view, then spun around to back into the strewn cover, sticks crunching against her thigh and flank. She lost traction and suddenly dislodged, charging forward with an irascible bawl, mostly sliding down the incline. The dog was nowhere to be seen. Calf and cow came together, the big calf wobbling, weak from too much fright and exertion. The two glanced into the forest behind them, then considered the worn downhill track they had so resisted—leading to the clearing where Tucker and Horse waited. With a heated swishing the cow took a step and for the first time revealed her lameness. As if in a cower she hobbled forward, her grown baby very close and brushing on her side. When the trail became more steep and narrow, the calf fell behind, but neither showed any intent of changing direction. Their defiance had failed, thought Tucker, no more places to hide. The increasing slope and rockiness made her progress more hesitant and painful; she began to hop in lunges on one front leg. They came closer and Tucker could see the unused foot, swollen with infection, the hooves splayed out as if pumped full of air.

The collie soon appeared one hundred feet behind, skipping lightly from rock to rock or tuft of grass as though crossing a stream. He began following too fast and had to wait and stand, seeing the broad cow struggle below him. Tucker watched him as he stood very serious, as though he were sorry for having pushed. The dog's eyes then lifted and met his own, with a haunting expression of confidence, confidence that Tucker was forever able—the man that would help. Never confused.

"You are wrong," he said out loud.

The cow reached the bottom of the steep drop with the calf's nose on her tail. She quickly stopped her halting bounce and returned to a brooding hobble.

Horse's head came higher and he began to walk and recoil in place. He would have reeled but Tucker held him and his tail flicked rapidly underneath, as if he had been stung in the belly. Without turning his neck, his eyes rolled as the dog approached. Tucker could see his nostrils pulsing with a quick fire of dislike.

"Patience," he said to the horse, "your chance to be useful will surely come."

As the trail became a road the broken sunlight began to pool, join together. A faint dust lifted, slight, just enough to coat the horse's hooves and discolor the dog's tail. The buffed hooves made a periodic click and the dust shed. The lead cattle slowed and the lame cow gained. A minimal cloud of heat and dirt drifted above their backs as they wound in soothing single file, life to life in an unbroken chain. Gradually Tucker felt a clearing congestion—like a preparation—the surrender, then acceptance into a brighter and more vivid place. He followed their lead toward the canyon mouth and a less shaded world.

Without guidance the entire herd traversed above the sawmill. A simple roof on poles protected the saw and husk; all else in the open air rusted and weathered. Tucker caught the new pockmarks of rust on the big blade in the shadow. A handful of plank, recently stacked and stripped, showed signs of twisting from the hard-bearing sun. At the end of the chain and arch where the saw's waste dribbled into a mound, Tucker viewed the large burnt-colored cone. It had a covering of fresh yellow. The new dust had spilled from the top in coarse lines like lava, too thick and grainy to continue. A pungent and familiar smell. Below the mill the hill extended, layered with ancient and rotting chips, dunes of organic sand. He had disconnected and removed the tractor that powered the big circular saw. The long, flat drive belt, still carefully rolled up, lay balanced on the near rollers. Horse's neck bowed as if to look: the iron and bark and sawdust, at once sour and new, a cluster of dark brown machinery half buried in the crumbs of past production and noise.

"Quiet now," he spoke, with visions of unborn children. He thought of Alice and himself old and gray.

"Someday...perhaps quiet forever."

The trees broke away. A quick downward turn and big numbers of cattle buckled and overflowed the edges of the road, as if reaching a lake and taking more than a drink, a welcome swim, the grass suddenly higher than their sides, enveloping legs and drowning the young. The haze of pollen lifted, then hung. Cows divided and milled among the vacant forms of the old Voss home, holding their chins high and lapping at the seed. The dog stood, watching, then finally moved to the shade of a lone pine. He sat.

He reviewed the herd as though he were making his own count. Tucker rode by and tipped his hat.

"Good Tom… Get a drink."

Now in habit of doing without, Tucker had not bothered to bring refreshment for himself. He felt again the crowding—clutter of his own passing life. Then he thought of Alice: had the boy come? Were they alone…and together? One hand tipped his hat back. The other held Horse's reins. He lifted a shoulder and twisted his neck, a glimpse of contentment touching his lips.

The dog swerved behind the cattle, bordering them until gone from sight. Tucker noticed a stirring in the tall grass, then caught his reappearance under the trees along the water. Some of the cows also noticed the collie's direction and were reminded of their thirst. Within moments all were in motion, a confluent black progression toward the clear waters of Jasper.

Horse was given grain, then released. Tucker crossed the first half of the yard as though he were tardy. The dog traced the scent of footprints; then each of them briefly considered the bike where it lay at the edge of the lawn. Tucker took his boot and spun the front tire. It coasted slightly untrue while the dog cleaned, combing face and ear in the soft bristle of green, then falling on his side to roll over. Tucker slipped his gloves free and slapped them up and down on the thighs of his pants with little effect.

Near the porch he could hear a mumble of voices. Still in the sun, Tucker removed the broad brim that shaded his eyes, then climbed the steps, moving very slowly, his assuredness deteriorated to an almost comical tiptoe and creep. The collie stiffened. Tucker turned his head to listen and he walked where the boards would not sway. The dog's alert changed to concern and bewilderment; he stretched up to be taller and also hear through the wall.

The voice was now clear: a convincing French accent, then one entirely different—a coarse male voice of force and few words, a swagger of muscle—interrupted by another man's throat with delicate slurs, refinement, and logic. Tucker did not catch every word but soon recognized the characters and the book being read. He readily imagined the lure and intrigue of a mysterious undersea world. Pride and pleasure filled him for Alice's total immersion, her impeccable expression. Such acting gave the old familiar tale a revived and immediate interest. Had he a chair he would have sat and indulged, bent against the house to the inside swirl of her variable phrase.

The dog's intuition to have them together created a shiver: the strange false tones too worrisome. He reared and softly growled.

Tucker released the latch and swung the door in. Alice caught their shape while her reading continued undisturbed. A frizzle came from the part in her hair. The boy's back was to the table with one arm resting on its scoured plane. He sat in a slouch with his head nodding forward and toward the window as though he were a sleeping old man. Tucker entered and the dog followed. The uncertain sound of toenails finally penetrated Ray. He looked around with pale faraway eyes and Alice stopped. A profound hesitation, then, as if he had truly been asleep, he flinched and sat upright. He stared at Alice, jumped to his feet with disheartening eyes, and looked past the dog.

"What you got to do, C-Captain...*Nemo*?"

Silver Mare

When Alice first lived in the valley that golden summer, Tucker was too occupied to teach her to ride. She thought of the solace she had found in books and stories then, how she had loved Jules Verne, how stories had pulled her along, helped her not to feel so…*untethered.* She knew now she wanted to attract the boy, hold him—pull him to the ground rather than letting him drift, likely to sail away at the slightest ruffle. Would Tommie and their company, *the valley*, be enough? Perhaps she could teach him to ride? Such unmatched pleasure under the big sky, in the free air, surely would draw him, make him soundly want to return again and again…

Tucker had introduced her to Lace—the ideal horse—given her a lesson in all the tack and safety, then left them alone to learn each other.

Though the horse was still young, Lace had given her the company of a bold but kind and protective elder. They entered the same essence and embraced each other with a delighted curiosity. Lace's ears were continually perked toward Alice, her long neck bending and following around her rump while the girl brushed her silvery coat, reversing and greeting her on the other side. She would not move her feet, unless Alice stood at least a horse length away. She refrained from swishing her tail.

"And *he* calls *you* Lace." Two prongs of affection.

Alice brushed the speckled gray of her neck and Lace's attention began to dawdle.

"You're not white enough to be Lace."

She came in front and petted both flat cheeks below the darkness surrounding her eyes. A mutual gratification.

"You wouldn't mind if I called you something else?" Her look rose above the horse for a moment and she let go a cheerful "*D-a-i-s-y.*"

She put the blankets on, then hoisted the bulky saddle, such a trim young woman alongside a heavy horse. After buckling the cinch she remembered to tighten when unexpected. She missed the next notch and became nervous. Daisy heaved, then slouched. One ear pinched under the bridle while Alice studied the bit; she worried it was on the wrong side of her tongue and shouldn't rattle so much on her teeth. At last her jittery fingers brought both ears up and tenderly combed her mane. Its kinkiness caught. She pulled the forelock from under the strap and gave it a light twist, molding a spear-like curve down between the horse's eyes.

"You will teach me."

Daisy seemed brimming with pleasure. She clearly enjoyed any touch from Alice. The delicate scratch of her fingernails so unlike any man.

Alice mounted without trouble and at once felt an untold awkwardness, as if balancing on a loose-skinned elephant. And the view, the pointed ears and the narrow neck drooped out like the horizontal neck to a giraffe. She found the other stirrup and laughed for the horse to hear; this was not the grace or comfort she had imagined. She twisted to see behind and noticed the powerful root to the tail, the giant handle to an expressive whip.

Alice guided Daisy into the east hills, rolling, with a deep carpet of grass. The horse swished. The mare abruptly paused, stretching her head out and blowing through her nose, following with a gentle shake of her entire body. Alice shook with her. They started again; she felt a quickening rhythm and consciously conformed. Warmth from the horse came up through the saddle.

"I think we'll get along."

Daisy flicked her tail.

The horse sauntered spryly over several rises. Alice smiled, feeling free, delighting in the health of the grass and the ebb and variation in the draws.

"This is my home."

Her disbelief would not leave. "This *is* my home." She needed someone to help convince and gave the horse a mild squeeze with her heels. Daisy broke into a trot and Alice lost rhythm as her eyes grew big.

"Whoa."

The horse fell back to a fast walk, as though suddenly losing interest.

"We won't do *that* for a while."

Daisy's head bounced back and forth coherent with her gait, an agreeable yes and maybe.

Alice bent forward and patted the swaying neck. In the bottom of a hollow they encountered a change in the undulant pasture, a grove of leaning cottonwoods, and further a small dam completely full: the trapped water so flat and still, a noncompliant blue element in a green world with nothing level or bare. Older trees had fallen. Their curved trunks lay bark-less and bleached like picked gargantuan bones of a long-ago age. Among the deadfall a package of yearlings camped. Only two were standing; the rest were sprawled or lying upright chewing their cud, partly buried in the litter but not lost, filled black bodies against the image of tremendous white bones. Their heads rose when Alice approached; more began to stand and stretch. Alice kept a wary margin, then came close to the water. Their eyes *all* followed, and most continued to chew.

"Surely, you need a drink," she whispered to the horse.

The cattle were a little frightening. The slope to the water steeper than anything yet and all awkwardness returned. She felt the mare's shoulders go down and her rear end come up. The horse stepped carefully but with a bit of a release, then jar. Alice pressed down in the stirrups, thinking it would provide relief, very conscious of her weight on the bowed string of Daisy's vertebrae.

"You've carried me a long way," still speaking as if to keep a secret from the animals in the shade, disturb no silent frequency.

The horse's hooves stood in pooled mud and resisted touching the water. Alice encouraged.

"You better drink. It's a long way back."

She held the reins up and forward. The front feet splashed lightly and broke the glassy surface. Daisy's nose went down and made ripples, and her upper lip twittered as though playing in a soda. She raised her head again, grinding her teeth, and the bit clashed. Her chin was dripping but she had not drank.

"Come on," Alice coaxed, leaning with the reins out. "I'm thirsty..."

The horse would not lower its head. Daisy stood and groaned with her neck hanging midway, seeming to stare across the clearing water. Alice began to see their reflection through calming ruffles, and sat back. Not so bad. The horse seemed very big and herself stable. A confidence tremored.

"You know best."

The cattle were leaving the shade to get a better look, noses raised, converging with a tentative interest; what be this new thing sitting above the horse?

Daisy showed a sullen distrust of *any* group when they came from behind. Alice felt the horse drawing her fragments together as she stepped back into the mud, facing the cattle, as though preparing for an impending conflict. They paid no mind. They appeared attracted and entertained by the object on top, her high, halting voice, long, flowing hair. Alice, with her lingering whiff of assurance, did not fully realize Daisy's unrest. With quick, stable movements the horse chose its own route to the sod. One sure foot slipped into the rut of a cow path and the saddle shifted. Alice tipped and rolled from her position as if she had fainted. A quick tumble and she hit the ground with a jolt, landing in the hard sand just above the mud. Daisy stopped in midstride and the stirrups swung. Alice spun and sat in surprise and embarrassment, feeling sharp pangs in the parts that had hit first. With a dash of sand in her hair, she used the heels of her boots to scoot herself further from the squishiness, immediate to hooves. Daisy's ears twitched. They went back and forth, independently pointing toward the encroaching cattle, then down to Alice.

"No harm done."

Alice rubbed an elbow and wrung her wrist.

"It's not your fault." She felt her hip along the seam to her pants.

Three of the yearlings hustled forward and Daisy jumped onto the grass bank with her ears folded back; the reins were undone, so she held her head high to keep them from catching. Her nose flared. Her eyes glared. The first three halted but those behind advanced in turn. Trembling chromium flanks: ears tightened against her head, which she now tossed back and forth, prancing, flailing the reins like a pair of whips. Suddenly her lips curled back, showing sallow teeth, and she charged with her mouth open—a fiery extreme from nose to tail. The heavy cattle forgot Alice and knew only the horse. They split and dodged. Some slid—tripped and fell in the bright grass but were quick to recover. They joined and ran from the shelter of the trees, racing halfway up the near slope, then stalling. All looked back in dull wonder over the wreck—such fury—then continued in a slow, complacent-like trail.

One rein had landed across the saddle and caught. The horse dragged the other alongside with her neck bent, her ears again perked. Daisy trotted lightly toward Alice with her tail softly snapping and whirling in a kind of *sashay*.

Alice rose, too astounded to brush the sand from her pants and hair: without wound, without damage. She considered her defender:

"I'm like your cub, your baby."

Daisy stepped carefully from the break in the sod and dangled the one free strap near Alice's boots. The horse's muzzle stirred in her hair as if better learning her scent, the hot breath loosening sand to trickle down her shirt.

Alice bent back so she could see more than a nose, "Awfully ferocious for such a pretty face," and took hold of the rein. She held Daisy's jaw and slowly blinked. She brushed her jeans, squiggled her shoulders, and took advantage of the grass stair to help her climb on…*re*mount.

Before long, the two would be galloping the hills as one, with the wind through their hair, caressing each young and confident face.

Lesser Resistance

It did snow, only a thin grayness over the land, and the boy's bike still worked. For three days they lived with a tinted sun, as if to create more surprise-prominence to the brisk fall air and the advancing color. High colonies of aspen, once hardly noticed, now were a loud yellow with tints of orange. These rapidly changing groves accented the wrinkled slopes, the lofty steep and coolest areas of the mountain. Below the rampart each bluff was underlined or cradled by the same. From the house, Alice could easily choose the trail leading over the top, the path to and from green summer parks or impassable winter snow. The cottonwood and willow along Jasper creek were fading. Cavities of scarlet formed in the undergrowth, the thickness and bramble of vine more vigorous and determined than ever.

Tucker returned to his fall farming. The boy and dog explored beside the water and deep in the shaded thickets. They disappeared for long periods, then came into the sun together, either farther up or lower along the stream. Tucker tried to imagine their ramble. The spring-tooth pulled easily, the dust hanging low and wispy. A steady breeze began to press his hat and he tilted his head going one way, then the opposite coming back. An invisible grit rose and caught in his teeth. He tried to never miss their re-entrance to the fallow field and often lost his bearing, crossing slightly over his previous pass, once leaving a narrow, uncultivated gap. He shook his head over the drone of the open-air tractor. With a wasted wipe of his smile, he began keeping his mouth closed.

Further down along the farming, older trees crowned and leaned, shading the edge. The summer storm that had stranded he and the boy in the building of the old Voss place also left broken and scattered limbs. Significant pieces, like fans with bent arms, lay shriveling on the crusted soil. They would be in his path.

The two adventurers were missing from sight for a long while and he waited for their return. They did not come and they did not come. New sensations of worry clouded Tucker's work. He stopped suddenly and brought the tractor to an idle. He whistled into the increasing wind. The collie bounded onto the freshly groomed ground, unsure of the whistle's source, the worked earth very dark but nothing like the ink black of his coat. The sharp milky white of his collar and chest struck an unexpected aversion to all that surrounded him, the dust and labor of the day in clear separation. The wind in the overhead trees had confused Tommie's senses: he first placed the buildings, then looked downstream to locate the tractor. A moment later Ray appeared in a shirt the color of a pink grapefruit, its ragged hem hanging over deficient blue overalls. The relief came as a surprise to Tucker. This world—always so familiar and tame—now carried a strange shade of risk. They approached as a pair with no one leading, the soft, damp footing apparent in the boy's walk and clinging lightly to the tread of his shoes. Tommie's tail blew to the side while Ray's hair and sloppy pants fluttered. Tucker shut off the engine and licked his teeth.

"What are you finding?"

They both looked up at him with a glow of perplexity.

"Oh...nothing."

Granules of bark and dirt had collected in the corners of the boy's eyes. Hidden partly by the hair, his forehead had a smudge of mud. A swipe of scratches curved toward one ear as though left by the claw of a bear, almost deep enough to bleed.

"Just looking," Ray said.

He had been kneeling in wet sand.

The dog sat with dignifying content—not a mark—no breeze combed hair out of place, merely particles from the farming like bits of black bread atop his paws. Tucker saw little similarity between the two, save the engagement of eyes, the same chaff and debris gathered, chunks big enough to impair the dog's vision. His tail flopped in the softness as if conscious and proud of his neatness.

Tucker dismounted the tractor and stood very close to the boy, so that he could speak lowly. He smelled the sap and oils of cottonwood, damp, sandy leaves. The breeze grew stronger; he could still feel the heat from the sun, absorbed and rising from the open soil.

"I think you found something."

Ray stepped away to see his whole person...from hat, to boots.

"*What?* W-What?"

"I think you found a good creek you will never tire of."

The boy looked behind to the string of trees and the twisted pockets of flagrant color. Everyone looked. Tucker watched his head trace the row, to where it began at the spring.

"I wish I—I don't go to school."

"There is time. It will turn cold and the school will be protected." Moving side by side, he touched the boy's shoulder: contact different than a handshake...with unforeseen feelings.

Ray reversed the direction of his search. Tucker watched as he now looked down the valley, under the bridge and past the last vague hayfield. His eyes left the stream, then seemed to catch on the swaybacked roof of the empty barn.

"I hate inside. It don't matter— It don't matter to me it gets cold."

Tucker lifted his hand.

He followed as the boy's head turned again and considered the lower distance. Ray had yet to go there: the season's moisture lay close to the land, a sleepy grayness. The trees altered and spread, regressing to a flat whorl of darkness as the valley lost distinction. For an instant Tucker felt doubt, wondering if there still flowed a stream beneath the far woods.

"I hope—I hope my mom and me don't move."

Tucker's wrist dropped as if it had been knocked. He felt the lurch of an empty void...he knew...considered how things were before the boy. Tucker pictured Alice cooking—reading stories—and began to squint. He quickly removed his gloves and knelt to clean the dog's eyes. Using fingertips he gently rolled away the moist pebbles, like little pearls, and brushed them from the collie's sleekness. The tail flopped anew and threw a wisp of dirt up under his hat. Something lodged. Tucker cocked his head and winked repeatedly, then stood and pointed.

"See those sticks? They are in the way. It would help if you dragged them off, threw them back."

Ray bounced a little, as if he suddenly enjoyed the cushion of the farming. He stretched taller while the collie circled.

"Yes sir." He prepared to dash.

The dog skipped to block his run.

"Whoa—"

The boy tumbled over his friend, then sat.

"Make sure they are far enough I don't snag them again."

He rose quickly and his knees were now black, his elbows stained. He nodded and withheld himself.

Tucker realized a rising restraint, all around, dull caution not to branch out or overextend. "And do not poke your eye. Try not to get any more scrapes."

Ray tipped his head, then brought both hands up and closed and touched his own eyes. By chance his fingers discovered the welts along one cheek.

"Okay," he answered, a little less wind in his sail.

Tucker swept with the back of his hand—for the instant oddly limp—as if dusting them away. "Go on."

Ray and Tommie galloped, the dog careful to stay at his side and know the boy's direction.

Pulling the harrow one way, Tucker could watch them. When going the opposite, they were at his back. He had to turn before they reached the first limb. He listened above the roar of the engine and the wind past the sag of his hat. He thought he heard a shout. He increased the throttle and after a long, sluggish pass faced them again and the dog was absent. Ray headed back, reaching for smaller sticks he had missed and throwing them with an exaggerated effort, often hanging them in the side of a tree or the top of a bush.

Tucker rocked closer and awoke to the tracks, the changed placement of several remaining limbs. He bent his neck and his hat blew away. Airborne, it twirled, then tripped on the earth and rolled just clear of the implement claws, flipping upright and resting. He released the clutch to an immediate halt and the tractor roared while he watched the dog prance onto the field balancing a long, heavy branch in his mouth. He trotted lightly along with one end jabbing the loose ground, causing sudden jerks to his face. The tractor idled and Tommie dropped his prize to chase after Ray, who was about to throw another. Tucker momentarily locked on the boy's image: facing the dog he launched a spatter of words, defined and clear with a flash of teeth but too far away to hear. He spoke, waving a small fan of rumpled leaves for emphasis.

The collie clearly was not listening, seeing only the waving stick and rearing back and forth, mirroring its swing or shake. At last Ray gave a mighty throw. For a mesmerizing instant it revolved and floated high; then the dog dove under it, into the thicket and on toward the stream.

Tucker had ample time to retrieve his hat. He slapped off dirt. He must finish his work. He reengaged the tractor and returned to his farming.

He could still see Ray stuttering. The boy placed his hands on inconsequential hips as his unruly partner came into view dragging a different limb. This one was too big to carry and he pulled it with great difficulty onto the fractured ground. Sprays of leaves did their own raking. Rear-end first, he pulled from one side then the other, arching his long back, digging in his claws. Finally he settled into a straight reverse line, his tail extended as a counterbalance, and proceeded to drag it further into the field than all the others. He had been in the water. His legs and front now a terrific muddiness; there were added pounds to his outstretched tail. He dropped his task, then turned and smiled at his audience, swallowing and choking, gagging a mixture of bark and mud from his quivering mouth.

Tucker began to shake, careful not to lose his hat again. It grew to be involuntary and temporarily replaced his breathing. He felt it under his ribs, uncontrollable spasms, in contradiction to the strained undulation of his forward travel. Laughter new to a lifetime. In his marvelous distraction he was late to swing the tractor, begin its turn for the opposite heading. He gasped and caught the boy taking a step, raising one pant leg to stomp his foot. The spring-tooth swung too far out. At first it tore heavily in the sod, then hooked on a root, hammering the hitch sideways. The tractor lurched and pulled, skidding the front tires—off track...

Ping.

Tucker ducked.

Something shiny flew through the air and buried itself in the freshly darkened wake.

On the ground again, with short eruptions of laughter but back on course, he studied the break and the remaining rows of silvery teeth. His boot swept through the warm, friendly soil where he thought it had fallen. His toe hit the familiar steel and the soft earth fell away. Brushing free its arch, he held it by the middle and extended to rap it against the rear row. The part made a sound like a clumsy tuning fork and buzzed through his glove. Using old rags he wrapped and nested this single piece in the tractor toolbox, as if he valued its polish. He continued with the one broken tooth: a little less whole, but with a purged remainder to the afternoon: a lesser resistance. Before completing his turn, he realized the boy had placed the dog under command.

Tommie lay like a muddy sphinx in painfully bright attention. Ray proceeded to clear the field. Several limbs were too big and he had to drag them backward with the same method as revealed by the dog.

Tucker laughed lightly one last time, then twisted to leave them at his back, in a fashion as though it would be forever.

Native/Outlander

Alice, puzzled by Tucker's broken implement—for he rarely had accidents or left things damaged—tried to learn from his slow patience when making repairs. Before he had left the kitchen, she chose the morning for going upstairs to mend her torn jeans, patch the worn elbows in several shirts, though it seemed she had no actual interest in mending, fixing. Alice did not expect Ray for yet another day. Perhaps later, she would go beyond mending and begin choosing and laying out fabric for wintertime gifts. She felt she might still enjoy the smell of new fabric and the design and creation of fresh things. She hadn't used her sewing machine since before—for a very long time.

If not for the collie's surge of happiness, Ray would have appeared in the shop unnoticed. No sound from the bike. An unusual quiet. Already absorbed by his gathering of tools and his plan, Tucker welcomed and accepted the boy through the open door without thought. "Hello—good morning," he took inventory of what still lay on the bench, "come with me."

Tucker rooted through old car parts, all hidden behind the building—axles and wheels, hoods and fenders void of paint, a brown pile of tin and iron, now and then an unknown hoop or buried bumper of bubbled and pitted chrome. Parts of history:

heavy iron wheels from horse-drawn wagons, the more delicate cast spokes from a binder, the intricate governor to a steam engine, and an overwhelming flywheel. The area was not organized, intently confined, not much larger than three shops, and made private by a solid board fence on one side and a thick barrier of low bushes and windbreak trees on the other two. A secret snatch of disuse and untidiness.

Ray and Tommie stood framed by the rear door, looking out. Tucker bent in the early morning sun, surrounded by numerous items covered with dew and crescents of frost. He cleared just enough path. Tucker laid a large wooden block beside a naked car frame and carefully wedged a long, rigid bar in between. The handle to the bar came down, causing a scrunching of wood and the remains of the car to pivot, partly lift, and hang. He tucked the end of the bar between spokes and under the rim of a nearby wheel; the enlarged end neatly lodged itself as though a ball into a socket. The frame corner and a single assembly of leaf springs remained vaulted. His hands were free. He took a rule from his pocket and re-measured the width and thickness of the springs. Also from his pocket came a cold chisel, then a hammer from inside his belt. After three smart and sufficient blows, the center bolt to the assembly popped. All but the top leaf fell with a dull clank into a pad of grass and other vague articles of metal. He stood the group on end, rapping it on each side. Abruptly it split apart. He anticipated this division and fall and kept his feet well clear. He chose a single leaf. The even lesser car scraped against other junk as he easily undid the bar, making the bray of an animal as it lowered into place. He considered the rest of the busy enclosure, then faced his helpers.

"Come carry these tools."

Ray and Tommie scurried over as though breaking from a huddle. Tucker carried the spring and block of wood. Ray followed with the hammer hurriedly laced in an empty belt loop. He struggled with both hands on the bar. Its heaviness swung and bounced in a surrounding crowd of rusty steel and tin, as though he were rowing through a turgid swamp. The dog stayed clear. The bar caught and spun, walloping the crinkled fender of a Model T, the only thing left of the vehicle.

Bang!

His young friend hunched.

Tucker made two big strides into the shadow of the shop, then cocked his head. "Good thing it is not a new one."

"I don't do *nothing*—not for attention," the boy answered defensively and dropped the steel on the edge of the concrete floor. It echoed with a pealing ring.

Tucker halted at once and reversed in his tracks. He could not see Ray's face for the sudden inside darkness, a simple stamped outline and the dog still in the clarity of sun.

His focus on the project began to slide. "Nothing can get hurt out there, in that scrap heap, except you."

No eyes. But he knew immediately the boy was toting an excessive baggage, some undertow of conflict from earlier in the morning or during the week, a disquieting sheen to his silhouette. He remembered it was not yet Saturday.

What is going on? Tucker waited, then spoke with calm assertion. "What is the matter? Something must be the matter."

Ray shook his head.

In spite of the brightness behind he began to see a face, a dilated look like an opening plea. Shadows under one eye. He was pressed to reach out, somehow affirm the quiet and steady.

"That *is* a long bar...a lot of weight."

Tucker felt a gripping of his insides, an increasing wonder and worry over the boy when he was out of sight. He propped the spring against his stiffened leg.

"I was older before I could do more than drag it. I still drag it."

His free hand looped out, then rose and came back and nudged the front of his own hat up. His gloved hand tried to smooth the ruffled hair below its band.

"It is a school day?"

"Nope."

Tucker closed his mouth, then puckered his lips as though sipping from a hot cup.

"Got parent conference," the boy said.

"I see."

"No school for three days."

"I see." *Three days…three days maybe knowing where he is…*

Ray knelt and took hold of the pointed end of the bar.

Tucker pulled his hat down, feeling more clutter. His part was no more than a fraction. He began walking again but very slowly, as though to move forward in secret. He heard the steel dragging and grating on the concrete. He set the block down and scooted it under the bench with his foot. He received the bar and added it to a leaning collection of shovels, rakes, and a post-hole digger. They left the dim of the building and stood out front, this part of the yard still shaded by trees, but a fresh opening with far less distraction.

Ray offered the hammer to Tucker's much bigger hand.

Tucker bowed back—hammer in one, the flat spring in the other—a slight flex in his shoulders, feeling like a big-hatted blacksmith standing before a forge. His focus returning, he took a deep breath.

"Let me show you how, how you can bend a spring."

With simple and intricate precision, he clamped one end of the curved leaf in an outdoor vise. Tucker spun the handle tight, then took the hammer and tapped the screw lever another several degrees, making the grip more sound than the jaw itself. The vise was anchored to a squat post, big around as a washtub. He returned from the shop with lengths of slender chain, a pulley and clevis and clamps and a peculiar collection of homemade weights. Like chosen parts from a physics kit, he laid them in the dirt in a special order. Without hesitation he began to assemble the pieces. His goal not at first apparent, then gradually obvious, he created a fascinating tension between the doorframe of the building and the extended end of the spring. In but a few moments, the chain began to roll through the pulley and tug against the secured steel. He added three more weights to the chain: his efforts all flowing together as if listening to a flawless, even-mannered speaker who never drew any air.

The dog watched the boy.

Ray watched Tucker.

The boy was totally absorbed, feeling the construction of some kind of mysterious and violent trap. The line tightened between weight and anchor, and Ray felt the loading in his own wrists, a leftover pulling from the oversized bar.

Tucker again vanished through the door. Ray heard shuffling, a loud pop and hiss. The collie's ears went up, then drew against his head. He backed away and sat on his tail. The man came out carrying a silver handle with knobs and a long copper nozzle pointing a small blue flame as sharp as a quill. He directed the torch carefully while he unrolled twin hoses from an inside source and approached the work. He adjusted the flame to give it softness and a less threatening hiss. Tucker had traded his hat for a pair of pitted goggles, and they perched on his head with lenses so dark and glossy they looked like two painted black checkers. Ray came forward. He showed interest in the flame, yet incapable of knowing the danger of its touch.

"Well... Well... It would be better if you did not look at the point. Blue eyes are tender." The elastic to the darkened glasses gave a diagonal part to Tucker's hair. A sprig pointed outward. "And it is not good for Tom." Seeming to think of something more, he ducked the torch down and behind the vise as though meant to be a surprise for a later time. Ray wanted to step around so he could get another look.

The dog wanting to leave, more uncomfortable than ever, the boy only smiled.

Tucker considered the leaf spring: caked with black scale, it appeared more like a brittle length of slate rather than something malleable. He looked down at his hands, remembering he had changed his hat for a pair of goggles, a completely new man to absorb: the sunlit pallor of his forehead, the rubbery strap and strange lenses he could feel rolling and pinching his hair, the artificial pressurized hiss—as brandished. He watched the boy come forward, then lean away, Ray's fascination attracted and spurned in the same moment.

Like *his* attraction...his own welling thought...of something deep, forgotten—Alice's—*their children*—had they been born earlier, they would be the boy's age.

Tucker swallowed and concluded, "You better not see." Touching his head, "I will pick up another pair and show you another time. You need a visor."

A loose fleck of carbon caught in the nozzle. It made a mewing sound as it cleared, far too much like a searching cow elk trying to pair with her calf, jerking Tucker's thoughts—the flash of an overwhelming herd in the field beyond the trees. He unconsciously wrung his shoulder and twisted his neck. He looked at the boy, totally removed. The sound had begun to haunt, rather than highlight the season.

He twisted the valves down to extinguish the heat and pulled the strap free. His hair went back into place without anyone's notice.

"I won't look," Ray said quickly, standing tall but obviously injured by a disappointment.

In the absence of the noise the dog's ears regained their composure, then perked as if expecting a new and improved direction.

Tucker looked to the foothills, *empty*... Time for them to be joining numbers, impressive bulls with their gathering of cows—the same as before—an expected invasion to the lower fields, and lingering... He watched the boy glance down, catching on his gloves, the blackened and smooth palms.

How *strange*: the earlier track of elk and August damage, leading him to find, discover—

"You two can go on holiday. Have Tom take you up the ridge and show you about." He pointed with the silent nozzle, feeling the hoses trailing on his lift. "Go tell Alice what I am doing and that I am sending you."

His arm dropped, but he had already signified the rocks of the hogback, distant, this side bleached and scrubbed by the fall sun—but with many dark pockets and unknowns: tap to a great root of adventure. He remembered a boy's eagerness, knew it could not help but rustle. A long-ago picture of his crippled father surfaced, sitting on the woodpile and pointing. Himself young, crawling the ridge, coming back to listen to more stories, then climbing again. His memories were not so distant. His father's stories had grown tattered, far away and vague.

"She will pack together your lunch," he told Ray. "And she will tell you not to climb anything too high. But get to the top so you can see."

Alistair: climb that hill with a view...understand where you are.

The long shade of the shop had moved. It fell sideways and cut Tommie in two. His head was under cover and his eyes relaxed while Tucker and the boy's were now in the bright. They each squinted from the reflection of the center yard.

"Tell her I gave you the same caution." With a fleeting twist he looked for his hat, then brought his hand up to protect his eyes. The torch made it feel like an overbearing salute, awkwardly attached to the coil of hoses at his feet. "There should not be snakes this late. If there are, Tom will tell you."

Thinking snakes, the toe of Tucker's boot pressed on the lines carrying the fuel to the torch, like a nerve that he could restrict, flatten to a closure.

Ray just stood, in suspension, beginning to rock up and down lightly on the balls of his feet. His hands hung by his thighs, empty and spread.

"Well...*go.*"

Boy and dog charged and collided, bumping together.

Tucker called after them and the boy slowed in acknowledgment but did not look back.

"Leave ample time to get home."

His glove wiped a fringe of soot from the torch tip; almost searing the leather, his hand drew back. He felt himself swallow again, watching the two regain a distracted speed, a jagged and suspect intent. Children and puppies. The screen door slammed and echoed. *Tatters and folds.*

Momentarily he heard Alice's friendly voice...*she knows they are in the kitchen.* When in her sewing room and *he* needed her, he would have to climb the stairs and call. *Must have been the bang of the door, as if to jar and refresh a memory.*

Children and puppies. He could not cry now, alone and outside—Alice and Tucker's *ancient* loss. He cocked his head and squinted, as though his eyes were poor, as though there were no hood above them formed by his arm and heavy hand.

* * *

Only a few minutes after the screen door slammed again, the boy and dog disappeared among the first small cliffs and could no longer be seen from the dim, empty-feeling entrance to Tucker's shop. Inside, an obscure tool tipped from the workbench and clattered to the floor. Tucker—hearing the drag of his own boots—decided he must finish his fabrication, return to his repair.

Ray carried a small brown paper bag, the top neatly tucked and carefully folded down. Naturally, Tommie took the lead and led them above the barn. They passed near an odd rock sticking perpendicular from the slope—Billie's gravestone, but neither dog nor boy knew the significance. Ray paused, then circled. The stone looked as though it had swollen and split—raised the weaker grass and silty soil. He came close and knelt, balancing the brown sack on top so that he could study the ground around its base without damage to what Alice had prepared...so carefully. The dog rushed in and snorted at the dirt, then went straight for Ray's low face. His tail tipped over the sack. Ray squirmed and laughed loudly until he noticed the lunch pressed against the rock.

"*Stop.* Tommie. *Stop.*"

The dog sat, leaning against the stone—his face and eyes bright with cheer. Ray could nearly hear words: *What could be wrong?*

The bank had a dampness underneath and the sun a welcome warmth. They were just beginning to catch a pulse of air from the valley floor: his and the dog's hair lightly lifted from an upward draft.

Ray cradled the snug little bag with mild concern, a weighted feeling. He had found a split beginning along one lower fold, and knew the carrying would be different from this point on. He had never carried such a risk. He lowered his chin. He raised his aquatic eyes in fake reproach.

The writing in the stone, *Billie,* struck his vision and Ray slipped from Tommie to stand. He thought of *Billy the Kid* and smoking guns. He circled again and looked around in puzzlement, Tommie catching on his heels. The red ground lay thinly grassed and smooth with no other rocks as if this one had landed from the sky. He imagined a giant blunt arrow thudding down and wounding the hill.

What happened to the shaft and feathers?

He decided to move on. He held the sack in one hand, now carefully from the bottom but with an attitude of dislike, as though its contents had little place in this new vision… He felt his stomach churn and licked his lips: knowing better. The dog stayed close, in front or on either side, entirely too—*carefree.*

Ray looked about for a stick, something to be his weapon-rifle, but the higher on the ridge, the further they were from trees or any wood. As the slope became more exposed, he began to crouch. He shifted his plan to a bow and arrow, twice kneeling to peer around imaginary medieval boulders, like *Robin Hood,* taking aim. He felt awkward with the package; the crinkle of the paper did not fit with his sneak, his undetected creeping. The dog's tail sloppily flapped and waved. Ray wished to be present but less an exhibit. So uncovered.

More than halfway to the top and he turned to look down on the buildings. The people were gone from view: no ring from a hammer, no smoke from a chimney. On the mountain beyond, all the aspen had lost their leaves. Below and through this barrenness

Ray could see the golden ground. Along the creek and about the house, the cottonwoods were in full yellow, only a week past but a very different place and time, something fresh and exciting. The house, the barn, the shop: soundless and nestled: under the mountain. For the first time he felt the protection of the valley, like a body...shouldering, nurturing. He felt it fingering its way around his own person. Never having known gentleness, he shook as the dog would, to shuck water or dust. The collie gave a look of wonder over what he might be doing. Ray dropped this unknown feeling and renewed his crouch to continue up the ridge, his interest in the high rocks a calming pull...to a higher step.

Ray's plan changed again. Still with bow and arrow, he was now a native, more upright and with a feather in his hair. The sneaking picked up speed and he began to zigzag with his shoulders tucked forward, high-stepping like a barefoot man trying to navigate cactus. His companion began trailing a little behind, not sure where he was headed. As they approached the summit, Ray couldn't help but re-notice the spires far across the valley, up the other side. He dropped to his knees and took another aim along the invisible shaft to his arrow, as if in response to a mounting invasion, something mighty and fearful. The giants across the way stood motionless—no shield in their hands. The brown bag, again forgotten, dangled under his chin with a growing tear. The collie tipped his head and his tail quickly dropped. Ray glanced over while placing a single finger to his lips in warning; he wanted no noise, nor any talk. The tail shot up. With a forward charge the dog knocked away his hand. The sack rolled beneath them as they wrestled.

Ray snickered softly, "You bugger," then quickly recovered. He saw the paper begin to unfold and a longer rip revealing things on the inside.

"Stop."

The dog sat, with the bag under one hind leg. Miraculously intact, Ray could see the polished red bulge of an apple. He had needed a bigger and more rugged container. It was overfull. He gathered it from underneath and held it against his chest, then became very serious and spied again, high over the fields of his past discovery. Blue eyes, creased and cloudy, older than his years. The castle-like spires stood as if two people, frozen in time.

"They're friendly," he said.

He now continued, at a slower pace and in a straighter line. Tommie clearly braced for the next imaginative scramble. The view opened up dramatically. He could see west *and* east, and now to the north along a string of two-sided cliffs and breaks like a thick and ragged fin. After all the climbing, the delays and distractions, with the cresting of the rim and the sprawling panorama, Ray's character jelled. He stood erect. He was a tall, strong Indian. *Almost* alone, yet leader of many. The dog was another brave but not as tall. They both scrutinized the distance to the north and east. Their land was being threatened and the bordering mountain was their refuge.

With a sudden sick feeling in his stomach, he again looked east. Ray caught something like smoke from a moving fire. He was so high…at first he thought of a faraway cigarette with its drifting band of gray, then a match, the drag of a wooden match across the pastures—the sparkle and smoke before any flame, or dust rising from an advancing and galloping cavalry. Then the gray disappeared, and reappeared, turning sharply to begin approaching on the same road as *his*. The winding leading lane that had been his alone. In more turns there were added sparkles from the sun's reflection: a suddenly slow-moving truck. His eyes strained, and not knowing why his fingers drew tight against his palms.

Brother warrior rustled and looked the opposite direction, over his shoulder to regard his home—reminding Ray, who turned and waved his hand, denying what he had just seen. He looked down on the ranch: something strong...something graceful. Quickly, the much taller brave also chose to avoid this direction. Instead he noticed the close and strange shale pyramid, skimming over it with his eyes, questioning and being drawn by its unnatural construction. It took hold and momentarily flooded his attention. Still without words, merely feelings—ones he had never before felt—he imagined a speechless curl in the air winding about his head, then coming to land on the very top of this pointed shape like a winged bird. He stepped forward with his role, approaching the laced rock with a sudden flush to his purpose. The rocks now stood as an ancient marker to a primary lookout. Thinking smoke, signals—somebody long ago had sent signals. From this footing he searched for the signs of soldiers: danger looming outside the boundary of his territory. He glanced again to the east, then hurriedly and completely wiped the intruding truck away.

A canyon from the mountain led to the empty barn, the appealing shed where the rain had beat upon the roof. His pretending vanished. Not losing sight of his view, he sat below the blank plates. The dog came and sat beside him. From this vantage he could see the abandoned house surrounded and disguised by the different leaves of its trees, more of an orange than a yellow. Like a returned torrent, the Voss place drew him and would not let him go: how it lay between the mountain and stream—the huddled colors of bush and tree—the meandering carpet of grass. Winter sun was not important. The protection, the security—something he did not yet understand but wanting to know like the man in his dreams. He considered living there and being married to a lady like Alice. He felt a flutter in his chest; it spread up through his neck and down his arms and he began to breathe deeper, and faster. He blinked to hold back, keep it in.

It spilled.

He again pulled Tommie to him and buried his face and knowing, drying tears, smelling the living, clean fur and body more attractive than any flower…

* * *

Tucker adjusted the flame until it lost its sharp point and concise definition. With a systematic motion the hissing passed back and forth and up and down. A band of spring began to swell, grow tones of purple and blue; flakes of rust crinkled, then popped free and fell into the dirt. From the darkness a glow welled and the steel began to waver, faintly distort, and bend. Buried in concentration, he heard a squirrel chatter. In the corner of his vision it bounced from the cottonwood beside the barn to lope across the yard, strangely passing between Tucker's anvil and the shop. Above the spew from the torch he became aware of a scratching noise climbing the corner of the building; after a short pause, the same sound came from the roof. The squirrel began to scold. Tucker stooped lower, preparing for the glowing area to bend more quickly. When looking to see a turn in the pulley, he was startled by the placement of a close pickup, empty, with its door hanging open like an impolite mouth. The squirrel carried on in a sudden panic. Causing a spasm in his lower back, he felt a man approaching from his rear and immediately raised the torch. The thick metal had bent unevenly. He knew an instant rub, opposition to the progress of the morning. The stranger loped away as if realizing his lack of forewarning, or alarmed by Tucker's size and abrupt movements.

He again extinguished the heat. A different quiet landed with no boy or dog and with it the shadow of worry over their safety. The man wore a casual uniform and smiled shallowly as he repeated his approach. Nearby parked a freshly dusted truck with an emblem on its gaping door. Colors were hard to define but the dash was exposed and an outstanding number of long white rolls lay in a jumble. Tucker looked down at the extra black of his gloves and remembered the goggles. He pulled them from his face and hair while the new black on his fingers left a swipe below one eye. The cups of the lenses left dents in his cheeks, even visible for him.

With a restless feeling he wished that Alice would look out the upstairs window, raise her head from the groan of her machine, the hum of the stitching.

The man came quickly, his walk like stepping over or through a continual attachment of clutter, and the pressed pants looking very showy.

No Ray. No hat.

"Hello."

"Hello, hello."

Tucker had the odd feeling he had just called into a cave mouth or down a well. He laid the torch on top of the post where he had placed the goggles, taking care to overhang the hazardous tip. He searched for his hat, and refrained from removing his gloves. Near, the uniform was less subdued: emblems on his chest, emblems on his shoulder: matching the somehow callow mood of the truck. No question he belonged with the truck, or the vehicle was his.

He came only so close as though still concerned over a residual fire and Tucker's big dirty gloves. His eyes remained wide while the abrupt sun turned his face rosy. "Mr. Black...Martin Daniels."

The man, younger, raised his hand and explained his agency, then division. A dry wave hung, detached from any action of a handshake. Tucker again noticed the rolls of paper on the dash…incongruous.

He nodded politely, but glanced down at the torch.

"One moment… I have a gauge that seeps."

"Sir?"

He touched below the other eye, leaving another smear.

He could feel the agent watching: Tucker needlessly ducked as he entered the arcane doorway; he sensed his own outline beginning to muddle, then break apart. In this sudden reduction of light he held a thought of the man outside, crossing his arms, folding long, smooth fingers under the elbows. Incongruous—not belonging—in a fashion almost aggressive, invasive.

Tucker's hat rested on the tall bottle. He took his gloves off and put them perfectly in place. He turned off each tank and checked the gauges. The molded gloves slid back. He *had* to duck for the hat. Eyes now shaded, he reached the sun with an obvious seasoning to his mood.

The stranger had shifted his position. He returned from his pickup with his fingers stroking one white roll. He stopped suddenly and cupped a hand over each end, as if he had just captured a wasp, or a butterfly. Tucker could almost hear rustling, a struggling to be free. The man was younger, yet stood with his feet apart, a distinct and professional attitude, as if he had received a great deal of training.

Tucker apologized, "I had to shut off the gas."

"Gas?"

"Oxygen. Acetylene."

"You have that inside?"

"Certainly..."

"This is quite the spot." The agent released one end of the paper and flung his hand over the frost-burnt hayfields below the buildings. "I had no idea."

Nothing flew out.

"Soon we will be in snow."

"Yes."

"We get more snow here."

"Yes."

Tucker reached for the roll with his black glove and the younger man lifted it away.

"This is a map of our management roads." Martin Daniels attempted to unroll it; then his hands became jittery for there was no place to lay things down and it kept curling over itself. He quickly grew more serious and stretched his neck as though his collar were shrinking in size, holding the dustless white tube across his waist like a military man with some type of baton. "This is *inconceivable* back here—" Now he looked hard down the valley, and the red of his face developed a minor throb.

Tucker tried for the paper again.

"U—uh," Martin responded and for the second time, pulled the roll from reach.

Nothing like the map his father had offered—guidance, as though drawn on a square of linen: he remembered being told to be slow of temper.

Martin considered the forceful ridge and mountain at either side. "People should see it."

Like a deflating tire, Tucker gradually lost reserve. He began coasting on a raw rim. He had been living with animals too long. A latent sense told him his visitor had nothing to grow, no one to teach, no magnetic pull…

"We have resource management roads, fire control roads on the other side." The younger man pointed straight up the slope to the west, using the unwrinkled antiseptic white as an extension.

No earthbound bearing or sense of distance, the sadness of only—

The stranger withdrew the map, then reasserted with a bare finger, as though harshly tapping on someone's chest.

Tucker was confused, waving at a fly. Any road was much further to the north. Martin seemed to realize the confusion. "They were built two, three years ago. They've been to access timber. We need an easement to connect with the roads on this side."

To Tucker, the man's authority blossomed while the paper gave him permission in places he did not understand.

"It's too steep," Tucker said.

Martin Daniels smiled. "We have engineers to assess, evaluate—who can overcome that."

He kept drifting over the uniform, as if one of a visiting soldier, from a new and developing country.

"We have too much snow."

"Yes."

"We are much higher here."

"Yes."

"We catch more rain and snow, and with this kind of soil, travel is limited unless—"

"The road would improve our ability to manage what's behind you...protect you from fire, manage wildlife, give us a quicker access."

The folds in his pants neatly buckled over the top of each shoe.

"You should address the elk," Tucker said. "There are far too many. They will become diseased."

"Elk?"

"Correct. Too many teeth."

The man worked his tongue as if there were something churlish stuck to the roof of his mouth. "That is not my branch." Martin slowed but was clearly undaunted. "An easement would be beneficial to you."

Tucker's mind rode horseback all along the perilous lip to the rampart—*get to the top and see clearly, understand where you are*: only one way down. "I believe it is too steep."

"As I said previously, we have engineers to evaluate the grade... We need the formality of a contract before we can get out on the ground."

"Mr. Dunbar—"

"Daniels."

"I suppose you have your cannons and tanks."

"We have everything that we need." Martin remained artfully friendly but scratched his forehead as though the sun were becoming an irritant. He paused. He held the unused map under an arm, creating its first wrinkle, and put his hands before his face in angles as though framing a small picture. The hands and fingers spread apart with a swaggering drama. His arms grew wide and his chest expanded, a corporate gesture. The partly flattened roll nearly fell. "This whole range of mountain, it needs to be shared… It belongs to everyone."

"That it does." Tucker pulled on an earlobe and made it darker. "They can get up there now." Like Alistair, his tone changed. It now had an edge, almost a bite.

The man's arms abruptly dropped. "On what? A horse?"

"And these." Tucker lifted each boot and pointed with his chin.

Martin looked away, careful not to nod or shake his head, and Tucker determined a burr had been placed.

The man's already bright face began to reflect. "You think about it." He rubbed his brow again and wrung the map, causing a mild creasing. His artfulness was falling to pieces but his stance remained broad.

"Climb the mountain with your feet; then you know where you are."

"You should think about it. I don't think you know what you've got to show."

"To show?"

"There is a value here."

"Value? My education is of other things." *Climb that hill with a view…above the low places—pushing and shoving…*

Martin Daniels could not help but tip his head down and turn it from side to side. As though waiting for more to unload from the truck, his smile languished. "People dream of something like this." He used the extension again and arched between the ridge and mountain as though daubing with a wand rather than a club, "A better road would bring interest. The effect would mushroom. This place could sell itself."

Tucker's eyes opened wide. He felt his shoulders and well-used back. He twisted his palms up and glanced at his gloved hands, no longer reminded of his failing father. *What is going on up in Alice's private room?* Quickly, the right leather came off and he held his hand out, damp, but clean and a similar color to Martin's. Broad, big-knuckled, grooved, construction hands. He stepped toward his visitor and Martin Daniels lost his height, his compartment. Tucker's hand clasped around his fingers with no intention of squeezing. The touch arrested and dislodged the stranger. He began his retreat.

Tucker made it simple. "I have got to get back to work. These days are getting short." With one bare hand, he followed the agent to his truck.

Martin backed onto the seat, giving the now puckered roll an agitated toss to land among the others. He looked grimly at a manila folder on the padding beside him. A small calendar stickered to the dash had alternating dates circled. He closed the door and leaned back, both hands on the wheel, "Mr. Black," they began to look snaky, "you think about it…*still*—"

With a failed gesture, the younger man looked straight ahead, and Tucker could see the changing whiteness of his fingers, a sudden deep absence of confidence.

"We are an easy agency to deal with." He was in the shade of the pickup but his forehead lingered with a splotchy quality. "You think—" his mouth opened wider, then clapped shut "—if you agree—it would serve for much better management."

"Thank you for the thought."

Tucker's bare hand swung high and thumped the hood directly in front of the windshield and driver as though swatting the rump of a persistently indolent horse. The heel of his palm left a perceptible dimple in the sheet metal and dusty gloss. Had he not seen the disturbance in Martin's face, the strike would have had more force. Pulling on his glove he walked back to the vise and spring, laid his hat upside down on the ground. Before replacing the goggles, he looked across the yard to the upstairs. If only Alice had lifted the sash to shout—*cry*...get rid of this pest far earlier: the deep waves rocking his mood and rippling back, over and over.

The engine started. Gears were shifted. Martin Daniels' foot must have slipped, and with an accidental acceleration, the tires spun in the loose sand, as if momentarily stuck in a warm and gritty snow. Fine bits sprayed onto the bordering grass.

Tucker's attention roiled—then fell away. He felt without plan. *She* would have—could have snubbed the prolonged interference. He looked down at the poor curvature of the discolored spring. He had wasted his fuel, his heat...

Forgetting to put on his goggles, he tried the flint striker to ignite the flame.

No gas in the torch.

He watched the truck depart, and stood in frustration, again looking in the direction of Alice's window.

Less than an hour later, in the lightless rear corner of the shop, Tucker took a small hand crank and gave the familiar, reliable flywheel a twirl. It started immediately, without alarm.

Pop, pop pop, pop...

The exhaust was loosely jointed out the back wall. The clamped connections puffed and leaked slightly until the makeshift piping became warm and a draft developed, the fume hardly noticed. Once engaged, a jackshaft sent many things in motion—rhythmic, mesmerizing busyness, *therapy to anchor his thoughts, straighten a sense of direction.* Unlike the dread and unrest Martin had set into motion. Belts, both V and flat, came off in different lengths and angles, like a *sewing machine* with a variety of bells and whistles: some might think it too much motion for indoors, yet not for him. Gears to a small lathe transferred speed to a slow, smooth power; a wire wheel and grindstone whirred; like the top to a giant eggbeater, the drill press worked in precision, changing a horizontal spin to vertical. He made pilot holes first. He held the arched tooth with the exact curvature of the one he had broken—as though he had made the originals. The cutting oil from the bit darkened the spring and smoked briefly as it started to bore and throw out curls of steel. The engine fired in response.

Pop-p-p-p-p-pop.

He thought he heard an additional sound, guttural, like that of a distant airplane, high over the worn October. After testing the fit of a bolt, he looked behind him and into the sunshine.

A woman in pants stood with her back to the open door, loosely combing her hair with her fingers. The hair was auburn and very heavy and long and shone in the brightness. She was quite short and beyond the top of her framed figure, he could see a smatter of leaves fall, a minor drift to the right. Tucker cocked his head, watching her figure lightly sway, as though something buoyant and out of place. Floating on the wrong shore.

Two in a row.

Tucker laid the replacement part on the floor and grounded the spark to cut the engine. The flywheel continued to coast, producing a strong smell of gasoline. He used his knee as a brake and his pants became ironed where he pressed against the thick and weighted whirl of momentum. This time he removed his hat and gloves and placed them on the bench. He scrubbed his face with a fresh rag, a faded flannel shirt that had once been worn by Alice. He ducked to get out the door with empty, stark hands. The lady faced him.

"Is Ray here?"

The lady was a girl: a young plump face with flashy brown eyes. She looked as though she had pebbles in her cheeks: not old enough to drive.

A two-door Buick sat parked in the same sand where Martin's truck had been, very low slung, with sun-scorched paint and treadless tires.

Better not snow, or rain.

Tucker's hands hung at his sides as though recently swabbed with something to make them numb.

"Ray?"

"Yeah, Ray. Anyways, Raymond. He says he comes here to work."

He made the motion of tipping his hat and she stepped very close, near enough to reach in his pocket or button his shirt. He noted a sour breath and a lunar paleness below her chin. He waved his arm, like the limb of a tall tree, uneasy with this nearness.

"He's on the hill."

Her eyes closed, a wink of deprivation.

"On the *hill*?"

"Why?"

"You ain't got him pulling weeds? Do you?"

"Not at all."

Her head tilted and her eyes flashed. "What do you mean? I see his bike." She drew on a coil of her hair.

Tucker whirled his limb again and clarified the direction. This time hoping that Alice's shade be drawn—tight. The girl did not look. She had the chest of a woman but the face of a child and stood very close. Tucker felt farsighted. His father's map had blank spaces. He looked skyward to place the sun. He felt his center to one side and stepped back and a half circle around until his shadow fell across her shoulder.

"What do you want with Ray?"

With a heavy breath, a different depth to her eye, "I'm April…I'm his mom."

She could have been the boy's sister, almost young enough to be Tucker's daughter. Shocked, Tucker glanced toward the porch. He turned back and passed over her again, now without reservation, as if studying his own female child who had suddenly reached more than maturity, motherhood. Inside her light sweater an abundant softness piqued, tight pants held comfortable hips and short thighs, a faint sign of freckle under each eye and a mole on her temple. Collarbones—boastful cleavage. Such heavy hair, maroon lips, the twist of her neck and the stance of her small feet all flirted an immodesty.

"I am Tucker." He limply offered his hand. "Tucker Black."

"It's a *frigging* long ways back in here." She reached—for the instant both giddy and anxious—and again stood too close.

Tucker made a tolerant swallow, as though he had bit into a pithy apple, and felt her hand: so unlike Ray, so unlike Alice: plump. He could smell cigarette in her hair.

She withdrew, with an abrupt and suggestive confidence, close and upturned, using the sun on her face and all that a man could see. She folded her hair to the side.

"He says…he says he come here to work. He doesn't say what he does. He doesn't say much about who's here… Where is he now?"

Tucker twisted his boots and stood firmly.

"They have been gone since before noon."

"They?"

"On holiday."

"I'd be in town. *Who* is he with? What do they do?"

"A dog and he—"

"They? A dog?" She impetuously leaned into him, without touching. "He never said nothing about any *dog.*"

Tucker did not believe her. It seemed far too late for her to play *mother.* He felt certain that Alice was watching.

"*It* don't bite? Is *it* safe?"

Tucker's voice stayed steady as he imagined his teeth slowly coming into view. "He is certainly safe." He held his hands as if she were offering something adhesive.

She began to sway.

"What do he do here? What do he *do* here?"

"If you look, you might catch them."

She glanced past the barn and partway up the slope, clearly finding no route to follow. As if from a new curiosity, she considered the shop, then the house.

"You work him?"

The white of his mouth disappeared. "He is pretty young. He is at that age to discover things. He needs room."

April's head tipped sideways again. One hand stayed busy in her hair: feeling for trinkets.

She looked at him as though he were flatfooted.

"Well. Are you working him?"

"He is learning. He is a little too young to work much. There will be plenty of time for work."

"He doesn't *know* anything."

Tucker's feet were immobile. It appeared she cared to break them loose, somehow pry on his height.

"He has a lot to find out." April turned up with a thick, creaming insolence. "He needs a *man* around—"

Tucker spoke dryly, unfolding a forgotten place. "What did they say at the parent conference? He told me today is parent-teacher conference."

Her eyes flashed, a garish darkness, and she seemed to struggle with an impulse to pull away.

"I didn't go."

"It is today. I am sure it is today."

She looked toward the sun, blinking. "It don't make sense. I don't have anything to do with that school. I don't like it. I don't like it. They're teaching him to be sassy."

"He is a smart boy."

She turned on him, with smoking brown eyes. "I don't like it. He'll be sassy soon enough. He'll be thirteen this coming June."

The weight of being too young bore heavy.

"I would like his help next summer. Light work—he could earn a wage," Tucker offered.

As if a madness had struck, she glared at him. "He won't get hurt around here?"

No answer.

"I don't want him riding no hot-blooded *lady* horse."

Tucker frowned.

With her eyes yet mad and without focus, April pulled her limber shoulders unmistakably together and forward. Her physical nearness her only remaining tool. "Like I says," with a voice of syrup, "he needs a man around." She reached to touch the elbow of his shirt and Tucker now moved.

She had won.

With total evasion the girl smiled and turned, heading for her car. Midway she stopped her humid walk and faced him, still with a madness. "We will talk more about Raymond—later."

The Buick also spun, but very differently, the smoothness of its tires bouncing lightly in the soft, blind ground before moving on.

Politeness

"She was here in our own yard!"

Tucker nodded, returning to the moment, unwillingly seeing April instead of Alice.

"You should have come for me."

As if out of character, his chin went up and to the side. He looked into the high corner of the room behind her. "There wasn't time. It was very brief." Then directly back to her thinning composure, "I am afraid she will visit again. Her name is April."

"What do you mean you are afraid?"

He wished he had said it differently. "She is very young. She should be his sister."

"They *do* look alike?" She bit her lip.

"No. He is so slim and straight. They are not at all alike. There is nothing alike."

"Is she pretty?" Alice touched her hair, then softly her own lips. She remained sitting.

The dredging of words, "I guess so. She is not very tall and a little too soft. She is a little pretty."

"What do you mean, too soft?"

"I don't know."

"Tucker."

"She is too soft. That is all."

"Tell me."

"She is carrying a little too much." He put his hands out from his own middle. "She has never lifted a hay bale or worked a spade."

"I don't think she cares very well for him. What color are her eyes?" She would not drop her look.

"They are dark brown. Very different. Very dark. Her hair is totally different."

"You find her attractive, don't you?"

Tucker made a motion as though he were pressing on his hip, then twisted to the side.

"When I was young my hair was lighter."

"I know."

With a classic but doubt-filled action, he reached for her shoulder, not sure how to tell her. He cared to pull the thorn out and throw it away. The boy and Alice were one, the same opening truth, the same chance at climbing out of a hole, rising from a rut...healing.

Alice and Tucker did not break their regard.

He lightly fingered his own thorn.

"It *cannot* be our territory," he said.

She looked as though she were going to cry.

The image of April stood at his shoulder, like a shell of disorder—and more—

"You are right. He is not well cared for. But I hurt for them; she is such a child... Something happened, or didn't happen. Her path started too young and too narrow, like a trap."

"Can we help?" she asked.

"I think it is past that. I believe."

"There must be something."

"Maybe—"

"I want to see her...but then, I'd rather...she disappear."

Tucker felt a sharp swaying from side to side, Alice falling from strong to weak, again and again. He lost heart in his telling. He chose to keep hidden his picture of walking trouble, lush exorbitance, *out of control.*

Alice pulled away. "Does he know she was here?"

"No."

"I am going to grow more garden this spring, a big garden, so we'll have fresh vegetables to feed Ray."

Alice stood on impulse, and stepped to the kitchen sink. With a sudden vacancy she studied the bare counter, then rose above the sill, through the series of small panes. The garden lay fallow and dark with faded remains of chopped-up plants. She considered how she would enlarge its dimensions and rotate the rows. When tipping forward she could see more than the close yard, an edge to the lower ridge. Between trees she saw but a sliver. Almost at once a boy and dog came skipping and hopping down the sunlit slope, into her view. Ray carried a long stick which he often used to give himself a vault—a purified height to his deer-like hop then skip. Each time when he landed, Tommie's tail went higher and gave a frantic spin. Cloudless and bright, but an evanescence to the light, the finish of a year. Ray changed his antics and began stooping to wallop the ground like a big bass drum. A faint smile pulled on her lips; she could feel her eyes about to tear. Consciously, very consciously, Alice kept turned away from her husband as she spoke.

"Let us find out more. We need to know *more*...before we should tell him—that *she* came looking."

Soft Yellow Road

Over the next few weeks, a prolonged cold settled in, but it did not snow. Ray pedaled into the yard one morning wearing a letter jacket far too big and thin nylon mittens too small for his growing hands. The jacket had a purple vest and scuffed and dingy Naugahyde arms, once white, now gray and yellowed. The letter was a tattered gold G with loose threads and dog-eared corners. The whole coat looked as though it had once lain on a sharp gravel road and been driven on more than once. He wore a black baseball cap with a clean white letter P, pulled tightly down with the tops of his ears tucked under its band. The exposed lower lobes and edges were red from the cold. The long bill completely hid his eyes and his nose ran.

Smoke came from two chimneys: first from the shop, then from the house. It rose slowly in two straight columns, then hung and floated together at a certain stratum, like a transparent lid over a small settlement. Frost covered everything equally, in sunlight and shadow. The smoke smelled of pine and cottonwood.

Ray parked the bike against the outdoor vise and opened the shop door, greeted by a strange, sweet-smelling, oil-hot dusty tin. No one stood at the window-lit bench or stooped in the cluttered corners. No Tommie. The sudden warm air made his eyes water, his nose run more, and the thumb to one mitten grew dark from

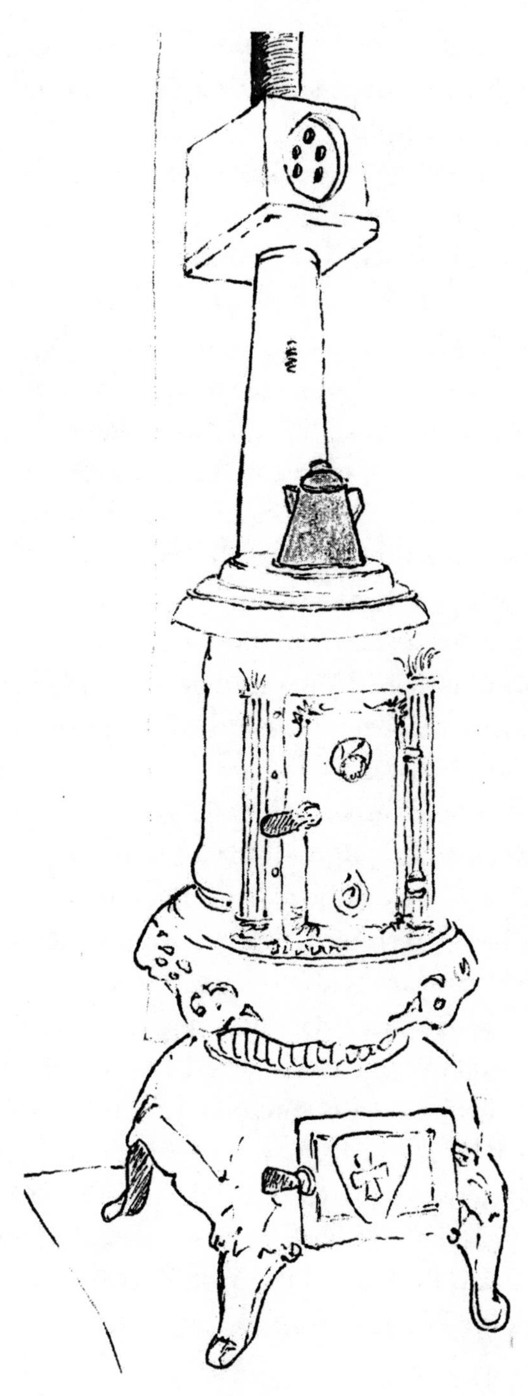

the drips. He sneezed. He heard a voice and a clatter coming from the house. Before he could reenter the frosty morning, the collie was dancing and wriggling on the floor before him. He carried more fur, as if overnight, a thicker and bigger dog. He had come from a heated space and now felt more inviting than a cozy winter bed. The hat bumped back and the mittens fell. They spoke. The thawing made his hands tingle. No matter how sick his head, the dog brought comfort.

Ray turned to exit and swing the door closed, and was struck—It lay on the bench with a cardboard pad underneath, with its lever fully down and forward, exposing the inside. Freshly wiped, the gun's finish was satiny and appealing. He pulled back his shoulders and looked around the room: all the tools and parts and storage like no place he had ever noticed. Even without a stove it would look warm, crowded. Not the same crowded as in the clutter of his mom's trailer. There would never be a gun. She'd yelled once, at a boyfriend, *keep it outta here.* If it happened it would be like poison and he would never touch, *never* get near. He crept closer to look where the bullet would go. There were miniscule pools of fresh oil among all the intricate parts. He abruptly looked out the door into the cold yard—mostly a place with lots going on. With his habitual shrug, he shook his head. Ray turned back. One bare hand came up, with the tense fascination of a boy about to touch a snake. He sneezed and the dog bumped his elbow. The stock pivoted and the end to the barrel hung over the edge, a menacing point to a row of paint cans along a sunlit shelf. His mouth slowly opened. He saw only minimal risk if he were to scoot it off, get the feeling. It was heavy. He rested the friendly end on one cold toe, then straightened his back, to peer down the internally polished tube toward the light of the open chamber. His hands were too numb for the inspection, and it tipped free to bump the wall, then fell from his shoe, lodging among the other propped tools of much less significance. He pulled his hat tight. He pushed the mittens down into his left pocket, then tried to untangle what he should have never gotten down. The butt kicked out and the whole thing fell flatly onto the sandy concrete. He heard the steel grate and the heel of the wood grind and dent.

"Son of a bitch."

Tommie wagged in answer.

The gun felt much heavier as he lifted it from the floor. He tried to wipe with his cold damp hands but the grains stuck to his fingers and he worried over scratching the hard blue steel and the mirror-like stock. It was cradled in the Naugahyde arms. He worked his fingers to make them stronger and rid them of their sand.

The dog licked them.

Too much time was passing. Ray could sense the heated air mixing with the bitterness from the open door. Again he balanced the gun on his foot, then held it tightly to raise and wipe each gritty side on the front of his leg. In spite of his streaming nose, he decided it was the oil in the gun so pungent and distinct. Diagonal streaks remained on the cotton of his pants. One of his hands had made fingerprints on the barrel. He hurriedly set it back on the cardboard and held his friend away who was beginning to prod. In the process his nose dripped. A large salty pellet curved down and parallel to the grain of the polished wood. It came to a stop just above the handgrip.

Alice removed Ray's hat and coat and had him sit on the bench-like door to the oven of the range. The heat seemed funneled only toward him. The fire crackled. He rubbed his sleeve over a shiny lip and she brought a box of tissues to within his reach. She hung his coat on a nearby chair. She set a kettle on so they could all have tea. It sizzled and popped.

"This dry cold is how you became sick."

Ray nodded.

"And your clothes. You don't have the right clothes."

"My coat is warm."

"That is not enough. Riding a bike in this weather, you need better clothes. You need more clothes." Alice took his spent tissues and opened the lid to the stove to put them in the fire. She turned toward her husband. "Tucker—you get something of yours to go under that coat. And get a proper hat. We need one with ear muffs."

Ray watched the dog look back and forth between Alice and himself, then finally lie down. He felt Tommie's nose nearly touching his foot. Ray bent forward and fished for the mittens now deep in his pocket. He put them in the oven.

Tucker stepped over quickly. "Those things can melt and catch fire."

Ray pulled them back and put them at his side. He turned them so the wet tips were facing the hidden rustle and draft, but nowhere near.

He saw Tucker considering the raveled and faded nylon. The ends were coming apart as though a small animal had been gnawing on the stitching.

"Your work gloves, they would be better."

With a noticeable squirming he tried to rub the stripe of oil from his pants. He could smell the gun and couldn't meet the man's face.

"My mom—my mom had her car worked on."

He caught a drip on the back of his hand. He looked up with a puffy sensation spreading over his face. "I left them in that car.

She says, she says they fell out somewheres and don't know where they landed." Ray tipped down and shook his head. "I know—I know I shouldna put them in that car. I been saving them. I hardly, hardly never put them on."

"Don't lose sleep. They are replaceable. You will need better for the winter."

Tucker reached down to compare his hand to Ray's, turning it over and back as though something he no longer recognized.

The kettle began to rumble.

Alice began to stir. She immediately placed the cups back in their cupboard, then wheeled about and disappeared down the hall. The kettle rumbled louder. As if carried by a breeze, she returned and swept by his shoulder, dropping something in his lap. In the same swing she moved the water to the side, where it calmed and simmered. They were leather front and back, a used pair, but still fresh. They had a thick wool lining the color of buttered popcorn.

Ray sat with each hand braced on the oven door, his mouth falling open. Her gloves lay on his lap and his partner rose to sniff. The dog thumped back into position more closely and his neck bent snugly against his ankle. Ray felt a chill. They *were* Alice. He would carry them this day like a totem.

Alice rattled the cups. "You keep them." She put teabags in each one. "Our hands are close to the same—for now."

He would carry them always. Never in the car. At night he would hide them under the bed.

She passed around the steaming drinks, each with a spoon and saucer. Tucker remained standing and walked slowly about the room taking polite little sips and blowing at the vapor, the cup and individual tray appearing far too dainty. Alice sat at the table and pursed her lips, watching *him*, who had not yet drunk from the tea.

"Would you like some sugar?"

His eyes were on Tucker.

"No."

The hat hung by the door behind Tucker's walk.

"No. No thanks."

The hat. The gloves. Tommie, Jasper Spring. The stove settled. A want was growing. He picked up the smooth leather and set the gloves closer to his waist. His regard came to Alice with a deep, immovable look; he felt much older than his years.

"Inhale this and it will help you breathe."

He did as suggested, then coughed. He took a long drink and felt the hot nearly burning his throat, as if killing his sickness. Ray put the cup down and rested both hands to cover the stains that would not go away. The smell of the oil seemed to come from his mouth and all of his body. His head changed, became more congested, and he snuffled in an effort to clear it. He looked out the window. The pile of hand-split range wood was covered with frost.

"I saw your gun," he said with a thickening voice. "I saw it was empty and I went to look at it and we knocked it down."

The dog lifted his head as though he realized he was part of the story.

"I mighta scratched it!"

Tucker raised his eyebrows, then continued with his tea. His head tipped back and he finished with a hefty swallow, then cleared his throat.

"It had just been cleaned."

He took his dishes and laid them by the sink.

"Guns are serious."

Ray nodded in sorrow.

"You were going to pick it up?"

"I did—oh, I did and I shouldn't have. I did."

The hot fluid and the oven and the release of truth made him feel as though he were melting. "No. It wasn't going to be no touch. My fingers was cold, Tommie came up."

"I know Tom—"

"No, he didn't knock me. It ain't his fault."

The dog changed to lie flat on his side, as if in display of his length.

"I don't want it scratched." Ray caught a brief amber glint from the floor and the tail lifted as though it also had eyes. "Oh, I did—I did. I know I done it. It is brand-new."

"Not at all. It is old. It was my father's. He taught me how to shoot and care for guns. He taught me respect."

"I know I done hurt it." His cup and saucer rattled and he shakily drank.

"Tucker will shine it up," Alice offered. "You will see nothing is hurt. But young boys should not be around such big guns—without a man."

The tremble of his cup began to calm. A quick feeling passed...like he needed to sigh.

"Tucker has been hearing big numbers of elk. He has to push them back up the mountain. Without snow, they should be staying high."

Tucker rested his height against the counter, blinking. "They discover the stacks and then waste more than they eat."

"You going to kill one?"

"I cannot do that."

"You ought to shoot one."

"No."

"Why not?"

"I will shoot at their feet and over their heads to make them feel there is a rule here."

"Will it work?"

"I don't know. They do not like rules."

Ray drew air from his cup and stood for himself, a tight hold on the gloves.

"More tea?" she asked.

"No." He could feel his voice changing even more.

The dog stood and shuffled.

"What are we doing today?" His eyes felt grainy, with an odd kind of itch. He rearranged his feet.

"I think you should stay inside," said Alice. "You have a redness to your face."

He lifted the battered coat and poked each new glove into individual pockets. He tucked its bulk under one arm. Holding it off balance left the sleeves dragging on the floor.

"I am only hauling sawdust," said Tucker.

"I think you should stay inside," she repeated.

"It ain't but a cold."

"We could read."

He considered.

"Where is the sawdust?"

"There is a sawmill above the old Voss place."

"Sawdust?"

Ray began to sway: toward the dog, then away. He wrinkled his nose and caught the glaze of his own lip. "Where?" he asked. He looked at the wall, as if through a window. "Where?" he asked again.

"Up the canyon into the mountain."

He spread his feet.

Tucker faced Alice. "I will keep him warm. If it gets too cold and damp, he will be in the truck."

Ray stopped his rocking and came back into the room. He kept hoisting the coat to keep it from touching the floor and his fingers felt how the Naugahyde had softened.

"What you want sawdust about?"

"For bedding. We will need several loads."

"Sawdust?"

"The coming mother cows and their baby calves. Alice spreads straw on top so that it does not stick to the wetness of birth."

"I like sawdust. I like sawdust. I never seen a sawmill." His whole person pointed toward the door.

The dog left his side and he looked down. He heard Alice giving in.

"Go warm the cab. I'll get something for under this coat." She followed Tucker to where he hung his outdoor clothing. She spoke lowly but not in secret. "Stop back for an early dinner. I will have something more."

It took some time for Tucker to return. They gathered at the door. Ray now had a brown winter hat with fleece-like earflaps and a wool scarf around his neck. The coat draped around him like a barrel. The pockets still bulged, a fresh handkerchief in one, and his hands were barely visible.

After all their close preparation Alice suddenly asked, "Where did you get that coat?"

He didn't answer. He let the man and the dog and himself get outside, then turned back with a stiff neck so he would not undo the scarf.

"I think it was—is—my dad's...the dad I never seen or know."

* * *

Alice's face grew thin and tired as she watched the exhaust steam around the truck and they left. The weather, a change to an assailing, damp cold. She kept hearing her own voice: *we need to know more, find out more.* A lone boy missing his father, an underage girl his only parent—not giving care… *Will I ever want to say—that she…came looking?* Alice reentered the house, which felt more than empty, as if the draft to the fire could suck her away. She took the forgotten mittens from the oven door and put them in a safe and hidden place.

Tucker had assembled sideboards in the stake pockets and hitched the wagon to the pickup. They started with the dog in the wagon and the two people inside. Immediately Ray looked back and saw Tommie trying to balance his front paws on the frosty top rail. He slipped and momentarily one white leg and elbow hung over the edge at an awkward angle. Tucker also looked back, then slowed the truck and rolled down the window.

"Get down. And stay."

They proceeded with an insulted companion now missing from sight. Ray felt a worry that he had fallen out the back, and in sadness and perplexity returned home. To great relief a head popped up, but only for a quick glimpse. Ray waited; quite soon two feet were again propped and this time stable on the sideboards. His friend pleaded over the edge with exaggerated mouth and ears as though the man at the wheel had grown quite dull.

"*Can't*…can't he be up here—let him ride aside us? Please."

The coat billowed.

Tucker glanced at the space between them. "With all these clothes there is not much room."

With the tips to his hands, Ray pressed the chest of the coat down, then scrunched himself against the door.

The brakes shuddered and the truck and trailer came to a more sudden stop. From the driver's side Tommie bounded onto the seat and curled his tail around to sit perfectly in the middle, his frill of fur already chilled and beginning to stiffen. He checked the wool about Ray's neck, then as if to confuse him turned instantly calm, without interest. Ray ducked his chin, expecting more, but the dog looked straight ahead with his mouth clamped shut. He pushed his nose into the warm softness behind an ear and his lip came away with less gloss. The new passenger panted but once, as if with a body language—*keep in place.*

"How come he never get a runny nose?"

Tucker rolled one shoulder and shook his head.

Too warm and confined, the windows began to cloud, an early fogginess from more than just heavy clothes and Ray's feeling sick. A thicker arc of condensation formed on the center windshield: proof of the dog's breath. He felt a rawness in his throat, but at the same time knew a comfort. He watched the road. As though loosening, the defrosting fan squealed and rattled, then picked up speed. The limited scene slowly grew, showing more and more of the midmorning glitter to the valley. He felt surges and jerks from the trailer. At any time he could turn and view his company. Lifting the bulk of the coat, he placed one arm on the seatback behind the dog which gradually slid off. A bare hand protruded and rested on the fluff of the dog's tail. He couldn't keep his fingers still.

They came to their first gate and Ray jerked up his arm so he could bump open the door.

"I will get the gates."

Tucker stood on the shining ground before he had a chance.

"You stay in."

The wire stretched long across the road so farm implements could pass. After driving through, Ray turned to watch. He could see the shoulders swelling underneath the bulk of Tucker's coat, as the drooping wires drew straight and the hoop to hold the gate stick fell into position.

A low-lying winter grayness hung below and beyond the valley. This morning it rose, slowly, as if from a tide to begin covering—everything so groomed.

Through empty fields, the truck and trailer made a gentle dip and curve, following parallel tire paths and a centerline of stunted vegetation, already stiff and full from a growing ice. Ray thought of crumbs or bits of silver sponge. It had been dribbled in a row like the middle of a track to pull them along. They approached a grouping of long, wooden bunks. These were heavily built from two-inch planks. The surrounding frost had been recently beaten away and the stubble lightly broken. For a moment Ray felt baffled—they had a shine—licked clean, with a well-developed polish from many seasons of callous lips and tongues and the rubbing of coarse hides: a fresh mottle of frozen saliva from earlier in the morning. A huge dish for eating. No cattle were present. The dark wood looked hardened, with a returning fragile white fuzz. There were wandering trails of shattered frost leading to the trees of Jasper Spring, as if those once here had a schedule calling.

"We will move the bunks soon or their feet will wear a hole in the hay land."

Ray glanced across the dog's back; he saw Tucker's profile and swallowed. He was the sole one not looking forward. He touched his nose with the gentler elastic of his sleeve and used his hidden fingers to pinch; he pinched again to keep from sneezing.

"We need snow. Something to wet down this dust." Tucker hunched his shoulder again as though fighting a stiffness in his neck. "It will bring sickness, just as in you."

He sneezed.

"I *can't* go in snow."

Ray looked back at the trailer with the racks bouncing and shaking, a continuous muffled commotion. He wouldn't be able to come if it snowed. It was hard to think of dust when everything seemed so frozen.

The dog suddenly appeared trapped in the cab. He sprang to his feet and lowly growled. Tucker watched him pressing his face above the dash, leaving nose prints on the glass. The hair between his shoulders rose as if by static, or as if drawn by the plaintive tone in Ray's words. Tucker pushed away the thought of snow and watched a party of calves gallop from under the trees and part the brush. They wove and bucked in a haze of crystals, blocking their way like barely contained bandits with a plan of interception. Once clearly in the road, they lost all restraint. They spun and danced and bawled over the sound of the engine and fan, pulverizing the fine white coating in the wheel ruts and raising a cloud of dirt. The dog's lip quivered and he freshly growled, still softly. The cattle dropped their drunken-like celebration and began to circle, swarming about the truck and trailer like a lumbering parent or provider. Tucker smiled, thinking not of winter but of huge puppies, trying to nurse. Tommie began to lean from side to side, intent on each window with nervous jaws. The sheet metal popped and buckled. He chose to step onto Ray. His front feet wobbled on the boy's small lap and he snapped at the glass, following with a high-pitched complaint. The pickup, moving very slowly, pushed one with the bumper, causing a kick, the contact of a hard thump. Calves began to wedge between the hitch and the tongue to the trailer. The truck halted, too engulfed by the crowd. Body to body—shoulder to shoulder—heads struggling, squeezed and plying as if reaching for air. Tucker smiled again for the boy's view: all he could see was the thick fur of Tommie's collar. Everyone could feel-hear the very close tremor and rustle, as if the doors were being damaged.

"They are a little too tame," he said.

The truck gave a mild shake and rolled in reverse.

"Too tame."

Tucker shut off the engine, then fan, and rolled down his window. "Whoa... Hey. Whoa. *Hey*... Tame, but a governable mob."

He forced the door open as though mindful of a bite by its hinge. "Hey...*scoot*...*hey.*" He made his voice quite loud.

Tucker gained his feet and with the proof of his whole person, a small round bubble of space began to form. His hands came up and waved, too much like the debonair and expressive director of a church choir. The cattle merely watched. With his first abrupt action, he clapped his gloves together and charged at their heads. The door swung fully open and the dog silenced to crouch behind the steering wheel. Those nearest—that could witness—were frantic to back into the others. The bubble surged and expanded. Tucker made birdlike flaps with his arms and jumped lightly. He flung his hands up as though shooing away peasants for the entrance of royalty. The collie met the ground and the circle parted with a spasm, like a living division of black hair to form a lane, an alley for their own departure. With a churning on each side, the entire group moved away.

Tucker wondered over Ray's impression. Through the open door the boy could surely catch their molasses breath, the smell of a steaming multitude. He sat big-eyed and a little shaken, as though Tucker and the dog were acting in a secret play and careless of the danger.

The weathered truck lost company, spotted from noses and drools, sketchily buffed and scoured but undented. The herder worked them into one big pool, then deep into the silvery field. They broke a new trail in the increasing frost.

Tucker and Ray waited for the dog to create a division. The truck door clicked closed but the window remained down. Low clouds now gathered: arms and tendrils were drifting up to greet them, a muddle of winter slowly reaching out to envelop all the sparkle. Like a stirring of low-hanging moisture, it came from new sides, filtering through the trees of the stream, a mass gray trilling over dormant tops.

Finally he gave a whistle. The collie made one last sweep, as if with an urge to tuck in the corners, tighten the wad. The cattle stood bright and in wonder, creating a fog of their own.

The door swung again and he leapt over Tucker's legs. They began moving at once. The engine came to life with a rev and the wagon jerked. They had overcome the obstacle of the crowd—and drove further...further into a breath of sweeping diffusion.

A billow had returned to his coat; Ray's head and hat twisted at its top like a turtle with a sustained look of discomfort. He sneezed into his arm.

"This is sickness weather. You had better stay inside."

"I can't stay inside. I can't. I got good clothes. I got to get out and stretch so my head don't plug."

"You sound plugged already."

"It can—it can get better, I know it can. I move around—around. I ain't able to set in all this."

Like a turtle awkwardly upright and propped on its tail.

And a dog.

Tucker gave a small cough and an abbreviated choke.

"I swear I'm fine."

"Do you feel hot?"

"Not any."

"Got a headache?"

"No sir."

"You might know. We will give it a try."

The suspended cold began to thicken. Crystals had formed on the outside mirrors; a heavier dusting grew on the edges of the hood. In total grayness they came to the forgotten Voss buildings. Feathers of cloud strayed between Ray's notice of the house—then the barn, as if with a pattern to accent one, then the other. He wiped his glass, believing condensation had added to the clouds. Everything had a delicate white mold. He felt a welcoming as though there might be a friendly human ghost standing in the opening to the barn or on the veranda to the house. All the paint-less wooden framework in white, distinctly outlined and detailed by a strange growth.

They entered the canyon. Rocks from the mountain made them sway and jar. They came to the mill and Ray's hands extended from his coat with a clear awakening. He sat up and pushed the front down, immediately centering on the large cone of their purpose.

"Ain't it froze?"

"There will be a crust."

"Looks awful froze."

"Not too thick, not yet."

From the bed of the pickup, he watched Tucker lift out a big scoop with a short handle and a standard square shovel. Ray stood beside him but didn't know what to do, for the trailer was parked way too far away. Tucker took the smaller shovel and broke through the frost and ice and dug a shallow hole in the diminishing slope to the pile. A few feet to the side, he made an identical hole. His breath hung under the brim to his hat and his ears darkened to a deep robust color.

"You stay back while I get parked."

Tucker made sure of where Ray and the dog had moved. Obediently they backed over by the chain that dragged out the chips from below the saw.

He called out, "Put your earflaps down."

Ray folded them down and pressed them to his head. He and dog stood still and smoked lightly from their mouth and nose in turn. The chain with paddles was heavily covered and drooped behind them like a giant diamond necklace. Tucker backed the trailer around until the rear tires dropped into place and the frame rested easily on the unbroken mound. Ray then understood. He broke his stay to drag the scoop high up the side of the cone, as if walking atop a drift of hard-crusted snow. He stabbed at the sawdust, anxious to see it fly. The shovel only flexed and bounced. At once he shook his hands, feeling the invisible poking of something sharp. Tucker came with the better tool to readily break the covering.

"Remember your gloves."

The scoop dropped and Ray felt his pockets in a definite panic. He looked down as he drew out the pair and another gift surfaced in his fingers: a red handkerchief neatly arranged in a small square. He touched his nose to its softness without undoing the folds, then replaced it in the coat. The gloves came over his fingers as a new experience. Watering and swollen eyes, but it could not stay inside; his face collapsed into a smile.

Tommie's tail was up and stalled, with an obvious interest in what Tucker was uncovering. He had reached the soft interior. A christening arc of sawdust flew over the moldy boards; several more and the opening began to fume. Ray came closer to see what was steaming, and his shovel slid from the icy crust into the shallow hole. It clanged against Tucker's. He sat and braced, to keep from joining and landing against the big man's legs. Tucker put aside the scoop and quickly enlarged the space so there would be room for two. The dog chased the smaller crystallized clods, as though they were escaping mice.

"Come around and get closer to your target."

They traded tools.

Ray stepped into the warm cushion, holding the smooth wood handle like a staff too tall and heavy. His shoes disappeared with his laces floating, slack socks stirring in the damp grains. He smiled even stronger and his nose dripped harmlessly.

Tucker began to fling large volumes directly into the center of the wagon.

In his smallness Ray struggled with the long handle and made a halting first throw. It twisted in his gloves; the light load glanced against the boards and missed entirely. His smile hardened. Steam rose and surrounded his face and he inhaled—then drew again, with difficulty, but more deeply, as if pulling in an incense of clean life and health—rising from a mound of ground and fermented pine.

They completed one trip before dinner. Ray sat tight against the window and now and then looked back at the heap following them down the road. With a shadowy pride he watched it bounce and settle, no more rattle. Next time he would top it up better, knowing how it shook down. The gloves were back in his pockets. During most of the drive, he had worked hard to clean the sawdust from their insides. Unruly slivers and bits had stubbornly embedded in the woolly lining, collected in lumps at the tip of each finger. Much of it was still there and the gloves grated on his hands, so different than when Alice had worn them. Something had started and this difference did not lead to frustration. He *did* promise—for the coming trips he would be more careful. He would avoid filling the cuffs when reaching so deep.

They were early, yet too late to return to the mill.

A whole chicken was baking and they *had* to wait.

Tommie rolled and gave himself a cleaning shake. Following Tucker's example, Ray stomped on the porch and brushed repeatedly. Upon entering the warm room, he left his coat by the door and it stood like a small tent. He placed the hat on the floor. Wherever he walked he left a light trail of yellow crumbs, but remained unaware. All the crevices of his shoes and socks continued to spill.

Tucker followed his path as he made his way to the sink.

"You will not get lost, Hansel."

Ray looked down and discovered the faint flakes of wood on the floor, leading only to him. He sniffled—then reversed in his steps.

"Wash, and *sit.*"

They had to wait...suffer snug chairs and the pleasure of simmering food.

Alice turned the light on at her desk. She read: a continuation of Jules Verne. All three listened to her story, poised in the dimness of the day to travel 20,000 leagues.

* * *

After eating, they began their second trip to the mill. Deep under the bank the sawdust remained thawed, elsewhere a newly formed stiffness and cohesion. Clouds would hide the upper canyon, then drift and dissipate, only to reappear with a slight change in identity. Not a bird in the rush of quiet: peace: but for the huff and soft motion of their shoveling.

Too calm.

The dog now joined in the work. As if he had carefully chosen the place, he clawed through the hardness to dig his own cave. At first with an eagerness, then a gradual frenzy mounted as though he had started a contest—to tunnel and meet them, or race the people…in a quest for some buried prize. Between each throw Tucker watched. The dog gave in to total temptation; sprays shot out from between his hind legs and he sniffed and rooted in abandon. Tucker shook his head at the sawdust balanced on the collie's nose, and the dribbling from his mouth like drool.

A big scoop, then small, their efforts jointed and mixed, adding to the whole. He sensed the boy's struggle to stay in rhythm and noticed his long, slender limbs, so different from the soft, short, coupled form of his mother, the girl he had met but once.

Active, cobwebs of frost grew on the dog's rear skirt and tail. Tucker's and Ray's hats and coats had developed relief, a sugary highlight of seam and texture. The trailer settled down in clicks, sinking in its own private hole. All too full of happiness, the dog stood and rested. Ray continued scooping until the contents began to shower over the sides.

They drove along in quiet. The boy began to fidget and brew.

"You ever imagine there coulda be a man have his own submarine?"

The phantasmagorical Nautilus hovered in the cloud between trees. The clumsy pickup towed its mundane cargo.

"Oh…possible…yes."

"That captain, he was crazy. He was crazy smart. Do you remember —see when that—they rammed into that other ship? He was mad. And he done it. He had his men build stuff stronger than anything else. They was safe as long as he stayed inside."

"Seems true."

"It must be pretty and scary so far under the water. Under water. Nothing but different animals and fish out through that window—underwater mountains and cliffs and forests and sharks—not a single people. I wouldn't want to go out and get my air through no tube, all those sharp teeth and rocks around. Would you?"

There was a loud breath in the closeness of the cab. Ray faced Tucker with eyes perfect for the story, enlarged and marine, not leaving time for an answer. "Maybe I would. I'd carry a long sword, not a knife. A sword." His hands came out from the coat, as if to guess at the length of a dagger. "A sword would be better in fightin'—fight shark or octopus. I'd poke right into their hearts. Harpoons is good but I'd have my men all swords." He nodded to himself, and this time left a space.

"Take a long stick and wave it under water? Wing a sword about and you might cut your own hose—" Tucker's voice diminished in the instant. His mouth sealed, sorry he had spoken.

Ray held his own throat and took another breath. "I don't know. I'd like it on the land." He ran one hand down the dog's back. He glanced behind, the trailer still full enough to rock and sprinkle a soft yellow-orange along the surface of their road. "I'd feel terrible closed in, no jumping, always a ceiling top my head. Don't you suppose you'd not get used to it?"

Tucker did not answer.

"I'd rather be on this—doing this. Some a these spears is like guns. That's right. I'd have that kind of har*poon* for everybody. Like guns for everybody. They'd shoot in and out of the water." He held an imaginary spear with a trigger and took aim at the stream. "No...I'd rather be out on a kind of island—or a place like this." He sat up and stared into a wonderland of frost. A blur had started on his window; the Naugahyde came up and wiped, only to smear.

They drove as though below a dim reef, slow, close observers to a fabulous growth of coral.

The boy pinched the redness of his nose but his cheer was untouched, as though he just remembered a stronger and attractive Alice—and her food.

What did Ray's own mother feed him, Tucker suddenly wondered. *Did she feed him?*

"Isn't nothin' better than this," the boy said, his hand finding its way down to settle again on Tommie's back. "Nothin'."

The wagon emptied. Ray made an effort to sharpen the peak of the fresh mound, wading in its newness, backing down and filling and smoothing his own footprints. With a smile as if satisfied, he placed the shovel in the back of his side of the pickup, lowering it down with care, as though its worn handle and rust-pitted blade could easily be scratched.

Their eyes met behind the rear window.

Tucker felt he had been embraced.

* * *

Now there was fog. They could sense the running forest but not see it, the boy's coat like an underwater suit. This would be the last load. Evening and night would be premature. Within moments there were wisps of gray on Tommie's shoulders and on the fringes of his ears. He had lost his enthusiasm and sat and watched with a lustrous but removed interest: a vacancy, but still listening to the deep cloud. The frost grew rapidly, like crystals of hair, fine tentacles and feelers to amplify everything. The boards of the wagon had doubled in thickness.

Ray's shoveling slowed. An ache and pull had surely come to certain muscles in his arms. His grip lost its power, moving closer and closer to the weighted end; a hold as though trying to remove a hidden root from the pile rather than a small scoop of sawdust.

With the wagon nearly filled—Tucker heard crashing in the brush, a shocking dissension encased over their heads. Ray quickly wielded his spade as if it were a weapon and looked about the circle, then upward, into the muggy and freezing air. His feet spread and his shoulders hunched, as though something might fall from above. One eyelash clung and bore a heaviness, while he blinked. And the dog grew rigid, all his attention again awake and pointing up the fog-covered mountain. Tucker made one more throw, then stabbed the pile, showing a freedom with his empty hands.

In *two* places they heard a popping and breaking of deadfall. In many places they heard a fluty and echoing chatter, treble squeals and an arrested bugle; everything padded in cotton but the sound held low and immediate, like a covert life and clamor inside the very sawmill.

In the style of a mule deer or pogo stick, the dog bounced and ended at the peak of the cone-shaped hill. He arched his tail.

"Elk," Tucker said, with a changed steam.

With the sound of his voice came a prevalent thrashing, shifting the noise from right to left—then left to right. Nasal calls, mewing.

"They *know*...they know just where we are."

Ray brandished the shovel higher and held his head forward with bigger and bigger eyes.

"Sounds like an *army*."

"There are many."

Tucker's gloves had grown stiff and he tried to loosen them by gripping his hands. He looked to the sides as though recording their weak flanks, preparing for an assault.

He could see Ray's excitement throbbing, on the brink of not believing: thoughts in his eyes about to make him cry.

A silence landed...

Like an explosion of sound, the blast of an organ echoed through the clearing. Tucker clenched his jaw—such mighty posturing of dominant force.

Tommie dug his claws into the top of the mound with a matching shudder in his hips, an almost violent flexing.

Tucker gave a short, sharp whistle. "Here, Tom. Here."

Too intent, the dog just stood, quivering, and clenched.

Tucker hustled to the pickup and thumped its side.

"Tom, *here*," banging once more with a louder exclamation, strong enough to pierce the fog.

Unexpectedly, the dog bounded down and over the truck side and into the bed.

The resonant horn from the bull elk blew again—with lesser force—followed by a short interval, then the sound of a clotted withdrawal, heavy and numerous. The unseen army was leaving. The chattering and calls and snapping gained elevation and softness.

The collie now stood with his front feet on the wheel well, his ears still tense and listening, as though he were able to see their ascent, their sudden rise in elevation. He stood as tall as Tucker. Maybe taller. He had become fantastic: a gauzelike mane, a down of ice over his shoulders and along his spine as highlight—tracing. Thin fragments came from his nose and he looked down upon the boy without the agitation or passing illusion of a dog's spirit.

"I need to get you headed home. It will be dark early."

Ray dropped his eyes to the ground and shook his head, a straw-like parting to his ducktail of hair. Tucker gathered his small and very tired worker. They stood beside the truck. He and the boy heard another call, further south on the rampart; a shrill, elongated bugle as though through an extended tube, pointed directly at them. Ray's eyes returned to a wondrous size and began to pool, tears enough to blur. The dog hopped to the ground and entered an open door.

"Is that the same ones?"

"Another herd."

"Ain't any snow, how come they're out? How come they keep coming down?" The hat seemed suddenly too tight for his face.

"They *do* know it is coming. And the new roads and people are pushing them out. There are too many—"

"But what if they come into the bottom, all them, and get all over you and steal the hay piles an— Isn't you coming back with that gun and run them away?"

"Not tonight."

"They got to know—they got to know. *So many.* Show them you own it."

Tucker shook his head and sighed.

"Father, Alistair," he said.

"What?"

"We don't own it."

"What?"

"It is ours to take care—"

"You got to, get them off. This is your place," his eyes now a blue reflecting from brass, "you got to own it. All that work and you piling hay."

Tucker considered the back of his gloves and brushed away frost, then turned up the leather and cupped his hands together as if he were cradling marbles. "It keeps us. We are not here very long." He pulled his fingers apart and one hand made an awkward motion as though following the curves of a river. In the same dim moment another elk called, faint, far over the timbered ledges. "We direct and *protect,* to bear fruit, so it can rear more."

He could see the elk talk repeating in the boy's head.

"But you got to. You own your own cows. You coming back with that gun? We—I be with you and help you chase. We k—*kill* one."

"It is past time for you to go home. It has been a big day. Too big."

Weariness swept the boy's face.

"It will be too dark to come back. I cannot shoot into this." Tucker craned up at their blindness.

"Go and shoot—shoot in this heap and scare 'em, scare 'em off." Ray pointed at the eroded hill, very tired. "Shoot in the dark."

The dog shifted his position inside the cab.

"I don't want to go. I want to stay here with you, and *Alice.*" He looked into the fog. Under the stiffness of the coat, his shoulders were shivering in jerks.

Tucker arranged his lips as if he were going to whistle, words formed. He traced the boy's outline with a sensation that he could not hold or touch, as though something were failing in the tendons of his wrists. He could not speak. When Ray turned back to him, Tucker's mouth had returned to a firm and silent nothing...

They rode together and all previous pleasure emptied. Looking straight ahead, the collie now slouched and the point of his elbow prodded through the softening Naugahyde. Such a sideling road. Ray looked down over the bank until the trail leveled and the sleeping buildings came. His head drifted from mirror to mirror with his eyes closed. He coughed without covering his mouth and swallowed several times, feeling a new resistance. An ache crept up the back of his neck and he tried to stop swaying.

"It will get too cold for that bike."

He opened his eyes. They had passed the old homestead. He had missed it, and turned to Tucker with a gloom and sadness beyond the man's reach.

"Alice will not want you getting sick over and over." In the overcast there settled a precipitate, something solid. Tucker tipped his hat back and could feel it rubbing on the ceiling. "I want you to come to work in the spring. There will be many things you can help with. It will be your first job."

Ray's head swiveled from the driver to the road, then back again. The collie pressed harder. The man's reach had extended. A warm light flickered on.

"We will pay you a wage, something for you to save and build on."

Tommie slouched completely, like he had lost all care to remain upright. His tail lay against Tucker's hip while his thawed chest and throat went down across Ray's thighs, turning them wet. Ray stroked the dog. The ache in his head slowly lifted.

"You don't need to pay me no money…Mr. Black."

Winter Frosting

The fog had lifted but a heavy overcast remained. Now Monday morning, Tucker was out in the yard much earlier than usual, loading the buckets of grain well before sunrise. He propped the gun on the seat by the gearshift. If there were elk, he would be ready. The dog sat by the window very conscious of the glossy thing jiggling and lightly rolling in the center. They came to the gate and there were no frosted lines and stays crossing the road. A wrap of confused wires and bright splinters of gate stick lay in the pasture on their side of the fence: tufts of thick hair from an undeterred force. Any track had covered over and obscured. Silently, Tucker cursed the new road, barely two years old, cursed the movement it forced on ancient patterns. He did not stop to untangle and review the damage. They approached the feed bunks with no sign of cattle and the dog rose inside the cab to begin searching.

Tucker opened the door to the passenger side.

"Unload."

They both stood as though holding their breath and looked and listened in all directions. He watched as the dog outstretched his nose and sniffed, then trotted among the legs to the bunks. After a tour around all the troughs, the collie again stood still, and gave a look as though questioning.

Tucker pulled an empty bucket from the truck bed. He turned it over and began to drum.

"Ca-alves… Bo-o-o-ies."

A style like no other.

The bucket rattled and carried, much louder than his voice. It mounted slowly, as if taking time to loosen and shed embarrassment.

"Bo-o-o-ies. Whooee!"

Propelled by the force of the drumming, the collie leapt into a bunk to see better and continue his search for factions of calves. He froze and pointed. Beyond the creek, off the farm ground and outside another fence, stood a small bevy of coming yearlings: lesser black dots on the east hills. They were scattered but could obviously hear. They each turned and watched, holding their heads high but making no response to come.

Tucker had the dog hop in back of the truck and they sped to the bridge and crossed the creek. Once in the next field he saw the yearlings begin to bunch and hold their heads even higher. Though the field was smooth, Tucker slowed and called from his window.

"Whooee!"

With the pickup still rolling forward, he opened the door, preparing to get his drum. The cattle nervously milled, circling each other as if for some mysterious purpose—repeat of a ritual. The steer with the highest head made a wayward choice and split from the perimeter. He trotted further into the overcast and forbidden hills, a distant and unknown horizon. He swung his head back and forth as if surly and horned. All the rest followed as if drawn by a net.

In the middle of the hay land, Tucker stopped the vehicle and ceased any noise. He unloaded the dog and had him stand on the ground for a moment. The calves kept trotting, escaping from home, going faster and faster. Very calmly he turned down.

"You stay out."

He stepped to his left and paused.

"Way on—out." The fingers to his right glove clipped the front of his hat.

The collie cast to the side with a trailing rope of nebulized crystals, loping adrift as though he might head for the yard, or unseen porch.

Tucker twisted his boots in the coated stubble, powdering the ice.

The dog curved and reached the end of the hay to duck under barbs of fence with no perceptible change in his course. As if in ideal placement, a hill rose between the dog's lope, his line to intercept, and the escaping cattle. Soon he also disappeared from Tucker.

The cattle proceeded, breaking into an easy gallop, changing shape often like a chaotic flock of dark birds. They were rapidly getting smaller. Tucker waited. He discovered the dog low and creeping: the skyline blurred for the lack of light and a heaviness in the air, his intersection precise. The yearlings—in unavoidable collision—scattered like quail. With exquisite and deliberate action, Tommie made large hesitant swings—delicate gestures against the cattle's fear...all of them turned but never stopped running. Never a grouping, never a huddle.

Tucker scurried to the pickup and motored to meet them before they reached the fence. His door popped open as if by a spring. The dog remained far behind, now stopping to stand on the crest of the hill and watch their descent. The calves approached Tucker with domed wild eyes, as though pursued by a lion. From a night of tearing through fences, several had sliced and blood-clotted ears, and one galloped with a deep horizontal gash across the hide of its nose. Tucker sidestepped and flapped his arms and shouted, without deflection; they were fixed. They plunged into the fence and he ducked his hat to the screeching wires and twang of staples. Three hung up and kicked and lurched, joining the others over the calm, sloping shoal of home pasture, in a race to nowhere. The air glistened with bangles above the fresh break. All the wood posts still stood while broken wires curled and flopped like loosened yet savage ribbons.

He tried to count and arrived at an unclear one-tenth. They spread and hid in the cover of the central stream.

Tucker called in the collie, bending down and patting his side.

"We will have to wait...let them rest—tame down—in the light of day."

He headed for the truck, with a plan to gather tools and supplies for mending the fence. The dog's riveted eye brought his attention to the mountain.

Across the valley lay a crust of winter with unusual dryness underneath, nothing fluid but the elk: an eddying mass among the aspen groves, without control but a definite stealth. Knowing their morning exposure, they began to shift into the shadow of the pine and spruce. They filtered through the barren stands, dark-bodied, in accent. Tucker thought of flies crawling through the thinner hairs of a carcass, crafty and slow-moving, yet stirring with argument and competition. Instinct made him feel a need to count, have a census. The need dwindled. One hundred and fifty. At least. Run yearlings—smashed fence—flattened hay: greed, too far down from the rampart.

Tucker drew from their slyness and refined his own action. With one hand he opened the door soundlessly and, without collision of the stock or barrel, lifted the gun to the outside. They knew he was there and far away. Still, he bent over the hood, careful not to produce any wrinkle or scrape, and drew the hammer back. The dog immediately backed away and pleaded. Tucker studied the bulls, the cows and calves, unbelieving of their number. He set the sights directly on the lungs of the lowest cow, still beyond reach. She had stopped to browse. He turned and pushed the dog further away with the movement of his hat and open lips. Closing his mouth he returned to the cow. He pulled the trigger, knowing the unseen bullet would fall well below the flesh of the coming invasion.

A reverberating *boom*.

Tangent to the heart.

There ticked a pronounced delay before the gun's report reached all the elk. A thin amount of winter frosting pulverized and rose, as though from a muffled underground eruption. They raised their heads; many seemed to read him. The adults began high-stepping, with their noses pointed skyward. Tucker watched their silent voices, a fuming chorus of calls and mewing. They advanced on the shadows with more intensity but a certain *unfear*—aggression in withdrawal—such a mass no single one felt threatened. The bulls followed, at once cautious and arrogant, a slowness in their lope.

Tucker took his hat off and waved for the dog to go yet further away. The brim to shade his face had held the booming down around his ears. He saw the young cattle still hiding in the brush along the stream. Laying the hat beside, he bent over tires and tin, working the lever, and shot again, buckling the hood—and again—and again; empty shells bounced before him. Repeated echoing. Not once aiming his deadly force and anger to *kill*, never raising the barrel the required inches so the bullet might reach, like Ray would have chosen. For once, Tucker made certain that it could not land in anything living, in anything breathing.

For the week the weather remained cold and dry. At last the clouds released falling moisture. With a continuing undertone of dryness, it snowed just enough. It snowed just enough to stop the boy.

The Outrun

Bizarre weather, it blew dust and snow for days, baring the ridges and whipping the trees. Charcoal streaks came from the corral, mixing with and eroding the drifts; high on the lane tones of red pointed to the southeast, clean white streamers in the grass on one side and a burnt pastel on the other. In low-lying, protected places, snow lay hard and tough, deep enough to high-center a truck, in draws, deep enough to high-center a horse. Tucker had trouble finding feed ground where he and Alice could still drive and the hay would not blow away. The land was either blown-open crunchy grass, or covered with snow so impervious—when they tried to drive through—it felt like lugging slowly across a drying beach; wheels would eventually chew and bounce, then spin in futility. Tucker thought of the old time when they fed with a team and sled. As usual he filled the wagon with bales, but now hooked it to the tractor. He drove closer to the tree line and promptly came to a halt. The cows gathered and fed themselves while Alice collected the strings and he shoveled. The collie seemed to wonder over all the trouble; he ran atop the wind-packed snow, when the tractor and its burden fell through.

After three weeks the dog began to watch the eastern horizon, not just the incoming road but the barren tops of all the hills.

When the wind remitted, his nose would reach and he would sniff. Alice came into the yard carrying the ash tin from the range. She held it with tattered hot pads and sprinkled a fine gray sifting over their path: squeaky snow, as if it were made of tiny particles of Styrofoam, not water. She watched her companion watching and could feel a longing occur, a pain. She and the dog both looked, absorbing the emptiness of the exposed and weathered lane. The dog sat up. He forced a yawn—as though in an effort to keep from howling.

"Oh, Tommie—" *Yearning* upon yearning.

His crystal sadness merely added to hers. With a blank feeling to the days, now the dog spread disturbance, a sharp concern over Ray's well-being.

Winter grew worse: its immobility, its indoor boundaries, the long hours of darkness. She thought deeply; was he given food? A bike could follow the ridges.

She drove for feeding, spread straw…cooking was worse.

Tucker had more relief.

He loaded hay, grained and doctored yearlings, repaired machinery. Calving started and each evening he and Horse and Tommie would gather those which were nearing their time. She watched them sort in the snow-covered pens before the loafing shed, working around the remaining pile of sawdust, Daisy hanging her head over the fence. Often, Alice could hear him rise in the night to make certain the newborn calves had nursed and the fresh parent was firm in their claim.

Alice knew she had a cloud wrapping around her, a cloud with a current of its own—beyond her control—of loss and loneliness. When the day had expired, as if in response, the dog headed directly for her. Whenever possible he lay his chin by her feet. She stood at the counter and he camped underfoot, often too close. She rarely made him move. She rarely went upstairs to sew.

Alice felt Tucker watching, with leaner shoulders, not yet braced for the state of a setback...another siege. It had been six years since her collapse into pieces.

Sight of the wobbly new calves helped, but the dreams still came. Dreams of empty upstairs rooms: clear scenes of Ray at their table. One night she awoke with a desperation wheeling in the dark. After much tossing and turning, she thought of the mittens. If in six months he did not come back, she would get out the mittens.

And do what?

Nibble them away.

The same snow lay on and on and became dirtier and dirtier. An arid cold. The wind went into a longer remission. Tucker put the blade on the tractor and in his own fashion cleared away the tinted drifts of the yard and the few on the road. He pushed the dry snow into banks, resembling loaves of bread and broken clumps, leaving smears of rust from the previously idle plow. The rust diminished but the formed white revealed veins of dust, a temporary record of the weeks. Many days and cold nights of isolation. People could once again make their way through.

A friend...an old friend telephoned that he was coming. Alice and Tucker prepared to have coffee: clearing off the table, placing clean cups and saucers, linen napkins. From the porch, they could hear him for a long while, an approaching increasing disturbance over swept-off hills and drifts of snow. Alice watched Tommie listening with a cautious eagerness as he tipped his head at the overbearing banging and shaking. The dog clearly centered on the lane, with the noise in the distance, as though he were in wonder over such a truckload: *broken cymbals—shabby drums*.

Milo Taylor came in a pickup with a twisted front bumper, bent in the center as though from a direct hit with a light pole or corner post. Behind trailed a topless and remarkably faded stock trailer. Every little bump or slip in the remnant snow made the trailer's interior gates bang and slam. As it came down the last hill, she and Tucker could see the sheep in the back. The collie began sniffing with a vivid look of disappointment and bewilderment. The sheep were unshorn and light-faced. Though with ample room, they stood tightly bunched and swayed with the motion like dirty cotton balls glued together yet free at the feet. He drove beside the corrals and shop. Baby calves galloped on the bare slope above the barn and their mothers raised chewing heads.

Milo parked in the level of the yard to an instant tranquility. He viewed from his window with a perpetual squint. "I've brought some sheep—a surprise—"

Tucker smiled lightly with his mouth closed. A look of thoughtfulness passed over his face. Alice caught it dissolving into a stern arch of his neck.

Milo considered Alice and the squint sharpened: an expression of bottomless cheer.

"Go see," said Tucker.

The black-and-white dog bounded forward for a greeting. He carried a confused excitement and circled their company, as if trying to find more in the truck and not this oddity of goats or deer confined in a trailer. With his familiar stretching tail, Alice felt a part of herself coming to surface, a mounting interest. She began looking too, for more than a single and weathered man.

Milo then glanced toward his passenger seat. He shrugged his shoulders.

With a carefully timed—*planned*—appearance, an additional sheep dog rose and peered over the pickup box, timid and shuddering. Alice quickly turned to consider their own collie. His greeting stiffened, then shifted to a more gallant pose. These brusque changes vanished as everyone caught an overpowering odor coming from the trailer. Tommie reared. He twisted and placed his paws on the closest tire, to better see between the panels. Alice herself studied the giant maggots. They had glassy eyes. Did the dog know this smell? Had he known these creatures in another life? Did the sound of them rekindle the bleats he'd heard as a pup on Palmer Divide? In worry, the sheep jostled and rattled their rickety pen.

The young dog in the pickup ceased its shudder and came to the tailgate—as if trying to win Tommie's attention. It had a meager, incomplete collar of white, but a wide blaze over a rounded very feminine head. She clicked her feet. She anxiously lifted and relaxed her ears, then began jumping from corner to corner of the empty box, like an entrapped dolphin about to dive out.

Sheep: unblinking ancient eyes, a rabbit could have dashed under Tommie's outstretched flank with no more effect than the wind.

Alice came to the truck side and rested her hands where the new dog could touch. Immediately it licked and nuzzled her fingers, wriggling, yet conscious of the bigger dog on the ground.

Milo swung his door open to catch with his foot, rapidly rubbing his hands together as though wet with a watery soap or dribbling cream. He shook his head so quickly his cheeks gave a lagging flutter.

"Oh, Lordy—it's been dry. Even your calves on the hill were raising dust."

Tucker tapped his friend's shoulder and pursed his lips with a lingering tension. Alice could feel both men watching. She petted the dog as though weights were dangling on her wrists. Milo's appealing squint wavered; his lips parted and closed several times with the same nervousness as his dog.

"This is my *Jill.*"

"Sheep have never been on my folks' place."

"No say."

"Ever."

"Ever?"

Jill went from Alice to Tucker, then back again, as if she had never been stroked and agonized for a touch. She stood on the wheel well, then straddled the edge, her front toes in protest and slipping, about to crawl into their arms. Tucker gently pushed her away, turning to Milo—

"What do you plan on doing?"

Milo looked closely into Alice's face, then refluttered his cheeks. "They're fresh young ewes. Skittish. They know a dog. Let's see what your Tom thinks." The burst of wrinkle about his eyes could soothe—encourage. "I want to see him gather."

Alice turned away. She could hear Tucker question:

"Gather? Gather these?"

"Jill loves sheep—I say she *loves* sheep. I bet he will too."

Milo's eager female dog again took the wheel well. With a dart-like strike Jill was able to reach Alice's brow with her nose.

As though waked by this dampness, "What made her so afraid?" For a fleeting moment Alice stepped out of her silence. "She was shaking."

"She's young. My first time at pulling a trailer behind—anyone would be hiding for that. She surely, I reckon, thought it was going to run over and flatten us on the road." Milo puzzled. "She can ride up front."

"He has never seen one." Tucker spoke. "He has never seen one. No sheep have ever been here."

Alice watched their Tommie; he propped on a different trailer tire and lowly waved his tail. He then dropped to the ground and went to Milo, as if with a higher purpose, and considered the slim legs and checkered shirt. He placed two front feet carefully beside one boot. Jill followed his every move, from above, down looking.

"He looks sad."

"He is lonesome," Tucker answered.

Milo pried his eyes wide. "How so? You got new calves—a growing family."

"We had a boy coming... He must have thought...he must have thought *you* had him along."

"Boy?"

"Boy."

"On a big old bike?" Milo brightened.

"That is his horse. It cannot make this snow," said Tucker.

"They live at the sharp turn in the road?"

"His name is Ray."

Milo flicked his cap off to better reveal his untrimmed gray wings and lively gray eyes—white creases in his forehead.

"His mother does not have a husband," continued Tucker.

The squint tightened into little slits. "A young girl with her boy. Have you seen her?" Milo asked, not pausing. "Kind of a wild one. She's been around town—can't keep a job without trouble. Our Joyce sees him in school—hears the teachers talk. They think she's hard on him—they reckon she's hard on him—some black and blue—"

He stopped, as though he had gone too fast and it was now too late to slow down, turn around. Alice felt a sinking, an unreal sinking. She caught Tucker looking at her like he hadn't for a long time. If there had been no company, she thought he would have come to hold, touch her, help compose, share the need.

Milo's wrinkles stayed but lost their grinning. Alice slowly and now listlessly stroked his dog: vibrancy too close. She looked across the pickup to where there were no people or animals and her hand fell, making a weak and hollow thump on the edge of the truck box. Milo shook, as if to suggest she had better look out, see something new.

"Joyce says, she says, he's talked about you in school. Your helping him read." He folded his hat very briskly, with a clear disgust, then jerked it from back to front over his head like catching his own loose ball. The hands assailed each other, this time as if kneading some kind of volatile clay or stinging dough. "Where can I unload?"

Motion and talk far too near.

"Unload?"

She heard her husband.

"We were going to have coffee," Tucker said with a tone of wariness.

"Let's unload first."

Tucker made reference to the blown-off places in the field below the buildings, well apart from the trees.

"You better hop in."

She and Tucker shook their heads. Tommie extended his neck, lifting a single ear.

"We will just walk..." Tucker added, "wait—"

Milo smiled at the empty seat beside him and repeated a shrug of his shoulders. "Suit yourself." He abruptly started the engine and drove forward.

The truck and trailer circled, leaving them standing by themselves. Tucker pursed his lips again. Alice paused, then ran her fingers through the looseness of her hair. Both of them wanted to connect—express their worries about Ray—but weren't given the time.

As though drawn by a clamorous vacuum, Milo's shallow tracks guided them through the softening snow. Between the gaps in the rear gate Alice could see the sheep riding, as though floating on their own springs. Jill disappeared again. Tommie followed.

Milo stopped at the edge of a wind-cleared oval several acres in size. By the time the couple arrived, he stood outside the truck. Jill stretched tall on the wheel well and watched them approach, partly shielded by the man's head. The sun reflected on his clean gray and her clean white. For an instant, Alice thought of him as a lovable but inept father, squinting more happily than he had done in the yard. All his movements were very brisk, before a background of brown—patches of white…wintry stasis.

"This will be fun—this will be fun. I can't wait to see."

The light seemed to brighten over each collie's blaze. Alice watched. They considered each other: now with a mutual satisfaction.

Milo unlatched the gate but held it closed. "You hold him a minute, until they relax. They might be a little wild. I reckon they'll run a bit in a new pasture…"

Tucker stepped forward. "I'm not too sure—"

Alice blinked and everyone diverted their eyes to the loud clanging of the gate.

With nervous feet the sheep spun about on the inside, excited by the same sound. The whole truck and trailer jiggled.

Alice noticed a drop in her husband's shoulders like she had never seen, as though he mistrusted this newness—and felt awkward. Man and dog backed away, as if to catch an unleashing. She backed away also, spreading and making the furthest wing, almost in the snow. She felt like a mole in too strong of sun.

The dog lay down without a word.

Milo swung the gate open with a face about to weep for his excitement.

Six sheep bounced and darted as though ejected. They swerved in fright. They passed Milo and Jill and galloped for the far end of the open ground. Fearful eyes, they shot right, then left in swift angles, leaning into each other as if afraid of their own shadow, partly blinded by their own wool yet certain of a pursuer. Thin strands of dust rose behind them.

Had Tommie been standing he wouldn't have been able to follow. To Alice, he looked rooted to the earth; between tires of the truck he stared in rigidity. When a tire intruded, he lay flat and stretched, under crankcase and axle an unbroken connection.

The sheep never slowed and met the toughness of old snow. The action of their hooves threw corn-size grains into the air. At last its deepening pulled and they curved to hear, discover the absence of any threat. They trotted back, hopping free of this granular ice, as if onto an island of greater safety.

She watched Milo's mouth open. His lips revealed his teeth and she could see a sigh.

"I thought I might lose them—a moment—they looked they were going to the next township." He spoke loudly for their separation, so many creases in his face they began to muddle. *"I hope he doesn't eat them."*

"What?" Tucker shouted.

The displaced flock stood with poor sight, ears twitching for the babble of far-off voices.

"He might think they are rabbits."

"No!"

"Their bones—he might splinter a leg."

"Now you tell me." Tucker took his hat off and headed for Milo. "We should have introduced in a corral."

"Naw." With an odd stiffness the elder man held both hands up. "Stay!" he shouted.

Jill's tail gave a flurry.

Tucker looked down the brown-and-white plain, to the knot of wool pillows.

"No guts. No glory," said Milo.

Tucker resumed his walking, returning to the truck, distinctly swinging his hat at his side.

"Just kidding—got to have fun. I trust him—*I mean, I trust him.*"

Alice could hear but began drifting away, not catching meanings, a different kind of listening, staring out at the sheep. One hand shaded her eyes.

Tucker and their collie assembled like a team. They moved well clear of the truck and trailer. Jill jumped from the pickup box to the roof of the cab. Milo beamed, a shining and higher level of glee. Tucker and the steadfast dog stood side by side. Tommie's shoulders protruded with his legs in a crouch. Tucker slowly put his hat on. As if in response to this hat coming up, like a signal of grave intent—the sheep bunched even more tightly.

"Sssuht."

Tommie sprang, cut slightly to the side, still heading for the snug gray package. He seemed to soar...like a gathering for flight. Alice could detect the forming radius: the dog looking ahead, then off his shoulder. He began to veer further away as they helplessly watched. Something about the style—shape of his run—drugged and dumbfounded their will. He curved out into the snow, drawing the perfect side to an upside-down pear, his arc so wide he hit softness and broke through in places like a skip in stroke but the line unflawed. Opposite Tucker he resisted and stopped. He burrowed down the blossom end and the small band bristled. They exploded directly for the tall figure standing perfectly alone.

Tommie mimicked their speed but kept his distance.

They ran even faster and whipped wildly.

He abandoned the fetch and circled, letting them run into the shadow thrown by the mountain. Allowing a great deal of space, he circled them again.

Tucker cocked his head and cupped his hands in preparation for a call.

The truck top dented and popped.

Milo stood with his fingers laced together and drew them in and out rapidly.

Tommie circled them four times and they began to slow, panting over more than their heavy coats. They were learning—he wasn't driven to hurt. The sheep ran again. At length they wearied and stood. He allowed them rest. They heaved and puffed, appearing to study this mystery. He resumed his fetch to Tucker and they mildly trotted in a straightening line, as if driven by a master with a cape.

Everyone smiled.

Even Alice.

Jill fidgeted on the edge of her perch to the screech and tapping of claws.

Thirty yards from his man, the collie made an unexpected and refined turn. Passing by Tucker, he guided them in a carefully chosen path to Alice's feet. All stopped as if bowing in submission. Audience to an anointing. Panting vessels of compassion.

She blinked at the strange sheep so close and unpenned.

Milo came to her side breathing heavily.

"Your gift. I have never seen the like."

She tipped a little. Silent.

Tucker walked over, a quick glimpse at her face.

Milo took his cap off and rubbed through the thinning gray as though to disperse heat. "How did you *teach* such an outrun? Did I really see that?"

"No." Tucker looked to the ground and shook his head.

"You need to breed him."

The sheep stood huffing and their master lay down.

"He's a *clean* dog—you need to breed him—he likes things kept together. You need to breed him."

Jill gave more applause from the cab top.

"He is connected to *both* of you like an arm to a shoulder—I've never seen the like."

"He's a definite dog that gathers," Tucker said lowly. "And he gathers more than sheep." He nodded to Alice, then lightly glanced over the rolling hills and eastward.

Alice's eyes began to water.

Milo twisted his head but his cheeks did not flutter. He turned up to the cloudless sky. He began reshaping the bill to his hat, then replaced it with a jerk: "At least it quit blowing."

"That is nice."

"I hear there is a plan to make more road."

Tucker regarded the mountains and made an unusual face. "Even cows have a better sense of direction than some..."

"Prancing monkeys," said Milo.

"A new kind of people." The broad hat tipped down but the words carried. "They are hard to understand."

Still without voice—Alice rearranged the pointing of her feet. The sheep stirred in response.

"I reckon they're going to get from Stewart if they can't come through here. I don't know if they'll pay him money or if he wants to sell timber. He always would sell."

The woolly heat stood as though listening.

"They've got to enlarge their sand box. Power rules." Milo could not stop watching Tommie: holding his suddenly tame sheep quite close to Alice, as if they were an offering. "Make-believe power," he said.

No sound or motion came from the top of the cab.

"If not some check—dollars they can get or logs to haul—nobody'd give a hoot about climbing the rampart." A wink and nod, then, "I reckon I'd use different words if a lady weren't present…

"To hell with us at the bottom—there's talk about closing the creamery. Glen and *your* dad aren't old enough to retire."

She could feel him searching, for a sign.

"Someday—*they*'ll not have enough to fill up their groceries. We will all become lawyers like brother George. And go before the bench of justice to squabble for our daily meal."

Tommie glanced up for the spew of words. The sheep had lost interest. They began to pick at the stubble with hurried lips—raising their heads only to breathe.

Alice continued to shade her face and her mouth sounded dry; she felt out of practice for words. "You think he should have puppies?"

"No doubt—too much talent in one place…sort of a prophet of what things will do. What if—what if something should happen to him?"

She shook her head very slowly. Her arm was getting tired. She needed to turn: look in a different direction.

This being the subject in Milo's target, he spoke with straight, thin lips and starbursts by his eyes. "My Jill is a natural wide runner. Her balance is perfect and quick. She is too nervous and fearful. I reckon if I could get a piece of your Tom, I might have myself a trial dog." He waited for Tucker's reaction. "You'd get the pick of the litter."

"You can keep your litter. If there is one. We only need one dog."

Alice gave a very different expression.

Milo took his cap off for the last time and pointed up to Jill, now still and quiet, curled up on her platform. "She already adores him. Would you consider having him be the sire?"

From her height, the belle with the wide blaze passed an obvious smile over her back and down across the way to the other, the other black-and-white.

There was a small wait, a communicative look, then all the people—even Tucker—nodded as one.

Complication

...does not have a husband
...a young girl with her boy
...a wild one

Lying in the darkness, their sides touching, trying to give comfort beyond the thought of a borrowed child, Alice and Tucker both contemplated in their own style. They must face the situation. Keep trying, all through the long winter. *Think of us.*

Alice sat up in bed, clutching the covers, looking straight ahead. It was difficult to see the opposite wall. "Why does everything have to be so—complicated? You heard what he said—he said Joyce said...I can't help it, but Ray is dragging a gloom—that girl...the girl—" Her husband turned toward her, remaining on his side, but silent. "What can we do?" she asked.

Tucker returned to his back and spoke to the ceiling. "We are still close to too much loss. It is hard to say, say out loud: *we have lost children.* You have lost children...I mean...they were growing inside, inside of you. I can't know what that is. I'm sorry."

Even in the darkness, Alice felt the cloud descend—self-blame, the burden of her failure, the inevitable loneliness. It was *her* body that could not carry...

"Space is good...we need more space," Tucker continued. "The boy, he *does*...bring sunshine."

She thought of Ray, the bruises Milo spoke of, the boy's need—greater than hers. "He needs more sun on himself."

"I shouldn't say—but what I want, what I *know* I want—he should keep coming when the road dries out, come all summer. I look forward very much to summer."

Alice sighed and released her grip on the covers, smoothing the edging. "What if—if the boy were in some kind of foster care—less to worry me."

"Nothing is simple. There is much we still don't know."

Her chin rose. "I feel it. I feel it—I think I know enough. Milo said black and blue. Don't you remember? *Black and blue.*" She finally turned her gaze from the dim wall toward Tucker. He blamed himself too, felt the loneliness just as keenly. "But where are we going to?"

"We need to move slow, go slow and watch how we make our decisions. That girl is very alive, very confusing...not some parent without a face, or lungs and heart."

"It's me—and you—and the sun on Ray. I've never seen her. Some people are very selfish." She faced the wall again. "I can't wait till I see him. Will I see him?"

"He will be back. It's a conflict of what is best..."

"Maybe—just maybe—good things come to those who can wait." Alice lay down, a lingering tension. "We have to move slowly. Oh, I hope, I hope we will be able to sleep, we need to still, sleep."

"Yes." Tucker shifted, their sides touching again, his hand resting on her thigh.

Yet Alice's mind kept stirring. For the rest of the winter, many nights she did not sleep. Too many trailing ends.

Blond Grain/Dead Wood

Blowing again, a portion of the drifts refilled. At the very beginning of the lane, a shiny pickup had almost stuck itself and struggled to back out. In backing it missed its own tracks and now roared, shifting with a clank and viciously spinning, mincing the broken snow until at last it found dirt and sped in reverse, to higher ground. With a great zoom it made a fresh attack on the packed white, bouncing and weaving for the squiggle of ruts. Two men sat inside, jolted and rocking like stuffed dolls. The next drift they rammed with an even greater momentum—revving and cutting through in one drub pass. The third trial was a prolonged battle. By the time they reached the tops of the hills where the going was much smoother, droplets of candy-colored red fluid were following them down the windswept surface of the road.

Tucker stooped, filling the buckets for tomorrow's feed, and heard the distant roaring. He parked the dogs on the clean brown grass by the granary door. Such a quiet morning, he could hear the tires on the dry sand as it came without force down the last hill. He thought it might be a different truck but easily recognized Martin Daniels, well before it entered the yard. He looked to the house, contrary to how he had felt before, with a clear preference that Alice remain unaware. She didn't need to deal with this kind of intrusion—her worries over Ray grown too strong. The air waited, dead still. By the dimness of the grain bins, he shook his head in privacy.

They drove up so closely they could see into the building. Soon they stood on each side of their cooling vehicle, faces an insistent smug and eagerness, identical caps with emblems set at slightly different angles and heights. They wore casual denim pants but still of matching color.

Members of a visiting team in intermission clothes.

With the shrinking sounds of the engine, Tucker felt—imagined—a waltzing voice: whispers from trim, out-of-town players critical of the competition and its lesser community.

"Fine-looking dogs." The stranger spoke clearly.

Tucker had the buckets all in a row, filled and ready. He looked only at Martin.

"You should have phoned."

"We were going by and I wanted to show Duane your place."

Untruth, an addictive habit, it leads to overcorrection. *Alistair: painfully crossing the yard and stopping to lean on the corral fence, Tucker could hear his lungs rasping: what you do is the measure.*

He stepped out of the granary with his mouth tight, as though clenching a thumbtack before his tongue. Seeing Duane's slotted observance of the dogs changed his conviction.

"You must be on recess."

"*Oh no*. We have come here on business. But this is something to see." Duane spoke without looking, then turned toward Tucker and thrust his hand before him, with a much greater seniority than Martin. Proud of his hand, he paused, an occasion for delay.

Tucker slowly laid his gloves across the blond grain in the closest container. He raised his fingers and the man stepped forward and jabbed with his own.

"Duane Parker."

"Tucker Black."

"Your ranch—surely could have been a robber's roost—who would have thought to come way back here? A good place to hide out, scenic or not."

Their truck continued to click and sizzle. Duane and Martin stood like veiled dominoes separated by the glistening hood. Duane had the most dots, an elevated socializer, an empty success *your mark, your word…not how you look.* Martin appeared taller in his cap. The same Martin, the same waver.

Tucker: in the comfort of his work clothes…

"This road idea—it's nothing—just a connection to the county network—a system of roads," the new man added, without coherence.

An inexhaustible hive.

Tucker understood why they had started with Daniels. They bent, each with one foot forward, as if balancing guns on their hips. It became more and more difficult to hold back, keep his manners. Nervous Jill rose and wagged her worried tail while Tommie appeared indifferent.

"You stay down."

She buckled without a turn and twittered the tip to her white.

"Have your maps shown you it is too steep?"

"We have chosen a route and the engineers are ready to stake."

"You move fast."

"The money has been set aside for this spring."

Tucker pulled a fencing nail from his coat pocket and knelt in the foot-worn dirt before the door. Other nails and staples jingled. Both men stepped forward as if to watch him tie a lace-less boot. At last his dog stood, with no motion in his tail. Tucker made long, shallow scratches with the point of steel.

"Rim rock all along here, one saddle, if wet or in winter, it is impassable."

He felt the two men exchanging glances over the faded back and shoulders of his coat. Perhaps there were smug smiles.

Tucker regained his height and brushed the powder from his fingers. Martin's face lost a portion of its color.

"There will be blasting," said Duane. "We have come from the back side and the center line has been flagged."

Martin spoke up. "You should see the elk. Hunters will love the new road."

He looked between and beyond the men. They were now in front and each placed a foot on the dripping bumper.

"It will be very costly and only usable in certain seasons—"

"That doesn't matter, the road is needed. People need easier access. The expense will be amortized over many years. To those who use it, it will seem cheap."

Tucker said nothing.

"Access through here would cut costs and be more direct. The road this far would be all-weather, raised, with shoulders and ditches—culverts."

He could not help but consider them as rectangles, leaning against each other. He turned to again see the buckets of oats: "A permanent toll, all this play leaves weeds and litter."

"We would pay for an easement." Duane's fluency rolled on. "We can go around. We'll have to build a bridge and it will be more expensive, but we can go around. The payment would be substantial. Martin says you would like a better road. There would be crushed rock all the way to your house—even in this yard." With a stale scrubbing to his face, Duane extended his hands like offering a platter.

You overcorrect without knowing and do not realize you have missed a turn.

Purveyor of disrespect, magician of consequence, enabler... "*Whose* money?" Tucker regarded the dogs. His own still stood as though something might escape, something without body he could no longer herd or surround. Tucker closed the granary and latched it. He had been moved: not by automatic transmissions or trails of crushed granite. He considered Martin, who brought his foot down and looked suddenly white. Alice had not appeared.

"My children are not for sale," Tucker answered unclearly.

Duane threw his hands in the air; the awards of his training and dress lost grip. Coolness in the morning yet beads of moisture gathered.

"Have you been listening?"

A flush of malice.

He could see his father's face, extremely pale, growling words: those who scramble, scramble in the low places...politicians of some kind of—other wealth...

Tucker stood aloof.

The sudden action and tone made by Duane brought the dog nearer. His lip quivered and rose, showing the length of his teeth.

"You watch your dog."

"I am." Tucker snugged his hat.

The two men moved closer to their doors.

"My recess is over. You can go around."

Tommie took two more steps and both dogs stood, no space for atonement.

Duane *stabbed* at the handle of the truck like he had *stabbed* at Tucker's hand. Martin reflected all his moves with a less descript style.

He could see the two men turn, speaking to each other as they drove from the yard.

Now void of human company, *the damn map had folded wrong and the lines were crossing,* Tucker reversed his closing of the building, wanting to be soothed by the smell and the full row of grain. Both dogs rubbed and wormed against his legs in false victory, misplacing their reward. He imagined kicking at the tidy line of containers. A skip in his creed. Only one would knock down and its seed would spill, falling through the rounded cracks of the well-seasoned floor.

* * *

High swarming and reedy honking, in fluctuating formation thousands of geese were flying north, swirling in vague confusion, moving on, but the men did not notice.

"He's crazy, crazy as hell," said Duane.

Martin's cheeks flickered, then began to relax. "He doesn't know what he's got—"

"Hell of a fool, an absolute…the old boy is sitting on a gold mine."

"Old?"

"I mean out of date."

With a rounded shoulder Martin turned to the side and caught the chance at seeing something *very* new, the same morning through the small framed image of a mirror, as if confined within the fragment of a broken windowpane: the clarity and clean of groomed, eager dogs around the legs of a tall man. A flash of perspective was stamped in reverse—a fresh approach that bounced and quickly swung from his view as the truck proceeded—realms escaping, groomed and eager around tall legs. "Those dogs," he whispered under a breath, then repeated with diminishing force. "The man doesn't know what he's got."

Duane drove over the hills consuming tread and raising more debris than necessary. In the padded truck, he spoke again. "If no one sees it, the old boy has nothing." He blinked at the modest road. "There'll be no *success* coming to him."

At the junction, though Duane was clearly the driver, he seemed strangely driven to assert his leadership, as if spitting out his presence. "Aw hell... Let's go to town and get something to eat."

* * *

That afternoon Tucker took Jill and Tommie to cut a load of dead wood, along the edges of the hay. He chose where the snow was not deep and looked particularly for bark-less trunks of aspen and cottonwood. Subdued, the dogs rattled in the brittle bushes until he ran the saw, then backed away and watched with their ears pulled down. The pile of wood grew. Moving to new locations they had to balance on the jumble of blocks he had thrown into the truck bed. He saw them through the back window: one on one side and one on the other, fresh young faces always pressing forward. He needed but a small amount to make a complete and rounded load. Tucker parked and stepped out to walk a north-sloping bank, without releasing the dogs. Among faint and feathery drifts of snow, he searched the dark stand for smaller, leaning aspen.

Noises came from where the truck and passengers waited. He heard a skitter, then a rustle on the road ahead. Moving for the trees to align, he saw the black-and-whites, down from their ride.

Prancing around one another, a bristling and vivid waving of fans, they pawed the ground, marking territory, then crouched with thin rumps in the air, trying to initiate play, a chase. Daring, dodging. Mane and tails in full bloom, skirts fluffed out. One would break and spin, clipping before the other. They took turns, then Jill became the more bold, in her element. Everywhere at home. A beautiful-perfect time. She made bigger and bigger loops and pigtails, trailing S's; trees, logs, nothing made a stumble. Tommie became the follower.

Tucker cut no more wood. He returned to the truck and the whirling continued.

His dog yelped for her smallness, her quickness.

Tucker did not try to load them, but drove alongside and let them run the north timbered slope high above the road.

The two raced, airborne, waiting for one another, then surging again. Reaching: heads rocking, shoulders pumping, flowing spines and tails. They stopped anew with thin arse in the air and made flashing charges. She broke free and loped out, dashing through the shadows lighter and faster. Both weightless, more speed and grace than a mare and stallion. Running through the sunlight and dark, leaping over deadfall and rocks, ducking limbs, swerving—faster than the wind—faster than the race of time and season.

Part Two

Early Thaw

In spite of herself—during the boy's prolonged absence, Alice's life with Tucker grew fluctuant, moody, again marred by grief and anxiety, overwhelmed by a frightful interior chemistry. She cried easily and her hands trembled.

Though imprisoned by the cold and the waiting, her connection to her home, all its life, remained a constant. Especially Tommie. She allowed herself his comfort: a profuse place to warm her hands and press her hollow cheek. She had not allowed herself an attachment to the female.

"Milo says—that Milo—he says the lane was much improved... Time for wet snow...or rain." Tucker brushed his boots and hung his coat and hat. "I will miss her."

Alice folded the blanket that had been Jill's bed. "She had made this her nest. Will she *miss us*?"

"She cared for our—"

Tommie heard what they could not, clamoring on the floor to reach the door. They turned their heads to hear the outside. It sounded again: the clash of tin, the clang of a chain.

Much ado came with the boy's return. Tommie forced himself into the doorway, nearly tripping Tucker. Alice drew two fingers through her sweeping hair and studied her hands, hurriedly clearing papers from the table to place at the desk. Her arm bumped a row of books that suddenly collapsed. Some folded open and splashed on the floor, just below the switch for the light. She glanced down but kept walking, drawn forward by a tremendous urge to go see.

After twelve weeks of winter, Ray looked older, leaner, almost a teenager. He dropped his bike and sat in the middle of the path and the collie quickly bowled him over. Together, Alice and Tucker viewed from the porch. Alice took a small step forward and lightly raised her hand, as though not wanting to interrupt. Tucker also raised his hand, then gave a soft touch to her elbow as she settled in her place. Suddenly the dog released the boy, standing back as if to assimilate reality. A welcome push and Ray went down again, clinging to the fur, seeming afraid to smile. The collie stopped kissing, then turned, squirming and rolling his back and shoulder against the young torso, a serious effort to absorb the boy's scent. Quench *everyone's* need: thought Alice.

Ray smiled, but with a shyness, as though shameful things had happened during their separation. She felt awkward—sensing the presence of something uncommon wedged between them. Quiet moments came, then eased away.

"We have been wondering over you," said Tucker.

"You—you still wants me in the spring. Like—like you said?"

"That is the plan."

"Yes," she added.

"If it snows I will meet you at the county road."

"And on the weekends if you can make it." She tried to think of reasons and had difficulty getting past the food and the reading. His hair was long again. All the skin exposed, unhurt, had lost its tan. His eyes, a blue pool— "Tucker will have wood to split."

"You need a phone," her husband said.

"My mom— We ain'ta gonna get one."

* * *

The days grew lighter and milder. Numerous clouds passed over. On the in-between days, which were many—for the school *had* Ray—if the air was gentle, Alice saddled Daisy and they went for long rides. The horse was in heaven: save the dog. The mare scowled, as if Tommie were too near, then threatened him with quick side steps and a whipping tail.

"You be nice."

The collie ignored the horse except for the hidden effort to keep Daisy in a straight line. There was no doubt that his mind was with Alice, his charge on board.

Alice untangled the horse's mane and stroked the fuzzy sides to her neck, but felt more keenly the dog's tangible but untouchable discipline. She felt his upward regard of boundless affection, and concern. She could never again reject him but welcomed this involvement, as she would be involved—and ignore her fear of losing another child.

Ray is back.

Some days she and the collie would walk without Daisy. They walked the lane. Returning home with a special slowness, she recalled her first entrance and her hopeful spirit...fifteen years of expectation.

"I was just a girl."

On a sunny day in the next week, Alice and the dog climbed the hill to depart with the same directionless pace. She imagined having to leave for the last time, riding in a carriage, then getting down to walk—her own small feet in the dirt—the finality of never coming back, and felt a constriction in her heart. She some-

how sensed that her husband was destined to leave first. He would go first. She turned to inhale the homestead, the blue-green mountain behind, the resting trees and brown grass, the thirsty hills. What would be left? What would happen to her home, the rolling land and life-giving stream?

She knew each of them thought of the coming spring, and then summer: strings of days all together one after the other. Empty nights.

The cows and calves were all turned out. They would soon be leaving for their summer graze on the mountain. One cow remained. She grazed alone, in a small pasture still touching a corner of the corral. On Saturdays and Sunday afternoons, Ray helped Tucker clean the stalls and bays. Often Alice would be near enough to hear them talking:

"Why the sad cow?" the boy faintly asked. "Nobody with it. She don't *look* different." They were hidden in the darkness of the loafing shed, working.

"Sad? You get to know them and they all look different. She is our pet, so mild and relaxed with us. Her name is Bunny." They each held a fork and took turns scooping wet chunks of straw and sawdust into a rusty wagon.

Alice stood around the corner from the open face of the building. She could hear a strain in Ray's breath each time he made a throw.

"She is giant... Why her name—*Bunny?*"

"When she was first born her ears were pressed back like a rabbit's, or so I thought."

Alice felt her lips part. When it became Tucker's turn she heard no sound, only the repeated thumps landing in a growing mound.

"They are all black, but study her face and you will see traits special to her—and like I said, she is gentle as a sweet pea. An old friend."

Alice stepped to see a little further around the corner and nothing was falling in the wagon.

"Several of her daughters are in the herd. None are like her."

"Why is she still—still here?" A growing interest rose in his words.

"Bunny is late to calve and she doesn't mind being alone. You watch, see her manner; she still returns to the corral for her water. Her daughters are very different. One will be a yearling—sassy, wild—like a teenager. Mostly in trouble..."

Different. Wild. April—too young a mother...

They spread the fertilizer in the fields. The garden soil still cool, they waited to spade and turn it. Ray helped Alice fix the woven wire fence and lift and reattach the sagging gate. He carried water to the special trees and bushes for the continuing dry.

She knew well it was pretend, and pretend she did, renewing her yearning for Tucker's stability and competence, his tedious commitment, his tall and quiet masculinity she had known as a bride. And she felt torn, with a vague straddling of an imminent change…in herself.

She said to the dog, "This time I will not leave you or anyone else. Like when the second little girl died. I will not forget what I have, or where I belong. I will do the best that I can.

"Ray is not forever."

Sometimes she could and sometimes she couldn't.

One night Alice had two short, indelible dreams.

The first: a vision of Tucker leaving the valley in a coffin carried by a horse-drawn wagon, a faceless driver, no mourners save a faint rise and linger of sparkling…*silt.*

The second, even more haunting: an unmanned crane parked too close to the homestead house, broken tree limbs and shredded bushes—groaning machinery—a boom and claw reaching up and out, tearing off pieces of roof and wall, exposing bedrooms where husband and wife had slept and made love, the structure of floors where the children of others had played and learned to dream. Whirring and crunching as if a mutant insect munching off the dormers, the covers of her soul.

Alice rode. She rode all along the ridge and down across the farmland, then up the other side to the high table where Tucker and his ancestors rotated oats and barley and hay. She wove between the Sisters and into the timber with the other hidden boulders, climbing, climbing. The dog led. She and the horse were careful of the degenerate snow and slippery steep. The day just cool and airy enough she wished to be in the sun rather than the shadow of the forest. Once over the top they found disappearing springs and isolated beaver dams, sacred pools, open and mirroring the sky and trees along their edges, still-floating wafers of ice over their depths. The dog and the horse drank.

Alice sunned herself and listened to the trickle of the overflow, then turned for home.

At the brink of the rampart she paused the horse, at the very beginning of the traverse to descend. Rock along the edge resisted the growth of trees and brush. She dismounted and stood in the shade while the land below her warmed in unbroken sun. Small cracks at her feet allowed unknown plants to root and spread, the adjacent moss a fluorescent green, plants without flower yet beautiful glassy leaves which grew nowhere else, fresh and sturdy, as though unaffected by winter and the deepening dry.

Through the opaque wet of her eyes, she blinked at the far-off cluster of buildings: the house, the hearth—dead babies. The body of the earth took her strong and clear and swept her down the valley like a vortex clenched. A halted rush. A tender release. As never before she felt an imprint in time—deltas from the canyons, buttes in the east—all the landscape and its flow detailing a force and erosion beginning long before woman or man.

Alice zipped her coat, then spoke out loud: "I belong. I will strive, give, possibly lose—but always belong…"

North, in the neighbor's pasture, rose a streamer of dust. Had she watched the collie's attention, she would have looked sooner. It led to a row of machines parked well beyond their fence line. Distance, and her mood, made the equipment appear like a proud lineup of toys drawn from a little boy's box, uniform themes to their style and color. They had already made a provisional cut across Malcolm Stewart's receding hills. She watched the dog. His eyes a reflection of the windrowed sod: winding like a snake all the way out to the county road. The distant artery, small, becoming no more than a white scratch on the leveling plain.

Alice withdrew from her outstretched conversation, the caressing of her home, her *loving* root and guide. She felt a stiffening of her shoulders. The noise, the severing, the building of undeserved access was about to begin.

* * *

Alone, Ray in school, Tucker held a flat piece of steel as a giant chisel; one end mushroomed from many impacts of a hammer, and hammered now. Back bowed over and moisture at his temples, he stooped above the unruly rear tire to a tractor, which lay flat on the ground. With fierce blows he wedged and drove the piece of steel between galvanized wheel and the rusted rubber bead. The three-legged tractor waited nearby, a bridging of rough-sawn blocks under the corner with the missing wheel. He worked in a circle, then back. His boots left a pattern in the well-tracked dirt. Finally the stubborn bead dropped down from the rim, and with strong hands and bars, he pried it free so he could reach inside. He took his gloves off for better grip and worked to pull out a heavy rubber tube. He laid it on top of the worn and sun-checked tire and aligned the valve stem with the hole in the rim. His fingers traced a white chalk mark on one lug and below it a distinct X.

A lime-green car came quietly down the hill.

Tucker looked toward the empty house, then stood and rested. He took a rag from the tractor tool box and wiped his hands. With his shirtsleeves he pressed his brow and the sides to his head: a new season, an abrupt change coming to the weather.

It was a different, younger model car and the boy's mother drove in softly. She sat for a moment looking first to the porch, then to him.

Their acquaintance brief, in an action to welcome her, Tucker tipped his hat back, then laid it on the tire and walked forward. April opened her low door but did not get out.

"You have a new car. How are you doing?"

"New!" She laughed. "Another piece—*your road*—I *hate* to drive it back in here." She sat with one foot on the ground, then reached to push the ashtray in. Her foot lifted. Her blouse lifted.

Tucker stepped to the side and rescrubbed his hands in the rag. He could smell smoke blended with the crass sweetness of a car deodorizer. "New paint," he said. He mopped a stripe of dust from the near fender.

Her feet came out but she did not stand, short pants and tennis shoes without any socks, a spring chill in the air. She stroked the dash with a hint of pleasure. "They try to dress 'em up and polish all the chromed-up knobs—ain't some working. I hope it gets me longer than the other."

Tucker felt speckles of roughness in the bright green; they had not left enough spray or used enough thinner. It did not flow. "What happened to the Buick?"

"Some trouble with the air cleaner being off and the engine wore out. I kept oil in it." She petted the dash and clicked the radio on and off. Bleeps into another world.

Tucker stood back and tried his best to look approving. "If you have trouble with this, any trouble, let me know."

"What?"

"If you need work on it, let me know."

"What?"

She laughed again and saw the tractor up on blocks.

"I got me a mechanic." April sneered. "And a *good one* too. And he's in town. Anyways, why the hell would I come way out here?" She wiped the dust from her speedometer.

Tucker said nothing and tucked the rag in his pocket.

She grimaced as if with pain to get up and stand, then abruptly sat back. A darkness came into her deep brown eyes.

"Oh...I might come out."

She lifted one hand requesting help but Tucker didn't move. With a jingle she pulled her keys and twirled them on a finger. "Anyways, what's your trouble?" She sat straight, to point over the hinge of the door, referring to the proneness of the rim and tire.

"There is a hole in the tube."

"Run over a nail?"

"Possible."

"How's Ray doing here?"

"Good."

"Anyways, school will be out soon. He turns twelve the end of this month."

"You said he was going to be thirteen."

"I messed up."

"He is learning a lot."

"In this good weather he oughta get something for his chores. I won't get no help from him."

Tucker nodded slowly. "What do you think?"

"Ten dollars a day."

He turned his head and closed his mouth, then came back to her, trying to find something she had passed on, trying to find a reason for their disconnection: the gap, the void of caring. He stepped away further. He shifted in the direction of his work.

"I guess he's just a kid—" Her volume went up. She took her fingers and strung her hair out and laughed an octave higher. The keys tangled in its thickness "—Five dollars."

She must have loved, hated the father.

He stopped and re-approached, careful not to bump the open door. He pulled out his wallet. Lingering bits of sawdust were stuck in the folds.

"You *do* feed him. And he ain't such a pain..." Her hand extended.

Without a fence to lean on or guide, an open and fruitless path—without instinct, he thought.

Calf abandoned.

He laid a twenty and a five on her palm without touching the skin, and another twenty and a five. "That's good for ten days. He chooses when."

She returned the keys to the ignition and struggled to get the wadded bills in her pants. She began rocking the steering wheel. "You got all this—" She gestured toward the valley. "Why don't you take that old tire to town and have some *flunky* fix it?"

"I guess I could."

"I wouldn't grunt over no tire." Her dark eyes glazed thinly over the yard, then stopped at the house. "Anybody home?"

"No."

The wheel rocked more lazily. *Blank places in the tattered map.* It made a sound like loose cartilage in a human joint. He sensed a meshing of April's gears.

"Nobody home. Chummy-lookin' little farmhouse. I'd like to see inside."

He straightened the worn creases and the lines connected. "Come back with Ray and Alice will have you in."

Jealousy stung the girl's face and she blinked with a shadow of being hurt...found out. The darkness flickered, a deepening coil. "I think I've heard enough about *that* one." In hesitation she let go her toy and twisted her pelvis, but her jeans were attaching to the seat. She spread her knees and placed one foot on the accelerator, her central remaining force. "You sure you won't let me in? You sure know how to shut down a friendly—invitation—" The key clicked and in one turn the forlorn exhaust pipe blew out black droplets and a light puff of blue-gray smoke, well-tuned but tired. She sat with one leg out the door and made the engine speed, then slow. The bright car body tipped slightly in varying opposition.

He looked over his shoulder to the still empty porch, grateful for Alice and the dog on a ride, the boy in school. As though hearing another click, like a sudden shift in his weight: he felt a returning pull to his proper course. His refusal was complete.

"You keep Ray," she said. "I'll stay clear...for a while."

April drew her foot in and closed her door. She put the lever in drive and quietly left his side.

There would be two payments: one to April, one to Ray. It would cost him twice, but that was not an issue. He thought of what he would unbelievably say—

Don't tell your mother.

The boy's eyes and motive from some other source—

Put it aside. Your gloves will wear out, and your tires.

Rolling and Vibrant World

In the span of two days, the high valley received an even inch and a half of spring rain. Everyone and everything felt marvelously refreshed yet hungered for more. The grasses immediately sent hopeful shoots, and the entire land changed its tint.

School was out.

Early the next morning Ray arrived to the glee of a tiny *red* calf alongside Bunny's huge shiny body, already nursing and twittering its miniature tail. Beyond his delight...he became worried over the calf's odd color in the bright new green.

"What's wrong, why—why—it's red?" he sputtered.

"It is in the breed. There are red ones too. Once in a great while the red just happens." With a soft touch, the man adjusted his hat: "Even if the family has been black for years. It is an ancient trait."

"Everything. Everything is black. The baby so little, so different—like adopted. It's my favorite. It...it *will* be my favorite"

Tucker tapped Ray's shoulder. "That is good."

On the windblown ridges Tucker dug postholes, not very deep; the ground, still packed and powdery, would not lift with the auger. In the truck they carried ten-gallon milk cans filled with water to dip from and sprinkle with the dirt so it would rise and later tamp. Ray watched Tucker pinch and scour his brow at the underneath talcum. All three people with Tommie's company built wooden corners and set wooden posts for the stretching of new wire. Ray carried the tools, and tins of staples and nails. He helped measure the braces and hold them for the saw. He and Alice had newer, matching canvas-backed gloves. Tucker's were old.

Ray delighted in the hills, their rolling temper, the job and its steady progression. The view from each hilltop had a fresh perspective. He savored the green at his feet and the endless unworldly air.

After very few days Ray was told to fold the gates back. "Allow Bunny and her calf to roam free," Tucker explained. The others had already been gathered for their passage up the Voss canyon and over the mountain bluff.

Now, Ray thought, was a good time to make friends. He stood in the gateway as Bunny passed. She stopped and he stooped to try to touch the brand-new calf. The cow just stood and looked down at him with big staring eyes. With wet, shiny nose and bright, curious face, the little red body skittered through and he missed entirely with his grappling hands. Cow and calf headed down the valley undisturbed. Ray shrugged, happy to watch them wander freely in such a big clean place.

Moments later, he told Tucker, "He is—it's...*beautiful*...so clean and fresh."

"She is a girl. That cow has thrown only girls. And they have been keepers—all girls and still here."

Ray lightly frowned for his mistake, then quickly grinned. "This one will be a keeper—it will be a keeper—I know it!"

On the level of the hay, still but a stubble, he learned to drive a tractor: how to start, the clutch, brake, throttle. He learned to decipher the raised cast numbers between his legs and find each gear of a different speed. He practiced with the feel and control of the steering. He was quick and made few mistakes, but the newness and worry wore on him faster than any physical labor.

As Bunny progressed to find the others, Ray was given the duty to open and close the gates. When she stalled because of a fence, he would ride down the hay field road to open the wires and let her and her baby through. Once, the calf became confused. *It can't see the opening to follow its mother.* Ray dropped his bike, Tommie standing at attention. "Bump her with your nose," he instructed the dog. The calf only turned to sniff its guardian: nose to nose. With his bare hands, Ray held the girl calf by her sides and gently forced her through the opening.

Six days later, above the Voss house, was the last gate. Ray watched them weave up the canyon trail—wondering when he would see them again.

Where the earth sloped more tamely, Ray was asked to bring the tractor with the swaying auger, and Alice or Tucker brought the pickup. When the grades were too rugged, he felt the rise of concern, like an infection—spreading to him. Alice then drove the truck and Tucker the tractor.

Ray had spaded the garden and the time had come. "The soil is warm now," Alice said. For several days, she stayed back to plant seeds and to water. Some mornings, Tucker loaded posts and wire while Ray hauled buckets of compost to help mix, stirring with an already rich dirt, for the future rows of vegetables and widely spaced hills of squash. With no apparent conflict, the dog spent the mornings with Alice and the afternoons with the pair of fencers.

Their progress on the fence slowed considerably. There were times when the man had to walk quite a distance to bring forward a vehicle. Ray's enthusiasm felt a downward pull, but quickly recovered. The hills were increasing steep and more exciting.

"You miss a gear or a pedal and it can be a wild ride."

Ray's vision glistened, as did his hearing. This feeling of height made his hair flutter.

"If you stay on."

Tucker developed a system and a momentum returned. They were troubled with little talk and no clumsiness. Still, Ray missed having everyone together, and certainly looked forward to the afternoon company and encouragement: of a pretty woman, and uplifting, sunny air…of an uplifting fur and tail *not just afternoons, but mornings too.*

The straight line continued for two and one-quarter miles, then joined with an existing fence. The day's end rang with a somber note as Ray drove in the final staple. His mind followed the turn of older barbed wire: the longstanding yet tight and evenly spaced strands, a wrought parade of weathered posts marching over the rolling and vibrant world, his hands ready and willing to sharpen all the countless barbs, stoop in energetic tedium without gloves and a flat file—to earn the right—if he could just belong, have this and the dog, and the red calf, a part of his home.

* * *

In the east hills, the disturbance from the progress on the new road was weak or absent. At the buildings, certain days, the unrest of construction funneled up the valley as though there were digging in the near hay fields, outsized machines digging deep and piling the black healthy soil, reaching under and clawing into unknown tiers. Alice and Tucker made repeated scans to assure themselves the farmland was untouched. They saw no highway.

The sound bore too much distress of rock and the breaking of many trees.

The dog went through spells of marked uneasiness. The grating and snapping, the spew of multiple engines, *had* to dishonor and carve on his instincts.

In a baffling fashion, Ray seemed to ignore it. Behind the shelter of the house or busy with a chore, he could be anywhere and sit: put his arms around Tommie, as if to shut off his ears, lose all intrusion by powerful incantation.

Alice and Tucker took deep sighs in the changed quiet of the evening, a relief from decay, hoping for an even louder chatter and song from the return of spring and the nesting birds.

Once, after the boy had gone, Tucker and the dog hiked the ridge. In the long shadows three miles to the north, he could see a broad swath had been cleared for crossing the stream. The pasture on each side was burdened, cluttered with large piles of roots and trunks and brush. Beside one particularly huge heap lay a long, reflective culvert, big as a silo. In the dimming valley it rested like a hoop of polished silver twinkling in the last sun. Tucker considered…the predictable future, an interruption in the channel, the shining culvert accent to all that is excessive and foreign. On a dry year the waters of Jasper would leach away, too intimidated to enter.

Less than two weeks after the nurturing rain, they could see directly. Beyond their northern boundary, but with the buffer growing disturbingly narrow, the road began to climb the mountain, at first an exposed cut, then entrenched in the taller timber became hidden, but for the knowledge, the indisputable shadow of missing tree tops. As it went higher, all the valley and more could place the source, the actual dust-smoke rising and stalling over the action-turmoil. Tucker and Alice watched. They were grateful for the distance, yet the scar cut deep, the first permanent alteration and gash visible from the porch.

Mouth of Needles

Alice sat at the kitchen table with a pile of books, trying to choose a future story that would interest Ray. The phone rang and Tucker answered, "Y-E-S?"

To the sound of Milo's grin and chuckle— "They're here. Jill has born the litter. You should be here—you should've been here—" a total dispersion of any gloom.

"They all right?"

"Everything is *hunky dory*. You should be here."

Tucker heard a crackling snuffle and whimpering close to the receiver, a puppy yawn. Milo himself was chewing, breathing, snickering, more than being verbal.

"How many?"

"Seven."

"Whoa..."

"They're big. He is written all over. You should see. *Ouch!* Teeth are like little needles."

Tucker laughed. He envisioned his friend's gray hair: blunt and nervous fingers wading through the cozy bed of a new brood, fumbling, playing.

"All muzzle, their eyes are still but little pinches. Come after they are open, and pick one. Come now."

"No thanks."

"What about Alice?"

"We have plenty going...with Ray...the drought."

"Pups don't hurt drought. You should see. You would change your mind." Then suddenly, "They're going to be *something*—They're wired—I can see they are wired—"

"They have no eyes."

"Wired. I can see, *even* if they can't."

"You have them in your bed?"

"Not yet, they are here in the pantry."

He set the phone down and turned to Alice: Milo, the midwife.

"Jill has delivered seven bundles. All is well. He sounds dizzy himself."

"When will you go see?" she asked.

He shook his head.

"I think *I* will."

"We have Ray and the dry to deal with."

"A puppy wouldn't hurt."

"He would want one and he has no home, no home to keep it. He would be better not to know."

Why...won't the man go look? Alice wondered. He should at least want to—look. Fears of things hidden: secret, slipping through her hands.

Blood of a Tree

Mid-June, visible changes to the high landscape like never before. The labor over the new road that skirted their northern boundary climbed nearly a third of the way up, in reaching the rampart… Tucker, in his rest cared for soft movement and quiet, grew to need—*noise*…a distraction to drown out the too obvious and unsettling progress.

They began with the collie in the lead—dog, tractor, pickup—heading for the place of sawdust, past the Voss place and winding partway up the canyon to the sawmill—this time to make boards. The tractor wove nonstop, its young driver looking forward and to the sides with such intensity and interest, Ray could have weaved into a bush or fallen in a ditch, had the early path not been so level and open.

"Shoo." Ray raised one bare arm from the tractor steering wheel, warning the dog. *"Get away."*

It looked as though he were waving at flying ants—the louder and more frequent the boy's voice, the closer and more smiling the dog. Too close to the spinning front tire and often in direct line with the treacherous rear lugs.

Tucker watched and nodded from behind the cracked and pitted windshield of the truck. Could the dog get run over? *Father, new lion…parent of puppies…* He pulled on his sleeve. Was this present closeness even remotely a danger? He shook his head: no possible hazard. He hunched forward and pressed lightly on the tension in his shoulder.

"Get away, get away." Ray's arms went up one after the other, now as though he were being attacked by a horde of insects.

"Tommie!" the boy hollered, with a feverish mount to his voice.

The open-air wheels began to weave in response.

Tucker, tipping further forward, smiled. His foot arched from accelerator to brake; then he opened the door, whistling for his suddenly mature and responsible dog to ride inside, to bring back order—straighten the start of the day. The boy's head swiveled only partway, seeing their leader begin his loop toward the rear, then returned to his driving. Both hands gripped once again. The tractor went perfectly down the trail, a flawless straddle of the center line of grass. It suddenly became clear, Ray knew just where they were going and how to get there.

After parking in the sunshine above the mill, the boy and Tommie stood under the shade for the big saw. Tucker wheeled the tractor around to drive into a specific slot and align with a massive pulley. He unrolled the wide and continuous belt still attached. This motion telegraphed to the coarse teeth of the saw, causing them to creep back and forth. Once unrolled, he lifted and tugged on the free end. Shaking off bark and shavings, he gave it a single twist. He slid the rubber-coated fabric over the tractor's much smaller pulley while the midpoint still lay on the ground. He mounted the tractor and rolled in reverse until the belt rose and maintained a mild stretch. Ray waited.

Tucker shut off the engine, then turned to the boy. "In the truck, there's a box—a crate—of sawmill items that I need." Ray ran to the truck and climbed into the bed, returning a moment later with an old apple crate in which were assembled used rags, an oil can, a grease gun, and an assortment of files. The thin wooden box was dark and shiny from oil and years of handling by dirty gloves. A cleaner rag lay tucked in one corner, neatly folded around a particular file. Tucker sat on the husk and unwrapped the tool. He huddled close, careful not to further shade the big blade, and counted eight precise strokes on each tooth. After the eighth pass he took his bare thumb and felt the faint wire edge. There were fifty-two teeth. The boy watched—his interest boldly sustained during all the sharpening, even through the final touch and dusting of metal fines.

Ray's head was full of many smells. The smell from the box: old rags and grease, the sawmill; more than just pine and rotting chips, he could smell the filings from the iron, and once again, the man's hat.

Tucker had Ray pump grease into the axles of the carriage and the pulleys of the feed works. While following this instruction, he watched the man puddle oil on the slides to the knees and fill the cups to the Babbitt bearings; every torsion and hinge and socket seemed drenched with fresh oil. In a fashion, he mimicked, looking for fittings at each joint that would somehow rotate and wear, forcing in grease.

At last Tucker restarted the tractor. Ray stood in a designated spot where the lumber came onto rollers. Tommie perched on the pile where they had mined bedding. Tucker engaged the power, and the flat belt rolled and slapped and the saw fluttered; at once the chain began dragging insignificant amounts of sawdust up toward the dog—who was beginning to fidget—with a clear effort to see only Ray. Ray stood with his arms dangling, limp, feeling as though small amounts of sawdust were being removed from under his own feet. Tucker tapped a little further on the fuel control; everything increased to a fascinating speed. Now there was noise: the engine, a quick flutter, the flap from the racing belt, a quickening, friendly rattle of chain over cast pulleys. The dog moved only a few feet. Ray could see his eyes flicker, while remaining bound in his direction.

Tucker stepped down from the tractor and signaled for Ray. With a strong but light touch from the man's hand, his shoulder was turned. The opposite glove scooped up dry chips and threw them into the rushing belt. Like a suction, they immediately disappeared into the driving pulley and were broadcast in a fan. Down the alley by the off-bearing rolls, Tucker led him behind the guard for the spinning saw. The man laid a piece of curled bark on the table over the husk. With a stick he gently scooted it into the close smear of rising teeth. In an unseen snatch it shot up between the rafters, *kawthump*, and shattered on the underside of the roof.

As though listening for the correct sound, Ray watched Tucker tip his broad hat as he tapped the governor back even more; the saw stiffened, like an anchored disk with a fuzzy circumference. The long, swaying belt smoothed out.

Tommie left the area of the mill to lie under a tree near the incoming trail. Ray watched his departure: a certain unhappiness in his walk...acceptance distinct, an attitude very different from earlier. All this simultaneous mechanical action which so absorbed Ray, surely repelled even the bravest collie.

With gloves and fingertip control on the carriage lever, Tucker eased the first log into the saw. Scintillating bright chips were thrown down like sparks from a grinder. For an instant Ray thought of blood of a tree. Once he saw a board made, it would never be the same: that place in the canyon much more than an inviting pile of sawdust. The waste and slabs to edge went across the alley onto removable wooden skids. The good boards went down the multiple rollers and were tipped off, landing on the chip-covered ground. He soon tried to tip them into different piles, according to their width. His protected hands petted the clean, rough grain and the changing knots, pulled from his deep fascination by each coming board. The noise and odor of machinery transcended to a vague cleanliness as the results gathered at the end of the rolls. A moist, fresh sawdust followed the chain and fell into the caves they had dug, a startling pale yellow dribbling over and making the old look stale and spent, as though it had been too long in an oven. The jackstraw sticks at the end grew to many. Too intense and busy to form an expression, he felt himself working with unblinking eyes. Tucker tucked his hat down and squinted for the showering chips on his side of the saw; they were divided by guards and a whirl of spinning razors disguised in a blur. All was safe within the hold of a careful-watching man.

Together they sorted and neatly stacked and stripped the lumber.

Tucker could hear the road being built, no pauses in the progress, no resting at noon, a nervous and pulling sound…yet to reach Ray.

Lunch took place under the same tree where Tommie waited. They both had a fresh sprinkling of sawdust on their shoulders; Ray had red bits of bark in his hair and on the tanning of his neck.

"What makes them so pretty? Them boards?"

Tucker took his hat off and swallowed, trying to forget the steady advance of outside machinery:

"The pattern of where the limbs were and how the saw crosses the growth rings. As you cut deeper, the color changes."

"You don't need no—any gloves. They're so nice and straight and not that rough. I'd rather touch them with nothing." Ray held his sandwich up between his fingers as if it were a biscuit of fresh-sawn pine.

The bothersome sound faded, as though from a wind blowing it away.

"They save you from pitch. Leave them an hour in the air and stickers grow; they will prickle through cotton. Supple now, they lose their looks. Some will cup and kink, ends will split."

"Them strips?"

"They help them dry more evenly. They still dry too fast. And curl."

"I'll come—I'll come—I'll put rocks on top. Hold them down."

Tucker tried to smile in spite of the *irksome* grinding and chewing in the *shrinking* distance.

The dog looked away from their eating and placed his chin on his paws, as if in a continuing pout; his ears well aware of the same sound as Tucker could not avoid, machines grating on his senses...from both sides.

The picture of a collie litter hovered, seven...*he's written all over*...then rippled and floated away.

"How old is those trees?" Ray asked.

"Sixty—eighty."

"Old."

"They are second growth. The overstory might be eighty...plus a hundred."

Ray looked up into the tree above them and stopped eating, a distinct maleness in the exposure of his throat. "You ever cut one a these?"

"Sometimes they are struck by lightning or blown over. If they are healthy they stay. Their generation has already been cut. They are left to lead and shade the young—make them reach and grow taller, and to watch."

Tucker considered the mail-order sawmill, with a noise of its own, built to last: all its clever gears and bearings, cogs and springs, wheels and belts—the coarse sharpness of the saw like the mouth to a shark. "Plank for barns, houses, corrals. This place had a growl."

He looked into the forest. "And then for a time, almost a fret." Tucker put his hat on and tweaked its brim. "We brought in more people and cut railroad ties, hundreds upon hundreds, perfect clean squares, product to sell and money for the towns—more, more—it can lead to addiction."

Ray had finished eating and looked a little sleepy.

Tucker watched, and let the boy sit *in the slash and insistence of nearing construction, the road, as if over their heads.*

He turned and remembered his grandfather's industry, the lure of wealth, the fatigue of accomplishment: for a moment a place to bury the energy, evade our smallness—our transience. After a time they heard beyond the *bugle* and the industry lost its grasp, allowing a return to life and family, return to wife—*his girl*— return from a war without conclusion.

Milo's Clan

One-half mile before the town limits, Alice turned onto the short drive to the pleasure of clean young lambs. They were gathered on one side of the road and on her approach formed a line crossing over the rutted center. Perhaps fifteen or sixteen and all very close to the same age: pink curious ears translucent in the sun, fuzzy white brows. She drove more slowly— as though the drive were a hot griddle reaching that essential turning degree, and they bright little kernels. Several *popped* straight into the air. Alice blinked, took a sudden breath, and pressed so firmly on the brake the car rocked forward. Like a string of popcorn they galloped down the bank. With a broad curve and tightly bunched, they ran through the small paddock of closely clipped grass, their circle tightening as they came to a halt. Alice began driving again and realized her own smile, completely relaxed. Still, she kept watching this fresh congregation, like a spring gaining tension. She parked beside Milo's house, feeling movement behind the window of its front door—inside the comfort of his kitchen, she imagined him flicking a switch to electrify the pasture. The excitable band lost their innocence and began popping and hopping. A contagion of jumping beans, butting heads, without plan or direction. She heard herself laugh. She couldn't help but compare the nearby mothers, insulated and dutifully grazing, not once looking up.

Milo opened the door with a phone receiver in his hand, a loop of coil leading to the wall hidden by its hinge. His eyes sparkled. For several seconds the corners of his mouth twitched, a stuttering reflex… "Daughter Joyce says—says—hello." He looked at the floor and his wrinkles began losing their edge… "It's done," he said into the phone, then hung it in its chrome cradle. His hands flew into the air and his cheeks shook. Now hatless, a wing of his hair pointed awry from being folded wrong.

He left Alice standing on the step while he quickly receded in the room. He jerked on a loose porcelain doorknob to reveal a cluttered cubicle typically open to the rest of the house. The door screeched and dragged heavily. Jill skipped and bounced in a sideways fashion to immediately snug against Alice's legs. No hint of shyness or worry.

"I reckon she trusts you," his eyes again shining, the near creases their familiar crisp, at once again magnified. "Joyce made me move them—she made me move them. She says baby sheep, then baby dogs—there comes a time they get too old to keep in your house—reckon *my* house…" His voice trailed as he backed further away. The room felt oddly rambling, larger and more complex than the small residence could afford. He sat in a chair by a chrome table with a Formica top.

Alice remained through the open door and on the step, with Jill like an anchor to her feet. She stooped to pet the dog calmly; the collie now completely void of the nervousness Alice had thought so marked.

Not true with Milo.

Both hands waved and his cheeks shook violently. "Lordy, Lordy! You better come in—you better come close that door and come in… My marble—" he touched his temple "—not pegged down ever since…ever since they're—gone."

Her first words unbelieving, a bit alarmed. "Where are they? Are they sold? Have they *all* been chosen?"

"Not a one."

Alice pulled one of her shoes out from under Jill, then paused.

"I reckon nobody knows but you and me and Tucker and Joyce. I let it out, they'll go like donuts—peanut candy..." Milo shrugged his shoulders, then clasped his hands and set them on the Formica as if in prayer. "Who'd want that?"

Alice lifted her other foot and Jill fell to her side for an instant, quickly rising and preparing to follow. Alice wondered how difficult her first birthing might have been. Opposite Milo another chair rubbed against the empty table. In Alice's grasp, it jittered over the floor. Rather than empty, she discovered a pair of worn leather boots with their laces dangling and touching the floor. The laces were mangled, almost broken in places, then fanning out: a nightmare of split ends.

As though with a sharp poke to his ribs, Milo stood and jerked the boots away. He winked and pointed at the needle marks on the lower portion of the chair legs.

"You are lucky you have Joyce, a daughter that keeps an eye—"

"Sit," he said.

"Without her you might—"

Jill sat immediate to the empty chair; for Alice's first notice the dog exposed, flaunted twin rows of swollen nipples. Alice knew solid reassurance: puppies were close at hand.

"Tucker oughta be here to see. Why didn't you bring him?"

Alice shook her head and lowered into the chair.

"You know he might be right...I just moved them out yesterday—to the little horse barn with bum lambs..." Like miniscule bubbles of response, his snickering came to the surface. "I have a little nest for the babies, but the triplets have their own room."

"Triplets?"

"Their ewe got sick and I couldn't save—Darla, Dandy, Dalila—my nursery. They have me now. How is Ray doing?"

Her composure slipped, but slightly. "Tucker and Ray are making lumber, running the sawmill."

He nervously tipped forward and laid his hands on the table, only this time flat with their fingers spread. "I oughta make us some coffee. That's what I need—a load of sawdust—those little dogs aren't housebroke. Smart parents but that doesn't mean they don't have to start at the very bottom, can't skip any grades. So far they're failing—it's hard with seven. I remember training Joyce."

"You mean Jill." The dog's nose poked her knee, demanding attention.

"No, Joyce."

"*Milo Taylor...*" Alice fingered Jill's collar, then under her chin.

One hand of Milo's popped up so quickly like a bouncing lamb, swiftly turning his head at a right angle: he pulled harshly on the crest of the ear closest to Alice. He drew her forward, intentionally keeping his mouth closed, in total silence.

"It seems your daughter is training you," she said, "or hoping to *keep* you trained." The need passed for her to reach over and straighten his hair. As though with a striking abnormality, he sat without a cap, like a man never seen missing his false teeth—Alice expected he would rise from bed every morning, a shoddy covering placed over his head sooner than a pair of pants over his lower half.

"That's what I get—that's what I get."

"May I see them?"

"I don't know..."

Alice slid back and rolled her chin, with a stiffening smile. She swept the room and her eyes caught the long cord to the telephone; it had been overextended and remained stretched with a series of knotted curls. Where a twist lay on the floor, she could see multiple puncture marks and small tears in its soft vanilla-colored coating. Milo wore a clean Band-Aid on his right forefinger, again bringing his palms together, then with the sudden turn of a wrist made opposing cups as if needing to warm all his fingertips. Jill nuzzled her left arm. Looking down, she felt the collapse of feelings, a smoothing alignment, the strong desire to slow Milo's hurry and confusion. Jill's manner and beaming posed a definite contrast—settled—with the time and the day and her company like never seen, her dark eyes and rounded head emanating new qualities... touching deep.

"Is she good at taking care—"

"You wouldn't believe—" he bounced up "—I kinda trapped you. *Aw*...I can't do it. I can't be two against one—let's go look."

Alice followed, almost reaching to grab his sleeve and make him relax. Jill was different. Milo was different. He failed to snatch his nearby hat as they passed through the door. In the sunlight she trailed further behind, not yet knowing which small building had the designation—*horse barn*. Jill immediately clarified the direction.

"The boy like doing the sawmill?" the sentence vague, overpowered by the sound of his footsteps.

She nearly requested a repeat, his speed in leading and the trajectory of his voice obscuring the words. The distance between them grew, and Alice spoke with rising definition. "Ray, with Tucker teaching—he's come to love rough boards and pitch. He seems to find fascination and attraction in almost *everything*."

"You know he's right. I hate to agree but I think he's right." His pace didn't falter. "His mom—she wouldn't—couldn't deal with the trouble—not a little dog like one of these—" He turned and in a sideways fashion took a deep breath, as if in his hustle his lungs had fallen out of rhythm. "High-energy wired pups, they get worse before they get better. I reckon no one would let him take a collie to school, Joyce says…"

"I—I might, what if *I'd* like one?" A stronger assertion grew with her volume.

He had reached the barn, now in sharp transition, standing abruptly still and waiting. Jill moved to sit in front of his faded pants, looking marvelously proud, as though Milo were also a factor in the product that gave her such radiance. With several yards remaining in Alice's approach, he squared his shoulders, then formed a sentence with a clarity new to the conversation. "And what do you suppose he would do, the boy?" He folded his arms across his chest. "Lordy. He has fallen in love with a sawmill." The wing of hair fluttered, without detraction to the sudden seriousness of his demeanor.

Alice considered the grass in her path, nibbled to the root and dry; it had lost all green. She stopped walking and they stood opposite.

"Go looking. It used to be easy, before our—*city* grew so big. Urban sprawl. Everybody—everybody knew everybody, and everything. I reckon you'll see her soon, soon you will see her."

Alice waited for him to open the door, break her sudden feeling of impatience, uneasiness.

"I can just see him. I can just see him with one of Tommie and Jill's litter. An attractive young boy whispering in a beautiful dog's ear—trialing, penning cows, sheep. He'd be known. He'd be famous—" His hands released, darting up to scrub his sunlit waves of gray. "A beautiful pair, beautiful pair—set up for a fall…" He swung the broad sawbuck door and Jill vanished.

Alice felt abruptly afraid, afraid to go inside…face the full glow of puppyhood, *of thriving offspring.*

"That boy, he's a keep—" Milo stalled, as if knowing he had gone too fast, again, missed the warning sign: *sharp* curve, dead end. "Don't fret. He'll do all right. Joyce says he's bright—more than— He's lucky to get to be with you. Joyce says it's more—more than a passing help... You'll stick in his mind. Both of you. Yes. And that mountain and valley."

He released the door and it began to swing closed. A quick hook with his fingers and in the same act the toe of his boot rolled a rock to pin the lower corner. Fresh scrapes in the wood covered the bottom edge. There were small high windows along the south wall, but the open door allowed the most light.

Alice peered indoors, a shock to her eyes after such a bright day. She could hear puppies feeding, not far away. Lambs began to bleat from deeper in the building. "I'd like...we'd like to do more."

"You and Tucker still sleep in the same bed? You know you are a very good-looking woman." His gray eyes, close and clear, unusually steady.

Alice stepped into the dim space before him, then blushed, a different kind of flush, unrelated to embarrassment. She turned, his unruly hair in silhouette.

"A couple who don't look they are even *near* forty. That's mighty young to me. Mighty." One thin eyelid began to droop; the other iris sharpened even further. Blue-green and gray, piercing eye...

"I—we can't have babies," she said.

"Forget that. Just be—show—be—" No blink, no movement. "I have one daughter—no one else. Wife *Myra*: not for thirty years... I reckon you and Tucker have got more than you know." He took her shoulder and pressed her to turn and lead the way. "Don't waste time."

Awkwardness…and her past emotions of loneliness…failure…nebulized. All he said landing so sketchy and vague, but what he said—straight from the heart. She wondered how it might feel if Tucker were at her side. An old familiar warmth rose into her forehead.

The lambs grew forceful in loud complaint, drowning out the sound of nursing, harshly resonant in the space comparable to a modest shed for storing wood.

"They want their bottle." Milo spoke with a sudden gruffness.

Alice led them to a tall panel tucked between the studs below a high window. Several hay bales lay jumbled and wedged against the free end, adding support. The bales were faded from years of daylight and imbedded with dust. Alice realized a low place in the makeshift wall, a notch that Jill could easily clear. "How did you move them?"

"Wheelbarrow."

"No."

"Yes."

Alice peered over the panel and down to Jill's smiling face, *cistern of wriggles, rectangular bales placed carefully in a circle,* flashing glimpses of scenes long in the past.

Milo stepped closely behind her and spoke lowly, nearly directly in her ear. "They sure were shouting—claws squealing on the rusty sides. I kept sloshing them as we went to keep them from climbing out. One spilled—"

"You didn't."

"Mother came along and saved the seventh one."

"You didn't."

"No—I put them in a gunny sack and dragged them over the ground."

Knowing not to comment any further, Alice didn't bother to shake her head or even look up. The lambs cried louder and louder, demanding and spoiled, but their grasp on her hearing began to slip. The puppies nestled, much smaller and less mature than she had expected. Their eyes so newly open they had yet to turn bright blue, fully open but without the capacity for clear recognition. She might just as well been another man, an intrusion of no distinct difference. They were more delicate than the bundles she had prepared to hold and cuddle. Already full bellies, they were beginning to squirm and change places: black-and-white worms. With a slender knuckle Alice stroked her eyebrow, considering the entryway the mother had used. She stood thinking, counting the puppies, wondering over each one's future—in *whose* hands would their remarkable loyalty soon land.

Milo diffused her intention: "Before we leave they'll be like little balloons and full of yawns. I reckon you know that skunky dog-milk breath...stickery tongues."

Milo had done it again. She smiled. She turned to consider him directly and smiled more broadly.

His wrinkles spread, then tightened to their limit. "You and Tucker are a team."

She approached the notch, intending to step over, to bend down and touch, lightly stroke, then caught the repeating gesture new to his habits—one eyelid began to droop. His sun-worn face not well lit, but having definite effect.

"You sure you want to do that?" he asked.

They stood facing.

"First you pull—Tucker pulls...then you pull together so you can get the stump out, clean the field, and farm—grow things... I reckon you'll grow something different than—"

She felt the urge to turn, at least look one more time into the nest, then felt a rising wisdom to avoid the tease.

Her hand shifted. She lifted it toward Milo's face to slowly open and brush his bristly cheek. His nervous mouth quivered with pleasure. In blaring contrast, with increasing force, the demands of orphan lambs reentered in mounting crescendo. The tantrum in the next cubicle invaded their space: too much echoing for such a tiny barn. Alice backed away. She twisted, to walk straight and swift into the light of the open air.

"THANK YOU!" she shouted without turning her head, leaving him behind, rushing in full stride to find a place of quiet.

Trespass

By the fifth afternoon the sound became intolerable. When their sawing of lumber stopped, the crunch and scrape and power bore down on them as though they stood between the very survey stakes, the markers to guide the advancing welter. Tucker could smell diesel exhaust. He pulled his collar tight and fastened the top button. Tommie clutched his ears continuously and even in the morning gave a look of weariness. Ray finally acquired a distracted look; it wasn't possible—to ignore such strong feelings, in those so close.

That day they shut down early. Before leaving the narrowness of the canyon, Tucker forked from the main trail. He turned the truck sharply. They followed a shaded switchback and broke onto the sunlit table, an unmistakably groomed field. Unconscious of the smoothness, Tucker drove to find the battle between engine and mountain, as if to inflict more insult and injury, before going home. He must know…know the exact location.

The sunny high field had been nipped by late frost. Singed oats wilted for two reasons: the bite of freezing and there had been no more moisture. The underneath grasses were green but ungrowing. Production here came strictly from rain and snow, no sub-irrigation as lay along the stream.

They drove the lower edge of the tilled slope toward an immediate roar—thrashing in trees far too visible. The collie's ears flickered and rose in contradiction. A white dust filtered over the failing crop from the disruption of rock and shallow soil. A thin wisp drifted around the Sisters like a transparent sash about their waist. Tucker could see the tops to the timber shaking and waving, slamming downward as they reached the boundary. A fence from below the bench crossed in front of the pickup, and as it marched up the steepening hill, it became overgrown. He was first, with the others following, stepping out from the truck and standing on the ground as if in a trance, deafened witness to a monumental happening. He could hear the overhead muscle of great displacement but not quite see it.

Tucker's eyes followed the fence line…as he searched a silent treetop slapped down across the wires, breaking a post and bringing them flat. Reverberations came down the line, a soundless strain, then shriek. In delay the top wire popped to suddenly relax and droop from post to post. Weaving through the growth, he led the others up the bank, and another tree flopped down, crossing and collapsing more of the rusty strands. At once came a vicious snapping of stems and limbs as though a monstrous thing were taking bites of forest. Dust fogged.

Tommie's reserve fell away, with a new distinction, a quick passion to protect; he took the lead, climbing quickly through the fresh ruin-detritus—they all saw the machine: one giant dozer. An operator sat on top in an open-air canopy, small and lifeless save for a random bouncing and the working of levers at his chest. His helmet was powdered.

Now between branches and brush, Tucker caught a glimpse of the dog's inflated shoulder, the beginning hunker of defense. He gave a whistle to stop.

More trees went down as if in answer to the call.

Tommie leapt upon a freshly fallen log, old growth and limbless, with a mammoth root wad reared up, lightly raining stones and dirt, poised and glowering, a power in his stance like a regal wolf—infallible—

Tucker caught the close fall of more trees, slapping near enough to flutter the collie's coat.

His legs tangled in the brush while he whistled a "come home," again and again, as shrill as possible, but it could not be heard over the crash and roaring. *Could not be heard.* An unaccustomed panic seized Tucker.

The dog continued on the trunk, a shudder in his creeping.

Ray struggled forward and was able to see—the urgency—the breath before a disaster. *"Tommie!"* he shouted and the boy's face turned a blistering red. *"Tommie!"*

The dozer snorted black smoke and its tracks cried. Tucker whistled with the roar and his neck filled with pressure.

A young boy's throat split the air in a cutting pitch more harsh than any whistle. A chilling scream.

The dog turned his head.

Two smaller trees swept down and knocked him from his perch.

Without yelp or howl he fell below the logs and trash and disappeared.

Ray's eyes began to run and he screamed again, pleading…at anyone.

Tucker held him back and with serious repeated rapidity gave a *come home,* tipping one way, then the other, searching through the insistent throttle and dust and falling forest, the brim to his hat quavering.

In a long moment the style of Tommie reappeared—indistinguishable moments—scrambling through limbs, intact. He first staggered to assess Ray, licking and loving. The perfect collie had a ripped ear, bloodshot eye, and a weep of scarlet paint in his faultless mane.

Tucker bent down and roughly pulled the dog away from the boy, feeling all his bones. In a flash his gloves dropped and his heavy fingers combed through all the fur, looking for more blood and any swelling or lumps. Abruptly he stood and bustled his shoulders. He considered the unceasing machine and the trail of waste, the operator too full of himself and his job to see any twilight periphery, never aware of his company. Tucker knelt and touched his lips to the concave of the dog's nose, then straightened, clear-eyed, raising his sleeve to carefully wipe his own cheek, as though removing a stranger's saliva. He turned and ordered the others to follow. They loaded and drove below the starving, brittle hay without a word, soon to escape the sight, but not the sound.

Ray was awakened: the happening of the road and anything about it became an enemy. He cuddled his beloved, caressing the split ear, a residue in his fingers. No small sawmill could drown or wash away this wounding, no clean place along the creek. He rode with a *terrible* unrest, a bewildering nearness and need—between him and the man.

"You've got to stop them knocking down the fence."

Ray watched Tucker studying the side of Tommie's head. The pickup missed skirting around a rock. They all lurched.

"I can see the road is moving away." His gloves again on, Tucker's right hand reached up and adjusted his hat. "I can see. We will go back and repair when they are gone."

Ray squirmed in silence, feeling more change. They passed the Voss barn, all the buildings like the quiet emptiness in the wooden cross to mark a burial.

"They will dirty their own house."

Ray's ears pounded. He listened more intensely than ever in his life.

The dog lay still.

At the bridge they slowed, crossed the stream, entering the next field to quickly lean and hook the truck around and see the mountain, observers of the climbing diagonal cut, even in the thicker trees. The dog sat up. Tucker's mouth moved but there was no voice. They sat for a time with the engine running.

At length, along the exposed stretch of road, flags of dust rose, waving to the south, following unfamiliar vehicles as they descended the hill and headed east.

Tucker cut the engine.

"They are like termites sailing in a wooden ship."

Ray could barely hear.

"They have eaten the mast and now are at work on the hull."

The engine restarted to calmly return them on the path for home, turning and progressing, with a furious peacefulness.

* * *

Other than the brief, raw explanation of the trespass, there were no words. Tommie sat prince-like on the entry rug while Alice bathed him with a steaming, almost dripping, light blue towel. Tucker returned from the shop with a strange brush, a series of comb teeth on its back and bristles on the front; he began to stroke. The thick texture of the cloth came away with rust-like traces, growing brighter as moisture softened where the collie had been hurt. Ray felt heat—joint movement, kind of an inside light between the couple new to his senses. They moved with caring, as though bound together. As they worked this closeness gained in strength, like the reminder of blood in the trailing towel.

In the evening the wind began to blow. It came with a certain stealth, sneaking up, easing over the rises, then turning on, fierce blasts, prolonged and skittering grit. The fragile new grasses along the lane that led to town raced in patterns one way, then the other.

Ray had trouble traveling straight. The bike swerved and tipped and the chain clattered for the sudden turns. He could hear the wind coming and would brace, only to have it spin around and slap him from a different angle, his balance in constant stress. At first he was relieved to reach the gravel road, more trafficked and smooth, lower, but it grew worse. Dust and dirt spiraled out of the ditches, and the fines of the hammered road base beat against his pants and stung his arms and face. He pedaled faster. As though angry at his speed and greater stability, different currents of air struck as if a fighter, left jabs, then a powerful right stroke. Sand hit his eyes and he ducked with a tightening squint. His tires left the packed track and entered an unruly berm.

He went down with a bang and *umph,* and the bike tumbled over him.

He stood blinking and huddled, repeatedly tugging on his gritty eyelids while the flying dirt continued. He had skinned his elbow and torn his pants; small rocks were embedded in the palm of his hand. The bike opposed him to the edge of the road where he hesitated, pressing hard on his arm. One handlebar grip had gouged the gravel, and the round protective end hung down by a fiber. He twisted and jerked the dangling piece to put in his pocket, now seeing the hollow of the chromed tube.

At the trailer house he parked beside his mother's dirty but still brightly colored car. He remembered it was almost summer, the longest day, and that he had not yet adjusted to this clashing, uneven color. He hurriedly went inside to wash his eyes. In the small mirror over the sink, he could see they were red and swollen as if he had been crying. He rinsed and rinsed. Through his blindness he could feel the wind rocking the long, temporary house.

Seeming like the girl had not heard her boy coming home...for all the scuffing, creaking, and the sound of sand peening the thin walls, she went outside with full hair blowing wild about her face to empty an ashtray in the driveway. She held what strands were easy to grasp in a single hand—the other held the tray. She bent down to dump and the ashes vanished. Many butts bounced and scattered over the dirt like bits of cork and caught in the neighboring weeds. The grass against and around the house was last year's, folded over without color, broken but with a struggling green rising from underneath. She now cursed, facing the stiff and stale growth, bracing for an even greater flapping about her head and clinging blouse.

Pulling hair from inside her lips, she regarded the bike, as though for the first time. It fell over as she stood, leaving a deep scrape down her fender. The very end of the naked steering bar cut through the paint and further, a gray feather edge peeled up from an undercoating of filler and primer.

Brittle weeds blew across the yard. She clenched her teeth.

She slammed the door and in the clutter of the living room grabbed a hairbrush from the sway of a card table. As if in rapid descent from stale frustration, she came up behind him in the hallway. She thumped him squarely on the head.

"Yeow!"

Still blinking for the soreness in his vision, he ducked under her raised arm and ran for the door.

"Don't you dodge me, you little wart. Your goddamn bike slammed against my car." She dropped the brush and began to work a slim belt from her pants.

He slipped through the door and around the back of the trailer but did not run, the sky darkening.

"You run from me, you little *bastard,* and you won't get no supper. I spent hard money on that car."

Ray turned with his itchy eyes going up and down and from corner to corner, not rolling or flippant, an outward effort reaching for control.

She came to him, clearly unconscious of the wind, a black depth rising up—disconnection in her face.

He turned again, this time leaving his back to her and to stand, unable to hear the complete strikes, embraced by the loud soaring of the heartless and escalating storm.

* * *

April had already eaten and made him sit at the table. The smell had no appeal, that of rusty iron pans and cold grease—cigarettes. She set a plate before him of scrambled egg mixed with pieces of hot dog. The egg was incompletely cooked and poorly whipped. He could see a thin coating of salt over all the pink chunks and pale yellow. He felt a blankness growing in his tired blue eyes, void of hunger.

"Eat it."

He twisted the plate around with both hands, as though turning on a huge valve, then twisted it back.

The kitchen light glared. She stood above him, holding the heavy skillet and a spatula, curls of hair across her mouth. "I cook for you—"

Chocolate brown eyes still hot with impatience, he thought: *I demand on her freedom…*

"—now *eat it.*"

He rose to get himself a spoon and fork, then sat alone and ate. Once finished he took his used silverware and plate and set them quietly near the sink. Before washing dishes he left for his bedroom. In spite of the outside howling, he could feel her rustling at the far end of the trailer. With a rush he opened the window and the faded curtains immediately cleared him, flurried into the room. He hung his upper body out as far as possible so that nothing would come back and touch or splash the aluminum trim or paper-like siding.

Bastard wind —thoughts too deep to break into words.

* * *

In not many days the construction had reached the cliffs. The sound became much weaker and delayed. After a long quiet the valley could see, Alice and Tucker and the boy and dog could see, then hear the blasting—a soundless puff and eruption of white followed by a faraway boom.

Mending and converging near Jasper Spring, its cleansing flow, ravage and division apart.

Special teams were brought in, carried by a slew of vehicles, some with ground crew and some towing specialized equipment: air compressors and track drills, powder wagons. Their progress and intent became clearly evident. They removed millennium-old patina and moss. A stark, reflective band was drawn, a curve and cut over the edge of the rampart. Rubble and ugly rock collected as a fill and underline. Tremendous dozers pushed riprap from above while ones below packed and formed it, like ants clearing a channel working from both ends.

At last they were over the top. The strife had ended and the system attached. There would be weeks of labor to smooth and blade, but no more drilling and blasting or breaking of trees. Defeat of the mountain was marked by a great exodus of trucks and machines, common colors; a larger than expected parade for many had entered from the western side. The homestead watched. The departing dust always leaving the new cut like a flag, a pennant—Triumphant termites proudly enlightened, waving the banner of a burgeoning nation.

Runaway

Ray had seen Horse and Daisy in the pasture yet not up close. Flicking tails and pricked ears, they were pretty, but he was short of curiosity. He stood, his interest and foundation astride the ground—with independent feet and beside his dog—then came the bike, and now the tractor.

Alice lingered in the corral and watched the horses eat grain out of individual hubcaps. Toward the end of their meal, they scooted them around in the dirt, leaving odd tracks, as though playing a private game with half-polished bowls attached to their noses. Horse's head came too close to Daisy's and she jerked her mouth out to nastily show her teeth, spilling the last of her grain, while squeezing her ears down. The game and treat were over.

Tommie lay partly on his side to wriggle under the rail, leaving Alice and greeting Ray. They spoke. Ray climbed the first two planks and considered the tall shapes of the horses with their opposite colors. He saw the little one telling the big one what to do and smiled at Alice.

"You need to build me some new grain boxes. Some of that fresh lumber will do."

"I will," he answered.

"They get crabby pushing these silly things."

"They are funny to watch."

Ray had more tan than she had ever seen. His hair was getting sun bleached, even that on his arms.

"Would you like to sit on Daisy?"

Ray shrugged. His blue eyes faltered and looked down, as though she were a girl his own age and had asked him to dance.

"You better try it. We might ride fence or cattle together. You want to see that little heifer again, don't you?"

He and the collie entered the corral. He helped carry the tack, then watched Alice brush off dander and endless loose hair. Though he had yet to touch, his hands began to feel waxy and dry as she bridled and saddled a very calm white horse. She held the horse's muzzle by the bit. Ray climbed on without hesitation or instruction.

Daisy certainly knew he was a man thing, but seemed to like his youth, his insignificant weight.

Ray felt natural, absolute comfort and unity—save no handlebars—through the thick leather of the saddle he pressed his legs, clinging to her sides without any thought of being cautious. He looked about, in realization of his new point of view, higher, and in separation from his main companion. Tommie circled unhappily. Ray also felt a stirring worry for their being apart, raising a leg to get down, still preferring the ground and its feeling of—

"Stay a moment." Alice held the reins up and put them together in one of his hands. She adjusted the stirrups.

He had looked down on Alice only one other time.

"Hold them together. You steer with the pressure of one alongside her neck. It doesn't take much. Remember they are hooked to her mouth." She pointed to his shoes. "Just your toes."

The dog stopped moving.

Alice watched Daisy as she took her first steps, then fell to a brisk walk. Horse played in the hubcaps while the mare followed the perimeter of the grassless pen, lightly swaying her head, bright and eager. Ray immediately followed her rhythm with an outstanding connection. This sudden satisfied closeness of the horse and such a young rider made Alice shiver. The dog lost his stop and moved about the center of the corral, reminding her of a circus man—directing elephants.

Ray swallowed, as the plank fence went by and the whole world revolved; he dismissed his unused feet for the feeling of a living horse and the earth coming up through her legs.

Pay me money?

He grinned again at Alice and smiled at the collie.

Alice turned in a matching circle as they went around four or five times; then the boy gave the horse an invisible nudge. Without raising her head or trotting, Daisy extended to a lope. The vigilant dog *broke*—bursting dust—in precise flying violence he whipped by Alice and flashed gnashing, hostile teeth, immediate to Daisy's brow. Alice jumped. Had Daisy not known the dog she would have screamed a horse's scream. The horse reared and snorted and threw her head, spinning around to kick. The boy, like a quick four-legged spider, not surprisingly stayed mounted, dropping reins and stirrups but locked on, bowed, gripping in all directions.

Horse pranced, bringing a bumping and ring from the empty tin dishes.

Alice could not talk. It was a blameless thing.

Eye to eye, Tommie waited for Daisy to move and appeared to be crouching for another fly. She stood panting through her nostrils with her head held low, fanning the dirt, the abandoned leather strips coiled and almost touching her mouth. Horse succeeded in flipping both caps over and the prattle and ringing stopped.

Ray began to relax.

Tucker came from the shop and rested his arms on the top board. He watched the mare breathing and the boy sitting without any strap or stirrup.

The lady horse.

He could see Alice sigh quietly and noticed her ruffled hair. He couldn't help but acknowledge the continuing change, a kind of twisting—comfort—

The dog slumped.

Tucker tipped his hat back. "Maybe we should leash Tom...until Ray gets the feel."

At the sound of a voice, Daisy inched her head up; her ears went back, then forward, as though grateful for the rider still attached. She looked at the dog as if being trained: yet jumpy and with a lifted tail, an obvious anger in slow submission.

Alice walked over and gathered the reins. "After what just happened, I don't think anything could throw him off."

The guardian wagged his tail and backed away.

* * *

Rain had been sketchy at best or none at all; still, the country became amazingly green. The east pastures seemed to have caught more, while much of the hay land suffered in a kind of shadow, too sheltered by the mountain. Most wild grasses were short, in contrast with the tame brome around the buildings. The pale green covering over the open hills came only halfway up a man's boot and was going to seed. The highland oats had already rounded a droughty blue, a dull, wilted blue, with stunted yellowing patches to match the patterns of the thinner and rockier soil.

"There will be nothing to combine."

And it had hinged like a page to become prematurely warm-hot. The noonday sun lay harsh, trapped in the valley lowness where there should be a broad, sweaty lushness and growth, baking the smart green and turning it limp.

The dry did not yet reach Ray; rain or shine, hot or cold, he was too in harmony.

The road slept.

Tucker purchased him a straw hat and it became signal to his presence. Never without motion—up, down, bobbing and twisting—Tommie often knocked it off. There were days when the early heat felt suffocating to Alice and Tucker. The dog kept distracted.

Ray barely noticed for he had lived places much lower and more bleak. In this world, through the wavy sun, he felt a flickering of sweaty wings.

For everyone there remained a fated cheerful width, the loops and curves of reliable leaching wet along Jasper Stream. This is where the dog and the boy played most. The flow underneath kept things straight and reaching. His companion tunneled in the clover while Ray showed a clear attraction to the tallest and very best hay, able to duck down and vanish at any moment. In certain places the leaves and stems grew so high he could be standing and all the porch could see was the hat, a wriggling, wandering bright disk in a ripening field. When the warm wind blew over the dry hills, it was like rubbing salt across a fresh wound; the boy and dog were hidden and unaware, making trails like a doe and fawn in the protective, moist green of the valley's heart.

Summertime and they used the wooden pegs in the wall under the porch roof, hangers for a coat and hat to keep the dust and pollen out of doors. Under the window sat a painted bench. Here they laid their gloves—an intended place to sit and remove never muddy boots—a community tin cup rested on a cooler filled with drinking water. Without rain a dullness settled on their hats. Ray's and Tucker's hung side by side. In the evenings the boy's came back to the peg. He refused to wear it while riding his bike.

Tucker studied the hay carefully. He looked for blooms and singeing at the edge of leaves and the base of stalks. Deer had been snipping at the tops of the alfalfa but their use was tentative and light. Many of the higher margins of farmed ground were already too failed and would be left for grazing, a normally heavy mantle now so faded and shrunken he could see through to the ground. As a test he would throw a coin out, then walk and recover it with little hindrance from the year's growth. Harvest began a full month early.

With a burlap bag Tucker wiped clean the smaller tractor that would pull the rake. He warned repeatedly: stay off any hills and away from ditches. Ray was taught how to operate and maintain the side delivery, how to windrow one or several swaths to the mower, how to turn sharply without catching or bending the implement's tongue. He liked the spinning and rapid lift of the teeth, the smoothness of the fields, the clean formation of a fluffed green mound at his back—an unbroken trail.

Tucker did the mowing.

Neither Tucker nor Ray had hay fever and they drew on the sweet smell of drying timothy. Having little or no dew, it took half the time to dry as on a normal year.

As a pair they worked to prepare the baler. Now hatless, Ray lay underneath searching for places to grease while Tucker stood overhead opening covers and hoods, checking the tightness of bearings, looking for worn plates or grooves in the chamber where the bales were made.

"Can you feel that roller...is it tight?"

"Pretty much."

"Any broken springs?"

"Not any."

A large tin cover caught on its hinge, then wobbled down, and a handful of year-old leaves and powder fell into the neck of the boy's shirt. With a deft roll and stand, Ray pulled the clothing up and over his head, facing away. In the tick of a second, Tucker realized the welts and at once knew their cause. He skipped a breath; immediate to the revelation he decided never to tell Alice. Ducking his brow, he could still see the deep color and raised diagonal stripes across the softness of the boy's loin. He waited for Ray to shake, brush, and redress before turning up. Lean shoulder blades: the knowledge stayed. Through the thin sheerness of the boy's shirt, the marks were inescapable. Purple and blue.

How could he protect? How could they change? Glimpses of the one responsible paraded through his thought. A briefly anchored boat...swaying. Younger and soft and plush...too plush...leaving a trail of hurt.

Tucker now knew, he felt total dispersion to any thought of April's newness——attraction. The flaunting of her resource turned sour, more than flat and gray—*dead.*

Alice would know.

He saw her very familiar arm work its way around, take hold of the boy's waist.

Who *is* healing? Who loves? She *has paid the price, has suffered and needs*—this touch— *triangular embrace*...wife-husband-youth... With an upward, circular reach, his hand came to his hat and tugged at the brim, as if to turn away a flow, the reception of impossibility.

Since the passing of summer solstice, and in the quiet aftermath of road building, Ray began arriving *every* morning without deviation. Early every morning, but Sunday, so shortly after dawn he nearly interrupted their breakfast. Without fail Alice implored that he join them. He refused. In perfect regularity, this refusal dissipated by noon, reservation fell away, and he often ate more than Tucker and herself combined. She caressed the long sunlight of the season, and the guarantee of Ray's coming. Each day seemed to grow in her eyes, in opposition to the deepening drought: a steady graduation, increased relief-pleasure surrounding the boy's help and play and indirect gratitude—until this one. From Tucker alone she caught definite rifts of uneasiness, as if he and the boy had had words of disagreement, a secret and dreaded scene removed from her view and hearing.

Ray had left with the supper hour close at hand, a meal for which she also offered he stay. Alice sat on the porch bench while Tucker half stood and half rested his thigh on the opposite rail. The one raised boot swinging, like a slow and dusty pendulum.

"I went to see Milo." She tucked a wisp of her hair within itself. "I intended to bring home a puppy, without your approval..."

The boot hung, lifeless. Tucker's broad, even dustier hat responded with a gentle tilt.

"I know we shouldn't have a puppy—I wanted more for Ray. I *wanted to give him,* as much as I can—I think I know better...now. Someday soon I'm going to go looking for her...when you two are busy, I'm going to go looking—" She hoped that her mood to confess would spread into him. Alice sat in silence, waiting... "What happened this afternoon? Something happened—as though Ray had said words that somehow cut—"

"Cut?"

Alice watched his brim lower and hide all but his chin, then turn to reveal the profile of his manly brow and sturdy nose, his eyes directed at the fading green of the close yard. "I have come back," she said. "I can feel what we feel together. Are we together?"

"Yes."

"Good."

"But what else do you want to know?" he questioned the grass.

"Did you argue?"

His foot dropped; he stood without bracing against post or rail. Still looking to the side, "We could never argue. I thought I just said I enjoy this time...very much like you." Facing Alice, his mouth closed in preface for a smile that never quite formed. "It is his mother: go looking but don't get close. Let us do what is possible—"

"His mother?" Alice felt herself turning pale, suddenly flooded by the urge to reach out and touch her husband. She left the bench and stepped smoothly over the outdoor floor, feeling starkly near to the width of his shoulders and impressive height.

His hat nodded. "She disturbs him. And. And that disturbs me."

Alice watched his eyes consider her lips.

"Much about her is not good for him. More than I want to accept. Our—*our* part is larger than we know."

Alice rose to her tiptoes as his arms surrounded her. With a mounting clasp and no hesitation, their togetherness transcended to a kiss.

Alice fell quiet, deciding she must give him time, wait for him to reveal in his own way the things going on inside.

* * *

Tucker, with the fast click and hammer of the sickle, led Ray down the valley. Where the clipped hay had paled and was dry enough, the boy towed his rake. Across the creek or up closer to the house, the dog followed the much quieter and less severe tool around and around. In the heat of the day he wet his lower fur in the creek. Weeping and darker, he lay in the shade, never to sleep, but to watch.

Tucker, with his quick, slicing trail of fallen grass, would progress far ahead. After a brief disappearance he returned to follow the boy. The lifting crank and punch of a baler left the stubbled field with long rows and curves of tidy squares. They worked as though partners in the product, a coordination understood. The sky remained so clear and dry, Tucker felt no hurry to build stacks. Still, some days, in the cool of the early morning, he chose to hitch the wagon and they gathered bales. Now Ray could drive and he and the dog rode or walked alongside, filling the trailer. These stacks were for the cattle and were built outside.

Ray began to understand and notice more and more about the cut hay; close to the stream he felt as though he were driving on a mattress. The rake turned without slackness and the crop rolled into a heavy mound. Far out the stems lay like a thin straw covering which the wind could blow away; the teeth freewheeled with a scratch and chatter, lifting at the air. He grew to like haying, even more than making lumber. He remembered the cows chewing, the quieting therapy: this parched, leafy *food* for the close and living.

"We sure getting down the creek fast."

"Without water there is nothing to slow us. We are leaving plenty uncut."

"Will there be enough for the winter?"

"It is too early to say. It will be close."

"Gotta have some rain, soon."

Tucker nodded, watching the faint movement of the boy's lips, recalling the movement of Alice's. Leaving Ray, he turned to the east, eyes skimming the distant and rolling tan hills. Drawn to turn back, he followed the line of the boy's features from under the funny hat. His mind would never tire of this youthful line—tracing nose, mouth, chin—Alice and Tucker's future interest forming more than a shadow, an illusionary mother and father—and then, the trigger to events long gone by... his own youthful eyes watching his father die...Alistair's marble cheeks and forehead resting above the pillow, never ceasing his effort to leave behind some shape of love and guidance.

* * *

At first the grasshoppers were a minor sprinkle about their action. As the weeks passed, they grew dramatically in size and number. Now a teeming presence. When Tucker or Ray drove the road or over the cropped land, it created a bountiful hopping. As they approached the final fields, the hoppers became large and fat, herding, thickening over the ground as though being crowded into their last retreat. Some flew so high they landed on the tractor hoods, quick to leave the baking tin. Others might light on their arms, quick again, a fleeting grip of alien claws.

On a rippling afternoon, not a waver of leaf, Tommie moved from under a tree to the thickness of a bush. He snapped at flies. Ray drove the dried carpet of grass and alfalfa with a bouncing before and around his wheeling machine, like a personal storm of sleet and hail. This particular hay patch had a welcoming feel, almost as though it were a living shape. He was nearing the Voss home, and the row of trees along the water made two graceful bends, like the finish to a bold—most definite...signature. The mowed crop folded and narrowed under the closing hills, their withering slopes more rugged and sudden as they rose from the flat. *Here* is where Ray felt closest to the feet of the mountain. The hay seemed better than anywhere else. Over his own, he could hear the dim race of Tucker's tractor, through the trees and totally hidden. Ray began to sing out loud. He found the words as he rolled along. He caught the dog lifting his ears and knew he was able to hear.

Ray paused, then responded to Tommie by rocking his head back and nearly shouting the words:

O-oh
Oh—I wonder where I'm goin'
I wonder where I've been

It ain't no wonder I'm alive
I got my sight up hi-gh—

A grasshopper hopped from the hot, reflective hood, arching under his hat and into his tipped-back face and open mouth.

Crunch.

He stepped on the clutch and spit. He spit again with pieces caught between his lips and found neutral before wiping. A brown tobacco juice color came back on his hand.

Yee-aawk!

Ray spit in quick succession, then wiped his mouth on his shirt front, tweaking his tongue. Without setting the brake he jumped down. He disengaged and raised the rake teeth.

At this vantage point the dog sat up, as if under an awakening sky.

Ray directed the tractor and implement in a beeline across the center of the field, the most immediate route to the water. Soon he felt an accompaniment trotting behind. In his haste he had not fully set the lever in its notch to hold the rake up. The field was level but the jiggling rake dropped. This jolt downward re-tripped the power to its spin. Of its own accord mechanized lifting came to life and began forming an uneven and jagged windrow, passing the mower swaths and throwing hay in the wrong direction. With the abrupt whirling the collie skipped to the side but did not lose stride. He skipped happily, seeming calmly curious of the destination.

Ray stopped when he came to the outside and proper windrows between his tractor and the creek. He remembered to latch the brake, then climbed down and bounded over the first row: two giant steps, then a leap, again and again, like a man slowly running hurdles and about to lose his hat. This timed jumping stimulated the dog, who proceeded to do the exact opposite, diving *at* the heaps of hay, a confirmed pounce into the fluff as if in pursuit of a rodent. Ray arched over. The dog went through.

Arriving near a thinner tangle of trees and brush, Ray found a path down to the stream. His mouth became too dry to spit any longer.

Perfect, the dog boiled—no mistaking his delight. An excess energy suddenly drove him to look for something—anything to drag or toss.

A fallen log lay from bank to bank, partly damming the flow; Ray knelt by the water and rinsed away the brown stain on his lips and inside his mouth, then drew in the cool of Jasper, his straw brim pushed back but still dipping and parting the current. The misunderstanding dog found a limb and worked in a frenzy to pull it loose. It hung in the nearby willows, then released. Just at the imbalance point of swallowing with his head down, the straining dog jabbed Ray's ribs with a sudden blow. The hat rolled away and floated. He slipped from his ledge and sank headfirst into a shocking chill. He gasped and choked in brief dismay, then sat up, a chilling through his pants. The dog splashed around in front, as if to newly recognize his dripping and shining face.

"You bugger!"

Tommie's ongoing expression of excitement and energy—a ruthless spreading of joy.

Ray grinned and threw water. His companion dodged and smiled back, with a dry nose. Using both hands Ray finally succeeded in dousing the dog. Tommie shouted sharply back with a single bark, then began springing from creekside to creekside with Ray splashing along, trying to catch him in midair.

On the more suffocating afternoons, Alice would hike down the valley with a lunch and something cold to drink. As usual she could hear the struggle of Tucker's tractor, the fast engine, the vague pounding and special click of the sickle. The harvest sound rebounded from the mountain and settled under the trees. This day there was something different: from Ray's engine no more than an idling putter, on and on. Arriving near the fields where they were working, she headed for the slack of his tractor. Through a gap in the water's growth she could see a trail, very distinct. The paling hay was half raked. In the flat center field rose a sloppily etched line tearing crossways over the patterns of the mower. There sat unattended machinery. The trail continued, only now in reverse, a path of broken windrows and scattered hay ending at a local curve in the creek. She laid her sack and containers down, weaved through the brush and vine, stepped through the water, came into the open, and began to run—a sudden distress in her face. She crossed the rows of hay, leaping and keeping in time. Before long she came within earshot, at first with the tension of grave concern, then a gradual slowing of her legs and drop of her arms. Her mouth opened. Above the putter of the tractor she could hear shouts, crisp claims to exasperation, then pealing laughter. She stood still and listened, then shook her head. Leaving the obvious trail, she headed straight for the voice. It had drifted more than two hundred feet, upstream.

Both boy and dog were wet from head to toe, standing partly in muddy sand and partly in water. They were in tug-o'-war with a black and slimy branch. Alice approached quietly, but the truant chaperone must have heard, and released his end of the stick. Ray sat with a splash. The dog froze, as if drinking in her whole presence with a sparkle of welcome. The boy turned up from his soggy position and sparkled too, soaked with embarrassment.

She wavered on the crest of the bank, half in shadow and half in sun. A still and near silence came to the place. Alice folded her arms—feeling the creep of a new discovery—her voice coming clear and calm over the babble of Jasper…

"You have any more merriment and you're going to have a runaway."

Curve of a Talon

They endured a series of sweltering hot days, like he could not find in his memory. Tucker cut down the oats on the high table. The new seed underneath had died. The action of the mower made a fog, not the dust of rust or grain and pollen but that of a fine, unprotected, and baking soil. Recent elk had been along the high edges; very little still stood to cut. In the middle of the field were big open patches, trampled and broken straw, stubble upturned and big pellets of manure to bounce and chatter with the blurred sections of the sickle. He could smell the urine and see crusty stains on the powdery ground. Always marauding at night, the herds were soundless and out of sight for the long heat of the day.

No grain for the coming yearlings.

"Why—why they do that?" asked the boy.

"Fences are nothing. Once they find oats, it is candy. There are too many."

"Why—why they in such *big* bunches?" he asked again.

"No predator, no management. We must harvest now or in days there would be no reason to be here."

"What—what if you shoot one—leave it lay?"

"No."

"I bet—"

"The law won't allow. No..."

Ray kicked the dirt.

"We have to get it brought home, what there is. We must hold our defense...as long as we can."

Hawks soared above the cleared land, swift aerial hunters: expedient takers of uncovered prey.

* * *

Alice struggled with her garden, keeping it green, watering-cultivating-watering. Alone, with Ray and Tucker in the final stages of gathering feed for the winter, watering—the moisture steaming, leaching away nearly faster than she could replenish. She took the house broom to chase out grasshoppers, not to damage plants; the edges of some already riddled with irregular holes. On the nearby dirt or sod, she smashed as many as possible with an aluminum scoop intended for snow. Exercise in frustration: the aluminum began to crack where it attached to the handle, too many repeated and angry slams. She could keep the larger animals out, but the wetness attracted mice and voles. She picked some things well before they were ripe, fearing they might disappear in the night, or get nibbled into sections, or be found like immature fruits cut from their stem and already shriveling. Her efforts still being rewarded—backing away—the diverse rows and sprawling mounds appeared lush, all yet retaining an appearance of defiant success.

Everything was drying too fast and at the same time. The standing nurse crop of oats still had a blue tone. As soon as it lay flat, the whole field became a glossy vanilla with brush strokes of faded purple. Ray could rake the grain into a windrow only hours after Tucker had it mowed. Tucker could bale early the next day.

Dust rose much worse around the rake than the baler. Ray was made to wear a scarf over his nose and mouth. The boy's shape softened and he began to look like a rear-watching bandit, racing to escape capture by the close and galloping cloud— Tucker considered the dog following, with a distinct air of disapproval: not for the dust and noise, but the severe change and covert look to his best friend's face. The corner of every eye filled with dirt. Noses grew tender for the lack of humidity and all the impure air. Shattered straw collected with sweat, having a different and more severe itch and bite than any of the grasses. All along the mountains the sky became stagnant, with a general haze and oppression, begging for a breeze or something to fall and wash it.

Ray went around and around while Tucker bent over the baler on the edge of the field, tools scattered over its main lid; he had replaced its frayed belt and now hunched, adjusting the tension of the chain to drive the knotters.

From nowhere a whirlwind appeared on the far corner of mowed ground. It danced across the field in zigzags and stalls, lifting chaff and stems and a funnel of dirt like a mini tornado. Unknown to Tucker, Ray smiled under his mask until the motion reached his windrows. It rolled a swath of its own and in several places stirred with such force, the row ready to bale disappeared altogether. Ray's eyes turned dark; then the spinning stopped. Only a moment later two more funnels began in different quadrants. They met with their joint debris rising high in the air just before reaching Ray. As though commanded by a spirit, the current relaxed and dropped its load, covering the boy's hat and shoulders with considerable straw and dark gray powder. He blinked and squinted to clear his seeing, wrinkling his covered nose as if about to sneeze. Ray slowed the tractor for a moment, only to bump the throttle even faster for an uphill pull.

Tucker left his work, carrying a water jug and a large rag riddled with holes. Smoke began rising from Ray's machine, as though its engine had failed and suddenly started burning oil. The smoke rose from around the exhaust pipe rather than through it. Just after the boy noticed the smell and a visible puff of heat, a small flame appeared. He quickly set the brakes, jerking all to a halt. As though timing his presence to perfectly coincide, Tucker stood immediate to Ray's tractor and sprinkled water through holes in the hood, looking for a place to punch in the rag. To a fierce sizzle and spew of steam, Ray's hands left the steering wheel and hung, while Tucker brought the roll of event into calm resolve. When reaching around by the boy's knees, to kill the puttering engine, he could see Ray's fingers shaking and a jitter climb into his forearms.

Still facing the tractor controls, he consoled, "You didn't know." Then raising his head and looking into the boy's dark blue eyes, "You didn't know. It would have been all right. The fan helped it ignite, and there wasn't much to burn…almost nothing to burn." Tucker removed one glove and felt the gas tank. "It is just so hot…everything so dry."

Ray's hands pressed outward on the fenders to steady his arms—*slow everything down.*

The next afternoon they worked until almost dark, hauling bales. Half a load remained but Tucker drew the line.

"No more lifting."

"They'll get into it, I know. They *won't* get into it?"

"We will just have to see."

"I stay and get it cleaned up. I will stay."

"Your mother...she will wonder. We cannot telephone."

"My—my mom don't want certain people to reach her." The circle of the well-used hat went down and hid his entire head.

The next morning every single bale was in pieces. Each had suffered an individual explosion, more than broken and spread but stomped and *soiled* on by the elk, like a meditated and vengeful strike.

Ray had had a dream about their return. This view of broken bales had not existed, such destruction too hard to absorb. Dreaming of a lofty platform longing to be hiked, better for a run, running across the high stage even in the dust and chaff, pretending he was flying...Tommie at his side. And here he was, having raked and picked up bales in such a special place—like meant to be. Nothing in his dream made his nose burn or eyes sting, no smoke or flame, no sign of elk to make him angry...

Tucker and the boy pulled chopped strings from the waste, then kicked and scattered the denser lumps. Ray re-raked the confused stems while Tucker re-baled, salvaging what they could for bedding, totally threshed of any grain.

Once again more shaded by the mountain, they returned to the lower valley: the very last field was just as dry or drier. The cool season timothy stood half height with lean, overripe stalks and brown shattered seed heads. Though not much to bale, Tucker enjoyed the cleaner pleasure of the grass hay and the absence of elk sign. They waited for dew but there was none. Hot, Ray began to rake. Tucker checked the windrow and the clover crumbled at his touch. He watched the boy's advance like watching fine, crispy sticks being thrown into a row. The tires of the tractor and implement were too harsh and heavy and left creases in the destitute field. Not yet nine in the morning and he could see parallel ribbons, pressed lines of pulverized leaves the rake could not lift. Tucker waited for the boy to make a turn, then waved for him to stop. They stood in a triangle: boy, dog, himself. He put his foot down on the edge of the brittle row, changing much of it into small crumbs and a chalky green. Even the grasshoppers had lost interest.

"It is disappearing as we work it," said Tucker.

Ray made his own test.

"We will have to leave it for the dew, or rake and bale before sunrise." Tucker turned toward the rampart. "Well before sunrise." He tilted the dirt-coated brim to his hat, then considered the near and unchanging slope of evergreens, dark, with a remaining coolness underneath. "Along the base of the mountain there is moisture in the nighttime. It will soften it. Can you be here when it is not yet light enough to work?"

"No trouble." Ray smiled at the need and bent to pet Tommie. "I can be here, whenever—in the middle of the night." *Overnight...*

"After dinner you go back and sleep. Get here as early as you can."

All night, stay the night...

Ray did not face the man but his hat flopped with a positive nod. His smile toward the dog grew lifeless.

* * *

In the center of the driveway, beside April's car, sat a stranger's truck. Its box had been removed and replaced by a custom flatbed. A chrome exhaust pipe curved up beside the cab as though it were a truck-tractor, a fringe of satin-like soot at its beveled tip. Without a standard box the vehicle looked stubby and light on the rear end. The driving mud and snow tires had severe tread but no weight to hold them down.

Ray laid his bike out in the suffering grass, well away from the sheen of cars. He gave the different-looking truck one last glance, then skipped up the narrow, deserted steps to his house. The door swept in without sound to a hot stuffiness, a smell of strange smoke like burning weeds, and the sight of living space in more disarray than usual. Knife to the vision: the sofa torn apart and on the floor a man's nude backside in the air, stroke of buttock and leg cut by the wearing of cowboy boot, thick neck and shoulders, black curly hair, faceless panting. Flash to an unwilling eye: his mother's lower plumpness and clutching feet raised on a collection of cushions and pillows—

Never seeing a face he turned and began to run…through the burnt, empty pasture behind the trailer, intent for a reason, a crowning ache and crushing fear of the truth. Over a random horizon he inhaled, then chose a course—the beginning to a draw—to slowly lose height. As the draw deepened the bushes started. Short and coarse and gnarled, they pulled at his baggy pants and shoes like crooked and boney hands. Colonies of oak brush gathered and grew taller.

The scene would not leave him alone: the glistening *nakedness*.

Finally in shadow, overgrown, he discovered a secret maze of alleys. Faster and faster he chose one, then another. The slope cut sharply and the bramble thickened. This dark passage narrowed and suddenly ceased yet he plunged on, unforgiving oak snagging all the parts to his clothing, clawing his unprotected face, ripping both fabric and weeping skin. He dove on, gasping and fighting as if to escape a mortifying snare. His hands reaching and swimming—quickly drew back and pressed on his eyes. Abrupt as the memory, he fell, then lay still: half suspended in the brush, puffing and accepting like a dying rabbit.

Long after the sun had gone, Ray secretly gathered his bike to pedal away... He waited on the hilltop in the moonless dark, walking his worn tires from one sandy limit to another. Through the blackness he could distinguish elk sounds scattered in the valley, faint mews and low grunt-like whistles. The night was warm yet his body shivered. He did not think of the hay.

The light would not come.

Tucker, after their early morning act of love—reach for *connection*—rose in the dark to depart for the fields. Hesitant, he turned to tenderly cover Alice's graceful spine and bare shoulder. She had nearly fallen asleep.

A glow came in the east and almost at once, Ray could see the elk, many with antlers, the darkness of the crowd milling, then grouping and slowly vanishing under the shelter of big timber: large numbers, power in the black of night. He watched them creep at the edge of fields, moving so slowly like cold-laden bees, a strange talk, low chant. He remembered their smell, like the smell of disease. With the swelling light a fresh worry landed in his mind, an understanding: the hay, the pastures, the fences. The crawling, consuming throng dug at him without relief. "They don't *leave nothin'*," he whispered. With a mounting disturbance, Ray watched...attack...on a home.

Like a wink in the night, sudden yellow shone from the protected house.

The elk moved no faster. Their leisure prickled and pulled like a jeering, an invitation for vengeance. At the very moment the last one disappeared from the mowed land, Tucker's pickup started. With a soft rumble from the peaceful yard and no headlight, it parted the seeming slumber of the valley, heading for the field Ray still wanted and needed to rake.

Almost time, a cobalt darkness on the west side of the world.

He steadied his bike. The elk were reappearing. They had crawled up under the canopy to hide, like guerrilla soldiers. Some re-entered the hay land, but most continued their climb, filling the lower edges of the table…from where they had just hauled straw. They kept joining and filling, covering the pale, high bench. Over the faint drone of the truck and its lone driver, Ray could hear talking again, distant chirps through the slow air. The numbers were huge, a mocking flow of darkness, as if with the approaching day, armies were joining, herds of *anything* bigger than he had ever seen.

He shuffled in the shop, without need to open his eyes. No light fell on any of the space in which he walked. His small, nimble fingers found the zipper to its case, opening to the inside padding and the unforgettable smell—feel—of steel together with wood, cool and polished. He lifted it out, touching the trigger, this time with a firm grip, no longer the fumbling child. He blindly rooted and found shells in the coat hanging by the door.

Once outside and able to see and aim—a loud crack through the early morning air and the elk veered this way and that, but slowed to a thick stirring and remained in the open.

Crack, boom! He shot again and they split into battalions. Ray wove and staggered. His shoulder throbbed. He heard a slamming from the house.

Alice now hurriedly wore nothing but a long white robe, marching with naked feet and it flying about her legs like the skirts to a fluorescent dress. With the dim, angular light, her face felt pointed, long hair tightly pinned, harshly bound. In blurred, uneasy transformation slender hands appeared—reaching, shaking—for more than a gun. Ray sorely handed it to her, struggling to get the stock off the ground, his bruised collar obviously tucked and burning as if with fire.

"Where did you get the shells? This is not for you."

"I found them in his coat—coat pocket—the shop—"

"You knew, didn't you?" Her shaking didn't calm.

"There're hundreds of them…hundreds… It's meant to be saved."

She turned upward and found the elk in utter dominance of her favored place, facing the yet-to-rise sun. They were leaving, milling in shabby and unhurried formation. She felt the hardness of the gun—battalions—her body stiffened.

"Alice," he said.

Her posture relaxed, the one time he had called her by first name.

"I'm sorry."

In weak illumination she caught a difference to his face, the hint of claw marks. "There's blood…" She laid the rifle on the ground.

As though just remembering he touched his own cheek and his eyes *were* changed. "I ran through some bushes."

She took his shoulder gently and turned him toward the shine from the house. The cuts were not deep. She pulled a tissue from her robe pocket and tried to carefully wipe; she felt an overwhelming need to use the moisture from within her own mouth; the wonder blooming, louder and louder, a shouting of doubt and anguish, taunting her suddenly steady hand: Did *she* do this to him? Scratch from the curve of a talon.

Dry Thunder

With the narrower boards Tucker and the boy built hay panels. Now bone-dry, several boards had their grain burred up as if with a fur of splinters. Some bore a smoother appearance but long, sharp needles were hidden along the edges; now and again one would puncture the leather of Tucker's gloves or the weave of his pants. The sting lingered, as if from the touch of some poisonous tentacle. He used the bed of the hay trailer as a platform. He laid the lumber out flat and nailed it together in a sawbuck fashion. He gave the boy a hammer. Each board was spaced two inches from the other. Once the first two were made, Tucker worked without the use of a rule; he used two six-foot pieces as a pattern and straight edge, marking with a thick wooden pencil. The floor of the wagon served as the square. Tucker laid out a dozen or more boards and cut them to length in a single pass.

Whack-tap-whack. Whack-tap-whack. Tap-tap.

As if viewing from the side—he could see the two of them, stooped, performing on a worn stage with only one in the audience: different speeds, different sounds. The dog watched with a distracted interest, uneasily changing from one shaded place to another.

Whack-tap-whack—tap.

Tucker considered this four-legged walk, a flexed neck, craned slightly as though the collie were suffering a bellyache or concern they were building multiple coffins, some pain in the sound.

Whack whack. Tap tap.

They had to be wary of splitting the ends to the bitterly dry wood. Tucker realized again the change in the boy's face—more damage, the growth in his arms—and clipped the edge to his thumb through the padding of his glove. There had been many questions, private thoughts of asking for help.

I ran through some bushes.

I ran through some bushes.

* * *

"We have to DO something... There must be something," said Alice.

He looked down at the dust-rimmed hat which he held in his lap.

"If only someone could witness, make things right. He belongs in a different place. He belongs in a place—"

Tucker stood and loomed over the table. He took his index finger and drew an indefinite pattern on its empty surface. "We need some rain."

"We could work to have him taken away."

For one count Tucker's eyes closed and his lips parted. "This is tough." *Wedged between boy and parent.* "And the girl— What will happen?"

"Tough? *I* know tough." Alice shook her head, then paused, only to repeat this negative shaking with increasing surety.

"She has no place," he responded.

Alice quivered. "You said it was too late."

"We could misstep and instead of open a door, close one. All there is now could be taken away… I remember too well…other times."

"What if they move? I need to find out."

"Let him get older…"

"She lives without a phone. They could pack overnight."

"We need some rain," he said—as if under the hover of a superstition.

"Rain?"

"This is not a thing easy or even possible to do. Surely you know what I want."

She pressed the table with a new resolve. "He is abused, I know it."

"Yes. Yes."

"I can—can I make an appointment with George, George Taylor?"

"If Ray were just a little older." Tucker made a motion as if he intended to put his hat on, then swung his arm down. "This drought breaks, we get some rain to bolster our fortune— We get some rain, then we will talk to the town attorney."

She studied his face in misunderstanding, bewildered by a trailing hardness, layers in his message. *We were apart too long*, she thought.

Tucker stroked his own cheek. He knew the depletion of springs, a drying land. He felt himself searching—reaching through the past, groping for a lost abundance—so that he could stand steadfast, choose a future course and shape a plan.

"We should not wait long," she said.

He stepped away from the table.

She stirred in stress and looked up to the broad shoulders. His wrists were crossed and the hat dangled from an unseen hold.

Then she recognized, knew, the shared memory of doing without ingrained in his eyes and the pose of his chin. She saw the stance of a lone man inside his own house, arms remiss and hands bound. An imprint of a boy to carry life forward crossed his face. Each of them a prisoner. *Prisoners*...of loss and hope.

She felt a force, a vague but strong turning within herself, turning—to reenter their home.

"We should not wait too long," she said, more softly.

* * *

The hay panels measured six feet by six feet, and they wired them together to make a snug square around two complete stacks, then ran out of lumber. Further up the canyon from the mill, Tucker selected more trees. He lopped the brush that Ray scattered and made all that he could into twelve-foot logs. With the tractor he skidded the logs in groups, then milled them one by one. Alice loaded the new wet boards, heavier but a damp pleasure next to the earlier bent ones—so stiff and dished.

Each day, passing the cropped fields they could see more and more sign: elk feces and broken stubble, the greening regrowth over the sub-irrigation getting shorter and shorter. The last day at the sawmill, they discovered tracks in the old dust over the bank.

The nails now sunk easily and the project acquired a completely fresh sound. Tucker's and Ray's faces grew speckled from the squirt of sap as hammer heads met and compressed the distinction of strangely wet wood. Alice didn't pound any but kept the bright boards laid out and the tins full of nails. When a section was complete, she flopped it from the trailer and pulled it over the resistant ground to the nearby hay. She cut repeated lengths of wire for tying the newly made cage together. Their stock of feed was a fraction of normal. Soon every blade and stem was shielded by rough staves of perfectly matching height.

They rearranged the horse hay in the loft of the Voss shed, jamming it up between the rafters, packing it tighter than ever, leaving an empty ledge, a buffer of security from tall and rearing animals. Tucker envisioned bales tumbled down, torn apart, and wasted more than eaten. There was no room for waste.

With a short lull in their thrust, the crew stood back and rested. The weight of the drought and other things stood at their side.

With more satisfaction than the others, Ray admired the work. He put his hands on his hips and the dog tried to root and bump them down.

"It should be safe now. Nobody can reach. *No-body.*"

Alice stepped into the shadow thrown by the vacant barn. "We've done our best."

Tucker rolled his shoulder and rubbed the back of his neck.

"Them stacks up the valley, they've all got pens around—we've got an armor up."

The man spoke. "We have never had everything put up so early. We will have to watch. With enough determination, that protection could still get broken down."

* * *

Late one evening a change overtook a corner of the sky, a forgotten mood. Clouds formed and joined together. They began to darken and cluster just above the rampart.

This strange notion of rain made Tucker and dog leave the yard, all the buildings. In the gloaming he walked onto an incline of uncut hay. Droughty, his boots crunched a path. Tucker stood in the open and inhaled the chances, having a secret belief exposure would help the odds. Both he and the dog heard a rumble. A drip or two fell on their heads and about their feet, no further change in the scent of the coming night.

Much too soon he saw a break to the west, a fan of dusty sun over the distant ranges, the darkening now from the day's end and not from an approaching wet.

The next evening was a repeat. The thought of rain came earlier and there were several glimmers high in the cloud. Following the previous trail they went out again. Elk caught his attention, a horde still far up the mountain but visible through the thinner trees of the rugged and rocky crests, returning from the steepness. Tucker squinted and the dog held his nose to the air. This herd announced no glamour—symbol of the sovereign—greed, imbalance, too much for the limited pasture. The sky flickered without sound.

He twisted the stiffness in his neck and came back to the valley. Among many shadows of relief, he soon placed the stack yards: the distinct outline of large square mounds, the valley's gold. Tucker thought of them as brimming cubical baskets of perishable eggs. The clouds brewed with a delicate foaming. Lightning struck at a horizontal high, and it rained in a quick, thin sheet, then stopped. The dog blinked. Tucker's hands stroked the faint dampness in the cloth over his arms.

They awoke in the dark of the morning to close flashes and loud crackles of thunder. At first Alice lay touching him and they rested, shoulder to shoulder, welcoming the sound. It continued too near, a flashing, as if an immense curtain of dry static and no rain on the roof. The softness of shared repose—transformed into a knot of anxiety until each strike made them wince. Between rumbles the dog's feet came down the hall, then turned at their door and went away. The turmoil shifted. Without light in the house Tucker rose, the break of day still an hour away. He looked from the window and even then could see a darker plume in the sky, departing smoke from a molten and fluctuant source, as if its heat reflected in his face.

"Fire."

Tommie was at the door again and Alice let him in, then stood at the window quickly tying her robe.

"I'll get the disk. You bring water and feed sacks and shovels. It's the third stack. At least it is away from the trees."

"Is there wind?"

"No."

In undershirt and pants and boots, Tucker backed the tractor into the tall and snapping grass where the implement was hidden. Partly by feel he pinned the hitch and connected the hoses. He wore no hat or gloves, and his hands came back oily and blackened. Soon big smears crossed his chest, a matching sign on his face. He sat the tractor and with more snapping and tearing raised the disk from its moorage. Wondering if the tires were sound, he headed from the buildings and into the open of his memorized fields. The dog followed.

Alice, in her robe and riding boots, loaded milk cans into the pickup and filled them with water using the garden hose. While they were filling she ran to gather sacks from the granary and shovels from the shop. Deciding whether or not to dress, she studied the sky. The smoke was dying. The light of day stole from the light at the fire's base. She ran to the house. She returned with her gloves and the belt from her jeans added to her waist. Her nervous hands secured the lids over the water. She sat in the truck. Before starting the engine she gave one last listen to the sound of Tucker way out in front—determined pulling, still without a load. The air current had changed and for the first time Alice could smell the burning.

Tucker and the dog, with a rolling noise and swaying implement, arrived at the short but significant pile, a radiant phosphor of intense heat. He saw few flames and not a single remnant to the wooden panels, no sticks, nothing but an inferno of lumps and pulsing ash.

"Thank God for the calm."

Without pause Tucker allowed the disk down to cut and chew and began his circle of the fire. In the sunless light he scanned the outer limits for any more smoke or glitter. He drove close enough to turn his face ruddy and the bare arm on that side. He felt the hood of the tractor and widened his repetitive loop. The collie mimicked this circling, at a safe and cooler distance; the incandescence from the coals made his collar look orange. More than tucked, his tail had disappeared. Tottering ash caved and brought a smatter of sparks. Tucker tipped his head in habit as though he yet wore his standard of shelter.

"Thank God for the calm."

Around and around, quick to destroy the crust of grass and leaven a flour-like soil with the power of machine, he sat upright. A dust pursued and hovered, indefinite lines to the trailing night.

Alice arrived and at once stood in the back of the truck preparing wet sacks. In one leap the dog cleared the tailgate, joining her, two parties rocking in a troubled skiff. As if by a miracle, all movement of air expired. A dozen burlap bags lay over the sides of the pickup, streaming and unused. As quickly as it began, her work ceased. With hanging damp hands she watched the last of the food burn, shrink, and fall. Tommie's fur reached above the rim of her boots, a welcome friendliness to her lower legs. Her lap was wet.

One loosened end to her robe's tie dripped like the burlap and dangled with the weight of a cold and lifeless tail.

In the dawning Tucker looked down the valley to the next yard, a huge picturesque cube without space or security between it and the row of trees along the stream. When his churning of the ground came nearest to Alice, he shouted:

"Good thing this is the one."

"Thank God for the calm!" she returned.

The sun rose. The disk made a wide, continuous firebreak like a puffed-up racetrack, leaving nothing to consume. The tractor idled a moment, then came to a total rest. Alice and Tucker sat on the tailgate, drooped in exhaustion from the throb of adrenaline. The dog sat behind them. Dust toned the whiteness of Alice's robe and took the shine from her cheeks. Dirt from the pickup left lines and smudges. Tucker's white arms and bare, darkened hands flexed, then relaxed. Their hair now a matching dull, Alice took hold of his nearest wrist.

Ray heard the tractor from the beginning of the lane, its low strain somehow glancing from the mountain and winding through the hills, a faraway and muted pull. Halfway and the threat drifted to his nose. He pedaled faster. Coming down the last hill, he could place the pickup and tractor and the missing stack, the perfect oval of farming and its black center like a slanted and ragged bull's-eye. Smoke and dust settled in the valley. He dodged the softness behind the shop and ignored the house yard.

By the time he arrived, only a few small heaps were smoldering, like the telltale remains to a completely devoured building. The heat from earlier had breached the square line of panels and burned the surrounding field in sags and fingers until reaching the vacant dirt. The event was over, exhausted.

As an oddity—the dog remained in the truck.

Ray rode up alongside and dropped his bike.

"Will there be enough hay?"

"Likely not."

All felt the lingering static. The storm had come and consumed their work, then passed with only a patter of rain, leaving a slow spinning, the dynamo—on coast.

Graffiti

From several places in the valley, they could hear trucks and vans, faint accelerations, and the trivial echo of smaller engines. Tucker quickly located the sound and recognized some kind of schedule, climbing and coming down the mountain. Alice and Ray were able to follow, with questions of concern, the miniature vehicles causing a boil of dirt and a distant but penetrating drone. For a week and a half, the tiny carriers ascended midmorning and came down early afternoon.

Conditions were desperate. In the deepest cool shade of the forest, even the ferns and sedges were wilting.

As suddenly as it came, whatever the purpose, the activity ceased and the road once again fell quiet.

In celebration for this return to a feeling of privacy, the foursome attempted a holiday. The pickup entered the canyon. Leaving its narrow floor, the truck made the same shadowy ascent as only fifteen days earlier, to bring home the last of the straw, only now they had *Alice,* Ray in the middle, Tommie in the back. The trail was shaded but not cool. Early on their way up, they discovered pawing and rubbing on the banks of the high side. Definite elk tracks. Sticks and loose rock had tumbled down and into the wheel ruts. Behind the cab the dog propped on a wheel well and his nose gave a rhythmic search. Both windows rolled further down to an odor much stronger than deer. The collie shifted from side to side in the open box, bumping and folding Ray's empty hat with an increasing excitement, obviously anxious to reach the familiar field—the possibility of another infraction. Closer to the bright opening, they found new-generation spruce and aspen, many recently mangled, as though by some broken and flailing machine. Random Christmas tree spruce had a foul nettle of crushed and torn limbs; several were to die, for their trunks were split and broken and their symmetrical tops pointed downward: weeping sap. At the edge of the sunlit bench, bigger aspen had large bites taken from stems of cleanliness. Saplings had their middle bark and branches stripped, shreds hanging, pieces drying and shriveling in their disconnection.

"They sure been here," Ray couldn't help but say.

Tucker frowned. "Sharpening horns, now the oats is gone."

"Like they are confined with nothing to do." Alice's shoulders seemed to stiffen as she turned away from the evidence. They drove onto the whitish and ruined crop of grain. "This is my favorite place."

"It got me—I got me dreams about it."

"You see all over."

Ray had never told anyone about his dreams. Letting one out, his heart began to flutter.

"The farming, nurse crop without result" was all Tucker said.

Like a runaway—Ray's feelings. "Ain't it like looking down on the snake-snake of a creek and the treetops sprawling up like vegetables—"

"Cauliflower, broccoli," Alice interrupted.

Ray's mood turned uneasy. An odd tingling spread from his hands to his forearms, never before told. "I remember sittin' on a mighty high bleacher and you see way far out, squint and see farther... This is better, like looking down over a hill and down—down into a perfect world."

Alice's eyes closed for a second, and Ray thought he felt a tremble somewhere inside her neatness, her pleasant presence.

They felt a motion behind the cab, and his hat was flipped upside down.

"That Tommie, he wants to get down." Alice's eyes again opened...she smiled.

"He ready to run."

Tucker paused, as though not quite sure of a choice. Ray watched as his boot pushed the clutch in. He thought they were going to park and hike. Ray saw the pedal then lift and the truck continued moving. There stood very little for the tires to harm, as if rolling over a shell, a pale dead skin. With little bounce, they rolled softly across the sloping field toward the fixed fence, the fading picture of a bad afternoon, bloodied friend. His arms would not stop tingling. The treetops Tucker had sawn up for Ray to scatter were already turning reddish brown, each strand of barbed wire freshly stretched and still stapled. Beyond this tidy repair lay jackstraws of wood and root, some kind of *big* tractor had scraped and rolled it, trying to comb the tangle and flatten the mess. He could see the small rise of new dirt at the foot of the post, which he had tamped.

He felt everyone look up, the fill of the new road tumbled down around rock and thin stripes of leftover bark and needle, leaves of oak brush, dark but weak lines from the old ground. The close, dam-like heap had settled into humps and bumps. Ray couldn't find any plant on the wide scar, but in one small pocket, a pale and splotchy growth of weed he could not name. His eyes tripped at the edge of the embankment over an aluminum can, shining like a speck of chrome.

"Why they do that?"

Ray knew that someone had slowed and stopped on the curve above, overlooking the Sisters—not to admire but to unload. There was more. A short length of toilet paper fluttered among the clods beside a splintered and dingy log—reminding his chest to pump. A paper bag had caught against their newly spliced fence as though hung out to dry, Styrofoam meat trays, empty plastic wrappers balanced in the undergrowth, waiting for the wind.

He watched Tucker leave the truck and slip on his gloves. The man bent over and gathered. Everyone else sat in hesitation, then finally joined him. All of them, combing the brush and under the trees, Alice climbed through the fence and found another sack with things inside; she did not open. Ray found a roll of plastic ribbon: bright pink and much unraveled in thinner tufts of grass and browse. He lifted it to show while the dog sniffed over the trailing ends.

"What's this?"

Tucker frowned—again. "Flagging, for marking borders or new roads." His gloved hands tightly wadded the wrinkled bag. "It fell from a pocket." Ray followed Tucker's eyes as they covered the ground more carefully. Near the fence they found drips of paint, a flat, thick orange, lichen color. "Yes. *That is it*: tree paint." Ray could no longer see Tucker's face for the broad hat, and the words grew muffled. "They have been marking timber, preparing a sale."

"This ain't the right side." Runaway feelings, tingling hands. "This ain't the right side."

Crawling through the fence had made the paint gun leak. It left a trail through the shorter brush toward the edge of the field. Tucker, their leader, followed. The dog bounced around in front of him and found the scent of paint *and* foot. Soon the bright speckles became very sparse but the dog did not stop or slow down.

Alice called out, "Where are you going?"

Ray had also passed Tucker but turned to call back, "We found a track."

He couldn't wait anymore and went after Tommie until he, too, was high on the slope. The dog was quick to get far ahead. Ray stopped again, pacing over the bleached high, jerking his arms, the ribbon flying up and down as if accent to a frustrated cheer. All on foot, Ray second and much later led them in a string from short to tall. He couldn't hold back; his excitement began to pound. He had to struggle with staying slow. Ray kept looking to the rear, clearly asking them to hurry. He and Alice and Tucker headed directly for the two spires: in such nearness like giant spirits—almost frightening—as though just under their surface, somehow living and about to talk, words spoken from shaded ledges, creaking and cracking to break the stillness. Their scout and tracker disappeared in the undergrowth: bushes and trees as if with a purpose, hiding some massive footing.

At last everyone caught up and Tucker whistled. The collie reappeared and led them around the thick brush and young trees. It was too close and too late. The dripping orange again—now the color of something foul and rotting—puny for the rock and close to the ground yet as high as could be reached and obvious to the road above. Someone had drawn a crude and magnified outline on each great column: private *man* parts—swollen and raised and pointing at the valley.

On and on.

Everywhere.

"Sons a bitches. Sons a bitches."

Ray backed into Alice, wrenching wan eyes, seeing her open, susceptible face. He dropped the tangle of flagging: again, with a definite hope of running away. Tommie dove quickly to loop out and catch, but the boy dodged and kept gaining speed. On the third try the dog tripped him. With sure, reaching strides, Tucker overcame them and pulled him to his feet. Ray squirmed as though his large hands were terrifically unwanted.

"Now, son—now, son—"

Alice came to touch and he fell into her kneeling front with one sob, gripping. She stroked his head and shoulders. The collie stood on tiptoe. Alice wrapped her arms around him. Ray could feel-hear the creaking of Tucker's boots as he placed them in a wide stance. Turning, seeing him take off his hat, his big frame curving down as though to lift, as though to curl his hands and fiercely grip something deeply rooted in the earth—too long and twisted—standing close and tall like a moving and silent statue of all their troubles.

His eyes met Tucker's.

From this new place on the burnt field, the embarrassment was hidden.

Ray shook with two lung-filling breaths, then stopped. The things—new cares that the spring and summer had taught him—returned, his close interest like a post, brace to keep him from falling. He felt Tucker watching as he tipped back, seeing the faces of the rock towers and the sturdy, unbelievable green higher on the mountain. The collie nuzzled his ear and Alice gently loosened her arms. Ray's small hand took hold of Tucker's. He came to his feet.

"You do so much...you know so much for this land."

The Crossing

Almost a year without a meeting, Alice began to discover—*hear*—more about April, from sources other than Milo and Joyce: at the grocery, at the post office, in the hardware, the north-side Conoco—even the Ranchers Feed & Seed, as if voices specific for her ears, in warning, consideration, ringing.

—I swear

—Got to be a devil

—There's her need, and there's *her* need

—You feel that dark web

—Hay hooks for the boys

—And men

—I wouldn't leave her...to work in my store

—Let her wait tables...the kitchen of consumption

No one spoke overtly about Ray.

Except the elderly Helen at the drugstore counter.

You're going to help him. He is beginning to grow up. I am most sure you are feeding him.

—As much as I can.

The boys at the lunch fountain...

—She ain't all *that* pretty

—What a *chunk*

—Until she gets close and *breathes* on you

Without an encounter Alice learned more than a rumor of her size and shape, the color of her hair and eyes, held an incomplete picture of her inappropriate habits. There welled no trust. April was never seen with her own child.

Surely, Tucker felt the same. The man of her marriage had to—have decided.

—A *me* person

—In pursuit of pleasure

—She told me I had fish breath

—She called me a tiger

Across the street and in the bank parking lot, Alice took notice of a short, round figure talking with a tall young man. At first she realized more the boy for his gaunt height, his stiff brown hair burred up and flat in the back as if it hadn't been combed after a hard sleep. He waved his hands in agitation. He stood like a slight bent stick, peering down and unhappy. The young girl circled closely. Alice suddenly knew. She went up the street, erasing all errands from her mind, and crossed at the stoplight to head back—maybe another look. Only a peek. The sidewalk felt far too immediate. Before the solid brick edge of the mercantile, she lost courage and reversed in her steps, retracing them to the corner and the far side of the street, hurriedly, as though she were now late to catch a bus. In safer view, again divided by the rare passing of a car or pickup, she discreetly considered the paved opening and the two young people. Alice stood, pretending to fumble for an item in her pocketbook. She was breathing hard and had difficulty staying in balance. She felt her heart racing, determined to see one thing.

Now the boy was smiling broadly and reaching for the much shorter girl. With an obverse tactic, *April* retreated in a zigzag over unused lines and vacant blacktop. Her auburn hair flowed from side to side, noticeably thick and shining and covering much of her face. The boy kept missing his attempt to touch a wrangling shoulder.

For a moment Alice's nonaggression took control. She quickly folded her small handbag and began to leave. She heard the young man's higher voice and curious laugh, then the huskiness of the girl. She felt certain any close contact with *talk* and she would lose… A deep commitment gradually welled, returning. Standing for an instant straight and stable, making little judgment, her role must go on.

In one of the girl's teasing sweeps, dark, proud eyes were uncovered. The wealth of hair fell away, the attention on the tall boy. She encountered the stricken statue of Alice standing all alone. At a very great distance, Alice felt they were seeing *into* one another, sealed with a frank, unflinching recognition. At once Alice knew the argument of crossing; she felt the cruel and narrow path, the utter disappointment like a prophesy.

She must harden up.

With a different wave through her breast, she remembered his words: Something happened. *Long ago*—or didn't happen. Who was the teacher? What was the parent?

In the lapse, the young man succeeded in getting a hand on each shoulder and swiftly bent to kiss April. His body concealed her face and shattered the contact. Only one—the only person watching could imagine the purpose, the upcoming evasion of cause and cost. Before the kiss was over Alice had scurried away and the incident remained…untold.

Water on Wheels

The well pump for the house began to suck air. Watering the garden, the groping trees, and futile grass to keep them from dying was too much demand. Alice and Ray were not keeping up. A hot wind blew, stirring past leaves and particles of soil. Tucker watched as the leftover sawdust drifted from its pile. Drying, catching in the brown curling, it collected in any depression or scorched rut until the wind blew harder. Sawdust lined the shop footing and hid around parked tires. When the truck or tractor drove away, the wheel marks disappeared like a mirage of moisture. One end of the yard began to have a strange woody smell, baked and sifted, graying and mixing with the dirt, misplaced granules from another life. Transported crumbs from the sawmill scampered away.

With a tractor and chain, Ray dragged an empty fuel oil tank to the work area before the shop. Tucker had set the intention—to build their own water-hauling fire engine. He and the dog followed the scrape and drumming as it slowly skidded and bounced over the uneven sod, leaving a skid mark. This indentation led back to the closed gate of the solid board fence: the ranch's junkyard, in Tucker's mind, the wooden wall to guard the secrecy of things broken, left behind. The pipe legs of the rusted fuel oil tank, nearly a three-hundred-gallon capacity, had been unscrewed and left behind.

Tucker, after twisting the cap off, turned the tank up, and Alice stood on a stool to pour a steaming bucket of detergent water into its extended opening. Ray brought a large tin funnel. Tucker took a spade and searched for the coarsest sand at the bottom of the lane. The boy balanced the funnel and Tucker reached up to pour the dry sand from the spade. Dust floated like a faint drift of odor. Tucker watched: the boy had no need to tap or shake, for it descended easily, as if through the polished restriction in an hour-glass.

"We don't want the water to be tainted."

"I understand," said the boy.

"This should work."

"I understand."

The lid was put back. With all hands they rocked and twisted the now weighted tank in a unified effort to be abrupt and quick and keep the coarseness suspended. Tucker watched the leaks around the cap foaming and bubbling. Tommie circled closely with his ears twitching. The rough, weathered steel rolled up with white scuff marks and swirls. At last, Tucker lifted it up on blocks. As before, *everyone* helped empty the well-used contents back into Alice's bucket. Tucker considered the sudsy gray with many dark flecks, a slight film of oil and cream of cleanser. They rinsed using another mixture, then twice with water only. Each bucket of waste Tucker took to a new location, flinging it several times in thin swags, watching it sink in the hot sand of the ended lane.

Tucker had Ray hitch and bring up the work wagon, while he measured and cut two timbers. He toenailed the timbers to the wooden bed at a spacing to stabilize the tank. The tank was mounted upright and chained. He put a cheater on the binder, and the chain drew so tight, he watched dents being made in the wood. Tucker bolted a small gasoline engine and water pump to a short, wide plank. The plank was then lagged to an empty corner of the trailer. He instructed Alice and Ray to lay out used pipefittings on the other side and arranged them with a plan to most efficiently attach a suction and pressure hose. This arranging seemed to take a very long time. The dog hopped onto the bed, poking faces, and caused fittings to roll off and into the dirt.

"You bugger."

"We work together," said Alice.

"What a help," said Ray.

"Get down…" He watched the collie jump to the ground, not understanding his sudden tone of authority.

With rough boards Alice and Ray built a border around the two coils of hose to prevent them from undoing or bouncing to the ground. Tucker fabricated a suction screen from a cut-off piece of pipe, hose clamp, and folded hardware cloth in the shape of a party hat. He made a spray nozzle from a large pipe plug drilled with many holes. Alice and Ray loaded the milk cans in the back of the truck and had them tied and filled with water before securing the lids. A discarded coffee can served as a dipper, and he bent the lip so it would pour more easily into the orifice to prime the pump. Tucker felt that the pickup was overflowing. It carried water and shovels and sacks and axes and saws—bottles of fuel and oil and boxes of tools—extra coats and hats and worn-out gloves—additional rope and chains and another length of hose. The rake tractor towed the water wagon. It was far too light but the heavier tractor rested, reserved for other needs.

He considered the truck with the tractor behind towing the wagon. A two-vehicle, three-people-and-one-dog irrigation and firefighting machine.

They pumped the clear, cold water of Jasper Spring and sprayed or flooded the garden, a modest area around the house:

trip after trip. Tucker drove the tractor. When loaded and the water sloshed, the front end would lift or skid. With a mild sense of panic, he used the individual brakes to guide, as if they were steering clutches. He could see Ray and the collie squatted in the pickup box, bracing on the many supplies and smiling at his finesse.

The close yard took on a cooler smell of displaced wetness. The house trees and shrubs grew more limber while those around the shop and barn and other buildings rattled and scraped and splintered in the ceaseless wind. Crispy green and brown-fringed leaves began to fall and collect in crumbs like the sawdust. While one end of the yard declined, the grass before the step turned soft and revived, as if nourished by an unearthly wine and mineral, water from the invaluable flow at the foot of the near ridge.

Elsewhere they began to walk only in paths, preserving the skeleton of the year's grass. Even the dog's tail seemed to wilt and shrink. On the lower portions of his coat, his cleanliness dried and wore out. Everyone looked as though they walked in a low cloud, and sometimes they did, but often this dullness was no more than a clinging and imbedded remnant of broken and lifted fines.

The east hills had suffered most, the least relieved from sun or wind. They had no life-giving stream and almost no tree. Every dugout and dam had turned into a cracked and hardened pockmark. Short but still thick, the different grasses rippled with a contrary mood, as though hurting and stiffened by a sudden old age: desiccated cloaks over the dust of centuries.

"We are going to sell down the herd."

"*A-awh,*" the boy complained.

"No question."

"Do the neighbors have hay?"

"Only enough for themselves, or less."

"You won't sell—sell the red calf?"

Tucker considered the boy and pondered a moment... "No."

The wind shifted and struck the ridge with such strength and persistence, it raised silt from between the root clumps. It shifted again. This sifting back and forth became a cutting action, a motion endowed with knives. Invisibly the grasses fell like miniature trees and flew into the sky. More and more rock became apparent.

The jewel of the park grew smaller. The remaining loops and low-lying places of green were heavily bruised and overgrazed by the many dependents, appetite without pause. The obvious patches of clover endured—a strangling, boundaries slowly receding. More and more the only things green were the trees and bush.

"You ever seen it this way before?"

Tucker's security, familiarity: peeling away, evaporating when in separation from the heart and its artery—Jasper Spring—save the house yard and the everlasting shelter of the mountain; the steep shimmering in aridity but staying a blue-green, a comfort of sameness.

"It has been dry before. I do not remember anything near this."

For a single day's use, Tucker reattached the mower. Ray was carefully told how it worked and the danger. He was directed to cut swath after swath. The tinder-dry grass fell in a circle to completely encompass the homestead. He did just as he was told around the ditches and stumps. Tucker pulled the dump rake, which Alice rode, and they combed the uneven slopes outward. They left a gray, closely clipped hill. They built small loose rows of drab stems, for the wind to blow.

"Don't it make sense to mow more—mow more at the other place?"

"It is so dry now, we could spark a fire. The timber there is too close."

"What about graze?"

"You are right. We will do that. Soon. It looks as though we will be bringing them soon. Cattle mow without noise, and we control where they go."

Alice agreed with a haggard nod.

Tucker inhaled her expression, with a quick translation: when—when did the land last truly drink? He almost took her hand, for Ray to see. *It must... It will...*

They hauled more water. Tucker hoped to restore a broader area around the house and reach some of the other buildings. They dampened down humbling patches of colorless grass. It no longer smelled like rain on anything living. Where they backed in to load, their track beat down and sank into two sharp ruts from the repeated weight. It was like backing into a sanctuary of birds and a flutter of leaves and shadowy coolness. There waited a clear rock pool where Tucker laid the suction screen, mesmerizing water over opalescent stones.

Without priming, the pump would run dry and never charge. Ray took the tin dipper and stooped to fill it. Tommie stepped in nearby and began lapping. The dog finished and returned to the bank. Ray submerged the can entirely, then paused, raising it to his lips and drawing in water. He passed it to Alice, who also paused, then tilted the bent container for her own taste. She passed it to Tucker. Tucker had not yet braced for the steady pouring into the pump cavity. He set his hat back, seeing the dog on the bank, whose eyes followed every motion: the can arched from each pair of hands, like a chalice. With his regard on Alice, he lifted the rusty tin above his brow, the mimic of a salute before his own drink.

"I remember the fog and frost—it must be a hundred years," said the boy.

The small engine of the pump clashed under the trees. The tank sides popped out and the trailer settled down, an increasing bulge where the tires touched the ground.

Each time when they pulled into the light of the valley, it seemed to have paled a little further, while the mountain darkened, a dry-dry, suffering green.

Once on their way home, a satellite party of elk crossed in front of them. The animals soon stopped to look back, as though they were confounded over such an effort. With this discourteous pause dead center in the valley, Ray quickly rose to his feet. He pretended he was shooting:

"Hey. *Hey!*"

"No standing."

The encumbered tractor could only strain drearily forward. Heavily the elk singled out and Tucker watched them begin to lope: an exasperating leisure, relaxed rocking across the finished land. At each of their heels rose a small cloud of dust.

The caravan drove within sight of two stacks of hay, the panels of protection still intact. Tucker considered them as trim structures, untouched islands with a blatant wearing everywhere else. They passed through the bright heat, a warming globe, then returned to the welcome yard like returning to a mother ship, the surrounding sea with a dull sagging to its face.

No wasted step or idle hand.

"Imagine just one year without rain."

"We done all we can."

In the evening Ray hung his hat before leaving the oasis. Tucker felt they were mostly ready. He and Alice and the dog stood watching. The form of a child pedaled its bike along the fading horizon. All that they depended on came from the sky.

Waiting Room

Alice and Ray had gone to the barn to brush and grain the horses, prepare them for the work in the days ahead. They left Tommie behind with Tucker.

Tucker quickly dialed, then stood at the window nearest the phone, with the receiver in his hand, the collie watching and upright while staying close to the door.

"Hello. Franklin and Taylor. This is Megan."

"Is Mr. Taylor in?"

"He had court and is at a business lunch. He is not yet in."

Tucker pulled out a chair, but kept standing. He repeated the local number in his head. Twenty minutes later he redialed.

"Hello. Franklin and Taylor. This is Megan."

"May I speak with Mr. Taylor?"

"He is gone for the afternoon."

Twice a week, Alice and Ray with Tommie would take at least an hour caring for the garden. He could see the barn, but only one slight corner of the garden. Alice had a small spray bottle with a special mixture of soapsuds intended to deter certain insects. Ray carried a hoe and a brand-new coil of hose, for ditching and flooding between the rows.

This time, Tucker sat at the desk.

"Hello—"

"This is Tucker Black and I'd like to talk to George Taylor."

"Sir, he is between clients and preparing a deposition. I will have him ring you."

"I will wait. Here. On the phone..."

"Tucker."

"George."

"My man...how is Alice—and the valley?"

He had been here before, after the death of each of his parents. Tucker had lasting impressions. George Taylor bore a face like Milo, but with thick glasses and a slow, hesitant manner, an almost aggravating calm. He also had gray hair: an identity to his scalp line in the shape of little gray horns, close cropped, like an owl.

"That valley, I would delight if I could be out there...out in the blue...what fresh air... No small-town wills, no drunken driving or bent fenders...no county affairs—how is it?" Milo's opposite. "And Alice?"

"Just right—"

"It must be dry—"

Tucker remembered a faint nod, a trailing swivel to the lawyer's neck. "—as everyone else," not having that staring look or steady rotation of an owl, but a clear resemblance to a well-satisfied bird, "unless you caught that rarity of rain, you sometimes do... My man—your niche is right... What-is-your-interest?" The sentences paused, without the pressures of time.

"Can we meet?"

"Is it—urgent?"

Slow and exotic. His jacket always dark, and a regard as though heavy, like a creature weighted with a large beak.

George continued, "I have a trip planned and will be gone for about two weeks." His voice grew dim from turning away from the phone, as though caused by a gesture to someone else in his office. Fastidious feathers, groomed and snug.

"Two weeks." Tucker also paused, seeing no action in the corner of the garden.

"Is Alice all right? I miss the profound pleasure of her smile—her *aura...*"

The call with such paucity. Tucker pulled a small picture frame forward on the desk, a snapshot of Alice in full glow, shortly after they were married. Her attractiveness—now...stronger than ever.

Her desk...*their* desk. He imagined the one where George was sitting: huge and with a roll top. He could hear him through the phone, leaning back, making a soft clicking noise with his tongue, as if something metallic were hidden in the brusque hairs of his mustache. He wore no vest with trim little pockets. His right hand missed two center fingers from a boyhood accident.

With a sudden increase in speed, "*My man, what*—is your interest?"

"We have a concern and think he is abused."

"Who?"

"Alice thinks he is severely abused."

George clapped his hands to the arms of his chair. "I know."

"We have a concern about Ray Connor."

Tucker saw the slow blink, the small bright eyes, still without ruffle.

"Shall we all talk together before I leave?"

"When you get back—and not everyone should know."

George came forward again and spoke with a new gravity in his voice, tenacity in his posture. "I assure you, all is private. What do you propose?"

"When you get back, as soon as possible when you get back."

The connection silenced. The ear and mouthpiece returned to its cradle, then Tucker stood. He wiped his brow. He wiped it twice, and stroked his pants. He felt his future in that other room—waiting room: *We think we would want to be a guardian.*

A man with hair in a room full of feathers.

Reprieve

In the darkness it settled, a flush of need: this time to the awakening of dreamlike rain. Alice felt a close-bearing tension that the rain might leave before it commenced—nothing like the sound on a hungering roof over your bed. It pattered against the lower pane of the open window, and no one rose to shut the sash. The close leaves rustled with its kiss, and the night opened, a welcoming sigh in the very air. Water began to drip from the stiff row of shingles. A pitch blackness in the room and outdoors, yet she knew they both smelled a rainbow. The drumming went on lightly but steadily, a longer breath, more than a short sweep and tease. Alice and Tucker held hands. High rumbles came, and a luminescence on the wall and sky, no white flashes or threatening booms. Tommie didn't come down the hall. The gentle but reaching lightshow passed and the rain stopped. The eaves kept dripping hopefully, then slowed. They released each other's hand, and Alice lay for a long time trying to hear another coming; at length her fatigue and the sympathy of sleep pulled her away.

In the morning the valley cheered. She watched Ray arrive to the smoothing wrinkles of a relieved land. Dampness clung to his tires and peppered the bottom of his pants. The park had sipped a temporary half inch from the fountain of youth. The collie, with a mode of persuasion, carefully greeted Ray. Alice couldn't help but enjoy Tommie's puffed-up chest and his fluffed-out tail, as though he had bathed in some new world conditioner, ready for a show. From the porch…she and her husband had to smile.

Alice felt Tucker's touch and they spoke in unison: "Let's go for a picnic."

Only from the window above the sink could she see the entire garden. Alice watched Ray and Tucker dig new potatoes while the dog rolled them with his nose. They placed them in a well-used box. The lid lay to the side, bearing a paste paper advertisement for West Slope Orchards. The faded colors and scuffed picture caught her eye: plump, ripe peaches she had tasted as a youth.

Alice prepared pieces of chicken. Ray and Tucker scrubbed and rinsed the overabundance of small round tubers, then laid them in a gleaming glass bowl. The boys soaped their hands, a mixture of perfume and the cleanliness of garden dirt. Tucker tumbled the chicken in flour and cornmeal and took over the frying. She watched Ray meticulously halve or quarter the potatoes. He dropped them into boiling water. Alice brought in consonance a unique blend of mayonnaise, spice, pickles, and chopped egg. While waiting for the others, she went outside and pulled a bouquet each of carrots and onions, brushing away crumbs of black. The dog weaved in the same row. She straightened her back and touched her brow with a single wrist. She inhaled the diminishing moisture. She couldn't help but acknowledge the first hint of fall.

They held a discussion as to where they might go.

"Just below the spring?"

"We been there a lot."

No one mentioned the table.

"We could go up the canyon and above the sawmill," said Tucker.

"The top of the lane sure got view."

Tommie clicked his feet and waved at each of them. He made the air in the room stir.

At last they reached a consensus: there had been rain but they still wished to be near water.

"Beside the creek."

"Lower."

"By that field I swallowed a *grasshopper.*" Ray smiled as he dried his hands on a clean white towel.

"We don't have a lot of choice if we want to be by a real flow," said Alice.

"Sit by the stock tank—"

"No, we don't," she interceded.

"You will—will you—keep your mouth shut?" prodded Tucker.

"If there is hopping?" Alice added.

The boy simpered a slight red of embarrassment, then ducked for the teasing.

"Perfect..." everyone agreed.

Alice and Tucker did not change their dress but changed its attitude. Tucker undid the buttons on his collar, and neatly folded his sleeves back as far as his elbows. The outstanding pallor and hardness of his forearms made Alice look twice. He looked like a country doctor preparing for a patient. After seeing this, Alice brushed her hair differently. With a silky scarf she tied together its ends. Her belt and buttons and crisp white blouse went untouched but the hat she had found altered everything: a shade hopefully to mystify her smile: gracefully drooping straw in stark contrast to Ray's. His wriggled stiffly, a mildly tattered disk with all the edges turned up like the lip to a dinner plate. She noticed that all the people wore hats, as if ready for a procession.

Ray carried a bottle of lemonade. Alice carried a thermos of coffee. Tucker swung a crudely woven bag that looked as if it were two rugs sewn together, with long, feminine straps as handles. It rocked weightlessly at the end of his arm, spreading the tall grass at the edge of the mowing. They curved, walking from shadow to sun, listening to the reliant stream. Under many trees the rain had not penetrated. She felt the return of a dusty cool.

"Ain't gonna seem wet—long."

The dog's tail drew a circle.

"I am afraid—" she said.

"But what a time now," spoke Tucker.

Ray and his partner led, looking for a particular place and seeming to hurry for the early drying out. The dips and curves of Alice's hat, the tone of fall, the waves and shine of the collie's coat, the march of Ray's brown and lengthening arms: she could feel her husband following.

"This is good."

Ray chose a shaded bank with a near border of sun. He and the dog quickly sat overlooking an old course in the flow. The sunken channel had filled in with willows not tall enough to block their view. To one side trees and stream, to the other a simmering flat: clarified seams, the velveteen yellow of dampened hills.

"We got everything."

Alice knew a sudden pressure on the inside, then felt it fading. The dog moved separate of the group and began licking his front paws. Ray took his hat off and laid it upside down in the tall growth. He stretched in full, leaning back and shaking his hair.

They paused, as though being immersed in a special light, reflections bouncing from all around. Tucker did as the boy, and lifted his hat to place at his side.

"Are you hungry?" he asked Ray.

"Not much—very much—we got everything." Ray lay back in the cushion of grass with his knees up, his face out of view.

For a *sure* instant, Alice's place drew a filtering of sun, like a silken hand flickering on her brim: mark of a new time—a new beginning. She felt calmness, a prowess like never before, her lips momentarily anchored and firm. Tucker passed her the carpet-like bag. She began dividing the food, placing servings on the specialty of paper plates.

"A reprieve." She finally broke the quiet.

"Liberation," Tucker answered.

The tallest brome along the creek had already turned fall colors, brush strokes of gold and rust, while the trees and bramble remained multiple shades of green. The sparse and final drops of rain slid deeper, like a vanishing and ghostly wet. Alice held the first paper plate toward Ray, so buried in his nest he did not know.

"If this ain't heaven—" He must have heard her action but his voice trailed high, as though to glide above the trees before reaching the ground.

Tommie appeared and nosed Ray's face until he sputtered and sat up.

"Thank you."

"Good potatoes."

"And the chicken."

"I never had *so* good."

Alice offered the boy and Tucker each a checkered napkin. Ray swallowed and wiped his hands on his pants before accepting. He used the textured paper for the shine on his cheeks and chin.

"I'll never get filled."

"You said you weren't hungry." Alice reached and put more food on his plate.

"Oh, man."

She poured lemonade for Ray and coffee for herself and Tucker.

While they were eating, she watched the dog curl into an unusually compressed ball. He kept his eyes open and pointed toward Jasper Spring, but they appeared clouded over.

Ray spooned and scraped his plate until it began to buckle and fold.

"More?"

"*Ouff.*" He spread his fingers and felt for room. "Yes, please."

Alice sipped while Ray continued. The angle of the sun made a marked shift, beginning to spill over the bank's rim. As always, she watched the boy chewing. His jaw quickly stopped and his vision became fixed. Through all the leaves, dapples of light now glanced from the not so distant barn, like splotches of sun on an apple, weathered wood, the streaks and coloring of a home: across the clearing, a tired veranda, pushing— She knew this place and how it had grown for him…she saw moisture gathering in his eyes.

"I ate too much," Ray said with a start.

Alice felt churning, an inversion, something deep inside. *Defeat…or rally.* "An absolutely beautiful rain."

"Nice rest," added her husband.

"Perhaps this will mean a new pattern—increase our chances."

Ray dried his hands, speaking with a distracted voice. "I been happy…just doing nothing."

Tucker replaced his hat, the bright of the open field deflected in his face. He looked up at the mountain. Though long finished eating and drinking, Alice caught him as he swallowed, hearing distinction in his voice. "The right place. The right place for more than a lunch."

Her straw tipped down, her eyes remained hidden while she gathered to the sound of water. The handles to the odd bag for their picnic fell inside. She drew them out, at first with a manner of weakness, then a steadiness, a returning calm.

The sun approached. Tucker spoke quietly of the summer, the chance for a better fall. He mentioned bringing the cattle home and deciding what they must sell. The boy and dog sat closest together, upright, attentive, clean, and naturally tended.

Handsome: Ray's profile and smooth skin, the long, sleek muscle growing in his back and arm.

Alice watched the collie rise, slightly arched, as though carrying saddle bags just behind his shoulders. He descended toward the stream. He threaded himself through the willows and brush and drank without wetting his feet. He went down the flow and disappeared a moment. Soon he reappeared and climbed the bank, carrying a short, water-washed stick. He returned to the group, skirting the shadows with his tail humped and his ears half perked, an attitude of purpose.

Ray had turned to follow the dog's path, deep in thought, as if there were more to be noticed. He muttered, "Some dog— No road—no troubles here."

Tommie gently laid the stick in Alice's lap. He nosed the perimeter of her hat, then pressed his forehead against her side; his eyes only lightly deserted the gift. She knew not to grasp or draw it in close. The straw hid her face again as she felt and petted the smooth wood.

"What do you have?" she asked.

With a reaching length and his tail again arched, he lifted the clean branch carefully, to carry and balance on Ray's leg.

"If I ain't—he's the best." Copying Alice he did not raise the stick, but briskly bent forward and hugged the collie completely, wiping his whole face in the fur.

The dog stood tall and allowing, not losing sight. The chosen object rolled from the boy's leg and he placed it back.

"You bugger."

For a moment Alice considered only the boy, as he propped back on his arms and lifted his chin; his blond hair fell away, leaving a dignified slope and the refinement of nose.

As if in answer, the collie raised his mouth: image to image. Ray tipped up and his hand came around, but the dog preceded him and took the stick to Tucker. It rested on the toe of his worn leather boot. Tucker sat straight, still as stone. The dog climbed the hill and stood beside him.

"Good dog" was all her husband said, swinging his regard to Alice.

The sun slid further down the bank and touched Tommie first. With a suddenness, like a parting in the trees, it became spotlight to his grand chest-thick collar-amber eyes. A rippling memory congealed: Tommie in the sun in a selfless pose as if he had risen from a weightless drift of fathomless, cleansing snow.

Pale Purpose

Not until mid-August did Duane and Martin actually drive, and see for themselves, the new and decisive access to the forest. It became a tour of curiosity rather than inspection. Duane was the pilot while Martin thumbed through the maps. Lieutenant, sergeant.

The influence of the recent rain veiled itself, leaving no trace. It had never happened.

"Where the hell are we now?"

"Somewhere on the south side of the main draw," answered Martin.

"These damn spur roads have no end."

They passed an expired log landing; an opening littered with cull tree forks and bowed trunks. It lay above the ditch and was taken over by remarkable plants with big dry stalks and tremendous leaves, almost as high as a man's shoulder. Some had spread to the road and they rapidly tipped forward to rip and tear under the callous truck, dispersing seed. Soon the invasive plant would line the edges of *all* the roads.

"We need more fucking turnouts."

Martin's head gave a twist. "We could have backed out at the beginning."

They came to more rock, ledges, and breaks in the north slope of trees. Duane did not slow the truck. The jumps and rebounds brought dust up from their feet; it seeped through the seals around the doors.

Martin began to hold the dash and duck, as though bracing for something to fall apart. Maps fell to the floor. "Should be getting close to the end. I see no more marking, no paint on the trees."

"Better be."

Groves of aspen began to dominate. The evergreens grew thinner and woody. At last they came to a shaded cul-de-sac surrounded by large and smooth white columns, though shaded, a luminous space. Duane sketched a short, quick turn, not needing to back up or jockey his position. They made their exit without pause.

"They're for trucks," he said to himself.

At the beginning of the way out, their return to town, he drove more slowly. Again, the prevalence of so much timber seemed to weigh on his foot, causing a gradual rush, like a nagging unrest. The vehicle began to rock and lurch, at first only lightly.

"Lots of goddamn wood."

"Some call it piss fur."

"Ah-hah!"

The automatic shifted lower. The pickup propelled forward as if by jet power, as though speed would escape the tiresome and evade the roughness.

"When will these roads all have numbers? They're like tree branches going who the hell knows where."

Martin bent to collect the fallen rolls of paper from beside his shoes. "Now, with the better access there'll be re-mapping, posts with numbers."

The pickup groaned as they started up a sharp incline. A shadow of recognition crossed Martin's face. His finger landed on a freshly folded map, green and white with numbers for elevation. It pointed north, very near the bold line of a bigger artery. The new construction had been drawn much thicker than the spurs, and glowed with the precise highlight of a purple marker.

"This would be a bitch in the winter," said Duane.

"No one will be here in the winter," answered Martin.

"We're almost there?"

"You're right... This still isn't as steep as the cliff."

"We needed a goddamn tunnel."

Just as they reached the bright and wider swath, Martin stiffly laughed and Duane smiled. Without hesitation they turned at the junction and traveled even faster down the new and settling fill. The dust increased dramatically. The corridor through the forest tripled in width. Their view expanded, their placement on the mountain now easy to determine. Out from the interior saddle, the trees were changing to pine and were heavily coated with the powder of the road. Duane began steering with only one hand:

"They did a hell of a job."

He opened his window, but the cloud eddied beside and an evident annoyance came to each man's mouth. The window went up. Duane glanced in the rearview mirror: "Ought to have a water truck. Get this whole thing graveled and I'd be impressed."

The smoothness gave way to an unpredictable series of humps and sinkholes. They hit a particularly severe dip, and the dust billowed out in waves, an action like slapping down a huge dauber into a tub of talcum. The truck's suspension bottomed out, to the sounding of a loud clank. Martin's head bounced off the ceiling.

"Need to run a blade back through."

"The dust makes the trees look sick." Martin held his stomach, then throat as they approached the breathtaking edge to an abrupt downward grade. His fingers tightly held the map as though it were a duplicate wheel for steering.

Most aspects of Duane came without warning. He began to ride the brakes and they came to the overlook with a timidness, as if peering over the brink of sore rubble suddenly losing appetite. Their slowing brought debris past the sides and over the top. Their view became momentarily blank.

They sat, in a fashion like waiting for a traffic light, the great expanse before them appearing very slowly.

"Damn dramatic country," said Duane.

"Very."

"Damn big empty country."

"Quite brown."

"Looks bigger than it is because it is so empty—the power of desolation."

"I do feel power," Martin answered, but lacking the note of any alignment.

Duane drove with two hands again and shifted down. He sat up, as though carefully watching for a pothole or protruding boulder. After all the broken rock, they reentered a clutter of timber but the steepness dwarfed the lower trees. The country beyond and below them had little interruption, only a few grayish treetops like a jagged fringe in the foreground. As they descended, the forest color changed even more, still dirty but less bitter, with fewer dead limbs. Both pair of eyes skimmed over the top of the granite Sisters and the dried-out field in their shadow. They missed the graffiti and the smashed growth. They appeared more and more attracted to the early valley: the abrupt beginning to the stream, the dark, wandering line of the lowland deciduous, guarding something.

Beyond the suffering evergreens on the mountain, this green was the only place left.

Neither man made comment on the aridity, the shrinking of the arable land. No buildings drew notice. The evenly placed stacks of hay stood characteristic to independence and a life of plenty, not clear enough to inventory among the tidiness, the evenness of the fields, the organization. The needled trees abruptly receded, leaving the pickup an open, downward ramp all the way to the culvert for crossing the water. On entering private lands, the color of the highlight to signify their access changed from purple to blue.

In the last step down, the richness of leaves and reaching spruce again hid the creek, dense and rising with abundance above the stark cut for the road, as though screen to a forbidden privacy those passing would want to enjoy: lush clothing to intimate lines and curves, the secret texture to a valley's essential.

Duane drove his slowest yet, almost to a stop. "Not even a rooftop—no sign—the place is uninhabited."

"There *is a man* there…there is a man there. Look at that hay…and the board fencing all the way around."

"Work. Looks like work…upon work," mumbled Duane.

They dropped even more after crossing the pipe. The immense culvert carried only a trickle. Beyond, the minor shine in the sand dispersed to a mere dampness.

Duane now spoke with a stark clarity, as though inspired by this crossing: "He needs instruction. He will not last. He has to move to the side or be run over."

Martin said nothing. The corners of his mouth flickered, then froze.

They turned their backs on the low fertility and the distressed green of the mountain.

Just before the entrance to the county's gravel road, they came to an auto gate. It had been recently installed. With a quick passing the truck made a rub-board sound and another clank as it bounced. The dust-imbedded tires lightly faded the clean paint, as if to mark its very first use. It connected to no fence. With small rocks clipping the fenders, they sped along the first section of marbly road.

On a blind corner they met a low-slung car, also speeding for the solitude of space. To have adequate room they each had to swerve, sliding out onto the softness of the road's edge. The bright green car slid the furthest, to the jostle of its passengers. It began to high-center on a berm of coarseness. Duane drove more skillfully and met the eyes of a slim young man, then a short girl, sitting very close beside. As their clouds joined Martin happened to turn; he ducked. A tailpipe suddenly appeared, causing sparks and vaulting through the air like shrapnel being thrown. The tube of exhaust rolled into the ditch while the car weaved forward, found its footing, then steadied.

"Going like hell," said Duane.

"So are we."

"Are they okay?"

"I think so, but they sure didn't slow down."

"That would have been a hell of a picture if they'd upset in the borrow ditch."

"Just kids," said Martin.

"Lovers... I wouldn't slow down either."

They exchanged glances, Duane with a smile and Martin rather grim, then returned to the empty road.

* * *

The green car swam through their dust and again took the more stable center. Paint was being pitted. They passed beside the newly placed cattle guard, then skidded to a halt. Without allowing the engine to slow, the young man thumped the transmission into reverse. The rear tires spun, throwing pebbles and dust up beside the windows. Like a rapidly backing snake, he overcorrected, nearly hanging the car on the swollen shoulder. The panel below his door began to scrape and grind. More spinning, they partly floated in their turn, then flew over the unmistakable thumping of evenly placed bars. The iron was at a different plane than the freshly crowned road.

Kalump. The voice of the car changed to an esophagus without a head.

April squeezed the young man's arm. A muffler lay in the middle of the road. He backed up slowly, leaving perfect tracks in the fine soil. He parked and left the engine running, then walked back to pick up the part. She reached over and clicked the key off, as though fumes were coming around and getting inside. As he walked, the dust rose above his knees. April's head twisted to review the perfect imprint of his tread, left in the fluff at the edge of the road, a strange record, like the trail of an astronaut walking on some other planet. He had very long, slim legs and almost no substance for a hinge, his neck a rigid post above sloping arms. The slenderness without a face made him look younger than his years. He bent to lift and his hands snapped back.

"Goddamn it!"

In a different line he came back to the car. From the window he pulled the keys.

"*Hot*... It's only a broken clamp. Damn hot. You got any rags in the trunk?"

"I never been in the trunk."

"Never? You don't know if you have a spare?"

"Stay off me for that."

He opened the lid and blocked her view. He found a rag stuffed beside a dusty tire and wheel and pressed on the rubber. "You got one but it don't have any air—

"Your jack looks bent."

Her short huskiness shrugged and she turned to face forward. She briefly looked across the dead pasture and on to the mountains, then raised one foot and leg and crossed it under the other as if to study her shoe.

The rag was dirty and torn and filled with fines from riding in a leaking compartment, but he did not shake it. He unfolded the tatters so the darkest side could wrap around the end still bound by a clamp. One hand lifted the muffler and held it out from his pants; the rag shifted, leaving a smudge on his fingers. The long, flat canister made a sound as though it were a shaker. A black powder sprinkled to the ground. He dropped it harshly in the trunk and slammed the cover.

The girl slowly raised her head, glancing again over the rear seat. There were four sets of human tracks in the soft surface of the road. With his arms dangling limp, he seemed to be searching about, then looked at his hands with an obvious question crossing his face. He finally stooped to thoroughly rub the bottoms of his jeans. Afterward, he stayed bent and beat the new dust out. He took the keys and climbed down into the car. She scooted close to him and touched his neck.

In the pause, the car had grown hotter. Fine beads collected in the hair that lined April's forehead and temple. The boy touched dampness in the creases of her clothes. With both windows fully down and a breathless rev of the car's engine, they again flew, only now over a native and powdery road, as though trying to cool, outrun the roiling talcum and fume. The broken exhaust increased the noise and disorder, causing them to hover in their own rather than race and get ahead. Through more cracks and leaks, a haze gathered in the car. They closed their mouths. A fullness gathered below each eye, a look of restriction. Their hair stiffened.

Hurry, get to cleaner air.

Up and over the crest of the rampart, they took the first side road with no recent travel. Once on a narrower, shaded surface, their haste converted. They drove slowly and began to wander, slouched in a soft suspension, a rolling easy chair through close trees. The naked sputter from underneath powered and prodded their afternoon: in settling heat. An obvious dust now drifted *out* from the car windows.

They reached a small clearing, a brief slew kept alive by water seeping from a shelf of big flat rocks. It had been dry for almost a month. The boy's shirttails were pulled from his pants and the front entirely unbuttoned. The car had just enough room he could drive forward and back several times and get turned.

"Wait—"

One tire hung on a stick; then it popped and flew up beside his mirror, thumping the fender.

"Holy cow—"

As if suddenly more determined, she now had advantage.

He missed a shift and accelerated in neutral.

She raised a leg to put over his knee and unbuckled his belt.

"I can't see. Hey. Hey, wait—*hold on.*"

"Sure."

At last the car was almost straight in the road, and he swung his door open as he shut off its resonant irritation and smell. More dust fell out. April crawled her fingers around under his loosened shirt, then licked his neck. His knees bumped the dash as his slenderness untangled and he stood. April released all, as if to regroup, and tugged on his flapping belt. His eyes swept quickly over the private scene, then stalled above the bright roof of the car: the depth of the slew. Above his youthful brow his hair bristled, below, a blink-less, disparaging face.

"Get the mat," he said.

He jerked on her hand.

"Get the mat—let's get away from the car."

With shining eyes, she re-entered the errant vehicle and bent over the seat back to feel behind. She lifted a long, bunched roll of loosely woven reed with a short blanket. From the front floor she gathered a pack of cigarettes and a lighter. The downward reach increased the color in her face, involved and thickened her hair.

The boy forcefully took her hand and they ran down the hill to the opening of grass. His shirt split like strange wings, and the buckle of his belt swung from side to side. The mat precariously bounced and sagged from the multiple items clutched in her opposite hand, this short run a terrible exaggeration of their quarreling heights and shapes—their differing strokes.

He relieved April of the roll and blanket. In the action, and by total accident, he encountered a new and striking surface between the trees. They were standing just above a struggling beaver dam, a diminishing pool but still clear. In the exchange she attempted the top button on his pants while holding the cigarettes by her chin. Seeming to ignore her effort, he took the cellophane package before it fell and led her more slowly across the lumps of grass. She stuffed the remaining lighter in her back pocket. Their footsteps made an inappropriate crunch in the broad leaves, and puffs of orange followed their heels.

Irreversible, their inward excitement whirled, faster yet faster. Seeing condensed and the world grew small.

Not quite to the water and the very tall, thin boy stooped to undo their padding. His hurried hands passed over an embedded dust. She tried for the pants again, then abruptly sat and slipped off her shoes. She wriggled her sticky toes over the dry reed with grit and lint in between. Reaching for her own collar, she tossed her hair back and a dark glance met the tranquility of the pool. Her nose wrinkled. Her fingers stroked the coating on the mat.

"I dare you."

Too much dry and dirty air.

"Say *what*?"

"I dare you."

Breathing as a pulse: short and tall, plump and slim; they stood at the water's edge with bare feet and watched each other undress with wide and fastened eyes. He kept his opened jeans while she shed hers and deftly sloughed the rest like a sweltering debutante. Her last article relaxed at her feet. He crouched lower and disarmed himself to the skin. In one simultaneous splash they entered the cool and moss, touching in fumbles, their faces an extreme white and fluttering mirror to emptiness.

The water too shallow to clothe his excitement, he sank to his knees. All clarity broke, a rank sediment stirred, he slapped the surface and shivered in his leanness, flinging turbid water, pressing himself against—she tried to kiss, as though in covet of his bones—his maleness. They splashed out. Feet drooled. Goose bumps in the warm air: shivering with areas more pale than their purpose, a convulsive shake as though to dry, the mismatched pair fell in the grass before reaching the mat.

* * *

They lay smoking. They shared a cigarette, looking up at the calm, late afternoon sky and mingled tree branches. The blanket fractionally covered her front. The soiled fabric neatly concealed his center and was tucked on one edge. The knobs to his knees and fluted shins lay exposed and led to mud-covered feet. Above, his ribbed torso rose up and down with the inhalation and blowing of smoke from the filter that she held. One long arm rested over the head of their bed, still touching the ends to her thick roll of hair. His drying toes pointed starkly up, well below hers—muddiest and curved like a ballerina's. Upright she measured a head and a half shorter; horizontal they aligned at the hips and the difference became split.

She gave him the cigarette, then lay reaching with her toes and fingers as though to match his height. She snatched it back and drew a pattern in the air with the ash-laden tip trailing smoke, taking obvious care not to have it above her own skin.

"I'm getting chilled."

"Cover up."

She propped on an elbow and raised the course of a dark reddish eyebrow.

Totally warm, his skin a blotchy pink, his hair gnarled, he reached for the cigarette and she denied it, holding it daringly close to her front and the slipping cover. More tan lines entered the view and a distinct placidness.

"Let's make a fire."

"Fire? I done *had* mine."

She did not smile. With smoke in her mouth, she rose up on one hand, her eyes prying—digging—her curls dangling. A faint rim of dirt traced where a wet shoulder had pressed against gritty reeds. She emptied her mouth and rounded her lips.

"You ain't cold…you're *hot*.

"You want to *burn* me."

Satisfaction, incomplete...

He grinned at the softness he could see and the loose, unembarrassed spiral, bits of grass. He rolled toward her without untucking. She turned away. The last corner of the blanket covered her hips. She took an obvious breath, with a nimble motion turned back and found her knees, draping her auburn wildness across his forehead as she straddled him, teeth showing, crushing the cigarette between her fingers. The cover dropped. Her back swayed. Among all the startling movement and sight, the young man's face lost color—eyes in full dilation—as though on the brink of blacking out. She slid from his new interest and ran into the trees, waving a faint sash of smoke over her head and laughing, mad laughter: a staggered grace, for her darkened feet had no safety among breaking grass and shed needles.

As though searching for a dampness from the ground, she faced him. Between raging hair, she attempted a draw on the last of the smoke with the broken paper and nothing came. Their gazes joined, as though one. She threw her head back, whipping her flame into permanent suspension. The blanket followed him briefly as the chase began. They tripped and stumbled separately for the barbs. She eluded him four times with swinging arms and twisting body; then her blurred pivot led him back to the water's edge where their clothes lay in thorough confusion. They stopped: breathing heavily, an indelicate dance, no laughter, no voice. With the pretense of nervousness, she stooped and her fingers fiddled with the undergarments. She tried halfheartedly to dress while he pulled and dragged on revealed flesh, leaving brash and temporary stripes. They struggled and he slipped. He fell from the bank as his arms clasped around her short, coupled legs, holding the very deep softness of her abdomen to his cheek. She took mincing steps while remaining upright. His feet splashed.

Behind them rose strange crackling, a sneaking of something: an ominous, undefined shadow. They looked up to a thick fog spewing and blending with the porous grasses, a pungency not to be forgotten. It was no bigger than the size of a picnic table, and the smoke fanned.

Had they had shoes, they could have stomped it down.

Had they held containers, they could have poured water.

Their total exposure flashed—a sure weakness, discomfort—while their pants and shirts lay as unused tools.

They could have beat it out, snuffed the birth.

They stood in stupefaction and the world opened rapidly.

In six seconds, it grew to the size of a house. A yellow began to leap, creating its own draft; smoke curled skyward.

Displays of panic swallowed them. They grappled together their clothes and ran for the car, no longer any dangers to their feet. Halfway and he turned back for another pass. He smashed the mat against his chest and held the blanket in his teeth, darting beside the water to quickly seize a loop of underwear. At the car he threw everything in her lap and gave the location a fractional scan. Beside their small trampling the whole clearing was choked. It now towered higher than the tallest of the trees. The bright green paint had a tint. He tumbled in and slammed the door: an unmuffled engine roar, spinning tires, he sped them down the road without looking back, traveling so fast all their track turned to powder.

Unlike her driver, the naked April did turn—wide-eyed and swept by revelation, enough to jar an undiscovered heart. She had run away, turned her back before—without caring—and she would run away again. She would run—this time in desperation and with billowing intent…

The dust they stirred grew insignificant. The smoke drifted into the surrounding trees and began to climb the slope, soon to overcome all—a rolling, thunderous motion, a tidal wave—

Unquenchable

Ray was there for the fire.

Changing oil in the water pump engine, Tucker was still teaching. Ray learned which boxes had what wrenches and where the drain pans were kept. All but the bottles for used oil had been toted from the shop and organized in the pickup, a utility vehicle for almost every need. A certain metal box with smaller wrenches lay on the passenger side floor, the bigger tools and bars went behind, outside and crowded together between the spare tire and an open carrier for saw parts and supplies, and so on. The funnels slid over one another and were wrapped in a rag for a cubbyhole beside the milk cans.

Tucker had Ray unthread the spark plug to wire-brush the carbon. They adjusted the gap.

"When this is over, we will burnish the piston top and valves."

Tucker felt an intrusion, a change to his perception of the mountain, the cloudless western limit where the sun would set. He stepped up to lean on the rough cool of the water tank and saw clearly above the battered limbs and leaves of the far yard, shadows already long across the well-covered slopes. He did not squint, but swallowed. In that ultimate dry he scoured his thumb and fingertips together, then thumped them on the loaded drum. A smoke. A smoke he could not erase: high, somewhere far in. It had a peculiar slant to the west and north.

"Put that back in."

He looked for any others and now made the wagon teeter and shake. He thumped again on the tank. The dog came from the shade underneath, showing wear from the heat.

"What are you seeing? You see something?"

Tucker did not answer. He lifted an empty hand and rubbed his brow. Ray climbed up and stood opposite, not much taller than the chained and rusty container. The dog hopped up too, as though the unmanned tractor were going to pull them all away.

"What is it? I don't—what?"

Just as the boy realized, Tucker spoke. "We have another fire."

Ray tugged on his hat.

"Another fire."

"Fire."

He jumped down and became level with the boy's face, in clear hesitation.

"Go tell Alice to call the town. Hurry. This will be a big one—a big one, quick." Tucker reached up and held the boy's arm while making a definite point to the ridge. "I will be up there. From that point I will know just where—see where it is going."

The boy did not move. His eyes were getting bigger and bigger. The collie shuffled, disturbed by the tone in their voices.

Tucker squeezed lightly and almost whispered the single word: "Hurry."

He squeezed again. "Alice can come out and determine how to get to it as well as anyone."

In an exaggerated leap to run, Ray skidded to his knee and his hat rolled away.

Tucker spoke up. "Say that the new road will lead them there." For a blink, he followed the boy. Then he turned. With a ringing he scraped together the tools without wiping them and put them in their places. He brushed his hands and walked very fast for the barn. He went in the front and came out the back as though he were passing through the building without the use of doorways: a stream in his head of plans-options-priorities, if the wind changed, and it would. He began the climb with determined strides and soon passed the first marker. The dog caught up with ears and tail in full alert and remained at his side. Soon, the boy was there. He could feel the struggle in Ray, the difficulty, the boy's young legs so quick and able to leap and bound going downhill, as the incline sharpened a lesser thrust and power than his own. He could hear him approaching from behind, his breathing and the holding of his wind, sucking it back. Glancing, sweat collected under the shine of Ray's now hatless hair, a heavy moisture where its length gathered at the back of his neck. The flick of a hand brushed the blond from his eyes and the part remained. As they climbed the fire grew, both for better view and a feeding of fuel, a release: the lower smoke with more motion and definition against a backdrop of darkening waves of forest. Toward the top, Tucker pressed on each striving knee with his palms.

They stopped at the second marker and Tucker's mouth grew firm. He opened his lips but held his breath, in hesitation, over the significance of this high place. He felt his shoulders pounding on the inside from more than a pumping. He began to breathe, then looked back to see Ray, badly crying. In questioning seconds he realized salt running into the boy's eyes—not sadness—extreme effort and concern. Tommie then curled his tail and sat very close to the pyramid.

At last the unreality and excitement overtook Ray and he began to choke and gasp. "What these—what are these rocks about?"

"Nothing." Tucker waved away the probe. He studied the smoke and began to squint. "*We do not want* that wind to change. The longer we have the wind with us, the longer—" Breezes drying and cooling his spine.

He heard the boy sputter, "Where is it?" Ray panted.

"Up beyond, up beyond. Up beyond where they connected the roads," Tucker answered.

Not stopping long, he wove them among the cliffs. Before Ray had a chance to question again, Tucker had found secret footholds, a staircase leading up a great stump-like protrusion, just big enough for all three to stand. Tommie was the last climber.

At this higher level the air pushed more firmly toward the edge. The smoke came from a depression of trees, drawing the line of an organized force, spreading as an augmenting bank rather than a plume.

From straining, Tucker's eyes also began to water and he blinked; then he coughed.

He could see a great deal of the road or its sign, a definite dullness in the landscape on either side. Guiding to or from, the road was empty.

Tucker coughed again. More and more sky fell victim to a high smudge. As though still standing on the trailer, he thought of the cattle: he remembered—he should have followed Ray's suggestion. He should have brought them home several days earlier.

"They can get—I can see they can get—" The boy could not stop panting.

"No one will be coming fast enough."

As they stood the suction at its base flared. Tucker saw the distant lifting of unburned material, a churning and actual flame in the remaining light of day, the mating of incredible fuel and fire. Crowns were already torching.

"A big fire makes its own wind."

Tommie's tail hung, a current fluttered and pointed its tip toward the beginning devastation. Tucker turned, feeling the muscle in his own face, and considered his new partner, taut indecision: more danger in the dark. Much more, more than cattle to be lost in smoke.

The boy watched closely.

"We will get the horses in, the proper tack for you. Tonight…

"Tomorrow…we gather."

* * *

Any motion from town was slow to awaken. Following Alice's call for help, the afternoon dragged on, on, finally reaching its end. Now, in utter shade of the mountain, several tanker trucks struggled up the great traverse, then dipped from sight, a feebleness in their ascent. In less than five minutes, they reappeared with their lights turned on, bouncing for the downgrade, traveling fast and rocking with their unspent loads.

The hidden burning on the mountain went uninterrupted. Alice watched Tucker's arms curve and flex, as though also from an inside burning, secret and acidic cramping—shared between them. The cloud of smoke formed a lofty, dreamlike slope and covered the falling sun, a marriage of heat. For the first time ever, the boy stood on the porch and she fed him a late evening sandwich.

"We get them *all*—will we get them all in one time?" Ray seemed hungry, but with little time for eating.

"You will be a good team. Two horses and Tommie, things will go well. I wish I could watch," Alice answered, outwardly smooth, spreading confidence.

"This season they are scattered." Tucker stood beside her and touched his temple. "They cannot but come home."

Between bites, Ray said, "I hope, I hope they come—come easy. I want to see them, all of them together, Bunny and the calf with her."

As the boy left, the shadows stretched to their limits along the north and south, and the final rays turned golden. Above the black of smoke, an orange coloring spread more than a thousand feet high, as if from a secondary combustion. All happened without sound or smell. Ray pedaled away in a greater dimness as though the day had confused itself and was coming to a close, with an untimely and sudden descent of winter darkness.

He spent the night alone, only slightly wondering when his mother would notice the fire. He made himself oatmeal and thin slices of bread with grape jelly. He made enough so he would have it again early in the morning. In his sleep he tossed and turned, restless, empty of dreams.

* * *

Alice and Tucker stayed awake. They massaged each other's tense and differing neck and shoulders, then lay closely side by side. Alice fondled notions of tangled legs—making love—to fend, press against the impending treat, like Jasper Spring, refreshing will, clearing mind. Too much worry in their hearts, they lay like opposing covers to a dramatic story, too much worry in their hearts to break the mood.

The night stilled and relaxed with an incomplete sigh. The flames calmed and hid, slept under a thick blanket that slid into the low-lying pockets and valleys while the clock ticked and the day began anew.

Light came with a soft, static tension. The sweet smell of a forest fire lay evenly with no particular drifting or source. All of the valley and more was enveloped by a vast sallow gray. With a misleading calm the lower smoke favored the west. At a certain fantastic height, it turned back, tracing an invisible ebb in a long streaming across the entire sky.

Ray arrived early and Alice offered him breakfast.

"I done had some. I don't want to be too loaded."

The sun came up and the smoke over their heads began to dissipate. The park slowly cleared. As they saddled, the white parts of Daisy and Horse and Tommie lost their soiled appearance. The morning settled with a temper as though being pressed on the ground, trying to wring water that was not there. In a glare from the yard, Tucker descended the steps, unfolding a pair of saddlebags, and threw them over Horse's rump. He laced them on. Alice handed him compact wrappers of food and bottles of juice and water. Without looking he took her hand; she could feel his gentle grasp.

She touched his arm, watching…hearing him speak with Ray. "I have slices of meat and cheese, rolls and drink. You say if you get hungry before we stop. I have water any time."

"I will."

"Don't hesitate."

"I will."

Her husband's walk—in *continuous* motion—pulled the boy into the purpose more effectively than ever before. Ray held both horses while Tucker checked their shoes. He ran his leathered thumb around the inside rim of each hoof and steel, feeling the flaking dry and the dust and the firmness. Alice left for the house, to reappear quickly with Ray's hat and two bandannas in one hand, a piece of toast and a tall glass of half milk, half coffee in the other. She took the reins while he drank the glass down and munched the toast. He gave her a muffled thank you and she smiled back.

"Don't need no hat. I'll just lose it."

She passed out the bandannas. "Tucker has water to wet these and put over your face if you get in smoke. I'll bring coats to tie on, just in case. You have your gloves?"

"Yes…yes." He stuffed the potential mask in his back pocket, and tied his gloves to the saddle.

She regarded his hair, as though it required a touch, then stepped away. "You need a hat for protection. Not a straw one." With a fidget in her hands, she glanced at the house. "We do not have anything."

"We need—we need another horse. You'd do better, but I want to go. I want to be part of bringing them. Saving them."

Tommie trotted close and sniffed the hoop that dangled from Alice's hand, as if it were something new and constantly changing. His nose brought coolness to her palm, triggering the memory… Not that long ago she stroked him with a damp towel, streaks of blood through his milky collar. Rising shadowy concerns restricted her throat, urging her to whisper, *Stay. All of you should stay… Maybe the cattle will come home, come home on their own accord.*

"I *can't,* I can't. I ain't good enough." Ray's voice flooded the yard, sharp, out-of-place panic.

"You'll do fine. You're stronger than I am."

"You'd do better—I know. I'm not as good. I know. And I don't know cows."

"Daisy does."

Alice caught Tucker watching as Ray stuttered in silence, a visible mixture of fear and disappointment. The dog's devotion fiddled in the boy's hand. The mare's head lifted.

"What if Tommie and the horse fight?"

"Just get going and tell Tommie you're okay." She stepped within an arm's length. "Once the work starts you won't even have to think about it."

The smoke was already building and changing rapidly, pulling everyone to the cause.

"That country's in your head—in your head—better not—in-in mine—"

"*No*. I'm staying here to get news from town, and to push them. I'll spray water and pump more as long as I have time. *Someone* has to be here." And guard the home.

Tucker mounted and tipped his head back to loosen his shoulders. He tied the scarf around his neck, then tucked it inside his shirt. Horse pranced twice, then Tucker squeezed and he stopped.

"Bring the coats. You be careful on that tractor. It is far too light for the weight it is pulling. Check the hay field gates. We don't want anything going east."

Alice reached forward, took the empty glass of milk and coffee, and offered the reins to Ray. He began to accept, then froze. She took the wrist to his empty hand and drew the straps firmly across the palm. His fingers slowly folded over and they were his.

Her chin rose. "Use your toes; remember the bit. It is better to lose a stirrup than get caught."

Before Alice made the last trip to the house, she closely followed the actions of the boy. Ray looked into Daisy's eyes and stroked her broad forehead. Working bits of hair in his fingertips, he prepared to climb on. He told the dog to back away. "Tommie, I'm okay. I'm okay. It's okay to be up high."

They walked fast until almost by the bridge. With a clear warning, Ray watched Tucker nudge Horse. He broke into a light lope and Daisy followed. Tommie loped on a front flank, a confidence showing that he knew their destination, the purpose. Watching him eased Ray's apprehension. They went just long enough to loosen the horses and center their gear, then returned to a walk. Ray had a hard time keeping the fire real. Out of nowhere his mother's face rose, an apparition. Why now? he thought, forcing it away. Helping him escape—he watched Tommie detour to the creek and soak his belly. Being horseback seemed to make the day cooler, as if by simple division from the hot ground. Deeper in the valley the view narrowed. He looked up at the arguing smoke and a new reality struck; a shock of gravity leapt at his insides, begging for a day before any fire—one *open* and *clean*.

Both heard the drone of a small airplane but could not find it above the clouds. Moments later followed the chop of a swooping helicopter. Its twirling shadow passed over the pastures and trees of Jasper. Daisy pranced under Ray and listed sharply. The necks of both horses bowed and heads jerked. The collie crouched as if to sneak, keeping under the cover of leaves. He sought the shelter of the spruce boughs as though there were threat of an overhead predator. Tucker and Ray sighted the plane; in the next breath the helicopter rose as if racing in pursuit. Horse grunted. Daisy gave a low nicker. Leaves shook and limbs quivered. The flying engines buzzed—throbbed into the distance. In a broad turn they crossed the sky before the swelling cloud: a darkening dragonfly and swifter hornet, clarified lone specks over a billowing backdrop of failing white. With a giant

S they banked to the north and disappeared over untouched ranges. With hesitance, the ears of the horses swiveled forward and the march proceeded: steadily progressing, on a changed world.

"Ought we do more gallop—running?"

"We have to conserve Tom. He will be covering twice the ground…at least."

Ray's chin fell to his chest and he felt sorry for his mistake.

"Is there water—water up there? Places to cool off?"

"There are springs and a few seeps. Some have stopped. The cattle should be where they can find water, unless…unless the smoke has come between and driven them higher."

"Can the fire get—" He knew the answer. "Where will they go—where will you take them?"

"We will bring them to the cut fields: cows, yearlings, everything—beside the pasture with the bulls. It is safest where the elk have been, where they have chewed everything down. There is still a little green."

"Ain't nothin' to eat."

"They will have to hustle while this is going. If it goes too long we might hay them, or pull the fence down and let them in a stack."

Ray winced.

"They cannot go east. Dry hills could burn as well as a forest—and maybe faster."

He could not think of fire all around. He wished that Tommie would ride behind him, perched on Daisy's back like another human, and stay fresh. He knew that Daisy would fight, hate the notion. He wondered if Tucker ever thought of similar things.

"This is a hot day to gather," Tucker said.

"Hot," Ray answered, seeing the worn and stained hat nod for his repetition.

A curl of dust followed them lazily while the trouble on the mountain kept growing with the morning. Ray carried a great load of conflict: too much to lose. He thought more about Tommie being in front; at least in the lead, the air was clean, bright, and dry.

"When it is this warm and this late, they will be holed up in difficult places. We should have been earlier. We should have been here—well before the sun."

They rode by the Voss home. Ray felt a passing concern…reaching even deeper. He compared it to a flower, the old buildings tidy and erect, fully opened and dried into a memory. Once in the canyon the main cloud was hidden. They could see a high, smeared fume still drifting to the west, thin, gauze-like dirtiness stretched and distorted. Daisy's sustained rhythm began to make Ray feel soft and drooping. Tucker's back pointed straight as a board.

With horses puffing and leather creaking, up the steep and over the brim, they could see too much. Lather came from under the saddles. Tucker let Horse and Daisy stand but a moment, for his and the boy's first witness of the fire's path. Privy to their eyes and the machines in the sky, four miles further lay flickering remains: mere underline to what lay beyond—violent, heaving, as though with an effort to climb out of itself, Tucker watched the burning ascend three slopes in the same moment, turbulent, unsatisfied, choking—forms of destruction rolling in magnificence.

Tucker saw Ray's eyes glaze with shock and disbelief, the boy's face now white; his lips fluttered, as if on the verge of collapsing, breaking into a cry. Tommie held his nose to the air, also trembling. Tucker thrust his gloved hand out like a rigid fan as though pointing with each and every finger over an abyss of loss and threat.

"Now would be the time. Now would be the time to draw a barrier... We are lucky—now. The wind is with us, on our side, for this part of the day.

"It cannot last."

Tucker rose in his saddle and scanned the foreground. He could see small clearings and breaks in the timber, like a privileged scatter of miniature lakes in a friendly forest, brown with grass. He caught a glimpse of cattle milling along one edge. He pointed until Ray followed and made his own find. With his hat in hand, his arm swept the gentler terrain.

"There should be more all through here. I will send you along the high side. Our dog will be making passes between. He will bring some to you and some to me. Take them and get them started toward the canyon, then go back and meet him for more. They will know something is wrong and should head this way easily. Except the yearlings."

Tucker put his hat back on and snugged it.

"He doesn't bark, so you will have to listen for the stock, the breaking sticks and the pairs talking. Do your own talking to yourself or Daisy so he can know where you are, and the cattle. Don't fight anything, let Tommie; he knows where things are and when they are split better than we do."

The horses walked together for a short distance. The shining black mount under Tucker began to go sideways and throw his head. Tucker gripped him.

"Sometimes he will go back for more too quickly. Make sure all the yearlings are pushed up and not left alone. When he leaves too soon, tell him to *wait*—and *look*."

Both Horse and Daisy exhaled, their muzzles nervous, as if for an action yet to happen. Tucker knew that they knew: *a difference,* like never before.

"I will make a far circle to make sure we comb in the big steers. You will hear my whistles and they will help tell you where he might be." Tucker stopped Horse and made him stand without fuss. "If the wind changes...and we get smoke, forget us. Give Daisy all her rein. She will take you home."

The dog looked up at each rider, very serious, as though understanding.

"The bandanna—" Tucker offered an empty hand.

Ray pulled his free and unfolded its cleanliness to lay across the open glove. Tucker poured water over the absorbent cloth until drips began falling to the ground. He passed it back.

Ray twisted the cloth lightly, then tied it around his neck. As if a wick, his shirt bled a darkness downward.

"Thirsty? Hungry?"

"No."

"You better drink."

"No."

He held out the bottle and Ray drank.

"I will meet you as we come back toward the drop. You will hear me."

Tucker heeled Horse and he spun at a right angle and headed downhill. The collie followed. They trotted into the dense trees and disappeared.

Ray was certain Daisy didn't want to be left alone. She continued very slowly. Her sides felt puffed out; he tapped at them, but she went as though sore-footed. After several trudging moments he and the horse heard a clear whistle. The note seemed to open her awareness and at once she looked up and walked briskly, just as he desired. Soon Ray heard cattle approaching. He tried to skirt the horse above them but they thrashed and climbed in response. He hurried, ducking under limbs and guiding Daisy through the maze of brush and downed trees. Suddenly cows were in his face and startled; some bawled. They quickly split and flowed around him on both sides while Daisy ground her teeth and shook her mane, as if angry over the clumsiness of her rider. Rather than slow, all the cattle began to lope away, into the unknown and impassable forest, the heavy cows swaying from side to side and the calves with their tails in the air. Ray's shoulders sank. He dangled his head. Unexpectedly he could hear a change in their hustling, the sweeping through trees and shattering sticks, veering back on itself—then coming to a stop. He heard babies and mothers calling, drawing together.

Talk, he thought. He had forgotten to talk. At his home, the trailer, he choked his words down. Here, it was different.

"Hey—*hey*."

As though attracted to his voice, he saw bodies, then faces.

"Come—hey. *Hey-oh*."

The cattle came quite near and all were visible before he realized the reason. The rear ones were pushing on those in front. Ray caught a glimpse of black and white. A rose of pride for someone else...then the foolishness of his own darkened his cheeks. As if arranging for a strange game, the cattle bumped into a shuffling semicircle, directly before him, waiting for the sign of some ability, someone to lead. Tommie left without pause.

"Sorry, boy. Sorry.

"Hey-oh. Hey-oh.

"E-a-s-y—ones. *Hey-oh*." In graduations he spoke louder, but not loudly.

Daisy now took control, using the expression in her face, the position of her mouth and ears, a swish of tail like a pointer from Ray's own mind. The entire group headed peacefully and directly for the trail dropping into the canyon. He watched them go over the edge and start down; huge bellies rocked like overfilled flasks, hooves skidded and jarred with a set caution. Calves hopped and stumbled lightly.

Turning back, Ray was again struck by the changing cloud. The fire boiled and the smoke stayed west, as though on another page. Daisy's ears were unsteady.

For an hour and a half, Tommie brought package after package, few yearlings. Ray made the transfer much easier by talking. Each drift had new cattle, yet with the right voice they appeared to know him. He tried to copy the style of Tucker. He then realized that they knew, smelled the other pairs that had already come and passed this way.

"Hey-oh."

The whistles were getting farther away. He ventured deeper along the slope. His eyes couldn't escape the dominating shadow, the growth, like a dream, a nightmarish dream. He spoke out loud, not for Daisy or the others, but for the ugliness of the hurt mountain and the dirty sky:

"Please rain. *Please rain.*"

A sound came nearer, including whistles—crashing and wrestling in the brush—a much greater uproar than any before. Large numbers of black bodies charged forward and broke into view, cluttered by too many trees and limbs. Daisy stood with a certain uneasiness and faced this difference of big steers: tall and long, slick, shiny backs with curls of hair on their thick necks, heavy, but with a speed and muscle and the fresh smell of smoke. At first Ray believed they had sweat on their brows, then with bitter understanding caught the rub and glisten of frightening soot.

"Easy. Come. E-A-S-Y."

He tried to have Daisy climb the bank and hold them on course. Their necks flexed with an instant attitude of unrule and argument. Daisy's hooves clicked together and she floundered in the tuft. Out of balance, then straightening, as if to stay under Ray, she lost her head start. He caught a flash of the secret dog in the higher timber while twenty or more of the lead cattle cut and ran. They looked too big and muscular—oversize of what horses and dog could possibly handle. They ran for the difficult height of the mountain, as though bitten in the heels. Somehow a stirrup disengaged. He tilted to the side and hung, but kept pushing Daisy to catch up, blinking at thoughts of falling. She reared slightly, then turned away.

From nowhere Horse and Tucker sliced through, snapping more limbs and cracking leather, huffing, "Son of a— Son of a—"

With a dazed rider, Daisy joined and order began to fall on the complex confusion, the last of a splintering tribe. Ray felt hopeless, as if now all they held—but a fractional few—were the smallest and somehow weak…still disappearing.

He heard Tucker hurriedly call: "Leave, leave the others—too far out. Grab hold, save what we can."

The flying apart, the loosing of pieces came to an unbelievable slowing then stop.

Using bared fingers Tucker gave a breathless whistle. He boomed a harsh, "*Leave it. Leave it. Leave it.* HERE!"

Horse's neck and flank had darkened with waves of wet hair. His nostrils quivered and dripped and his sides heaved. He pranced and floated in place as Tucker allowed him.

"They will find the others we have lost. We will get them tomorrow. The damn…*rascals.* I saw no red calf." Reaching up, he pinched the crease in his hat. "We will find them tomorrow."

Horse continued to pace and cool as they waited for the collie. The cattle puffed and coughed.

Ray began to worry. "Is he coming?" A stark instant of feeling alone and afraid pounded in his ears; he wondered if Tommie could be crushed by a hoof, or be pushed *too* hard. "Could he get—could he get—run over?" As if his own legs had run all the distance, he felt short of air.

"Tom was way out in front before he heard. He is to sit and wait, let them pass."

Ray caught the sharp difference in the dog's colors, then quickly lost him again in the low limbs. He waited without moving, able to hear nothing but his own uneven breath.

"He's done enough," Tucker said.

Ray smelled the sweat of Horse and the residue of smoke brought with the cattle. The sooty matter had collected below many eyes.

"They been close to it?"

"Some could have cooked feet."

"Oh-oh… *Oh-oh.*"

Tommie slowly appeared at the edge of the remaining cattle, a look of defeat in his overused shoulder.

"He has done enough."

Ray's head rocked. It had no direction while only his lips repeated the words. He watched Tucker remove one glove, then surprisingly bend down, severely to the side, tipping the saddle to reach below one boot and stirrup with a single hand. Horse skittered and stood. Tommie came and nuzzled his fingers, then wagged his tail.

"Good collie."

Horse's ears folded back and the dog moved away.

"Go around," said Tucker.

Ray knew Tommie *had* to be exhausted. With a seriousness, he watched him curve out and continue as absolutely quick and tireless as ever, a great smile of effort. The cattle remaining now trailed as if there had never been a problem—there had never been a scramble or rise of voices. Several stumbled and coughed. Some limped.

"Will they—they heal?"

"I don't know. The coming rock will not help."

The smoke rolled north and with a drama of its own, like a scene from a *bad* movie, out-of-control waves headed out now doubled in the width.

To the grate of eight steel shoes, Ray watched Tommie's feet. The socks stained by a brackish dust, no ash or blood. Bare, sure, fast: he wanted to cry.

"We must keep them moving until they come together, then we can break," said Tucker, looking straight ahead. "No more fighting with yearlings, until we return tomorrow."

Ray and Daisy tipped over the brink to the downward trail, following the darker horse. He felt like the last soldier in a peaceful retreat, with a pressing of sun, then shadow on the back of his shirt. This same pattern of light slid over the hat and the man's dismounted form leading their way...

Tucker unbuckled the flap to the saddlebag. He lifted the water out and brought a distance between himself and the horses. Ray watched him kneel. He poured into a palm, then wet Tommie's nose and head. The dog tried to lick the man's eyes and mouth. Tucker took his hat off to turn upside down and prop between the nearby rocks. He made a small pool in the felt. Lapping began without pause. He poured more, then dipped his fingers in, to again dampen the dog's head.

"We found no water, no water on this side. The cattle are cut off. These springs are—have dried."

They parked on the steepness and Ray dismounted to eat and drink beside Tucker. They used the mountain as their chair. Tommie leaned against the cool of a rock with his tongue dripping. The eastern sky appeared a very clean blue. The horses dozed, each moment shifting from one leg to the other for the awkward grade. Sitting, eating. By some unknown calling, Ray thought of the *faraway* trailer house: its closed-in and stuffy smell, the small bed in a pinched room, a whole other world. He had no father…mother? Sitting, eating, in a whole other world.

* * *

The five-gallon container lifted easily. Alice expected more weight. She misjudged and tilted it too quickly, causing gasoline to spill over the top of the fuel tank and flow between the cooling fins of the small engine. The deceptive dampness vanished as she watched. Another vague urging triggered a search of the valley. This time she refrained, rearranging the thick and thin coil of hoses wound beside the water pump. Alice shaded her eyes, not from the sun, but the sight of the mountain and the overwhelming battle. From her angle a row of tired cottonwoods hid the lower fields. She saw no cattle but imagined an added haze, a sign in the still air from the shuffling of many familiar feet. In the foreground the riders appeared, parted from the wooded creek like returning hunter-gatherers. She felt a growing stiffness come over her lips and touched them cautiously.

A most welcome sight: two men on horses with their help in the lead, across a flat trimmed of all growth, dried to brittleness. The horses trod slowly and lightly, yet a fine dirt rose to tone and distort their approach.

Alice did not wait; she stepped straight forward, holding her chin high.

The collie paused, showing a strange discomfort, lack of decision, then recognizing her form began to lope, stretching out with tempered speed, a worn condition. Well in front of the others he kissed her hands and wove before her shins, making her stand. Alice stooped and hugged his chest, lingering, stroking, grateful for his health...his lean body fully in its prime.

The riders nudged their horses and were soon at her side. She felt a rising, the tightening of muscles in the small of her back as she rose from one knee. She studied their faces and swallowed a false relief, the fleeing confidence that the great trial had been overcome. Moving between horses and the settling dust, she touched each pant leg and surrounded them with her voice, her own coming together.

"Are they home? You are the ones that matter—" She switched each hand to a different leg and turned to face east. "If I could write down a moment, this would be one... Are they home?"

Hours later, after an uneasy rest in the kitchen, they stood outside and watched Ray diminish on the crest of the gray hills. After hearing the riders' story—a boundless overhang of worry while in their home—even worse in the tainted sun, Alice felt herself unravel, suddenly empty of the internal converging she had come to grasp, unable to stop her questioning...doubt over the boy's comfort and safety through a cheerless night. Both she and her husband *knew* he had cheerless nights. Like never before, everyone together feeling it, the surface desire to *stay* together and fight the danger—undivided: without word, without gesture.

Alice broke the silence. "I have a new—" She turned to Tucker and lost her thought. "So much is happening." Alice pointed toward the smoke-covered mountain with a single finger. "We *all* need to get through this—like some morning soon he will not be coming—"

Tucker tipped his hat down, then answered with an unusual softness, regarding his own calloused hands. "I talked...I talked to Milo's younger brother. George is gone for a few days. I don't know if it will lead anywhere, but we will be seeing him."

"Thank you. *Oh,* thank you." Alice pleaded toward the dull sky, then glanced to her feet. "I ache," she said, leaving his side to go indoors.

* * *

The next morning Ray entered their house well before daylight. He was breathless from pedaling through unclean air. When the dawn came, the morning remained dark with smoke, much thicker than before, as though someone had placed a domed lid down over the whole earth, a genuine heaviness and restriction to the air, no more sweetness. Everything had contracted an odor resembling the stale insides of a wood-burning stove, stuffy ash, creosote. The smoke lay like a permeation around every tree and bush, inside buildings, inside bedrooms, within every lung—as if leaking from the very mouth of Jasper: no taste yet to the water.

They assembled in an overcast yard. Alice and Tucker and Ray had long sleeves and buttoned collars. Ray's hair fanned out below the quilting of a welder's cap. Tucker thought of the people having damp tea towels to pull over their noses and mouths, and each having a bright-colored handkerchief stuffed in a back pocket...while the dog and horses had nothing. He watched Ray making an effort to keep his breathing shallow, only through his nose. The boy's struggle failed. His mouth opened. Everyone must have felt compression on their chest. No one coughed.

"Shall I spray the house?" asked Alice.

"Wet down the shingles as much as you can; keep them wet. Spray the siding closest to the trees and lilacs. You may have to cut bushes. Wet the foundation—don't overwork." His regard left Alice and he considered the other buildings, but made no suggestion.

Tucker waited for the visibility to improve, unaware of where the fire had gone. The early day commenced, still and hot, the first of its kind, as though the smoke itself refracted heat. Eerie, he couldn't place just where the sun was shining, if indeed it was. Then the ceiling brightened and lifted and every element of the valley turned a fescennine yellow: yellow trees, yellow pastures, yellow skin—yellow Daisy.

Tucker gestured toward the town. "What are they doing?"

"Glen told me this morning they are building a fire camp where they can cross the creek."

"Fire camp?"

"They thought they could pump there but there is not enough water."

"Jasper?"

"He hasn't told them about Jasper. They are still full and aren't going up the mountain."

"Will they help us?"

"The trucks are all six-wheel drive, brush trucks, reserved for the forest."

"Maybe the volunteers will come. Neighbors want to come."

Tucker watched as Alice tucked her hair back. "They won't let anyone in. Certain officials made the county road the tentative front. A man named—Parker—ordered: no civilians enter."

He ran his tongue along the hardness of his front teeth. He turned to Ray: "Did you see any patrol?"

"It was pretty—still pretty dark—too early." The boy finally coughed. "I'll go cross-country if they stop me. They can't *keep me*. I didn't see nobody. Not this morning."

The yellowness faded and through the somber Tucker could see the rampart, a dusky mood to the west sky, as though past when you would turn on headlights. The fire had crowned the first ridge. With a show of independence, it now struck out to the north, a soaring range of smoke in itself, several miles of ruin behind. From the very yard they could see flickering.

"You be careful," Alice said, her eyes traveling from man to boy, horses to dog.

Realizations were spreading but Tucker's choice—to not surrender? Unfaltering.

"It may not get any better. Let us start."

He watched Tommie circle, the white collar sickly in color. He worked the fingers on his gloves to fit more deeply on his hands. "Just finding them will be a chore. We may be late getting home."

Tucker mounted and the boy followed. From Horse's back he looked down on Alice, then considered the water tank and the trailer-tractor:

"Do not overdo. Keep some energy."

The two rode away with the dog at their side. Tucker could hear Alice starting the engine. Before long the ceiling lowered again and obscured the unstable horizon. As though held under a fog, the sound of vehicles glanced up the valley. Alice must have emptied the first tank, and in the renewed quiet he heard the slam of doors, cars and trucks coming and going, almost a voice, almost the static of a transistor. No sound of heavy equipment.

The multiple vehicles speeding back and forth over the dirt road left no clear track. They crossed Malcolm Stewart's empty pasture, so numerous only a heavy powder lay in the newly formed ruts—no tread lines—and a thick buffer in the grass on either side.

Dusty Shoes

Tourists came all the way from Marshal to park along the gravel road. Many had binoculars, some had telescopes, and almost everyone had a camera. Several crossed the ditch and walked through the dingy grass to lean against a fence post and steady whatever they held. Those with sandals remained in the road. Some sat on cars. The more animated paced, as though waiting for any light to glimmer through the deep overcast and improve definition. The prevalent gloom and haze, an arousal and disappointment to all who watched, much of the time no flame could be seen.

Until night.

The spectators first to arrive began to leave, while others drove in and filled the space.

Just inside the auto gate, an official car was parked with its door hanging open. A man sat with his feet propped on the doorsill. If any of the public slowed and attempted entrance, he stepped from the car and stood, raising both hands. They pulled up beside him, requesting information.

Before speaking, he waved the dust down and repeated with a scowl, "Pouuff!"

"Why can't we go further?"

"Safety..."

"There's no forest out here—"

"There are fire crews building a fire break around an encampment even as we speak. It will be a headquarters."

"Where is the camp?"

"Just back from the fire, a place where they can get water."

"Let us go to the top of the hill so we can see, see more."

"No sir—

"No ma'am—" A crackling spilled from the officer's open car, a loud radio like a carefully timed interruption, prompt for the coming gruff answer. "*No sir!* They have only hand tools. The road MUST REMAIN CLEAR for the delivery of equipment."

Many frowned, as though more than discouraged, offended by his manner. A track broke in the grass and expanded where people were directed to turn around.

One young woman did not ask to pass. She asked how it started.

"*That*...is under investigation." Without coherence he added, "We *will not* compromise anyone's safety."

Two marked cars and a pickup passed while the officer stepped aside, holding his hand over his mouth, each window with a blurt of static. The dust was getting in his shoes and mixing with his socks.

No one tried to enter as a blacksmith or gardener.

The Rescue

At the top of the canyon, smoke was pressed. Ray followed Tucker's guidance and pulled up his mask as they continued more slowly. Horses coughed. All morning and all afternoon they found nothing. They made long cuts across grimy slopes. In the dimness, Ray could see Tucker straining his eyes, looking for any sign: ruffled tuft, broken limbs, manure. Through the muffle of the drying towel, Ray heard the man's voice, turning down to ask the collie:

"Any cattle?

"Any bo-oies?"

All eyes teared and the dog's sense of smell was surely filled with the residue of burning.

Ray noticed the timber growing thicker and spindly, and the visibility even worse. Forage disappeared.

"Ain't nothing to graze."

Tucker pulled his filter down and swayed as Horse climbed over rocks. "They are not looking for food. They are confused and looking for water, and a break from the air."

"No air…" Ray answered. "How many missing?"

"Twenty-two…and fourteen pair."

"They shoulda leave—shouldn't they leave a trail? Oughta be something." Ray noticed a difference to his own voice, his own tone, as though preparing for a return to Alice with nothing accomplished.

"If they are in bits and pieces, scattered...maybe not. Your throat, how is your throat?"

"Some sore—isn't bad." His words were muffled while Tucker's were free.

"We are not going much longer. We will head home soon."

A long, tedious search, Ray couldn't tell there was any pattern, any order. They were almost to the top of a second swell. He heard a cow bawl, then jerked his mask down and straightened his shoulders.

"What we do now?"

"Talk."

"I'll make a wreck."

"No. No."

The man rode close and Ray felt him tapping on his hat. He let Tucker re-dampened his towel. They each pulled them up—as if to trap all the parts of their face in only their eyes. Ray's began to water even more, like this new dampness in the cloth underneath brought a stinging vapor.

The cattle looked genuinely pleased to see the two horses and hear the man's voice. Ray only whispered and clucked his tongue, knowing no one could hear. Some were bedded under the dark of trees while most were standing with their feet well apart; even their hooves were spread, as though weak from the weight of such big bodies. Tommie circled easily through the undergrowth. One rustled in the trees separate of the others—

"The red calf!" Ray shouted. He quickly touched his mask to make himself quiet, his eyes weeping so badly he had to squint. The morning so filled with alarm and depression...he had forgotten the calf. He felt he'd been a traitor—somehow neglectful. In

their being apart, the calf had grown so much, it looked as if it were a different animal, no longer bright with a curious face and innocent eyes. It was tired and dirty.

They bunched together in peace, seeming to wait for a signal. Tucker quickly made a count. "Everything," he said, "is present."

"How did they get here?"

Tucker twisted his neck, then rubbed it with a leathered hand. "I don't know. We are lucky."

The red color had deepened; unlike the others he could clearly make out blotches of soot on her forehead and black stripes along her back. Ray felt a stirring in the trees and caught Tucker looking up. It seemed as though the man were reading or counting something in the air.

"Maybe this will clear."

Ray swallowed hard and held his chin…

The cattle were tame but kept breaking apart and drifting at the wrong heading, wishing to avoid such tangle, and the endless forest without any grass. Tucker took the lead and he and the dog the rear. The man called and wove them between patches of dense deadfall. Ray felt an odd nearness to the end—a close, like the sure setting of a lost sun. He watched Tucker keeping the yearlings in check, seeming to make the line as straight and gentle as possible. If the slope was too steep, they made traverses and avoided slides of rock. The movement of air in the trees grew louder, then stopped. Like a rising floodwater, little feathery curls of smoke circled Ray, then began to roll over the ground and between woody trunks. Tucker scoured his brow. Ray saw as the man recorded directions like reading a compass. He sensed Tucker pinching Horse as the two of them hobbled down the slope, leaving more room. A pressing breeze returned, the beginning of a wind.

"We are getting close," Tucker called. "Be ready to swing out and help push, push them over."

Even as separate as they were, Ray could hear Horse's shoes crunching on rock as Tucker made him prance for a moment, while he distinctly tipped his hat and studied the blank steepness on the right side. He must have decided it was still too early to cut down. Skipping and bouncing, a half-dozen deer crossed their intended path and vanished without sound over the edge.

The sway in the rampart, the only way that Ray knew to be safe, was yet to come. Tucker called repeatedly to the cows, now obviously wanting an increase in pace. They seemed on the verge of stalling, keeping their calves very close at hand. The steers began to push, crowding, almost to brush against Horse's rear. Squirrels were chattering and scolding. A distant coyote called. Smoke came with a quality thick and brown, and the light narrowed into a slit as though being snuffed. Ray felt as if a thunderhead were building, a fanning up from the forest floor, receptive to a crackle and boom. He thought he saw flames just over the rise—hot and airless all the way around—

Then...*everyone* heard soft crashing—the crisis call—a chorus of chirping, screeching sirens of elk.

"Come. Come here. Be quick."

Ray watched as Tucker pulled the mask from his mouth, jerking it to the side, then whistling lightly while cattle began to pass, yearlings clearly in front and beginning to raise their heads. They stayed in one stream and Ray and Tommie swung out, primed for an order. Too many things to see—Tucker pointed with a rigid arm toward the approaching charge: the increased crashing of the elk.

"We must take them over now—before—"

Horse and dog loped left through the slash. Tucker did his own crashing, flailing the hand and arm without reins, breaking limbs, *more than a violent movie.* The cattle sensed a coming event and tried to get away. The collie hurdled forward and met the lead force. In a downhill lunge the first steer tried to leap over and beyond. The dog leapt in the same moment—chewing and slamming against his forehead, then tearing an ear. Black-and-white fur rolled into the brush as though limp. The beast turned just enough: barely enough to change course, over the edge and into the steep. Just enough.

In an instant Tommie was up and holding a continuing turn for the others to follow.

Stunned, Ray and Daisy prodded at the final cows, but the fighting had them bewildered. They stopped to bellow. The wind began to stir from below the bank and refreshed Ray's face as though an invitation to new air. It shook old needles from the trees. He looked up and the gray fogginess was lifting; he could see a towering cloud...shaping, like a cyclone.

Ray heard more breakage and a rumble and the elk came, different cows and calves and horns in a frantic blur, dashing through everything and shattering the last of their effort. Their own cows and calves cried in fear. Some were pushed against fallen timber; some were sucked down the slope: a coming together of elk and cattle into a waterfall of chaos. A larger calf scampered without balance, to trip and roll over the edge, feet in the air. Wild, suffering eyes. Ray sat stricken atop Daisy. Four of the cows cut back. His throat suddenly burned.

Now in a real dust from the stampede of hooves and vaulting sticks, Man and Horse and Dog disappeared into the thickness. Within moments they returned with the missing four. The one red calf! Ray watched it go over the cliff without falling. He could see new stress in Tucker's face. They heard more elk with a shrillness and terror, as though divided and running from a nearby blaze.

Even elk…who would ever save— "You are not mine!" he heard Tucker shouting. Waves of darkness followed the man's words: "We cannot go back—no going back."

Ray led as they inched over the unfamiliar edge, with the feeling of an exit. He allowed Daisy to carefully choose her footing and follow the dog. He could hear Tucker close behind. The wind persisted. Ray's eyes began to clear, then reversed, dripping and stinging for the smear of grit, his tired bandanna, sagging and soiled, flapped and fluttered. The cattle were gone: in a vague and vanishing stampede for home.

The elk? Scattered, burned? There *is* fire…right over the hill.

As if for this absence, the wind grew angry. Ray lowered his head and falling brown needles now struck at his face. The darkness of the cloud overhead filled the sky, a hovering power—no sound but wind. Trees shook and fell quiet, he more than imagined the rising glow. In this lapse, Ray heard and felt the passing shower. Through the dimness, pieces of singed yet unburned bark and needle landed in Daisy's mane. Particles rolled from his thighs. Storm on the mountain. Tempest of consumption.

* * *

Not long in the canyon, on a more gentle and widening trail, the collie began to lope and the horses began to trot. Around a blind corner they each met the steamy rustle, the black blotch of cattle and the reason for their ride. This sudden nearness made the cows shy forward and skitter from the road. Without speaking, Tucker and Ray pulled back on the horses. The cattle began to realign and return to the trail. Night fell—like the closing of a curtain.

They trod behind, hearing but not seeing those in front; those once lost now pulling the train. Tucker felt a slackness approaching, a well-remembered static. Both he and the boy caught the minimal flash, revealing for an instant a long row of shiny backs, then held their breath to listen: soft spasms of thunder. The dim lead shadows began to bounce, then broke into a slow and unavoidable gallop. The horses were allowed to follow.

They passed the outline of the sawmill and Tucker spotted headlights coming from the valley floor. The lights shuddered and swept sharply to the side, then flickered. It began to patter, cool, sooty tears.

"It ain't *rain*!"

Tucker and the boy sat damp and streaked from sustained effort and the heat of horses, little from the sky. Tucker could hear the truck coming, Alice driving. Horse and Daisy had quivering, sweat-soaked hair and pumping lungs. The dog was getting difficult to see. After a heavy flickering the lights went out and the pattering stopped.

He heard a voice in the dark.

"I was frantic—" Alice feared voicing her worry, as if her voice itself carried danger.

"I think we have them all," Tucker answered.

"I've come to meet you, hoped to find you, twice. The news I am getting is not good." She stepped near and could hear the sound of her own touching, stroking Ray's knee. "I was frantic. Are you all right?"

"Yes, I am."

"No hurts?"

"No."

"It is like an explosion up there, a meltdown—" Alice raised her chin. Barely seeing their shapes, she felt Tucker and the boy turn, as if just now having the time to look behind, reflecting drained hope and fascination. She knew their disbelief as they swallowed what she had been watching, something too close for them to have seen: a growing and vast indirect light, like the bombing of a high city hidden by the near crest. Tucker and Ray's faces bore blankness, a shape without eyes.

Breathlessly she spoke to Tucker. "Is everything all right? These horses are wet."

"They are blown. We ran into elk."

She felt his tiredness and the horses shaking.

"Some will get burned."

"What?"

"The elk. It is not my call."

"Where is Tommie?"

"Must have gone to the creek."

"If he ain't somethin'...he saved everything. I can't believe—I just can't believe..."

It began to patter again, big harsh drops: wind, more in the treetops than on the ground.

"We will push everything to the other side. They are watering now. Calves might get sick."

"You can't see. This boy needs to get inside." She pressed his leg. "Where is Tommie?"

"We have come this far and we will finish." Her husband whistled, steadfast, then the boy spoke.

"We got to, we got to finish."

"We will get them across, then will walk them, the horses. I will walk them."

She could hear Tucker thinking. "You can't see," she said, her ears still searching for the sound of Tommie.

"If it *does* rain they should be inside. They are soaked. Horse is blown. *Our*—Ray can be in the truck and I will bring the horses to the old barn."

"I help and get—get them across. I don't stop now."

She heard another weak rumble. The horses began to work their feet. Horse coughed. The saddles sounded different.

He finally came. Tommie. She could not see but the phosphorescence of his collar as he shook to shed a load of water. Her hand felt the wet of his nose. She knelt and wrapped her arms around him. She rose with soot on the ridges of her sleeves and the breast of her shirt.

"Put your coat on," she said to the boy.

"I'm okay. If it comes—if it comes, I want to feel it."

In the dark, she gripped his leg and smelled Daisy and the smoke in his pants. "I'll stay parked until I hear you. I'll meet you at the barn. Put your coat on—put your coat on if it rains."

"I will."

The cattle did not want to cross the depth of the creek channel, and the dog and horses had to take them beside the silhouette of sleeping buildings, then to the shallows used by the hay wagon. Standing outside, near the pickup, Alice heard the collie stirring in the grass to the sound of swift kicks and heavy hustling. The cows stayed quiet and trudged through the dark. At last she heard hooves venturing over washed rock and splashing. They trotted into the open and stopped, on the other side of Jasper…

As they approached she could hear Tucker saying to the boy, "Everything brought home. What a sigh…I think."

"I can't believe—I just can't believe."

By the light of the truck cab, Tucker and Alice unsaddled, then rubbed down Horse and Daisy with dry burlap bags. While scrubbing with the sack, Alice made a silent plan to bathe and rub down Tommie in the light of the kitchen. Over the water of an open milk can, Ray rinsed his face. To Alice, the quilted hat looked adhered to his head. Tucker led the horses into the blackness of the retired barn. She could hear Tucker locking Daisy in a near stall, then pulling Horse deeper to a much larger one where she remembered milking stanchions, dust and cobwebs. He must have had to feel his way.

As he returned to the shine from the truck, he set his hat up and rubbed his eyes. She thought his legs appeared permanently bowed. The pants over his thighs were pressed while the joints to his knees stiffly wrinkled: like a tin man.

"Close enough, close enough. This humidity should make it lay low…unless it blows," he said.

"You must have gone far."

"Very. This boy will be sore." Tucker patted Ray's bizarre-looking hat and smiled. *Our boy,* she could hear his thought as he gestured toward the ink of the doorway. "The horses should have grain."

She answered quickly, "I know. I know I should have brought some along…you or I will come first thing in the morning."

Alice could sense her husband's mistake as he shut the truck door and the light went out. She heard him open the tailgate and call for Tommie, then a falter, the scratch of claws and a definite fall. In the immediate second try, Tommie succeeded. Tucker hurriedly swung the door again and renewed the light. The dog did not have much place for his feet among all the tools. They both held the collie by the jaw. Alice softly petted his forehead while Tucker studied his coat and his legs, each paw.

"He gathered them all," he said.

"He done more than anybody. He done the most," the boy offered.

"My prince." Alice fed him a large piece of bread she had torn with her hands.

"Poor—poor boy. I just can't believe." A new layer of dampness flooded the boy's eyes.

"You have got to be tired," said Tucker.

Tommie had a look of great content while all the people loaded in front. Her husband started the engine.

Everyone felt a muted flinch. In a sudden swipe, the wipers went squealing across coated glass. They left an arc of soot and grime before coming to rest. Alice passed out rolls she had sliced and buttered. They tasted like smoke. The headlights brought a roughness to the hood, dried water drops, crumbs of bark and ash and curled needle: fallout from a catastrophe in another place. No one had the energy to speak. Ray fell asleep.

In the home yard, Tucker drove beside the bicycle and swept it up beside Tommie before Ray had a chance to awake. He jerked, then searched for the latch to get out.

"You ain't— takin' me back."

"We have to. It is too dark, and too late. You need to eat. But your mother needs to know."

He found the handle. Tucker mildly roared the pickup and they turned at the shop.

"I been in the dark a lot. This is nothing. Let me out—let me out at the top of the hill."

On the hilltop the man continued driving.

"This is nothing. I done this a lot—" Ray felt himself shuffle, rock in a puddle of tiredness and confusion. "You can't, I don't want..."

He could hardly notice others, but their driver closed his eyes—then quickly opened them. Alice tucked her hair.

"I could stay. She don't care."

Now fully awake, Ray watched Tucker speaking while looking straight ahead. "She has the right...she has the right—"

"I can do it. Leave me out. I can do it." He could see the fire in the mirrors.

A quiet seemed to billow, catch Ray's unknown feelings like a parachute with fraying strings. The truck neither slowed nor went faster. This voiceless evenness turned into an ache. Something sharp festered in Ray. For the first time in their year of knowing, he felt an *arrow* of anger, deep and black, a snarl of depression. He could not cry. They came to the gravel without comment, this silence like the probing forward of an acid splinter. The truck rumbled down the road. But two curves away and he began to fidget in jerks. His eyes felt like they were swelled: by the leftover glow of headlight and dash...a truck traveling in the dark, rattling and dusty.

"What if a patrol comes? What if a patrol comes? They won't—they won't let you go—they won't let you go and you might get stuck—stuck on the outside."

He watched Tucker straighten his arms and press against the seat back.

"You can't come. You can't go—you *can't. Let me out!"* Ray opened his door to the threatening sound of fast tires and tumbling rock.

He felt Alice gripping his arm. He could see her hand also on Tucker.

The man raised his foot, then bent his head. They pulled to the edge of the road. They all looked behind and could still see the fire. Tucker lifted the bike over the side and turned it upright to rest on the ground. Tommie jumped up to balance on the cream cans. He looked down on everyone. Alice tugged at Ray's sleeve.

"You be careful," she said, and stayed inside. Her voice rang clear, but trailed with a note he had never heard.

Tucker held one end of the handlebar while Ray prepared to leave. "Now you listen, I care— Sleep in tomorrow."

Ray caught the sight of paws on top of the water cans. In his tiredness and hurting delirium, he was driven to blurt, "I—*I* saved the red calf—" As he spoke he removed his sweat-soaked hat and threw it...to be lost in the truck. He avoided looking at Tucker. He could feel his hair lying plastered to his brow. He left Tommie waiting, wondering. He rode beyond the blinding beams, sensing an increasing division, as though he were an anchored weave and pump while the idling truck went backward, reversed into the night.

For the couple waiting, all disappeared but the shine from a broken reflector.

* * *

Alice and Tucker slept hard, as if by a drug, Tommie asleep at the foot of the bed. Too weary to talk, express their disturbance over Ray's departure, his bitter mood, they lay vaguely comforted by each other's touch. Tucker had combed her hair with his fingers while Alice held his opposite wrist. Like a dimming candle...one last wink—they were out.

The hot wind returned and made limbs talk on the roof and the house strain and creak; surely the dog heard. All humidity, the insignificant vein blew from the world. As though with a scheme the fire abandoned its slumber, spreading arms to cover the rampart and north, creeping east, coming down, confined to a descent on milder slopes. By midnight several fingers had reached the base of the front-range, well below the culvert for crossing the stream. The wind shifted. Momentarily the flames turned back on themselves and rested. A draft began, a flow up the valley. Like a sneaking cat the fire kinked and curled its tail, to prepare muscle, sink claws. As if on a turret and flowing down a channel, the wind shifted, twisted further. The cat rose: aimed-poised—for penetration.

Bearing down, fluttering, it leapt into the dry and rolled.

While Tucker and Alice slept, with a scurry of lights and nighttime dust, a sudden parade of vehicles headed to the east. The fire camp depleted, save the lonely outline of portable latrines: a feebly scratched-out circle, strewn paper plates and Styrofoam cups.

In solitude the health of Jasper thwarted the savage, drove it back on the mountain. Like a chimney fire racing-climbing only one side, at first so fast the burning was incomplete. It slowed in the aspen and blazed in the pine and spruce. Flames lined the sides of the new road, gulping and swallowing trees as though knee-high weeds. Brutal singeing skipped and flashed across the table, then settled into a crematorium, over and into the canyon where the sawmill waited. Machines cauterized together and partly melted: maelstrom of hell. The faces of the Sisters cracked, then sloughed.

Tucker sat up in bed, sweat on his brow, his chest, down his back: remembering only a fraction of the dream... *Flying like a bird over meadows and hills, the home ridge...thoroughly covered by stone promenades and paved decks—nothing sheltered for the weather—immense open-air terraces, no quiet families sunning themselves, no children, crowds eating, talking—too busy to see the coming, the boil of darkness, the crumble of artificial rock and fabricated brick and mortar to a rubble.*

Tommie rose and paced in the hall. At last Tucker heard him scratching on the floor near the bed. His mind cleared. He now smelled a different smoke, not sweet or sour but strong, a new burning of leaves and grass. Reality struck like the blow of a hammer. He stood and laid his finger on her cheek. Though very light, she awoke at the touch, placing her hand in his.

"I have got to get the horses out, let them free."

Tommie had a limp. When he jumped onto the cab seat, he stiffened. Seeing the extreme change Tucker drove the night valley, leaving gates thrown back, a fast stride.

The trees above the Voss house were in flame, skeletonized and diminishing as he approached. Even then he felt a heat, a wickedness. He watched the devouring of the growth around the veranda's base, then the torching, as if the structure were not truly there, but a facade, a sheer curtain of flammable gauze rather than a dwelling made of wood and plaster. The fire burst, spreading from house to barn across the rank and shelled-out grass like the feet of a giant stomping forward. He and the dog ran for the scream of horses trapped in their shelter, an intemperate sound above the rush and fall of limbs, whole trees crashing on the hill. Tucker felt his own shape disappearing as he entered the wooden cavern. The dog refused to enter. With his hands he searched and in his blindness found the hook to release Daisy from her stall. A sound kick reverberated through his glove and the door splintered, falling from its hinge. He heard a hateful shiver and neigh—then a gallop. Daisy reached the outdoor unknown and veered from sight. He followed her to the light of the doorway, to see again. The background was leaping and alive. Flecks of fire tumbled from the sky with an undecided wind. The grass had ignited on two sides of the barn and followed the footing of the broken and weathered siding with a hiss and spitting like that of a fuse. Left inside, Horse careened and reared, crying out with a vengeance.

With a quick turning Tucker reentered and the clear flash of the dog followed, hunkering. The light of flames began to shine through the cracks of a wall and revealed Horse to his owner, surging and thrashing in a horrid cage. Thick curls of smoke grew trapped in the overhead hollowness of beam and rafter. It fanned into the low corners. Yellow fire lit the bottom of another wall and Horse fought and raged, damnation of candlelight and fume rolling in his eye. Tucker jerked at the stall gate, then threw it open. Crazed, violent flailing knew no exit. Dreadful froth flew from Horse's mouth. Tucker brought his arms up and tried to move, to comfort Horse. Treacherous rearing and stamping threatened him.

Tommie slipped silently into the open stall in a low crawl, no other call needed. Firelight flicked across bared teeth and wolf eyes, beyond fear—faith. Tucker tore at the buttons on his shirt to use as a hood for the horse's frenzy. Whorls of gray smoke rose and he gasped, *Get back*. Twirling, scrambling legs, chrome hooves flashing and the collie was brushed against low boards. Sections of decayed roof fell like flaming cards, leaving a red-rimmed hole, brief stars, and a passionate draft. Fire entered from all sides. Horse bucked and spun, sweeping past Tucker, who locked his arms around the hot neck and was dragged, hearing clashes with

Tommie, clicking teeth and an odd thump, at last pounding his hip and thigh on the gate post and skidding well down the main galley before letting go. Horse thundered on. Part of a wall folded in. Tucker rolled over and peered through the far gaps to see—More wall buckled to the brief glimmer of night sky before the suction—

Between low gaps the dog lay: flat, arched, a knot of muscle. A tremor. Tucker stood hunched and unaccepting. Timbers came crashing and he could no longer see beyond the intolerable dust and ignition. He heard a rustle in the stanchions. He coughed and stopped breathing. Glowing boards teetered and swung, twisted from the ceiling, kicking his hat off and striking like a beast with claws of rusty nails. He went down again, this time severely stunned and suffering for the lack of air.

He awoke, sputtering, a blackness in half his vision, bent and stumbling into the furious night. Bare-headed and a new rain beginning, his mouth could not whistle. He called—sick—choking. By the light of the all-consuming fire, he staggered to find Tommie, surely somewhere lurking and wounded.

The Voss house collapsed in a fountain of departure, emblazoned spark and cinder shooting like rockets. He called and he called, his desperation floating and circling in the sky, then landing at the barn, now completely engulfed. He bowed his head, his face feeling the heat of burn, his voice having fallen to a silent plea...that Tommie did not feel pain and never woke.

No Entrance

At 7:15 in the morning, Ray opened his eyes. He heard a trickle from the trailer roof and watched a thin, oil-like coating slide down to streak the window. A stain on the inside panel had already turned dark. With a clean shirt and stiff bread and crackers in his pockets, he left while his mother was still sleeping.

It had been a good rain by the sign on the road and in the ditch, a wash and packing of dust, a trace of little streams.

It *did* rain.

The fire lay far along the tops of the mountains and still smoldered, as though trapped and guttering on each fringe, a great deal more black. His hovering tiredness and sleepiness gave the day a slant. The fact of water and the bright sun had trouble getting in. He stretched to get over the bike and felt a needling, reminder he had ridden very hard in a dream—driven and desperate pedaling to deliver a message. The pad to the seat squished water and revived a damp smell of smoke.

At the entrance to Alice and Tucker's lane parked a patrol car. A man sat inside with his head down, as though reading a newspaper or following the lines to a map. With the quiet of his bike Ray went unnoticed and almost passed. The officer must have felt his shadow, for he suddenly looked up, at first with surprise, then a quick friendliness and rolled down the car's window.

"Hello, boy. *Hello, boy.*"

Ray had to stop.

"You wondering over the fire?"

"I got to get in this place."

The man in uniform smiled broadly. "You can't go in. Not much to see now. You can't go in, unless you're already there...or this is your home."

Ray felt a heat rising in his chest. "I live in that trailer." He pointed with a clear knowing, across the pasture behind him.

The policeman shook his head, as though abruptly certain of a mistake, or an outright lie.

"I have got to go—go in. I *can't*-can't stay here."

"Why?" He opened the door and soon looked downward. "What do you want to see, a burned-up mountain?" The officer's eyes quickly rose and seemed to be searching for clouds in the sky.

"I been their help... They need me."

"I don't buy you being a hired man. Where did you come from?"

Ray rubbed his pants as if he might rid them of their smell. He closed his mouth, to stop the escape of a stale and miserable breath. With his hand as a muffle, "That trailer—"

The policeman now patted his hip and swung his arm to range after range of blackness. "We should get a handle on it now." With a toothpick, he fiddled at his teeth. "No young boys, no sightseers, we don't allow people in or around an old fire. You could get hurt."

Ray felt the prickle of heat rising even higher into his cheeks, around his eyes, then up his forehead. He lowered his head, glancing sideways to where he needed to go. The burning of the mountain came all the way down to the hilltops. He felt a threat to his yesterday, all the moments of summer. He turned, twisted away, and hurried: without a word.

He *did* look back, seeing the officer study his tracks, the crossing curves in the damp dirt and a much lighter imprint showing on the gravel. He wove, then swung around to look over the opposite shoulder, this time catching a tablet in the man's hands, and a pencil lightly scratching over its blank surface.

Another car waited at the painted cattle guard. This entrance also blocked. Ray switched direction in the center of the road with his head down, pumping. Once out of sight he began to go slow, looking for a cross-country passage. The first draw he came to had too many head cuts and a sharpness to the banks. The next seemed better. He drove into the ditch. He chose a place where the fence wires were furthest from the ground. He jumped off and quickly tipped the bike over to tuck below the strands. The grass thoroughly moistened and tougher than he expected—a pedal caught. The chain and rear tire spun and stems became wrapped. Hearing a slow car approach, Ray crawled under to be able to pull from the other side. His clean shirt snagged on a barb and ripped in a long, narrow strip. He jerked the bike free, standing it up, then jogging to a depression where they both lay flat. He reached up to stop the spinning of a wheel. Listening for the car, which continued as though lost and looking for a junction. He raised his head just enough for a glimpse. Another patrol was passing.

After a short pause and an empty sound coming from the road, he hurriedly mounted the bike and began bouncing across the pasture, searching for the best route over the hills with the least exposure. The slit and the flapping tail of his shirt made him feel he was trailing ribbons. He did *not* look back. A sensation overcame him that if he was caught now—stopped now—the morning, day, every day of his life would disappear. He pedaled fiercely up the increasing slope. At the very last of the climb, Ray stepped off and began to push.

The black kept getting lower and lower. The faces of the Sisters sloughed, flaked colors: he sailed the smoothness of the lane, swearing it be untrue—

Cattle were scattered below the homestead house. The two horses stood together and among them. They were taller. More missing hay.

Black sticks
Revealed plate
A steaming battlefield
The rock in everything never more sure
The core

A long, bright scar sloped, stripped of all cover. On one side of the valley floor, the fire had eaten—destroyed all grass. Ashy remains. The green trees of Jasper now dull, a changed and blotchy pattern yellowed and singed from below.

* * *

"Leave me to tell him," said Tucker.

She had been crying in stages since 4:00 a.m. Her eyes were badly puffed and she was still shaking as though with fever, then chills, a physical illness.

"Say to him I will want to see—" She ducked her head. "I am bare and broken inside, like only you have seen—my tears—and Tommie..." She regressed to more trembling, shaking harder. Alice lifted her face to meet her husband's. "Give me but a moment..." She ducked her head and hurried. Hurried to hide within the kitchen, the same place she had hidden on Ray's first arrival. Why did he then choose to visit? What purpose?

Tommie

Tucker waited for Ray by the coming sound. The man's clothes hung soiled and stained, a splotch of dried blood imbedded in the cloth above one shoulder. Though hands and face had been washed, he had neglected the fine furrows of soot in the bleached skin of his forehead. Black lines.

Then suddenly, the boy was there. He dropped his bike and without breath, "I seen the mountain and canyon... I been worried it mighta taken your house. I seen the mountain and canyon. There is still something. I been glad to see the house. I been glad to see the house."

"It burned all the Voss place," Tucker said. "It burned all the Voss home," he repeated.

"Where is Tommie?"

Tall and strong, he twisted his neck but kept his hands down. "We had to free the horses, free the horses."

"Horses? I seen—"

"He got caught—"

"Where *is* he?"

Tucker could feel Alice stepping through the door and onto the deck. Her walk soundless, she stood on the edge of the sloping floor. With her presence behind him, he cared to see inside Ray's mind. He thought he felt it turning. The boy's blue eyes growing dark, darker than the deepest water.

"The barn was burning—the horses—"

Tucker could hear the pounding of Ray's heart, louder than anyone's voice.

"Where?"

"He got caught... Old barn came down...Horse went mad, Horse went mad—"

Ray was not hearing. Under the snake-like encroach of haunted nights, the boy searched the yard with his eyes. "What? Where?" Alice descended the plank stairs and stood on the ground.

"The old building—he went down—"

Ray's eyes were no longer a boy's, but a man's, searching, disbelieving—

Tucker repeated, "Horse went mad. Tom was kicked...knocked out—cold out—"

"No!"

"He didn't suffer." Tucker felt his own hatless head turn from side to side. "I do not have him."

Ray's look collapsed into a boy's, sudden childlike fear and confusion. He searched the yard again, not seeing Alice, or the garden...or anything.

"We do not have him...he is gone—" He heard his own voice with a deafening permanence.

"No-no!" Filling with spasms of rage, he flared and viciously stomped on his bike's front wheel, bending spokes.

Tucker accepted, opening himself for the feral lances, the coming accusation.

"You pushed him. You done it—*you*. You always push—pushed him." Ray kicked the bike away. "You killed—you killed—you killed… *Bastard,*" he shouted.

With two giant steps he stood immediate to Tucker's waist, then hurled his small fists as high as he could reach, spewing with anger, hateful, blind, dripping: supplication for a lie.

With a nagging shoulder, Tucker's hands went up and back in the difficult air as if to uncover himself, prepare for the clutching of his own head, brace-embrace all hysteria. Ray's knuckles slid lower on his chest, arms at once weak and falling as though made of lead. Tucker now spread his hands in an outward reach—but did not touch. Almost instantly Ray was back on the bike, one last glance, wet pain. Tucker watched him weave through the puddles with a wobbling tire and clench his teeth, an agony grit to power up the hill. He discovered the tear down the boy's thin shirt, the long ribbon of cloth. He turned his head, searching for something different to see.

The barn: corral: sawdust. No upcoming children. Supine window to another life, he had lost a boy's dog—the great gatherer of hearts—a mere dog…

…the family's mountain.

Where was the opportunity? How could he ever bury? Dig a hole deep enough and bury?

The yard lay in suffocation, subdued, conquered, to ruffles and wavers of resurfaced emotion. Tucker turned to Alice. He saw clearly that she no longer shook. He waited. He suddenly expected her to leave, quit…after all that had happened and him to blame. *He should have stopped the road.* He should have tried something with the girl, young April. Why couldn't he—? He stood lame—in hiatus—waiting in astonishment as Alice looked only his way. She straightened her arms and walked directly toward him.

The Gift

Despite days of neglect, the garden had survived. Following the reign of disaster and the *rain* to revive, Alice continued with her watering. The land would need weeks—months of repeated moisture to defy the drought's grip. The pesky insects she had fought were temporarily at bay. The fact that there had been assistance from the sky made her effort more successful; the water penetrated more easily, not to puddle so badly in bowls of dust. Where it did pool, residues of smoke and ash appeared like a telltale scum. Her activity and the smell of spring water attracted red-winged blackbirds, out of season, the welcome warble of friends she had not seen in two months. Upon her survey, an amazing amount of vegetables were actually growing, to be gathered before the first frost. Alice cultivated between the rows—she held an image of Ray returning: to share in what he had helped produce. But she understood his anger—the blame—must fade. And that would take time.

A *dead* wildfire in over half her view, with its ugly odor slowly weakening; she could again smell the rich garden earth, so addictive to her senses since the very first days of her marriage.

Through the porch window she carefully watched Milo following the path, a stiffness in his hips, optimism trailing him like a waif about his heels. He bent forward and his chin and neck had a strange cast as though he had just slipped and thrown a bone out of place, pin to a nerve. His head remained turned, in clear refusal to witness the fire's destruction. In the shadow of their house, his lips began to quaver; not even his eyes appeared sound—too much private loss and suffering and no clan left.

She sensed him thinking: *More people should care—realize...*

Her husband stood outside the open door and looked past Milo's approach, then lifted one hand and turned the palm up slowly as if to receive or offer a gift.

"I have something for you—I have something for you to see," said Milo.

Alice watched as Tucker looked down the valley, dead center, no guarded angles.

She stood in the doorway already knowing what Milo had to show. "I will be out. Soon, I will be along."

Milo clasped his hands without allowing them to come together. Alice received a glimpse of his clean, warped fingernails, the mark of a well-aged father.

From the shade over the step, she watched Tucker and Milo walk toward the truck. Two young heads rose. Alice caught Tucker looking again into the fields.

"Brother, sister—out of the litter. I reckon this is his only daughter. She's a Bess—I named her Bess."

When Alice arrived, Tucker rested his wrists on the edge of the pickup box. Bright, clean children came. They shifted from each of his hands as though each in turn concealed something precious, important. He appeared to be studying their shine and figure, but looked away from their eyes.

"She's yours—I hope. I—will you take her?" Milo asked.

Tucker stepped in reverse and dried his fingers on his shirt.

Alice stood holding an elbow, watching the puppies reach and extend.

"He'll take her," in a bold voice.

Milo opened the tailgate and lifted them down. He helped the sibling of matching size into the cab. His decrepit hat stayed put. A convulsive limpness came down through his arms and into his hands. "You can—maybe ought to...change her name." Alice could see tears beside his nose. "I reckon you will."

Once they were alone, they sat on the ground and held the dog's chin, looking into her face and eyes for a very long time.

I know you. I have been here before.

The *strength*—grandeur of the valley—had made their pain smaller. Now in the same stroke of losing Tommie, crushing Ray's fragile hope with the burning barn crashing down, folding to a ruin—the land was maimed, beaten, and their comfort broken—*almost* broken.

* * *

Bess. Though still to grow, a wisdom in her pose, she had the same rear white socks as her father. They petted the stroke of tan on her cheeks. The white collar hung lopsided like a broken and twisted band of windblown snow, her blaze in a tip. Her first time in the house and she soon lay flat and rolled her eyes and flapped her tail on the floor: a most effective seduction.

I know you.

In the yard, she had the habit of resting with her front paws crossed, long white gloves, an exalting decoration to her eyes. She handled her tail with a pronounced femininity. Once she caught you, she began to look sleepy.

Bess. The flower, ambrosia. No changing her name.

Each in their way, during the course of passing days, they watched the lane for the boy... the echo of Tucker's own sorrowful and defeated howl.

He spoke out loud but with no one present. "Ray has had enough time. I have given him time. He needs to see, see Bess." *And her.*

And you need all three —

With Bess in the truck bed, Tucker drove through the cattle, deciding what to ship. The young dog's face leaned over the side, her feet too hesitant to balance on the wheel well. The truck rumbled toward the buildings, then went past and up the lane and over the hilltops to the county road.

At April's trailer there parked no bike or low-slung car, rather a mud-splashed station wagon with fake wood panels and a motorcycle with broken upholstery and worn-away foam. His boots were loud. A man opened the door before any knock. Tucker stepped forward and filled the frame. The stranger gripped the door edge to stop his entry. He stood with more weight than Tucker but less height. His shoulders were sloped, as though *worn away.* On his head perched an equipment hat markedly raked. Tucker felt pressure rising in his own brow, without shade, without band.

"What's up? What do you— What's up?" the man sputtered with a sharp mistrust.

Tucker leaned hard on the flimsy door, and with a hard glance covered all the corners of the room.

"What's up? What the hell. Who the hell do you think you are— *Man.*"

"Where is, where is," Tucker held his hand out, "where is the green car?"

"Get the hell back—" The hinges cringed. "I have cops come by, who are you? Who the hell are you? You're no cop."

Tucker suddenly stopped his pushing. He stepped away. Bess began to fret and whimper from the pickup box. The dog sounded as if she were right at his heels.

"She and her kid picked up and moved, moved to Marshal. She says. She says everything in a big hurry...leaves a mess. Damn. Now I've taken over. This isn't hers no more."

"Where? Where in Marshal?"

"No—that ain't true. She's not in Marshal. Sure as hell you're not a cop. Don't waste your time. Don't waste your time looking."

Tucker considered the strange and narrow ceiling, in disbelief.

"I knowed her a long time. Somethin' happen, went haywire—*bad.* She's disappeared. I knowed her to disappear before... Was it you? You cause it?"

Tucker shook his head slowly. Struck by a sweeping sensation, intoxicated in some secret, uncomfortable way. As though with red and bleary eyes, his desire to go inside shrank into nothing. He absorbed the news. Bess kept crying and started to claw: a grating expression, spreading through his head... *One last try—*

"You've *got* to know where she is."

"Give it up, *man*. She picked up and left. Just days ago. Nobody knows where. Another time...before she come here...another time and from another town—she been gone over a year—vanish into the air—" The short, heavy man shut the door with a *woosh*. Tucker heard it clicking into place, followed by a *thunk,* the harsh twisting and slide of a lock. He stood for a moment, then turned and headed to the pickup. As though to apologize, Bess readily placed her chin over the edge, nose down and eyes up, a modest display of two white crescents. Her familiar face like a touch—reminder of better days. He lowered the tailgate and helped her to the ground. He opened the passenger side and rolled down the window. He had her jump in. She tucked her tail around and looked straight ahead.

Tucker drove from the county road, over their east hills, then descended the last of the lane and into the homestead yard. Indecisive as to where he should park...pulling up close to the shop entrance with the truck idling. Bess would not look at him. He paused, then with an uncharacteristic clash of gears backed away in an arc. He drove forward and stopped immediate to the walkway for crossing the lawn. Below the porch roof he could see Ray's straw hat hanging, snug against the wall, on the peg nearest the window. After a pause he thought to himself: the hat would remain...waiting for the return.

He made a *here* sound with his tongue and lips, coaxing the collie to his side of the cab and onto the ground. Before he closed the door, Alice appeared on the steps. He did not shake his head, he did not look down, he squinted... She began to turn, then refrained, continuing to face him. Her head didn't duck or shun away. Her chin distinctly rose, as though to see beyond the boundaries of the yard—a view further than the porch could reveal. Tucker felt a movement, indescribable; he watched her slowly cross and curl her hands, a palm on each wrist, eyes and mouth with fleeting expressions of sorrow and strength—no hint of withdrawal.

She knows.

This time, he went straight to her.

* * *

Megan had them standing before a door of frosted glass. Alice briefly glanced at the brass plate above the panel, with thick letters inscribed and blackened:

George Taylor
Attorney at Law

She could hear Megan take a breath and softly rap one knuckle near the door knob, followed by a muffled, "Send them in." The door swung. Alice entered first with Tucker trailing. He carried a new hat. He held it distinctly before his waist, level and with both hands. They were standing in one of the tallest buildings of the town, thick native sandstone quarried in the time of Tucker's grandfather. George's cluttered office nestled on the outside corner of the second story, looking down into two quiet streets. A massive desk behind him, the attorney rocked back and placed his arms on two padded rests, pausing… Tucker began stroking the crown of the new hat…

"Dear friends," George gestured to the plush chairs before the large window of each wall, "have comfort, my friends…sit down."

Her husband nodded for her to be first. Alice felt as if her body were sinking, out of view. As though intentionally facing just her, above the rolltop behind Milo's brother, perched another plaque: Attorney at Law…she couldn't help but remember her lovable adviser, and in his flurry of nervousness—what he had said about his brother's profession… *Go before the bench of Justice and squabble…*

George blinked very slowly and tipped his nose down, as though it were excessively large and heavy. "The fire…" His hair lay neat and snug, a symmetrical swirl above each corner of his forehead. "…I am grieved."

squabble…for the boy, our boy.

Tucker spoke. "Shall we talk about Ray Connor?"

"What is your interest?"

"We talked before."

"Yes."

"We would like to be guardians."

So unlike Milo, other than the gray of his hair. Alice felt her discomfort growing, and joined the discussion. "He needs a home. A true home."

"Where is the boy?" The attorney repeated his blink.

"They have disappeared," said Tucker. "I thought you knew."

George began clicking his tongue, speaking with an aggravating calm. "This is a small community. All things have been surrounding the fire—what an epic event."

"April, the boy's mother, has moved out and taken him with her." Tucker continued stroking the fresh hat. "We would like your help."

"That girl, very cautious." He quickly scratched his brow. "She knew not to leave any sign." A hand left the chair arm, reaching up to comb his mustache. The other entered his jacket pocket as if to hide. "I heard from Joyce, my niece, Joyce. A while back she gave me many clues—she is sure but it is all hearsay—speculation. Nothing was ever visible. What do you know?"

"They have disappeared," Tucker repeated.

"About the abuse." The clicking sound ceased. "When we spoke before my trip—I thought you had more, something concrete."

Alice intervened. "I have something concrete. I know it in my heart."

"That is not my question."

She shook her head. "We are honest people."

"Dear Alice, that is not my question either."

Alice felt herself wanting to stand, get up from where she sank.

Instead, Tucker's voice rose, with a suddenness. "There were scratches on his face and welts on his back. I saw things up close—his naked back."

"Was there more?"

Alice stood.

"Please sit down. We need to be thorough—calm."

She remained upright and alone.

"We are on the same side." George bent forward, pulling his other hand from its pocket, holding it in her direction in a caring fashion.

Alice caught the missing fingers. She quickly sat down. "Were you abused?"

"No." He kept trying to smooth his mustache, the whiskers bristling out, opposite to his tidy, well-trimmed head. "I was six years of age, stooping to feel the sharpness of a serrated sickle. Brother Milo—always in motion—kicked it with a curled-up boot. I still see the boot, and my fingers too… Boys…scrapes, bruises, black and blue… Boys."

Tucker's voice became impatient. "Will you help us find them? We have to find them, before we can move forward. We need to focus." He placed the hat on the floor near the chair, as though it belonged to someone else.

"Just right. Of course. However, that will be a difficult task. We have no charges, no motivation." He began again to click his tongue behind the obscurity of his mustache. "I can only ask—suggest to the local sheriffs—have a notice out to their officers and keep us informed." His eyelids grew heavy, deep in thought… "A profound question. Do you believe the girl, April, had anything to do with the fire? My man, if that be the case, everything would alter."

Tucker pondered a moment, with an expression questioning Alice. She shook her head, the one chance and she shook her head. "No," he answered. "She complained driving into our valley. She would never drive into the forest."

Alice added, "Ray rode for cattle to save them…right into the fire. He was our Godsend—is our Godsend. His mother, whatever she is, couldn't be responsible. She could never be involved with such a risk."

"Suppose we do as I stated, inform the sheriffs—and then we wait."

Alice heard herself in silence, *no resolution here, no resolution here.* The realization awakened slowly. This time she stood politely. "We have taken enough of your time. And are appreciative."

George also rose to his feet. "Very dear Alice, I miss your smile, the pleasure of your smile."

She looked down on Tucker. He was slow to stand. She noticed him leaving the hat on the floor. "We need to take care of Bess. We need to take care of—things."

Tucker shook hands with George. "Thank you." And in the same moment as they went through the door together, she caught her husband looking down to where the new hat remained.

* * *

September. October. The first snow arrived early. It began harshly, showering down in hard little pellets, stinging the leaves and their hands and face, so bitter it made the dog wince and tuck her nose. The flakes gradually grew soft and enormous, until they began to drift and flutter like feathers. A clean, shallow white to blanket the burn. The very next day, while fixing fence high on the ridge, Tucker felt the valley leaning toward the sun, and the snow seemed to disappear—even as he blinked.

Two mornings later, he caught Alice searching the bookshelf for a particular volume. Finally she found it. She dusted the hard-bound cover, laying it on a delicate table that had recently been moved to the corner of the kitchen. Tucker recognized the table: one of Alice's nightstands. The book contained several favorite stories—over which he had heard discussion. No question, the worn cover sat waiting for a certain *someone.*

When the snow had been gone more than a week, it still left a change in the air, a fleeting warmth to the shorter days.

In front of the chicken house, two shovels lay with their handles crossed but not quite touching. One had a small square head and the other a more rounded, much larger scoop. Bright wooden packages with metal strapping were heaped beside the door: sawn cedar shingles. Tucker had propped two ladders against the roof, one on the south side and one exactly opposite, so that Alice could join him without facing dust. He climbed the north ladder with the smaller shovel. On the mossy eave he began jamming it under the old shingles and prying them up. They were stained gray and black, badly misshapen and split. After the entire edge was peeled back, he went down and retrieved the scoop. Now he worked much faster. On this shaded side he made two dark piles of broken roofing and rusty nails. With the broom for the shop floor, he swept away the splinters and crumbs. He carried packages up and set them above where he would begin. Once he had stopped throwing trash, Bess came around to where she could look up, keep an eye. He had a work belt and chalk line and hammer and a paint can full of nails. He put a row of shiny nails in his mouth.

Tap-tap.

Tap-tap.

Over the high crest of the roof, Alice appeared as though from thin air. Bess jumped up, suddenly rearing and whining.

He looked down and answered the dog, "Don't worry, doll...I will not let her fall."

Bess kept dancing and leaping, reeling.

"It's okay, girl. The sooner we get finished, the sooner we'll be down."

Alice sorted for width and handed him shingles, then nails. Not once did she hesitate.

Bess finally sat still and panted, in full attention. While reaching for the pail of nails, Alice stepped close to the edge. The dog ran to the other side of the building and barked in her blindness. When she returned she growled. Her eyes blazed, then gradually calmed, a compliant plaint.

"Don't worry so."

Between hammering they heard a cow bawl in the east hills. Tucker considered with confidence: somewhere out there, and grazing in peace, meandered the red calf and Bunny... waiting for the return of a young boy's eyes. A near tree limb rustled its pale yellow leaves. The time as a cow-calf pair was coming to a close. November would be the month to wean. And the red calf would be a keeper, a future mother cow.

Alice's slender hands began arranging the nails with their points all in the same direction. Tucker emptied a package and stood. He uncurled his shoulders and made a motion to throw the metal strapping into one of the piles. His decision paused, then reversed. He slowly folded the metal into a tidy strip.

"He will find his way back...

"We want to return to our beginning." He glanced at Alice in the very moment that she rose and their eyes met. Her face remained steady, calm and focused, her hair neatly held by two barrettes. "A place—the place where we feel some sense of direction... He will find us—"

"Some are not so lucky as to have that kind of beginning," she said. "But he is changed. My prayer is...my prayer is—I think he will not forget. *I am sure* he will not forget."

"I should have gone for him sooner," Tucker answered.

"*We* should have gone to get him sooner," Alice added without hesitation.

Bess at last lay dished to the side, starkly clean, swallowed by the fluff of her own collar and tail, the grass, as though absently watching and listening: outside herself.

They moved higher on the roof. Tucker briefly looked along the weathered peak. The same roof that had been *poor* Tommie's shelter, as a once neglected puppy.

"The mountain will green again," Tucker continued, still holding the folded band.

He watched Alice face the lower scar...sensing the new tan on his brow, the tone of gray in his own hair. As though the small piece of metal had become significant, he stroked its layered edge, while hearing—

"Ray was looking for fissures, places to put his feet." Her eyes traced the long, bleak road and its black surroundings. "Somebody gathered him. I believe he is changed..."

Tucker left his work and stood even taller, a clear intention to speak. "We—"

She felt her fingers pressing his lips. "We are changed," Alice said. She pressed a steady and silent assurance into her husband.

To the sound of her last words, Alice looked down to the young dog turning upright and bracing evenly, resting her belly against the cool earth.

Alice could not help but see all of the corpse, the mountain, the long, pale scar climbing above Tucker's head. Her eyes began to fill. She and Tucker came together and held each other atop the chicken house roof. Tommie's daughter lay on the ground patiently waiting, shining— promise for a new time, resurgent lush fields and crystalline spring.

* * *

the end

Thank You,

This is not a long goodbye, however there is definite need to express gratitude:

To my wife Pam for the tedious transfer of an obscure hand written story into a computer document, with crucial correction and suggestion.

To Kent Myers, author and educator, for his generous *hard* read of an early draft. He gave expert advice balanced with encouragement.

To long time friend, Page Lambert, author and editor, for her wise and detailed guidance in making *Jasper Spring* more complete and accessible.

To tall John Gritts for his fine drawings, his friendship and support.

To our son Tyler with his perfect pose for the cover photo: "Have you finished the book yet??"

To the border collie Spur, the loyal and devoted model for the character Tommie.

Thank You

CPSIA information can be obtained
at www.ICGtesting.com
Printed in the USA
LVOW07s1243300717
543152LV00004B/640/P